Kate Evans is a writer of fi[...] Donna Morris series is ba[...] North Yorkshire coast where she lives and [...]. Trained as a psychotherapeutic counsellor, she is interested in the connection between creativity and mental wellbeing. She has an MA in Creative Writing from Sussex University and has taught creative writing. She currently facilitates creative workshops with an emphasis on wellbeing.

Also by Kate Evans

A Wake of Crows

DROWNING NOT WAVING

KATE EVANS

CONSTABLE

CONSTABLE

First published in hardback in Great Britain in 2022 by Constable
This paperback edition published in 2023 by Constable

1 3 5 7 9 10 8 6 4 2

A CIP catalogue record for this book
is available from the British Library.

ISBN: 978-1-47213-477-6

Typeset in Caslon by Initial Typesetting Services, Edinburgh
Printed and bound in Great Britain by Clays Ltd, Elcograf S.p.A

Papers used by Constable are from well-managed forests
and other responsible sources

Constable
An imprint of
Little, Brown Book Group
Carmelite House
50 Victoria Embankment
London EC4Y 0DZ

An Hachette UK Company
www.hachette.co.uk

www.littlebrown.co.uk

To Mark and all the environmental activists who speak the truth even when few are really listening. And to the 'bottom enders' who (with volunteers from all over) preserve the history of the town at the Scarborough Maritime Heritage Centre.

Before

The last few days have been happy ones. Like a fairy tale. She still loves fairy tales, even though she knows she is way too old for them. It was only seventy-two hours – she had tallied every golden one of them – yet it feels like she's been away for years. She had been able to forget her mum's black eye and cut lip drooping across the Christmas dinner she had prepared and no one could eat. It was truly rank in any case. Her mum couldn't cook beyond baked beans on toast. It was another thing which made her dad mad. She had been able to forget the angry look on her brother's face. He had descended on them on Boxing Day, for a whole thirty minutes. He said it was all he could spare. She had been able to put it all out of her mind. Almost.

Until now.

Her pace slows. The Toogoods live not exactly round the corner. There are several corners. She has been counting each one. Their home is on a similar street to her own, rows of 1930s semis, each with their own smartly painted front door and patches of garden behind the privet. Yet it's like the Toogoods' house is on another planet. A planet where nobody shouts. A planet where everyone says please and thank you. Where fathers don't hit mothers. Where furniture doesn't disappear when the rent is due. A planet where everything is brightly coloured, warm and cosy.

What would happen if I ran away? She stops. This isn't the first time this has occurred to her. Would anyone miss her? Miriam Toogood would. Her bestie. *But she'd get it. Miriam'd understand.* And it's not as if she wouldn't come back ever. *Gilbert Grape went away and everyone forgave him when he returned,* she reasons. She had gone to see the film with the Toogoods just before Christmas and everyone had cried, even Miriam's elder brother, so she supposes it's OK that she did. *Only the main thing is,* she tells herself, *is that Gilbert left his mum and brother 'cos he couldn't stand it any more. Couldn't stand them any more.* Gilbert drove away. Which she can't do. Another three and a bit years before she can even start lessons. Her age, of course, would be an issue. They would try looking for her. Where could she hide?

She begins walking again, mulling over an escape plan. It strikes her that if she does go and she is found and brought back, then everything would be a hundred times, a thousand times, a millions times worse. *I have to disappear. Some ruby shoes like Dorothy.* She wants to click her heels and for it to work. Then another image comes to mind, from a sitcom repeated over the holidays, a pile of clothes on the beach, the main character going into the sea. *He pretends to drown himself. And it's a joke.*

Before she realises it she has arrived at her front gate. She grips its slender metal curlicues. The hedges on either side seem to have grown since she was away. They appear to be crowding round her, telling her not to go in. Though she can feel every muscle in her body rebelling against it, she goes

2

quickly up the path. As she opens the front door she calls a tentative, 'Hi.' No response. This could be good. Perhaps her parents are miraculously both out. Or it could be bad. Very bad.

Even she, after years of it, could not have conceived of how bad it turns out to be. She reaches the kitchen at the back, aware of an aroma she cannot identify. It reminds her of a butcher's shop an uncle owns in Hull. Stepping over the threshold, she's confused by what she sees. Her dad, her mum, slumped on the floor in awkward positions. It doesn't make sense. They are like wax works set up to portray a scene. A bloody scene. The smell makes her gag. One hand goes to her mouth. The other reaches out to steady herself. She touches material over the back of a chair. Her brother's jacket. She grabs it, holds it to her face, something to blot out the grisly tableau. Then she turns. She runs. Back the way she came.

Chapter 1

'Fuck you. No, I won't do it.' She's angry now. He has done his usual. Come in all friendly and charming. Wheedling. Then bang, when he doesn't get his own way, he weighs in with the very criticism he knows will fell her. She's not up for it. Not up to it. Not up to his standards. Like he's the arbiter of what's good and righteous. Well, she won't tolerate it. She won't let him belittle her. She stands facing him. Her hands go to her ample hips. A gesture she has inherited from her mother. She doesn't like it. She thinks it makes her look like an out-of-date pantomime mother-in-law. But it gives her strength. This distaff gesture passed down to her. 'It's all right for you, you don't have to worry about earning money – Mummy and Daddy will make sure you're OK. Well, I can't afford to mess up this job.'

At his full height, he's a good fifteen centimetres taller than her, and he's muscular.

Prides himself on those biceps, she thinks sourly. Then, briefly, wonders at the damage his fists could do to her, before she sends those thoughts packing. *He wouldn't hurt me. Not in that way.* The problem is his words can be equally crushing.

'We can't afford to do nothing,' he says pompously. 'We're in a crisis. People are dying.'

4

Like I don't know! Like it's my fault! Like I'm not doing my best! The phrases she wants to throw at him get all mixed up and clogged in her throat; nothing but a strange strangulated screech escapes. She is beyond arguing. *There's no point,* she tells herself. *He is beyond listening.* She wants to pound that self-satisfied chest until he sees her point of view. Until he apologises, for, for being so bloody minded, so bloody mean. 'I thought you were my friend,' she shouts. Ridiculously, she knows.

'What's that got to do with it? I thought you had some backbone.' He turns abruptly and walks the short distance to the door of her flat.

Once he has snapped it shut behind him, she yells, 'Fuck you, Orson Reed!'

Fifty-nine hours later, five hours into her shift, Alice hopes Orson has abandoned his plan. How wrong she is.

She was in charge of the set-up and is now coordinating the service. People had started arriving at seven-thirty on the dot. They are dressed as if they are on some fancy cruise around the Caribbean, not at a party four days into January on the North Yorkshire coast. It has been a long time since Alice has seen quite so many flashy jewels and furs – even if they are mostly fake.

The rowdier mob arrives around ten p.m., already tanked up. Alice has another go at pulling up the plunging neckline on her uniform and at pulling down the skirt. As she passes through the crowd, male hands 'inadvertently' stroke her bosom or land on her bum. One set in particular. She has to sashay her way around him. And he is everywhere she is. A gnome in an extravagant cravat. She does another sidle, bangs her tray down on the bar and says she needs to pee. The staff toilets are down a narrow corridor. At least they are as new as the rest of the venue. She takes her time, using one of the fluffy hand towels to cool her face and neck before discarding it in the basket provided. Perhaps Orson was correct, she is a traitor to the cause. She promises herself she won't do another gig like this one. Knowing she will. The money is too good to turn down.

As soon as she exits the corridor, she is aware that something untoward is happening. The hot air is as stretched as stale toffee. The chatter has died down. Everyone is looking towards the middle of the main room. Some are craning over others and asking what's going on. Firmly corralled to the rear wall, Alice finds a low coffee table to stand on.

Orson is addressing the assembly as if he has been invited to do so: 'Each one of you is killing the planet with your excess and your ignorance. You are sweeping the crisis under the carpet because it suits your pockets and it is not you who are suffering. Not yet.' He is dressed in his khaki combat trousers and grey hoodie and is carrying two wooden boxes, stencilled with the words: 'Moët & Chandon Jeroboam'. He must have fashioned them himself, Alice concludes. There is no way he would have purchased them. She can also see he has his bodycam attached to his top. He is filming it all, either for live streaming or for later release.

By now, several people are beginning to work out that Orson is not the delivery man they took him for. There are movements forward to stop him and to get the security guards to eject him. Sensing this, Orson quickly flicks open one of the boxes. It is full of rotting fish. He lets them tumble to the floor. The smell hits everyone in their craw. Some retreat from it, others turn away, hands to mouths, greening at the gills. Then Orson catches sight of someone. He launches forwards with the other box, shouting, 'This is for you, you bastard. Don't you worry, I've got enough to bring you down.'

His sudden movement brings animation to others. A large man with a dark thatch threaded with grey grabs at Orson's arms. Though the effort brings a deluge of blood to the man's face and almost causes an apoplexy, Orson's progress is slowed enough for him not to reach his cravat-wearing target before the burly security guards appear. Through the hubbub which ensues, Alice gathers there is a discussion over whether Orson should be arrested. She breathes out when she realises his erstwhile victim has vetoed the idea and, instead, Orson is marched off the premises, his second box intact.

Alice wants to follow, to make sure he is all right. Instead, her boss for the evening appears with cleaning equipment and Alice is set to sorting out the rotting fish with another colleague. *Thanks Orson*, Alice thinks as she shovels putrid mess into plastic bags and scrubs the carpet.

People, the more sober and more offended, leave. Others stay and Orson's exploits get twisted to emphasise the bravery of those who stopped him.

In a spare moment, Alice slips onto the balcony. The cold midnight air scours her out. It is damp and foggy; she can hardly see to the harbour. Orson is not within view. Her concern for him is tempered by her crossness. As usual, he

7

did not consider who would be (literally this time) cleaning up the mess he had made. And somewhere in there is the guilt: he did what she felt she could not. Maybe he is right. *No backbone.* She calms her helter-skelter thoughts. At least he is on his way home now. He will be pleased with himself and his footage. He may not have changed minds at the party. In any case that would not have been his aim. No, he will get the response he wants from his own framing on social media. He will cause outrage.

Chapter 2

DC Donna Morris climbs the steps to the paved top of the harbour wall. It is a curved limb, sheltering on one side yachts and an assortment of in-shore motor boats. Donna faces the other way. It is the first Tuesday in January 2014. It is the hour presaging dawn. *The opposite of dusk,* thinks Donna. She cannot wrangle out a term for it. Perhaps there isn't one. *Der Morgenstunde*: the German comes to her quicker than it has done in years.

The sky is turning from charcoal to ash, as if the fine rain is dousing any effort of the sun to set the horizon alight. A pace from where she is standing, the edge of the wall is a steep drop, sharp rock armour crowding around at its base. The sea is a heaving reflector for the sky. From the jagged water, oarweed raises its broad fronds in greeting, a chorus of slick brown hands. For a moment, the swaying gives Donna the impression that it is she who is adrift and about to topple. She clenches her hands in her pockets holding tight to an imaginary rail. She knows someone has tumbled over. One of those waving kelp leaves had turned out to be all too human.

Resolutely she turns to walk down the centre of the harbour arm. She can see there is activity at the wrist. A large light has been erected and there are two figures illuminated in its glare. As she approaches, one of them, a young PC, comes over. He is familiar. However, after only four and a bit months as a probationer with the Scarborough force, she can't put a name to the face. He obviously knows who she is. He is eager to update her. Donna remembers this eagerness from when she started in uniform. *Ten years ago.* She'd begun later than this youngster, after having children and several years as a Special. It's not as if the eagerness wears off – Donna still greets every work day with enthusiasm (well most of them anyway). It is merely that it becomes tempered by the knowledge: a dead body creates its own swell.

'Micky Harleson, thirty-seven years of age, found the body.' The PC is reading from his notes. Despite his local accent, he can't be that local or he would know the Harleson family as having fished in this sea for generations. The current owner of the boat catches lobster and crab. He was coming in after checking his pots when he noticed a marker buoy for a fellow fisher family's pots had come loose and was bobbing around by the harbour wall. Attempting to retrieve it brought him into this field of oarweed. The PC indicates to his right with his pen. Donna glances over. The imperceptible lightening of the sky is giving everything more definition. But, as if in opposition, the tide is rising, gobbing up onto the walkway, and engulfing the bobbing heads of the seaweed. 'He'd almost run over the body before he realised it was there. He called the inshore lifeboat and they pulled it out.'

'Him,' says Donna quietly, automatically.

'Him, yes. They took it, him, to the lifeboat station and from there he has gone to the mortuary. He's described as male, anywhere between late thirties and early fifties, quite well built, of average height.'

'Stab wounds,' Donna prompts. 'Somebody noticed stab wounds?'

The PC nods. 'The coxswain.' He pronounces it smoothly, correctly. You can't be five minutes in the town without learning how to get your tongue round coxswain. 'Thought one in the side. He can't be certain, he said, the body has been bashed about a lot and probably been a good supper for some of the wildlife out there.' He looks over his shoulder and for the first time loses a modicum of composure.

Donna lets her eyes follow his gaze. On a morning like this it is easy to believe in sea monsters.

The PC turns and adds quickly, 'That's what he said.' So it is the coxswain's lack of sensitivity, not his own.

'Good work,' says Donna, rousing herself from thoughts of Leviathan and colossal squids. 'The damage to him probably means he was in the sea for several days.'

'The coxswain thought maybe since Friday or Saturday. Any longer and there'd be even less of him.' Then he dives back into his notebook. 'The body, ah, he was wearing a Gansey. They're the pullovers knitted up and down the coast—'

'Yes, each place has its own design, so the drowned can be identified. Was it a Scarborough one?'

He nods.

'But Harleson and the lifeboat crew didn't recognise our guy?'

He shakes his head. 'Harleson didn't see him and, as I said, the face was apparently very damaged.'

'No ID?'

'None that the coxswain could find.'

'Probably at the bottom in there by now.' Donna inclines her head to the sea. She can hear its swooshing and farr-umphing onto the rock armour. It sends a tremor through the concrete spit she is standing on and into her feet. 'Thanks.' She begins to walk towards the other figure in the lamplight, Ethan Buckle, the crime scene manager.

'Erm, DC Morris, can I go now? It's the end of my shift.'

Donna pauses. Is it for her to say or should she leave the decision to DS Harrie Shilling, whom she has called and is on her way? She looks back at the PC; all at once he appears rather vulnerable. *Younger than my daughter and son,* she thinks. *Having to deal with too much for his years.* She wonders what her DI, Theo Akande, would do. Over the months she has found this a useful guide. She smiles. 'I'll just have a word with Ethan and then probably yes.' She doesn't add that it's the end of her shift too. She feels suddenly weary. But she will stay to hand over to Harrie and do whatever is required. 'Meanwhile, keep your eyes stripped.' She sees his look of incomprehension. *It's peeled,* she remembers. She adds by way of explanation, 'Make sure we are not disturbed.'

With the approach of day, some hardy types are out for their morning constitutionals, most with dogs, some running. The big glaring light is garnering interest. The PC tucks his notebook away and pulls his jacket up around his ears. The wind is sharp. The rain is still falling. Even so, he grins again and nods.

Donna reaches Ethan as he is putting away his camera. 'Is this our crime scene?' she asks.

12

'Your guess is as good as mine.' He is squat, shorter than Donna, and wider. Ex-military. In his late forties, he is a tad younger than Donna, though he hardly looks it with his pale bald pate this morning covered by a woollen hat. 'He was found down there, but whether he went in from here is debatable. Knowing how long he was in the sea and the tides and currents over that time might give us a clue. I've had a good scan of the walkway and not found anything of particular interest.'

'No pool of blood, for instance.'

Ethan returns her smile. 'Unfortunately not, DC Morris. Anyway, over the weekend there's been plenty of public traipsing through, not to mention the wet weather and overtopping. All adds up to an unacceptable level of contamination even if this is where our poor chap met his end.'

As if to prove his point, a wave slams into the base of the wall spitting up a spray of salt water to mingle with the drizzle already splattering their jackets.

Ethan picks up his camera case. 'I think it might be time to leave.'

Donna feels reluctant: it would be inadequate for 'our guy' if she doesn't probe further. 'Murder weapon?'

'Not that we've found. And if we go searching down there' – he nods towards the rock armour – 'we'll need a specialist team.'

He calls for the PC to help him with the light. Donna tells the youngster he can get off once he has completed the log at the police station. The two men retreat quickly along the narrow catwalk towards the town, people, traffic and, no doubt, a hot beverage of some sort.

Before she follows her colleagues, Donna takes one more look around. The sky and sea are now both pigeon-grey, with dark curtains of rain being pulled across by the stiffening easterly. Herring gulls, their wings spread, ride the wind, seemingly enjoying the rollercoaster, occasionally screeching to each other. A short walk away, behind her, Donna knows there are cafés and shops. *Even so,* she concludes to herself, *this is a cold place to die.*

Chapter 3

'Have we got enough glasses?' 'Have we got enough wine?' 'What about juice?' Wanda Buckle, the curator of the art gallery, is fussing. Alice Millson does not let it intrude on her calm as she carefully continues to set up her refreshments station. She is not surprised Wanda is practically having kittens. This photographic exhibition is a coup, Sebastian Hound's first since he emerged from his self-imposed seclusion. 'You'll be ready?' Wanda's voice has taken on a higher-pitched twitter. 'We'll be opening the doors in just under ten minutes.'

Alice looks up and grins. 'I am ready, Wanda. I was born ready.'

Wanda responds with an uncertain curving of the lips. However, Alice's reassuring expression is obviously enough as she moves away and flaps around the two meeters and greeters on the door.

Alice knows she gives off the air of being flaky. She still treasures the comment: 'So laid back as to be almost horizontal', from one of her sixth-form teachers over fifteen years ago now. Yet, in reality, she is rather good at organisation and time management. She completes the trays with fancy hors d'oeuvres which she and two colleagues will take turns in circulating, just as the man himself arrives, fashionably cutting it very fine indeed.

These days Sebastian Hound is a humble type. He'd found notoriety young and had squandered it, been arrogant, forgot fame is fickle and talent no guarantee of continued, or any, success. In recent years he has become sober. Without his coterie of acolytes around him, he could have been taken for a rather shy gallery assistant or a benign fatherly figure smartened up for someone else's festivities. He has his overcoat taken off him and assures Wanda several times that he is in perfect health and the drive over was just fine. Then he begins to warmly greet the staff and volunteers milling around. He reaches Alice, grasping her small hand in his ample paws. As he accepts an orange juice from her, she feels the graze of his electric-blue gaze over the length of her torso. *Rumours of him having a liking for buxom women – or any women, as long as they are in their twenties – have not been exaggerated,* she thinks. Neither her smile nor her fingers waver as she hands over the glass, but she'll give a brief warning to her younger co-workers. At least for this gig they don't have to wear silly-length skirts and skimpy tops. Not like at Saturday's party – frou-frou costumes comedy French maids would be proud of. A nun would be comfortable in the calf-length dress Alice is wearing. Burgundy to match the tips of her dark hair bobbed to rim her round face.

The gallery was once the fine summer abode of the aristocracy. Its large entrance hall is two storeys high with a black and white chequerboard tiled floor. At the level of the first floor is a balcony on its four sides. Below this, Alice is standing in front of the hall's ornate Carrara marble mantelpiece. Once the doors are opened, the place becomes thronged and Alice is occupied with making sure people have glasses which are periodically replenished and are being offered the plates of hors d'oeuvres. At the height of the preview, the noise in the hall is tremendous, voices and heels on tiles ricocheting up to the roof. After the speeches, when the crowd begins to thin slightly, Alice takes the opportunity to escape up the wide staircase with a basket to collect any abandoned glasses. There are several. If she were to see them, Wanda would get twitchy about the possibility of an accident resulting in broken glass too near the art-work. Alice quickly gathers them up. There are a few people up here, but it is altogether quieter and less frenetic. Alice pauses to take in some of the exhibition. She will come back, probably more than once, to study the technique. For all his failings, Sebastian Hound has a talent which Alice is keen to learn from.

Hound was barely twenty-one when he made his name in the mid-1990s. He started out with taking stark black and white photos of people caught off guard and landscapes in the throes of decay. His reputation detonated when he began to talk his way into select parties and it was celebrities who appeared in unposed awkwardness. His downfall came when his craving to be part of the in-crowd extended beyond his need to make art and when he added colour to his repertoire. In this exhibition he's back to monochrome, to stark clean lines, making the ordinary extraordinary. On the balcony, Alice leans in to examine more closely a collection of images taken in a market: butchers alongside fishmongers, greengrocers and booths hung with bags and underwear. The stallholder or customer often caught staring into the lens, challenging and challenged at the same time.

For a moment, she is so engrossed, she does not notice the woman standing just to the side of her. Alice's attention is drawn when the woman emits a strangled little whimper. She is tall – then most people appear tall to Alice – and stately, her ash-blonde hair in a large clip caught up severely away from her angular face. She has a long-fingered hand clamped over her mouth. She looks like she could be about to throw up. *Wanda would not like that.*

'Are you OK?' asks Alice. *Maybe the hor d'oeuvres were less than fresh?* She takes a step towards her. 'Can I help in any way?'

'What?' The woman turns to her, more surprised, or even afraid, than sickly.

Alice is relieved. 'You, you seem upset. I wonder if there is anything I can do to help?'

'I, er, I, this photo – it reminds me of someone.'

Alice looks at it. The image is dominated by the Humber Bridge. The woman is pointing at a small figure edging out of the frame. The body is made androgynous by a heavy formless jacket. The face is out of focus. The woman's fingers are now practically on the canvas, either to stroke the figure or maybe to scratch it out.

'I don't think you are supposed to touch,' says Alice, though gently. She can sense the strength of emotion coming off the woman.

This snaps her into action. She says sharply: 'Where's the photographer? Where's Sebastian Hound?'

'Downstairs, I think,' says Alice.

The woman marches off and Alice grabs her basket to scurry after. She halts, watching Wanda and Sebastian meet

18

the woman at the turn of the stair. Wanda starts doing the introductions, 'Sarah Franklande of ScarTek.'

ScarTek? Alice puts her basket down. Now she's definitely interested.

Wanda continues with less assurance: 'We've been so lucky to get funding for this exhibition from ScarTek. Leonard Arch, the owner, you've probably heard of him . . .'

The grabber of arses Saturday night. The night was really one to forget, for more reasons than Alice is prepared to consider fully. Even so, her cheeks burn at the flitting memory before she quashes it.

'Sarah facilitated . . .' Wanda flounders in the face of Sarah's angry features.

Sarah Franklande fills the void: 'Where is she? Where is Sylvia?'

Sebastian Hound smiles warily. 'I'm sorry?'

'The photo up there, with the Humber Bridge.' Sarah's words are distinct; she points upwards to the first floor gallery. 'Is Sylvia your model?'

The man remains cautious. 'I don't use models.'

'She's in one of the photos you took, the one of the Humber Bridge. Please.' Sarah's voice crumbles. 'If you know she's alive, tell me.'

'I'm sorry, I don't know who you mean. I don't pre-plan these things, they just materialise.' He holds his forearms up as if being threatened with a gun.

The people downstairs have gone quiet, captivated by the kerfuffle on the staircase. Now it looks like it might be Wanda who is sick. Then one of Sebastian Hound's companions, perhaps his agent from the luxury skirt suit and high heels she is sporting, approaches the trio. She takes Hound's arm and peels him away, murmuring something about an interview. Wanda gratefully follows them as they pad down the stairs. The audience below loses interest and conversations start up again. Only Sarah is left, stranded, it seems, on the turn of the stair. She puts a hand out to the broad banister. Alice notices it trembles.

She goes down to Sarah, giving a quick scan of the more than half-empty hallway. Her colleagues can be left to cope. She makes a decision. 'You OK?' she asks, touching the other woman's arm, which is holding her steady.

'I'm fine.' Sarah snatches her arm away, clutching it with the other one across her stomach. She juts her chin and nose up into the air.

'Well you don't seem fine. Maybe you'd like to sit somewhere, have a chat. I'm a good listener.'

'I have to go.' And she does, walking quickly but jerkily down the stairs, across the hallway and out the door.

'Your coat . . .' Alice calls. Sarah must have had a coat on an evening like this.

She does not appear to hear; she keeps on going. The door shuts behind her. Alice hurries down to the refreshment table to check she is not needed, then goes to the cloakroom and, with the help of the volunteer staffing it, retrieves Sarah's coat. A top-quality wool coat, flared from the shoulder, the colour of camel hair.

Outside is perishing, especially when compared to inside the building. Alice hesitates, thinking she should get her own jacket. *No time,* she tells herself. She steps out of the ring of brightness thrown by the lights from the art gallery and looks around. No one is moving. There is no sound from a car. *Probably she's already gone.* Even so, to be sure, she wanders over the road and up the steps into Crescent Gardens, from where she can see the street curving round to form its loop before exiting to the main road. Sarah is sitting on a bench, hunched over. When Alice approaches she can hear Sarah sniffling; she is wiping her cheeks and nose with her fingers.

'I brought your coat,' says Alice, sitting down. 'And I have tissues.' She offers them.

Sarah takes one and blows her nose. She also puts on her coat.

'Who is Sylvia?'

'You heard?' Sarah breathes hard. 'You're not from around here or you wouldn't have to ask.'

'No, I am not. And I am asking.' Alice knows she has to go slowly for her plan to work. She doesn't mind, she is truly interested. Other people's stories, particularly tragic ones, always pique her curiosity. 'Do you want to tell me about her?'

'No. I don't even know you.'

'My name is Alice Millson. Sometimes talking to a stranger can help.'

'No,' Sarah repeats crossly. She blows her nose again vigorously and turns towards Alice. Then something arrests what she was intending on doing or saying next.

Alice feels it too. Unexpectedly, a connection. She leans against the bench. They are sitting below a wide-spreading copper beech. Leafless, yet forming a canopy. A smudgy creamy curve is caught in the top branches. The moon is momentarily revealed through a crack in the clouds. *How romantic.* Alice tames her smile. She has a job to do.

However, Sarah is moving towards getting up. 'Thank you,' she says stiffly. 'Thank you for getting my coat. For the tissues.'

'Will you be all right?' asks Alice, realising she is genuinely concerned.

'I'll be fine. I have my car parked over there.' She is on the verge of leaving. She does not leave. She says, more quietly: 'I made a fool of myself, in there. It wasn't Sylvia in the photo. She died twenty years ago. I just wanted it to be her.' She lets out a heavy sigh. 'It's the season, I guess, the season for remembering losses.'

It is rather more poetic than Alice expected. 'I'm sorry,' she manages to croak.

Sarah stands. 'I must go.'

Alice notices Sarah's mouth is a smidge large for her face and lopsided. It now slips into a rather cute smile. Alice realises she is going to miss this opportunity if she is not careful. She shakes herself to say quickly, 'Yes, I must get back anyway, shoo out the last few punters, tidy up. I wonder—'

Sarah glances at the gallery. 'It was a good evening. Good turnout.'

'Yes. I wonder . . . I was wondering . . .'

'Yes?'

Deep breath. 'Would you fancy a coffee sometime?'

Sarah's mouth twists, perhaps showing her indecision.

'I'm new around here, I don't know many people.' Alice tells the half-truth fluently.

'OK,' Sarah says finally. She searches in her bag and pulls out a fancy monogrammed business-card case. She extracts a card and hands it over. 'Give me a call.'

'I will.'

'Good,' Sarah says. 'I'd like that.' There's a moment of awkwardness, then she adds, 'I mean, I'd like the chance to thank you properly, buy you a coffee.'

'Perfect.'

'Goodnight.'

'Goodnight.'

Still Sarah lingers, before she turns abruptly and walks away.

'Dr Sarah Franklande,' Alice reads on the card. 'Senior Managing Biochemist, ScarTek.' Then a mobile number and an email. *Perfect. How civilised,* Alice says to herself. *Coffee with the enemy.*

Chapter 4

After being relieved by DS Harrie Shilling mid-morning yesterday, Donna slept enough to feel relatively perky for the first case briefing on 'our guy'. She still finds the transition from nights to days unsettling, and normally she would have forty-eight hours off to adjust to it. But with a murder and the recent staffing cuts to an already small force, everyone who can, gets in at nine. They take their seat in the main CID office, the ops room for the investigation. *All hands to the pumps*, Donna thinks, pleased she has discovered its true meaning is a nautical one. She notices even DC Brian Chesters is here on time and (through his banter with others, she learns) on his day off. He places himself at the back of the room. He's had his hair cut. No longer gelled into spikes, it is more of a buzz cut. Despite his thirty-six years of age, his expression of extreme indifference would gratify a teenager. He adopts it as Harrie comes in accompanied by DI Theo Akande, taking their places at the front. Donna can sense the anticipation. It's that moment in a case when all seems possible.

Harrie stands, a reflex to give herself more presence. In her mid-thirties, of medium height, slight build, with blonde hair and pale skin varnished by a tanning cream, she is used to being underestimated. Not by her colleagues. Most of them, at least. Donna snatches a glance at Brian. *He has his eyes closed!* She tunes in to Harrie's summary of what they know about 'the deceased'. The story of how he was discovered is familiar to Donna. Then Harrie moves on to the autopsy.

'Our vic was about thirty years old, five foot nine, or one-point-seven-five metres, and just under thirteen stone. Brown hair. In good health, fit, before he ended up in the harbour. Professor Hari Jayasundera says there was one stab wound, in the side, as if our victim was turning away. The weapon was probably a chef's knife, one of those with a big blade, very sharp. The prof says the stabbing would have been lethal without immediate treatment. However, the deceased's lungs have water in them: he was alive when he went in the water. There was some bruising on his knuckles, as if he landed a few punches before the knife came out. Presumptive toxicity reports have found low levels of alcohol in our vic's blood and' – she pauses to look at her notes – 'possible presence of something like a sleeping pill. Confirmatory tests will tell us more. However, all in all, given the deceased's physique, he would have been difficult to overpower, which means the prof is suggesting two attackers. ToD is, as ever, relatively wide, up to eighty-four hours before the body was found. Undigested stomach contents show the man ate some rice and chickpeas a few hours before he was killed.'

'Could have been a Friday or Saturday night brawl, then,' someone offers up.

Harrie nods. Untimely death by another's hand is not unknown in the little town. As they are all well aware, where it does happen, beer and a fiery temper are the most likely contributing factors.

Harrie sits. DI Theo Akande takes over. He is only a tad

taller than Harrie, ten years older and of a slim build. He is wearing a dark suit. The green of his tie matches the rims of his glasses. He has his hair in short, neat cornrows. The only black face in the throng of white, plus his sexuality sets him apart, he nevertheless commands the room with hard-won respect. He remains seated.

'Now to what we don't know,' he says. 'The two main things are: we don't know who our victim is; and we don't know where he entered the sea. He was wearing a Gansey in the local pattern, which suggests a fisherman from the area.'

'I doubt it, sir,' says PC Trevor Trench, shifting his bulk in his chair. 'If you don't mind me saying, if Micky Harleson and the coxswain didn't recognise him, can't be from around here. More likely a yachty.' Trench himself comes from one of the older fishing families. The boat had to be sold in the bad old day of the 1970s, and he joined the force when he came of age.

'You make a valid point, thank you, Trevor,' says Theo. 'Unfortunately, rocks and sea creatures have made our victim's face barely recognisable.'

Most of the incomers consider this with varying levels of horror. The natives nod grimly.

'So how are we going to make an ID?' asks Trevor.

'If necessary, we will have a computer-aided face reconstruction done.' There's a pause into which Donna (and probably everyone else) supplies: *Good luck getting the funding for that.* Then Theo continues, 'Meanwhile, we've got DNA, and we follow up the usual channels of databases and mispers. We have dental records which we can approach local dentists with. We start talking to people. And there's one more thing, Harrie?'

Harrie taps into a keyboard and an image appears on the screen beside them. There's a delicately drawn large fish curving elegantly across white skin. It looks like a dolphin to Donna. She is mistaken.

'Our deceased had it on his right upper arm. The prof tells me it as a vaquita,' Shilling says. 'A kind of porpoise which is critically endangered because it keeps getting caught in illegal fishing nets. We need to check with tatt studios, see if any of them will own it, and, more crucially, recorded who they did it on.'

They all take a moment to admire the creature's grace and colours, then Harrie snaps them to a list of tasks. She asks individual officers to start the searches of the databases and queries with the dentists and tattoo artists. 'Trevor you will take a team to the harbour to start asking questions and do the usual searches of dumpsters and the like for the murder weapon. Brian you will start retrieving CCTV—'

'Where from?' Brian retorts. He goes on sulkily, 'We don't even know if the body went in from here or somewhere else on the coast.'

'Exactly,' says Harrie as tetchily. 'Which is why Donna will go down with Trevor and also have a conversation with the harbour master about tides, currents and weather. Everyone OK? Let's get moving then.'

Donna stands up. She makes a sign to Trev, she just has to go to the '. . .'. He nods; he understands. She leaves the room on the way to the toilets, passing Brian who looks deep in thought and as if a thunderous storm is passing through his brow.

27

Chapter 5

Despite the lid of cloud resting on the rooftops and the mizzle, they walk. On the whole, Donna prefers to walk, as does Trevor, though some of the team are less keen. However, even they have to admit it is usually quicker. The direct route is down the pedestrianised high street. It is busy with people getting their lunch from the bakeries and cafés. The officers cut down Bar Street, the extent of the medieval town as it crept up the cliffs from the sea. It retains its retro flavour, though, of Georgian times, with the bow-fronted shop windows. A few paces from its end and they are perched as if on a slumbering giant's shoulder, the bay the curve of its neck. Below is the beach and the harbour, its boats and buildings a child-giant's abandoned toys. On a day like today, the palette is grey on darker grey, the horizon obscured. Even so, Donna pauses to breathe it in, released from the crammed CID room, the squabbles between Harrie and Brian, the tensions in Donna's own life. *We are small,* she thinks.

Her movement is easier as she takes the steps down through St Nicholas Gardens and onto Foreshore Road. Slightly enviously, she has been listening to Trev expound on his recently born first grandchild. Now he asks after her kids. She starts about the one who is easiest to talk about, Christopher, her second born. He and his wife came to visit his parents when Donna had spent Christmas in Kenilworth. Home. She uses the word home to describe the house she lovingly tended with her husband all those years. And after a few days there, it does take on a home-like quality. However, here feels like home too. She feels stretched between the two places. Kenilworth, where Jim, her husband of thirty years, is. And Scarborough, where she's chosen to come to be close to her daughter and, a little to her surprise, she's building a career, an independent life. Currently she does not know how to resolve these conflicting claims. So, more often than not, she tucks it all away.

As they reach sea level, they can hear the waves. They are consoling to Donna. 'Sh-shush-sh-shush-sh,' they seem to be saying. *No need to find answers quite yet.*

'Architect isn't he, your son?' asks Trev.

She nods. 'Setting up his own practice now, in London. He's doing well.' Christopher has his path set. She doesn't have to worry about him. Though she still does, on occasion. A mother's prerogative.

'And your daughter? Did she come home?'

Trev is not one of the ones 'in the know'. Donna does not enlighten him. She shakes her head.

'Shame, not having all the family together. You had a good time, though?'

'Yes.'

Trev is no longer really listening; he does not hear the uncertainty in her voice. She had set off to Kenilworth determined to confess to Jim about how she really left Germany in the 1980s. But he had folded her back into their old life,

29

and she had found it delightfully easy to slip into her role as doting wife and mother. The trip back to Kenilworth was a missed opportunity and she knows it. Somehow the words would not come. She turns her attention to the present.

Trev is rallying his troops, the three other PCs he has been assigned to start the enquiries. He repeats what he has already told them at the station. He has a ponderous style; even so, they hang onto every word. He tells two to go off and start the dumpster search, which they do with more enthusiasm than Donna would have mustered. She always hated the smell and the bags of unidentifiable mush. The other PC is sent to begin questioning people working at the businesses along the foreshore. Before joining him, Trev takes Donna to introduce her to the harbour master.

The harbour master turns out to be a harbour mistress. A solid woman in her forties called Irene. She greets Trev like an old friend. They take several minutes to swap greetings and family news, before PC Trench takes his leave. Irene gets Donna a cup of herbal tea and herself a coffee. They are upstairs in a long, brick-built building. It is on the fishing quay which creates an open pincer with the harbour wall. The office has a large oblong window giving a good view of the harbour, with its raggle-taggle colony of local boats and the pontoons where the sleeker yachts are tied up. Beneath the window stands the chart table. It's here Irene takes Donna. She recognises the outline on the chart as that of the North Yorkshire coast, but it is as if it is a negative image to the road maps Donna is used to. Apart from around its edge, the land is an undifferentiated mass, whereas the sea is brought into sharp relief with colours and sweeping contours. *It is,* Donna thinks, *quite beautiful.*

In her no-nonsense way Irene is explaining about the longshore drift, which basically moves sediments and objects down the coast north to south. 'But we have this.' She points to the protrusion which is the castle hill between the two Scarborough bays. She does a little twirl with her fingers. 'Currents get turned back on themselves here on the north side. And in South Bay we have equally circular currents set up.'

'So a body could not have ended up on this side of the harbour wall from North Bay or from South Bay?'

'I'm not saying couldn't. Less likely. You still don't know when he went in?'

Donna shakes her head.

'Given time, he could have worked his way round. But from our report from the RNLI, it doesn't sound like he was in long enough.'

'Could he have come from a boat at sea?'

'Yes, that is possible. However, according to the coxswain, the body was hitched to the flagpole on the top of the buoy. It had gone through the front of his Gansey.'

'So?'

Irene straightens and uses her hands to illustrate. 'Imagine my fist is the buoy. It always keeps the flagpole upright, that's the point of it, to mark where the pots are.' She sticks her left index finger upwards, then moves her right hand sideways towards it. 'If a body comes in from this direction, brought in on the current or tide, it's not going to get caught.' Her right hand shifts to above her left and then down onto it. 'From this direction, it could.'

31

Donna feels a fizz of excitement. 'You're saying, in all likelihood, our man came off the harbour wall onto the buoy with its upright flagpole below?'

Irene shrugs. 'It makes sense to me.'

'The buoy had come loose, right? Do we know when?'

'Not precisely. It was where it should have been Saturday morning.'

'And Mr Harleson found it by the harbour wall Tuesday morning.' Donna thinks this new information over. 'Could our man have fallen off a boat onto the flagpole and they both come in together?'

'Possible. However, with the tide and currents as they were, a man's body snagged on what is essentially a bit of cane, it's more likely the pole would have got snapped off if it were further out from the shelter of the harbour wall.'

'Which means we're looking at our man going off the harbour wall above where he was found?'

'It's my best guess.'

Donna thought any best guess from the indomitable Irene was probably a very good one. She left the office with a lighter step.

Chapter 6

'Where's Orson?' asks Alice as she plops herself onto the sofa in Fareeha Gopal's flat. It is in the same large building as Alice's, a former Victorian boarding house – or bawdy house, as Orson would quip a bit too frequently. However, Fareeha's apartment is more extensive. Her lounge, which also incorporates a tiny galley, is at least separate from the bedroom. Alice's lodgings, up another flight, is one room with a cubby hole for a bathroom partitioned off. But then Fareeha has her bookkeeping income and Ian to share the rent with. Alice has to pay it all herself.

Despite its diminutive proportions, Alice is comfortable in her room. She imagines the original occupants: maids who spent their long days cleaning, fetching and answering the needs of others, the attic being the only space which was truly theirs. Perhaps two of them shared where Alice now lives alone. She likes to think they would have listened to each other's troubles and rubbed tinctures of rosemary and camphor into each other's aching shoulders and feet. Besides, from her dormer window (enlarged once the maids had left), Alice can see over adjacent roofs to a slim scrape of sea meeting sky.

'Haven't you heard from him?' asks Fareeha. She brings over a tray of tea and home-made zeera biscuits.

Alice can smell the butter with hint of cumin. She bites into one of the biscuits. 'Mmm, Fareeha, these are the best.'

'Thanks,' Fareeha says dully. She lowers herself into the armchair and puts her swollen ankles up on a woven pouffe. Patterned with stylised lotus, rhododendrons and tigers in rich reds, indigo and gold, she purchased it on a trip to see relatives in Pakistan. It is one of the few things she brought with her on her progress east: from Bradford to Scarborough. 'I dropped Orson a WhatsApp this morning to remind him,' Fareeha says. 'No response. He shared that photo of a robin on his Insta account on Friday, with the comment about pesticides being a danger to wildlife. Nothing since.'

Hasn't he posted the footage from Saturday night? Alice hasn't wanted to check.

'Have you spoken to him?'

'No.' Alice's denial (though factually accurate) rings off-key even to herself. She takes a gulp of tea. Her mouth has gone dry. She ends up choking, taking several moments to recover.

'What?' asks Fareeha, fixing her with a shrewd glare. 'What are you not telling me?'

Why hadn't she told her friend everything when she had given her the brief description of the penthouse party? It had been since Ian moved in. For some unexpressed reason, Orson didn't like the man and this has made Alice cautious.

Now she has divined from Alice's expression there is stuff which is not being said, Fareeha won't let it go. She chivvies and calls on the honesty which is supposed to be the bedrock of their friendship. 'Come on, come on, Alice.

34

It can't be that bad,' she says. Then she leans forward slightly. 'Bloody hell, it is that bad. What did he do this time?'

'The party, at the penthouse, he was there.' Alice's gut does the same dive it had when she saw Orson as the fulcrum of the wheel of smartly turned-out revellers. As she explains what happened, she re-hears Orson's words: *I've got enough to bring you down*. She sees again the fury in both the faces, the visage of the cravat-wearing Arch going a particularly vivid puce. 'It was as if they knew each other,' she says to Fareeha, as she realises it. 'It was as if it was personal.'

'Everything's personal with Orson,' retorts Fareeha. Then after a few moments she says, 'And you didn't tell me all this before because . . . ?'

Alice takes her time in answering. A sip of lukewarm tea, a nibble of biscuit to replenish the energy recalling Saturday night has taken. She decides she can't mention Orson's antagonism with Ian. 'I was angry,' she starts, recognising she was. Is.

'Angry? You, Alice?'

'Guess who had to clean up the mess? Muggins me. Orson didn't think about that, did he? And he—' She stops herself, the misery caused by her last argument with Orson still impactful.

'What?'

'He told me he was going to do it. He asked me to help. I told him no. I told him why. I couldn't risk my job. And he wouldn't listen. He had no . . . no compassion for me, no understanding.'

'Pretty typical Orson, then.'

'He listens to me.' Alice is abruptly defensive, protective

of the friendship she has with Orson. 'He's kind, usually.' She runs out of steam.

'Yeah,' Fareeha says carelessly. 'Until it suits him not to be.' She rests her mug on her pregnancy bump and stares down into it. Impending motherhood is not treating her well. Her normally smooth olive-wood-toned skin is decidedly grey. She is in an uncharacteristically scruffy set of sweat pants and shirt. Her long black hair is tied up in a greasy knot.

Glad to be free of Fareeha's microscope, Alice transfers her concern to her friend. 'You not doing so good, huh?'

Fareeha sips her tea. 'I haven't felt good since . . . since? Oh yes, since before I was pregnant.' Her tone rises in a crescendo. She flops forwards.

'Can I do anything for you?'

Fareeha shakes her head. A tear dribbles down her cheek. She swipes at it.

'Ian? He's looking after you?' Alice glances around as if expecting Ian to materialise.

Fareeha searches out a tissue and blows her nose. 'Don't know where he is.'

'What do you mean you don't know where he is?' Ian had one of those jobs – some kind of construction site management, Alice thinks – where he has contracts which would take him away from Scarborough for weeks at a time. Sometimes even abroad. But Fareeha always knew where he was. Approximately.

'He said he had a job on in Thurso.' Fareeha answers the rucking of Alice's forehead: 'I googled it, it's right up in the north of Scotland. He left Saturday morning. He hasn't answered his phone since. It says the number is not available. He's left me, Alice.' Fareeha crumples. She begins to hiccup sobs.

'Oh, sweetheart.' Alice rushes over. She takes Fareeha's mug before it tumbles to the floor and puts it on the nearby occasional table. Then she tries to enfold her friend's bulk in her arms. 'I'm sure he hasn't,' she mumbles into the crown of Fareeha's head. Indeed, Alice can think of several other reasons why Ian might not have been in touch, none of them good. Car crashes of various ferocities go through her mind. However, she is not surprised Fareeha's thoughts have gone the way they have. Ever since the unplanned pregnancy was confirmed, Ian has been halfway through the door. He would get the award for the least committed father-to-be, if there is one, and Alice would be glad to smack him over the head with it. Especially now.

'There's more,' says Fareeha through her snots and sniffs. 'Ian said he always worked for one of two companies, Lightfoots and Rimridge Constructions. I started out by seeing if they had a job on in Thurso. But, Alice' – Fareeha turns her face so Alice can see into her eyes, her dark brown irises floating in pools – 'there are no construction companies called Lightfoots and Rimridge. They don't exist.'

'Perhaps—' Alice starts.

'No, Alice, they've never existed. I went through Companies House records. And' – her fingers clutch at Alice's arms – 'there's no big construction project in Thurso. Ian said it was a bridge. They've already got a bridge,' Fareeha finishes, as if this is the clincher.

'He wouldn't just leave,' says Alice. 'Not with the baby.'

'Don't be sentimental, Alice,' says Fareeha, her tone becoming harsher. 'It's the baby he is running away from.' She pulls herself out of Alice's embrace. She stands, pausing to get her balance. Then she walks to the bay window. The street is a residential one, with similar Victorian villas on the other side, each with their own gated front garden. Some are tidier than others. Luckily for Alice and Fareeha, the retired teacher downstairs keeps theirs neat and is happy for anyone from the house to sit in it. Today, though, no one is sitting out. Those who are braving the rain hurry past in raincoats. This close to the Esplanade, which runs along the cliffs above the South Bay, umbrellas are no match for the wind; they end up battered and turned inside out. 'Mum said she didn't trust him,' continues Fareeha. 'I said it was only because he is white and she was being racist. Well, Ammi, you were right, you were fucking right.' She shouts this at the pane in front of her.

Alice picks up their mugs, going over to the kettle, offering to make another cuppa. Her friend nods, still staring morosely out at the street. Once she has prepared the tea and taken it over to her, Alice tentatively suggests the police.

'When did you become such a fan of the pigs? Don't we spend most of our time trying to avoid them?'

'I've got nothing against them as individuals; they are just people, like us, trying to make a living.'

'Are they? You sound like my dad now.' Like this is a fault to be wary of.

'I was only concerned that Ian might have had an accident.'

'And Orson is kind. Oh, Alice, you always think the

best of people. But the truth is people – men . . .' She puts the emphasis on the word as if it is in capitals. 'Men are irresponsible. Men are unreliable. You're right to renounce them, they're not worth the effort.'

'I never said that,' says Alice, feeling a tad prickly. She doesn't like being misrepresented. 'I've got nothing against men—'

'I know, you prefer women. You tell me they are sexier. I wish I felt the same. Look where fancying a man has got me.' Fareeha strokes her bump gently. For the first time this afternoon, she smiles.

Some of the tension slips from Alice's shoulders. She gives her friend a peck on the cheek.

They both return to sit on the sofa. 'I knew Ian would let me down,' says Fareeha. 'Eventually. But I did think Orson was more dependable. He's never missed a meeting before.'

'I could cycle out to his caravan. Have a look around.'

Fareeha inclines her head to the window. 'Horrible day for a cycle. Leave it until tomorrow. He's probably just forgotten. Or he's too absorbed in deciding what to do with the film he captured at the penthouse party to worry about us waiting for him. Let's do something useful. Take our minds off useless men. What's on the agenda?'

Chapter 7

The morning has drifted into the afternoon and Donna is feeling decidedly less lively. She has spent more time than she wanted cooped up with a woman in one of the souvenir shops. She didn't have anything useful to add to the current investigation, but had taken the opportunity to moan about the lack of police action over shoplifters and when her car was keyed. This last was in Bridlington, so not North Yorkshire's jurisdiction. When Donna explained this, the woman had said the police always had an excuse for doing nothing. Donna then tried to get more information on the shoplifting and the woman proceeded with a rant in general about young people. Despite her good intentions, Donna stopped listening, more aware of the surges of heat stampeding through her and the drill bit beginning to screw itself into the side of her head. In the end she had to take her leave without having placated the woman. 'And one of those brats kicked in the CCTV camera at the end there,' the woman said as Donna left. 'Not a week back, it's the only one we have this end of the harbour.'

Convenient, Donna manages to squeeze into her broiling brain, as she steps out into the air again. She heads to a bench to take deep draughts from her water bottle and dose herself with painkillers. It's at times like these she wonders whether she is up to the job. *I am not sick,* she tells herself severely, *just peri-menopausal.* Slowly, she recovers some composure. The stiff breeze wipes her face like an abrasive cloth dunked in ice. She is glad of it. The water in the harbour lifts and falls in a soothing rhythm. The tiny sanderlings, refugees from the Arctic, scamper on their improbably long, thin legs, as if constantly behind schedule for something. Donna is reminded of the White Rabbit. This in turn makes her think of reading *Alice in Wonderland* to Elizabeth and of her daughter resting her head against her shoulder, for once quiet and attentive. Donna sighs. Had she valued those precious moments of intimacy over twenty years ago? *On the whole, yes,* she tells herself. She imagines the older Elizabeth with her now, sitting close. Her light brown hair is less silken, her face more sallow, but she would still giggle at the antics of the sanderlings and gaze at the grace of a cormorant taking a dive below the dark surface of the sea. *Maybe one day. Maybe one day soon.*

She goes to find her colleagues at the little café in the armpit of the harbour wall. They are devouring coffee and bacon butties. She joins them on the latter, realising how hungry she is. Their haul of information has been relatively fruitful. One of the young lasses working on the doughnut stall was down here on Saturday night at the pub by the fishing quay, the Kiss Me Hardy. It was busy, raucous. Could this general rowdiness have tipped over into violence? Donna's younger colleagues think yes. In any case, it would all need following up. Plus there was a party at the new penthouse above the amusements. Not only is it closer to the harbour wall, it also claims panoramic views. But most satisfying of all, they have found a knife. A chef's knife, discarded into a dumpster.

Chapter 8

Alice stomps out her annoyance into the pavements. The rain has eased. However, from the Esplanade, the castle keep's ruins, hunkering down on their promontory between the bays, have cloud for a muffler. At the bottom of the gardens sweeping down below Alice, the Victorian Gothic spa buildings are in dark outline, their honey-coloured sandstone wet. The low cloud laps around them, as if part of the sea she can hear shushing at the heels of the cliffs.

She continues into town, already beginning to forgive Fareeha. Her friend, with dissecting precision, scratched and nipped at Alice's suggestions. Inadvertently echoing Orson's cutting words, she said at one point: 'Is this the best we can do? People are dying.'

But Fareeha is grieving, she's scared, she's been abandoned. Alice understands this. And it's not like she doesn't have a point, or several. A litterpick and a newsletter asking people to grill candidates for next year's council elections on environmental issues are not going to change the world. 'It's hardly a gnat's bite on a rhino's arse,' as Fareeha eloquently put it. *Better to be doing something,* Alice tells herself. The despondent wrap-up to their 'meeting' meant Alice didn't tell Fareeha about her chance encounter with Sarah Franklande of ScarTek and how she intends to exploit it.

This nugget she holds to herself. She realises she has unconsciously brought her palm to her chest, to cover her heart.

She heads inside the library. She has done some preliminary googling and has plotted Sarah's career trajectory from the ScarTek biography. She has deduced that Sarah left the Scarborough area around 1994, when she was twenty-two, after completing a masters at York University. Unlike many of her generation, Alice is fond of libraries. She is especially attached to archives of local papers. Sarah's words the evening before, 'You're not from around here or you wouldn't have to ask', suggest these might be a place to start.

A helpful assistant sets her up with the microfiche. Alice begins at the end of 1994, working in reverse, her notepad by her side. She doesn't have to search for long before the yarn starts to unwind, backwards. Hence she comes across the third death first. Sylvia Franklande, aged thirteen years and eleven months, walked into the sea and drowned, ten days after she had found her parents dead. Alice puts her pen down and rubs her hand over her face. Up to now, this had just been a fascinating story to unpick. But this cuts deep. A young woman – a girl – at the start of her life in such a state as to decide to kill herself. Alice has never felt that low. She has known girls who had.

Why had no one stopped Sylvia? Why had no one been there for her? Where was Sarah? Alice searches her notes. Sarah's name appears several times, listed as one of the children, along with Roland, her elder brother. Twenty-two and twenty-four respectively. *What is it with local papers and ages?* Even the age for one of the police officers is given. Then she finds it: Sarah was away, travelling in Spain. Alice sits back. For a moment she allows herself to move her thoughts away from the Franklande heartbreak, to recall her own backpacking trips through Europe ten years after Sarah's. What would it be like to travel with her? *Stuffy, planned and over-organised*, Alice tells herself quickly. The opposite to the way she likes it.

She wonders about leaving the rest of her research for another day. But she must be nearly at the beginning of it all. She might as well carry on. She turns back to the microfiche. Sylvia had left a note for her distraught best friend, Miriam Toogood. The wording is reproduced in the paper. Sylvia wrote that she needed to get away and, intriguingly, had added 'Gilbert Grape' in brackets under her name at the bottom. Alice wonders what the significance is and decides to do an internet search later.

She continues to wind back. The Franklande family hardly fall off the front page. Finally she gets to the opening stark headline. Saturday the 8 January 1994: 'New Year Tragedy.' She reads on: 'Yesterday the bodies of Philip Franklande, 48, and his wife June, 43, were found at their house on Peasholm Crescent. Both had been shot. They were found by their youngest daughter Sylvia, returning from spending several days with a friend.' The piece goes onto record the disbelief of neighbours, both Phil and June being 'a lovely couple, quiet and friends with everyone'. Having read later articles, Alice knows this tune will change.

She slaps down her pen. She takes a breath, as if she is surfacing from being submerged in murky water. *The season for remembering. The season for losses.* Sarah's words come back to her. Then she makes the connection. *This happened twenty years ago, on the nail.*

She presses the button to fast roll the microfiche onto its spool. It makes a satisfying snap as it finishes. She knows enough about this part of Sarah's life for now.

Outside, the day which never really dawned has turned to dusk. Alice checks her phone, which she has had on silent. There is a text from Fareeha. She has talked to her mum who has said go to the police about Ian. Will Alice go with her? Alice is glad of the distraction. She texts: 'Now?' Her friend does not respond until much later; she has been asleep. They agree to go the next day, after Alice has checked on Orson.

Chapter 9

There is a buzz in the CID section. Donna can sense it as soon as she arrives. She picks up the gist of it. The body has been ID-ed. DC Brian Chesters (working late) got the break – through luck or graft, depending on who you are listening to.

At the briefing, DI Akande confirms the rumour. 'The deceased has been identified as Colin, or Col, Flither,' he says.

This does not quieten the buzz. It only increases, as if bees really have taken up residence in the room. Donna glances around. She's too new to know what is bothering some people, including Theo. She merely notices the absence of the usual sense of relief at this kind of news.

Trev stands up as though needing his heft to make his point. 'Col Flither is too well known hereabouts for Micky and half the RNLI crew not to recognise him.'

Theo nods. Before he can respond, Brian cuts in: 'His face was bloated and eaten.'

'Even so,' says Trev stoutly.

'He's been away nigh on three years,' Brian continues. 'People change.'

'Not thirty-year-olds. Not that much,' says Trev. He carries on more quietly. 'And he's not been away, lad, he's been dead—'

'Missing,' Brian snaps.

'Dead. Down with his trawler, off the Faroes.'

'Missing,' repeats Brian. 'Nothing proven.'

Theo intercedes. 'Enough discussion, gentlemen, thank you.'

Trev sits. Brian scowls and folds his arms.

'However, I am grateful that you have clarified the problem we have. We have an ID for someone who is presumed already dead. Sceptical as some of us may be, we need to follow the lead.' He glances over at Trevor. Theo's expression brooks no argument. The experienced PC doesn't give any. 'Donna and I will be going to talk to Patricia Flither, Col's mother, this morning.'

Donna has been so busy watching the unspoken interplay around her, she is surprised to hear her name. Surprised and pleased. She enjoys working with her DI and the situation intrigues her. She now understands why he is wearing his sombre-coloured suit and navy tie, why his glasses are his round lensed, wire-rimmed ones. Dressed for a visit to the bereaved.

Brian is less than happy and bursts out, 'I pulled it in, I should be able to close on it.'

'Who is talking about closing anything?' asks Theo. 'And you speaking to her last night is the very reason why Donna is coming with me today. I want a different perspective.' Brian opens his mouth. Theo cuts him off: 'I am willing to overlook you taking Mrs Flither to see the body last night without my permission—'

'She insisted,' says Brian. 'You're the one who says we should listen to the victim's family.'

Theo continues firmly: 'We will do this my way from now on, DC Chesters. You are so sure our deceased is Col Flither, you find him on CCTV.'

Brian folds in on himself.

Theo looks round the room for Harrie. She is sitting to one side, like Donna, like all the others, observing. Harrie has one slender, tweezered eyebrow arched. Her lips are pulled into a flat line. Donna thinks there could be something of a note of sadness in the droop of her shoulders. Harrie straightens and takes over the briefing. The knife is with forensics. She sends a team down to the harbour once more, specifically to the Kiss Me Hardy, and sets another one on finding out more information about the party at the penthouse.

'Are we only asking about Col Flither?' one of the PCs dares to ask.

'No,' says Harrie. 'That remains only one line of inquiry.'

Everyone, including Donna, holds their breath for a response from Brian. None is forthcoming. He studiously examines his feet planted on the carpet in their two-tone leather shoes.

New? Expensive? thinks Donna.

Then the surface tension is broken by Theo standing, catapulting them all into movement, like stranded boats lifted by a tide.

The Flithers are 'bottom-enders'; one of the families who have fished out of Scarborough since for ever. They live where town meets harbour, in terraces along streets squeezed between foreshore and the castle hill, which turn sharply and steeply as they cling to the incline. The house Donna and Theo has come to is in mourning. The grief feels old. Deep-rooted and gnawing. It is seeped into the walls like stale tobacco smoke.

Patricia Flither opens the door before they have a chance to ring the bell. She is a heavy woman, her face lined, her grey hair tightly held back. Donna knows no more than a few years separate her from Pat, but the other woman looks at least ten years older, well into her sixties. The only bits of colour about her person are provided by the bold turquoise pattern on her bulky cardi, which she clamps about her with rigid arms across her abdomen. She leads them into the front room. Its window gives straight onto the street and a dense net curtain shrouds the outside while the double glazing deadens the exterior sounds. The large-screen TV dominates, there are books and magazines on a small book-case, other shelves and the mantelpiece are crowded with photos.

Theo and Donna have been offered the overstuffed armchairs, while Pat Flither sits on the sofa next to Doug. According to the police log, he also accompanied her the previous night. Doug Prichard is Pat's brother-in-law. He is five foot seven or eight – similar in height to Theo. However, Doug is stocky. He is wearing a baggy brown pullover and cords. He is in his seventies. The hairless crown of his head is patched as if with the skin of trout and the flesh of salmon. His white face is round and jowly. His eyes are navy. At the station, Trev had given a brief biography for both of them. In her late teens, Pat had married a salesman from the Midlands who took her away from the sea. It didn't last. She returned to Scarborough with twin babies, Emma and Colin, and never used her married name again. 'Em's a teacher,' Trev had said. 'Lives two doors down from her mum, but Col, well he was always a bit of a handful.' As for Doug, reluctantly retired from the sea, he has cancer, probably terminal.

Donna watches admiringly as Theo apparently disregards the slight stiffness which has greeted their – or is it just his? – appearance, to address Pat Flither with genuine warmth. 'I know this is a difficult time for you, Mrs Flither. Losing a son is painful, especially under these circumstances.'

Pat nods wearily.

'Could you tell us when you last saw Colin, Mrs Flither?' Theo asks.

Doug answers for her. 'Eighteen months, thereabouts. He had his berth on a trawler working off the Faroes. We told that young constable of yorns last night.' One of his chins pinkens, there's a dewiness in the corner of one of his eyes.

'He's gone sentimental,' was Trev's verdict back at the station.

Theo relaxes. 'I know, Mr Prichard, but we need to go over things, to be sure we've understood the sequence of events.' He looks directly at Pat. 'Could you tell us, Mrs Flither, when you last heard from Colin?'

'She answered all this last night,' says Doug. 'It's been a while.'

'I was wondering, Mrs Flither, if you could be more specific?'

She's not meeting his eye. Donna follows her gaze across the throng of photographs. There are black and white images of what are probably grandparents and great aunts and uncles receding into the past. Some have the stiff poses of studio shots, some more casual with boats and the harbour as scenery. Then there are the colour ones. Donna can trace the twins from their birth to toddlers to children to teenagers. The boy's grin going from cheeky to defiant. Pride of place is taken by the photos of the girl grown into a woman: receiving her degree; dressed for some posh dinner; at her wedding day; with a child; then with two. The narrative for the boy seems to halt abruptly with an out-of-focus snapshot of a young man on a fishing boat; he is sturdy, his arms muscular and his hair is razored short. It's difficult to glean any particular likeness to their deceased. Thinking about how the photo-story of her own daughter, Elizabeth, came to an end, Donna asks, 'Is that Colin, Mrs Flither?'

She nods.

'Is that your most recent photo of him?'

Another nod. 'He didn't like having his photo taken. Daft superstition.' Her voice rasps as if underused.

Donna catches Theo's eye; he indicates with a slight nod he approves her intervention and she can carry on. 'Tell me about Colin,' she says.

'He was a good lad. There's many ud say he wasn't, but he was. He'd have been coming for my birthday, that's why he was on his way home.'

'When's your birthday, Mrs Flither?'

'Middle of December.'

No one points out Col would have been almost a month late – better late than never appears to be enough for his mother. 'And he was trawling?' asks Donna.

'No choice, had he?' Pat snaps.

Theo and Donna may be outsiders, but even they understand the divide between the inshore fishermen and the trawlers. Fishing folk in Scarborough used to catch fish. The herring haul was legendary and was the origin of the fair immortalised in song. No longer. The EU quotas and the trawlers took away livelihoods. The locals complain about the number of licences given to trawlers. These bigger boats, with their large metal chains, cut through the lines which tether the crab and lobster pots set by the local fishermen. However, some young people choose the money and adventure offered by the trawlers, especially if the family boat has been sold or it can't sustain all the offspring. Trawling is preferable to taking a job on land, even if it is the cause of some strained nights in the pub.

'There were people who didn't like him trawling?' asks Donna.

'That's as maybe.'

'Enough to start a fight with him?'

'He could defend himself, our Col.'

A brawl, then, which turned nasty, thinks Donna. She shifts forward in her seat. 'The tattoo, Mrs Flither, there was a tattoo of a vaquita on the victim's upper right arm. Col had such a tattoo?'

For a moment Pat loses her composure, loses the rigidity in her shoulders, in her neck. Her fingers have found a thread loose from around one of the buttons on her cardi and they are pulling at it.

'Aye,' says Doug quickly, 'he had a tattoo.'

There's a pause. They have come to the nub, and they

agreed Theo would take this part of the interview. Donna is glad to sit back and watch him.

He asks: 'You didn't know Col was in Scarborough?'

'He'd have told me when he was good and ready. I'd have got to hear.'

'And you didn't hear?'

They've had her attention. There's been some loosening around her jaw. Now she flinches away, to stare at the grate with its coal-effect fire.

'Mrs Flither?' he prompts.

Donna is suddenly aware of the heat in the room. And the lack of air. She imagines them all as fish stranded in a waterless aquarium.

'We said all this last night, lad,' says Doug. 'We hadn't heard from him in a while. We weren't expecting him or nothing. We don't know how he ended up in the harbour. But, aye, happen it was some daft fight gone too far.'

'The truth is, Mrs Flither,' says Theo, directing his gaze towards her and leaning forwards. 'Your son was on a trawler which went down all hands off the Faroes—'

'Not all hands.' Pat's tone is sharp and too loud for the space.

'So he survived. He didn't contact you knowing you would think him dead?'

'I never, never gave up on him. He'd a known that.' It is as if she is chiselled from stone, her hands neatly folded on her lap.

'He took eighteen months to come home, saunters into town and doesn't even contact you?'

'I don't have to explain it to you. It's what happened. I

53

saw him, I saw him last night, lying there in the morgue. Are you calling me a liar?' She glares at Theo.

'I am just wondering,' he says gently. 'I am wondering if you could have been mistaken.'

'I know my son.'

They lock stares. Pat Flither's is hostile. Theo maintains neutrality. He gives way first, nodding at Donna, handing the interview to her.

She asks Pat Flither whether they have a hairbrush or toothbrush of Col's they could have.

'There's nowt of my boy left in this house.'

For the first time, Donna knows the woman is lying. She suggests she have a look upstairs, a stray trainer would do.

'No.' Mrs Flither breathes heavily and focuses on the grate beside her.

Donna asks about a doctor or a dentist they could contact. She asks questions about friends, people Col would have been in touch with, about his sister. Pat stares resolutely away and shakes her head at each enquiry. Donna feels her frustration rising: *what's the matter with you?* Doug suggests a couple of pubs where his nephew-in-law might have taken a couple of pints. Donna makes a note. She maintains a steady tone as, for completeness, she asks what Pat and Doug were doing on Saturday night. Mrs Flither keeps her mouth firmly shut. Doug summarises his Saturday night: 'I had a half at the Leeds Arms, that's all I can manage these days, then went 'ome. My lass'll tell you. My daughter was with us, and Pat and Em came ova. Satisfied?' He seems decidedly uncomfortable. A dense navy shutter has been drawn in his eyes. He shifts in his seat and puts a hand on Pat's shoulder.

Into the pause, Theo asks what Donna has been thinking. 'Mrs Flither, don't you want the person who murdered your son to be caught?'

All at once, Doug stands. After the stillness in the room, it's akin to an earthquake. 'I think we've had enough for today, Inspector Akande.'

Theo breathes hard. Donna can feel him blowing out his dissatisfaction. Nevertheless, he gets to his feet and she follows his lead.

Pat Flither remains seated. Her voice is cracking. 'When can I have him, have him to bury?'

Her pain twists into Donna's chest. 'Not yet, Mrs Flither, but as soon as we are able, we will release him. We are very sorry for your loss.'

'I lost my boy a long time ago, lass,' Pat says quietly. She does not move as Doug ushers them quickly out.

Outside the rain has returned and, dodging puddles, they hurry to the car.

'What do you think?' asks Theo as he settles behind the wheel.

'She's holding out on something. Could we get a warrant to search for something of Col's for a DNA match?'

'A warrant against a grieving mother and a dying uncle? We'd lose the cooperation of the community. Whatever rivalries there are down here, and they are legion, they'll melt away if we are – or specifically I am – seen to be bullying.' He starts the car. 'But you're not wrong: Patricia Flither is not telling us the truth and I'm blowed if I know why. She's taking me for a gawby.' His accent has taken a deeper intonation, the vowels heavier. 'And I don't like it.' The windscreen wipers swipe from side to side; it's as if they are going through a car wash.

'Gawby?'

'Vernacular for idiot where I come from – Brum, Birmingham.' His smile returns.

Das ist doof. Her mind supplies the German slang. She enjoys the taste of it.

Chapter 10

Alice follows the Cinder Track out of Scarborough. It was once the railway link to Whitby, twenty miles north. Established in the 1880s and axed, like so many others, by Beeching in 1965, it is a popular walking and cycling route. Even today, with the louring cloud, Alice meets a fair few dogs and owners and is overtaken by fellow cyclists in Lycra. Alice is wearing a short woollen dress under a bright yellow raincoat, with leggings and her purple Doc Martens. She is sweating and puffing by the time she has ridden the five or so miles to Cloughton. She pauses for a sip of water, and to divest herself of her raincoat which she ties round her waist. Her bike was second- or third-hand when she got it, more suited to city streets. Orson helped her repair it and showed her how to maintain it. She painted it purple, white and green – Suffragette colours as she had had to explain to Ian. It is now splattered with mud. As are her beloved Docs. If Orson turns out to be happily tucked up in his caravan, gone offline as some protest against the season of consumerism, she will have a few choice words to say to him. This had occurred to her last night. As had the thought that he might be lying there ill, or even dead. Worry for him is trumping her crossness with him. She presses on.

She exits the Cinder Track at a bridge that would have

carried the railway over this narrow road leading to a farm at a dead end. It would probably have been no more than a path when the railway was built. Even so, the builders dispensed with none of their ingenuity to create this perfect little red brick arch for Alice to cycle under 129 years later. She is headed towards the sea now; she can smell it and hear its throaty groan. It still thrills her after landing on this bit of coast over two years ago and not meaning to stay.

Orson's caravan, an old-fashioned one with a rounded rump, which he rescued from the scrap heap, is parked on the edge of one of the fields. It is up against a hedge which affords it some protection from the wind scudding in over the waves. Orson has permission to stay, plus a share of kindling for his stove and veggies from the farm garden, in exchange for his labour. Over time this purely business arrangement has grown into a friendship. Once Alice has knocked on the caravan door, tried to peer through the windows, and walked round the three sides free of the hedge, she heads over to the farmhouse. She finds Viv, the woman who owns the farm, sitting in the kitchen having a brew. She and Orson have a casual, though tender, amorous thing going on, so she knows Alice and is happy to invite her in. Alice welcomes the warmth and the cup of tea, not to mention the hunk of fruit cake. But she receives no firm news on Orson, except he was there Saturday morning and gone by the late afternoon. Viv cannot be certain where he is. However, he did mention going to a potential fracking site in the north-west at some point in January. Maybe he has gone there?

Alice turns down a further cuppa and piece of cake

and heads into town. In Viv's bright kitchen, the idea that Orson is at an anti-fracking camp appeared plausible. *But why the online silence? Unless he's planning a clandestine action? Yes, possible.* She can't help feeling slightly put out that she wasn't judged trustworthy enough to be told. *He couldn't be concerned by my friendship with Fareeha? He couldn't think I wouldn't keep a confidence could he?* She, and she alone, had been privy to his suspicions about ScarTek.

She arrives home more sweaty and no more reassured than when she left. As she hoses down her bike, she turns over all the possibilities once again. If it was some legitimate action, he'd be shouting it from the rooftops. However, as Alice knows, Orson's activities could be decidedly murky. He often argued anything was justifiable if it furthered the cause. Despite his frequent use of quotes from Gandhi, Orson was not a disciple of non-violence. He'd got away with it. So far. He could take care of himself when it came to a fight. And he was expert at disappearing at just the right moment, often leaving others to take the rap. One of his less than endearing characteristics, Alice has to admit to herself as she puts her cycle into the little lean-to she and Orson had fashioned for it.

In her flat, as she cleans her Docs, puts her leggings in the laundry basket and takes a shower, other possibilities come to mind. Orson's love life has its own complexities. Viv is cool with not being the only one. Perhaps others aren't? And Orson is not adverse to going to dives and dabbling in what many would consider risky sexual behaviours. *Perhaps he is lying beaten up in a hospital somewhere?*

Alice dresses in cotton dungarees and a cotton rollneck, putting a large flower-printed scarf around her hair – her land-girl look, as Fareeha would say. Then she heads downstairs, meaning to talk to her friend about calling around hospitals in Leeds or Manchester. She checks her phone as she goes. When Fareeha opens her door, she is smiling and holding her phone up, a reflection to Alice's expression and pose. 'He's sent a WhatsApp,' they both say together and then giggle with relief.

Alice is happy to sink into Fareeha's sofa. She had not noticed the emotional weight pinching into her shoulders until now as it lifts. Orson's message says he's away for a while visiting a sick aunt. Fareeha and Alice question each other on whether they knew he had an aunt, realising how little he spoke about his family, his mother and her profession with the oil industry in Dubai coming up once. Then they discuss at length whether they are still going to the police about Ian, each becoming more or less keen as they cycle through the various scenarios.

In the end, Alice says: 'I think we should go. It's not like with Orson – Ian never had a thing about the police, did he?'

Fareeha gives the waggle of her head which she has inherited through her parents from her Pakistani ancestors. It is assenting, though could be interpreted as equivocal.

'And,' Alice continues, 'they can decide whether to take action. It will be their responsibility.'

They agree to go. However, first Alice has to eat and insists Fareeha does too, a nourishing soup which Alice makes from scratch. It is some time past mid-afternoon, therefore, when they walk down to the police station. They both hesitate on the threshold, look at each other with a grimace, link arms and go in.

After giving some details to the desk sergeant, they have to wait maybe thirty minutes on hard chairs watching the flow of people. Each time the door opens, a blast chills the fug. A couple hanging onto each other, much as Alice and Fareeha had done, but for reasons of alcohol or possibly drugs, stumble to the counter. They are emaciated, in jeans and sweatshirts which don't fit properly. The desk sergeant jokes with them as the man signs various bits of paper before they unsteadily exit. Then an elderly woman comes in. She is panicking about having lost her keys. With infinite patience, the desk sergeant suggests they give her bag one last search. Even though she insists several times she has already turned it inside out, they find the offending keys tucked in a pocket deep in the cavernous depths of the bag. She weeps. The desk sergeant assures her it happens all the time, says she can sit for a moment to compose herself, offers her a cup of tea. Finally, she asks whether he would call her a taxi to take her home.

As he is doing so, the door by the side of the counter opens and a middle-aged woman comes in. She is white and about Fareeha's height, around five foot seven. She is wearing a cardi over a blouse with a cord skirt, all in different shades of green, all fitting snugly around the sturdy curves of her bosom and hips. If Alice had encountered her anywhere else, she would have thought bank clerk. Having said that, the woman's hair, clipped neatly back, has an unexpected swathe of grey running through the brown, a pale feather in a grouse's plumage.

She glances at the desk sergeant who, while on the phone, nods towards Alice and Fareeha. The woman comes over and introduces herself as DC Donna Morris. Alice automatically shakes the proffered hand, feeling some comfort in the woman's steady grip and friendly smile. She leads them back through the door, along a dull corridor, up some institutional stairs and into a room which is set out with easy seating and a low table. She offers them refreshments. They refuse. Alice explains about the recently consumed lunch. Then winces at her reflex polite oversharing. They all sit, Fareeha and Alice side by side on the sofa, DC Donna Morris on one of the armchairs. She picks up a notebook and pen from the table next to her and asks them to tell her what has happened.

Alice glances at Fareeha. She is gazing down at her hands and doesn't appear ready to speak. Alice can feel the stiffness which has come into Fareeha's body since they were sitting companionably, almost light-heartedly, downstairs. The situation has become heavy. Alice meets the expectant look of DC Donna Morris. Alice tells herself it's OK, they have every right to be here, and begins, 'Our friend, um, Fareeha's partner, Ian Renshawe, has gone missing. He works away a lot and he left for a job on Saturday, but he never arrived there.'

Something in DC Morris's expression shows this has piqued more than a passing interest. It gives Alice some confidence. 'But what Fareeha found out was that there never was a job for him to go to.'

'And his phone number has gone to unavailable,' Fareeha adds quietly.

'OK,' says Donna. 'Let's get some particulars. Shall we start with your names and contact details and Ian's?'

Fareeha has reverted to scratching at the chips in her nail varnish. Alice, therefore, gives over the information, adding what her friend told her about Ian's supposed jobs and the companies he was supposedly employed by. DC Morris asks about his car and its registration number, which Fareeha finds to the rear of a photo on her phone.

'Do you have a photo of Ian?' asks Donna, motioning towards the phone.

Fareeha shakes her head, 'He didn't like having his photo taken; he always turned away when I tried. I deleted them. They were blurry.' She sounds sad.

'Can you give a description, then?' asks the DC gently.

'Oh, about six foot, six foot one,' says Fareeha. 'Dark hair, he wore it kinda long. Brown eyes. Fit, you know, liked to work out.'

'White?'

Fareeha nods.

'Tattoos?'

She shakes her head.

'Did you see him as he left? What was he wearing?'

'Um.' Fareeha tilts her head upwards as if bringing an image to mind. 'Black jeans, a black rugby shirt, his black puffer jacket.'

'And you're worried about him? I mean this is out of character?' Donna has leaned forward, is keeping eye contact with Fareeha, as if coaxing a nervous kitten.

Fareeha sighs heavily. 'Not entirely. I mean with his work he comes and goes, but generally his phone doesn't go to unavailable, I can get hold of him.'

'So he's never gone off, out of contact before?'

'Yes he has,' Fareeha says reluctantly.

'He has?' asks Alice surprised.

Fareeha turns to her. 'Once or twice, before I met you. I guess I would have to admit he's not the most reliable . . . And with this . . .' Her hand goes to her bump.

'He's not totally on board with being a father?' asks Donna.

'No.' Fareeha pauses, then says: 'To be honest, I didn't expect him to stick around, but I didn't expect him to pull a stunt like this one, either. I thought, at least he'd say good-bye, you know. And maybe thanks.'

The three of them take a moment to digest this type of behaviour. Alice feels the pain soaking through from her friend.

DC Morris then carries on crisply: 'Friends? Family?'

'Ian was estranged from his family,' says Fareeha. 'And we're his friends, us and the others in, well, you know, in our circle.'

'Have you spoken to them?'

Fareeha nods. 'Everyone except . . .'

'Yes?' the police officer has her pen poised over her pad. She is looking up.

Fareeha turns to Alice. 'Well we haven't spoken to Orson.'

'Orson?' asks Donna.

'Orson Reed,' supplies Alice a tad reluctantly. *Why did Fareeha have to mention him? He wouldn't like his name being bandied around at a police station.* 'We've only just heard from him. He's gone away too.'

'Oh? When?'

'Saturday,' both young women say in unison. The word

64

hangs in the air for a moment and DC Morris appears to be considering it from all angles.

'Do you know someone called Colin Flither?' she asks.

Alice and Fareeha shake their heads.

'How about Ian?'

Alice glances at Fareeha.

'How do I know?' Fareeha bursts out crossly. 'Seems like there's a lot I don't know about Ian Renshawe.'

Alice takes her friend's fingers in hers and gives them a squeeze.

DC Morris's expression is sympathetic. 'OK, anything else you can tell me which could be useful. How did the two of you meet?'

'In a pub, in Leeds,' says Fareeha. 'Just an ordinary night out.'

Alice knows this is an untruth. It was the night out after Fareeha had led a successful 'die-in' in the foyer of a clothing firm to question the environmental credentials it was claiming. But DC Morris does not need to be told this.

She asks, 'And you were living there then?'

'I was. I don't know about Ian. I'd come to Leeds from Bradford for work, but he was always a bit hazy about his past. It never seemed that important to get it out of him. Until now.'

'You both moved to Scarborough when?'

Fareeha looks at Alice. They'd met on the beach, volunteers for Orson's clear-up, after which they dumped what they had found on the doorstep of the MP's constituency office demanding government action on single-use plastic packaging. 'End of the summer 2011. I came first. Ian followed. I didn't ask him to.' Fareeha turns to Donna and says firmly, 'He chose to come.'

'You have no reason to believe that he is in danger of harming himself or others?' asks DC Morris, rather formally.

'Blimey,' says Fareeha. She glances at Alice, 'What d'ya think, Al?'

Ian hurt himself? Certainly not. Others? She's never thought about it before, though finds she can't really say.

However, Fareeha says quickly and with conviction, 'No and no.'

DC Morris writes something else down and then closes her notebook. 'OK, what we're going to do is this: the Salvation Army has a website where you can list a missing person, you cover that. Perhaps you can also use social media? I'll put Ian into the police system. Then I will talk to my DI. I may be able to follow up using the information on his car and his phone number. I'm sorry I can't do more, but he's not really in the vulnerable category.'

Fareeha lets out a yelp of something like laughter, 'Ian vulnerable? No.'

Alice feels her friend sink against her. Perhaps from tiredness. Perhaps from disappointment. Ian might not be vulnerable, but Fareeha is. She wants to tell DC Morris this, then decides it won't make any difference. She thanks the police officer. DC Morris takes them down to the front door.

'I hope you get word from him soon,' she says. She sounds authentic in her concern.

Alice feels compelled to politely thank her again and shake her hand, before the police officer goes back inside.

The door snaps shut. Alice notices the damp cold in the gathering dusk. She wraps an arm around her friend's shoulder. Fareeha appears to have shrunk to bone. 'Come on, my love,' Alice says. 'Let's get you home.'

Chapter 11

It's Friday, it's mid-morning and Theo has called Harrie, Brian and Donna into his office. As ever, it's a bit of a squeeze. Harrie is going through what she has learned about the trawler Col Flither was on.

'It was owned by a big Danish company called Fiskeri-Line. They have trawlers, factory ships, container ships, you name it. Basically, if it's fish and it's farmed, caught, frozen, canned or pickled, then Fiskeri-Line will have had a hand in it. The trawler had a mixed-nationality crew. The captain was Danish and Col was the mate, but other than that we're talking from Africa and Malaysia. The Danish coastguard and police are convinced it went down all hands. The insurance company has paid out on the boat.

'There's your motive then,' says Brian. 'Col's life insurance gets paid out. He turns up. His mum would have to pay it all back again.'

'Pat Flither stabs him?' says Harrie. 'On the harbour wall?'

Perhaps she, like Donna, is struggling to imagine Pat heaving herself onto the harbour wall to confront her son. It might explain her caginess, but Pat a killer? Donna knows murderers don't have a neon sign on their heads declaring themselves. *You can't pick them out from a crowd.* She also knows what desperation can do. She won't let her thoughts stray to her daughter's violence. Or her own.

'Doug, then.' Brian ploughs on seeing Harrie's expression. 'Or one of their strapping nephews.'

Harrie shakes her head in disbelief. 'Why did Col not contact his mum for all that time? It makes no sense.'

'Maybe he got amnesia, brought on by nearly drowning.'

'He did drown. No nearly about it. That's the whole point.' Harrie and Brian are almost nose to nose.

'Enough,' says Theo firmly, though not raising his voice.

Brian slouches in his usual attitude of one ankle resting on a knee and arms crossed. Harrie settles herself more primly into her seat. Donna wonders whether she is going to be asked to sit between them. *The aunty between two warring teenagers.* And to think they had once been best buddies, when they were both DCs, before Harrie passed her sergeant's exams. And Brian didn't.

Theo looks at Brian. 'Do you know Colin Flither had life insurance?'

Brian shakes his head.

'Right, let's not work on conjecture. Let's work on what we know or, at least, can find evidence for. Have you got Col on any CCTV in the town?'

Brian shakes his head again. 'I haven't quite finished yet.'

'That's your task for today, then: to get it completed. How about around the harbour?'

'The main CCTV camera is broken.'

'Convenient,' says Harrie.

Theo continues: 'So get down there and unearth the

69

private CCTV footage. I want some proof that Col Flither was ever in Scarborough.' He turns to Harrie. 'Social media?'

She shakes her head. 'Can't find any profiles for Col. Doesn't seem to have been his thing. On a more positive note, we're getting a list together of those who were at the penthouse party. Plus we've got some witness statements from punters who were at the Kiss Me Hardy on Saturday night.' She looks at Brian. 'No sightings of Col Flither and no reports of anything beyond the usual Kiss Me high jinks, which, as we know, can get pretty tasty. We'll keep at it.'

'Good.' Theo moves his gaze onto Donna. 'I have decided against a warrant to search Mrs Flither's house, not until we've tried other avenues, anyway. We're going to do this the old-fashioned way. Can you do a sweep of the local dentists, please, for the one Col was registered with? No one got to the end of that.'

Donna nods. Not the most exciting of tasks, but she'll enjoy the contact with people and the methodical aspects of it. She realises the others are readying to leave, so she quickly breaks in with a summary of the report on the missing Ian Renshawe.

'I saw the log,' says Harrie. 'You think it's connected? His description doesn't match that of the deceased.'

'He was last seen Saturday morning,' says Donna. 'I thought it a coincidence.' *More so if you add the Orson Reed fellow into the mix. But he's not missing.*

'His girlfriend's pregnant, isn't she?' says Brian. 'He's taken off because of that. She probably tried to trap him with the baby anyway.'

70

Theo cuts in. 'Brian, keep that kind of misogynist claptrap to yourself. Donna, I would imagine Ian Renshawe wasn't the only person to leave Scarborough Saturday morning.'

'He's the only one who has been reported to us as missing.'

'Possibly missing and certainly not vulnerable.' Theo pauses, then gives a rueful smile. 'OK. I can't sanction a warrant for his phone records. However, you can ask traffic to do an ANPR on his number plate. But it can't be a priority, OK?'

She nods. *'Not a priority' equals 'if you have the time'. And who has the time?*

Chapter 12

The tops are dusted. Icing sugar sifted over brioche buns.
Up on the moors, the rain falls as sleet and snow. Donna is
mildly surprised, then she reminds herself she now lives at
sea level. She follows the familiar road as it dips and climbs
and loops. The faint seams in the grey above are edged with
a dim glow. If only the sun had the strength to rip them
open. Donna would like to see it again. The short days of
winter did not seem to linger as long in the south, where
she's been rooted for the last thirty years of her life. Here the
expanses – of moor, of sky, of sea – swamp human endeav-
ours at lightening the darkness. She takes the next turning
onto a narrow private road. Before her are the buildings
which make up HMP North Yorkshire. Home to more than
a thousand souls, and even it cannot do more than weakly
glimmer under the clouds.

The entry procedure has its usual mix of tedium and
frustration. Despite the continual turnover, Donna knows a
few of the staff. She makes a point of greeting them whether
she does or not. She is also on greeting terms with some of
the visitors, though it rarely goes beyond a 'hello' and 'how
are you?' No one really wants to talk about how they are or
why they are there. Or if they do, it will be to declare injus-
tice and the innocence of their relatives. Donna doesn't want

to listen to them. She is wholly aware people are in prison wrongly and, often, for too long, especially black men and women in general. However, this is a Saturday, she is here as a mother, she holds tightly to her right to be off duty, as if to a mackintosh in a gale.

Donna takes her seat at one of the tables in the visitors' room. She is glad she has been able to bag the 'usual' one. It is near the wall with (high up) the narrow apertures onto the outside world. Donna watches Elizabeth come towards her. She is tall like her mother, stocky like her father. Her chalky skin has developed a healthy tone from the time she is spending on the prison farm. Donna is a tuning fork to Elizabeth's moods. This afternoon she can tell immediately her daughter is in a peaceable frame of mind. She's taken up the offer of some Buddhist teaching to combat her addictions. Perhaps some of it is soaking in. Elizabeth even grins broadly as she comes over.

'Hey, Ma, you've stopped dyeing your hair. Bet Dad hated it.'

Jim had indeed not been appreciative. His comment had been, 'Unusual.' His code for 'why can't you be like the other wives at the golf club?' – biddable and ready to laugh at their husbands' jokes, however many times they have heard them. Many of them work, have responsible jobs, but they don't make a 'song and dance about it', as Jim would say. Insisting on joining the police in the first place; not to mention going onto CID; and then arranging to do her probationary year here. All this is, in Jim's parlance, a veritable operatic aria accompanied by some foot-stamping flamenco. However, Donna does not want to add to her daughter's catalogue of things her father gets wrong. She merely asks what Elizabeth thinks of it.

She nods approvingly. 'Distinguished. I didn't realise the colour had gone so completely.'

'Nor did I,' says Donna, a tad dolefully.

'It's kinda like a swan's feathers. Nice.' Elizabeth picks at the skin around her nails. It is already chafed and pink.

Stop hurting yourself. The injunction remains unspoken. It had not been well received in the past. If Elizabeth isn't picking at her own tender spots, she'll be scratching at those of others. Donna waits for her daughter to speak.

'How was it? Christmas? You and Dad getting along?'

'Of course.'

'No of course about it. You're up here, he's down there. Long-distance romances, they don't often work out.'

'We're hardly a couple of teenagers. We've got a solid marriage to hold us together.'

'Solid, yes. But now you're spreading your wings.'

Donna is aware her daughter might be one of a minority children who would actually like to see their parents split up. However, the more she goads, the more Donna hangs on in there. *If it ain't broke, don't fix it,* she repeats to herself one of her husband's favourite's idioms, though it doesn't sit well on her tongue.

'We're fine,' she says, then thinks how inadequate the word is.

Then Elizabeth wants to hear about Christopher and his wife. Also a tricky subject. The siblings fell out irrevocably when Elizabeth chose the occasion of her brother's wedding to steal cash from his future parents-in-law.

'He's not forgiven me,' she says mournfully. 'He didn't send me a Christmas card.' She focuses on the ragged edge of her finger.

Donna sees a bubble of red. 'Stop now,' she says softly.

'Mmm? Oh.' Elizabeth notices what she has done. She rubs the blood off on her sleeve and clasps her hands on the table between them.

'He asked after you,' Donna half-lies. It was actually Christopher's wife who had quietly made the enquiry.

'Only to make sure I'm safely stuck in here, I bet.' Elizabeth's eyes drip and she finds a tatty tissue to dab at them. She snorts in a snotty breath. 'At least I've got Iris. She cares about me. They say your found family is more loyal than your blood one sometimes.'

Glad of a change of direction, Donna asks who Iris is. Her pleasure that her daughter might have found someone to talk to, maybe laugh with, is tentative. Since her late teens, Elizabeth's friendships have often meant trouble. Over time they have become more combustible.

Iris, however, does seem genuinely kind towards Elizabeth. As she talks about her, Elizabeth cheers up. It appears that as well as having fun and watching each other's backs, they have some pretty deep conversations. 'Iris says I've got to understand my white privilege. If I don't, I'm part of the problem of racism.'

'You're not racist.'

'I didn't like it either when she said it like that, but I've been thinking about it, thinking about what she said. Lord.' She presses her palms to her forehead and then lets them fall again. 'If we've nowt else here it's fucking time to think.

Does my head in, it really does, Mum. Enough to drive you to drugs.' She gives a sly smile. 'Don't worry, Ma, I'm clean. I could get all types of gear, but I've kept out of it. Iris has been good about keeping me straight. And, you know' – she leans forwards – 'I think I owe her to take this seriously.'

'Of course, we should all take racism seriously.'

'Do we, though? Do you? Do I? In reality, do we? We slide through this world with our white skins, it doesn't even occur to us what it might be like to have a different skin tone, have that be the first thing we're judged on.'

'Everyone can be prejudiced.'

'Yes, but racism isn't about prejudice only, it's about prejudice and power. Don't you see? Our history, in the UK, in Europe, in the USA, colonialism, the riches in this country, they are all built on racism. White supremacy rules.'

'I am not a white supremacist.' Donna is feeling decidedly uncomfortable. 'I've met white supremacists, one of my first shifts as a Special was to patrol a National Front rally. I heard what they said. I was disgusted.'

'Course you were, Ma, you're a good person. That's doesn't mean you don't benefit as a white person from a system of white supremacy and white privilege. Just like a man benefits, whether he wants to or not, from a worldwide system of patriarchy.'

This is something Donna can understand. She nods.

Elizabeth continues, 'Dad, of course, is happy to benefit from and hold onto patriarchy.' She sighs. 'Just read it, the blog post Iris showed me. It'll explain everything.'

Neither speaks for a while. Donna has the impression – which has become familiar over the years – that she and her daughter have ended up seated at the bottom of a large dank container, with the sky mostly obscured by a heavy lid. The stuffiness in the room doesn't help. And a toddler at one of the other tables has begun to grizzle. *I don't want to feel more rubbish than I do.* She had thought this might be the day when she would explain everything about her childhood to Elizabeth, come clean. *You know I told you I'd been born in West Berlin, well, that's not entirely true.* She is nervous enough about saying it. For her own sake, she cannot risk a bad reaction. She now sees this is not a good time. Instead, she considers various ways of clawing the conversation back to its sunny beginning.

Before she can find the right opener, Elizabeth says, 'I haven't told Iris about you, about what you do.'

Donna is not surprised. She imagines Elizabeth is better off keeping it quiet.

Her daughter gives a thin chuckle. 'Trading places, eh, Mum? I guess you kept most of what was happening from the golf-widows of Kenilworth, your so-called friends—'

'They are my friends,' Donna responds defensively.

'You didn't tell them about me, though, did you?' She pauses, then says more resignedly: 'Whatever. And I don't suppose you tell your colleagues about me—'

'Some of them know.' *One, to be exact. DI Theo Akande.*

'You good at keeping secrets, Mum?'

More than you can possibly know.

Chapter 13

Alice had to wait seventy-two hours for Sarah's response to her text sent at nine a.m. on Wednesday, the morning after the preview. She had almost given up and was beginning to think about the wording for an email without it sounding too needy or just plain weird. Sarah's reply is brisk: she will be at the café suggested by Alice, at midday. No 'looking forward to seeing you' nor other ameliorating sentiment. The agreement feels dragged out of her. Alice wonders at her motivation. Had she imagined the moment of connection? She normally has an instinct for recognising a woman of her own 'kind', although she has been disastrously wrong in the past. *Make no assumptions, Alice,* she tells herself as she gets ready. *In any case, this is a job, not a seduction.*

It's taken her longer than normal to choose an outfit. In the end, she's plumped for jeans, a rather tame burgundy-coloured blouse and small silver earrings. *No need to scare the horses,* she thinks as she checks herself for a final time. Before going out, however, she does add her purple Docs, her yellow mac and a long multi-coloured scarf wrapped up to her ears. For which she is inordinately grateful as she walks vigorously around the exposed Marine Drive at the foot of the castle mount and into North Bay.

The small café is a hubbub – chat, steam and the

continual hiss of the coffee machine. Alice sees Sarah at a corner table by the long window overlooking the beach. Alice is on time. Sarah appears to have been in residence for a while, a half-drunk coffee in front of her. Her light-blonde, shoulder-length hair is loose around her face, softening it. She is wearing a caramel-coloured rollneck and similarly toned slacks. Alice goes over. She is surprised to sense the relief with which she is greeted. *Had Sarah doubted she would turn up? Was she that bothered?* After divesting herself of her outer clothing, Alice offers to get Sarah another coffee and maybe something to eat? Alice could demolish a sandwich, but doesn't want to eat alone. When Sarah agrees to a tea-cake, Alice decides she will have to settle for the same. To make up for it, she gets herself a vegan hot chocolate with all the trimmings.

Once she is seated, once they've done the usual 'how are you?'s, followed by the polite, inconsequential responses, and once the teacakes have arrived, there is a blank moment. Sarah seems a bit at a loss. Alice is cautioning herself not to dive in too ferociously. In her head, she runs through various openers. In the end she comes up with: 'Must be interesting working for ScarTek?'

'I enjoy it,' says Sarah.

Alice waits for more, but when nothing is forthcoming, she asks, 'What do you enjoy?' *Poisoning our groundwater and, no doubt, our seas for generations to come?* She keeps that thought for later and her tone light.

'Oh, you know.'

'Not really. I don't know anything about the biotech industry.' Another lie, it comes easily. 'What does it even do?'

'Oh well, it's about innovation, using biochemistry and the latest technologies to create products which are useful to, well, to everyone.' Sarah takes a sip of coffee. Maybe it warms her up, for she goes on with a bit more fluency. 'Leonard Arch started with his first company near San Francisco, oh, about twenty years ago, no nineteen, in 1995. I worked for him out there when I finished my PhD in 1997. We were creating cleaning fluids for energy companies.'

Cleaning fluids for energy companies – it sounds innocuous. Chemicals for fracking, less so. Alice makes the effort to keep her expression open and encouraging. *Innocent.* It seems to do the job as Sarah goes on.

'When Leonard started up here, he invited me over to manage the lab and oversee the R and D. The research and development.'

'And is it still cleaning fluids for energy companies?' *Not a note of derision. I should be an actress.* Alice smears her tea-cake with extra peanut butter and takes a salty bite.

'Mmm, we're exploring the possibilities. The old company, before Leonard bought it, was creating products for the food industry. There's innovation possible there. And Leonard is interested in moving into pharmaceuticals – vaccines and the like.'

'Could be useful when we have our first proper pandemic over here.' Alice cannot help the mild provocation, though she says it as if she isn't completely convinced.

'What makes you think we're going to have a pandemic?'

Alice makes a whole show of stirring out the last of the chocolate and oat milk from her mug while she forms an answer. 'I think I read it somewhere. Human activity encroaching on animal territory, the growing demand for what some people consider is wild meat. Viruses hopping species. Wasn't that what AIDS was about? And we've become so complacent over here, we'll just let it roll on in.'

Sarah nods. 'It's a possible scenario. But there are plenty of things worth looking for a vaccine against. Malaria, for instance. Currently, there are over four hundred thousand deaths from that worldwide; sixty-five per cent of those are children. Or cancer. All valuable areas for research.'

And commercially advantageous. But Alice is not here to argue over the way the pharma industry makes unseemly amounts of money from human misery. She wants to know more about these cleaning fluids. Before she can form her next question, Sarah intercedes.

'That's enough about me. What about you? You said you are new to Scarborough? Where have you come from? What brought you here?'

'This.' Alice sweeps her hand across the view from the window. The grey sea is choppy, it has withdrawn from the beach. It has discarded a looking-glass in the sand for the sky, another texture of grey.

'And you work at the art gallery?'

Alice shakes her head. 'I was only there doing the catering for the preview.'

It sounds very grand the way she puts it – better than part-time waitress and barmaid ready for hire. Sarah's expression shows interest and curiosity; Alice responds to it. She explains how her paid work sustains her real passion: art and photography. Then Sarah says with a smile (and she really does have the most appealing lopsided smile)

81

that Alice is an artist. Alice beams and finds herself talking more about her approach and then about her travels, the two being inexorably interlinked. The real reason for this meeting becomes subsumed in a rather pleasurable conversation as they find things in common: shared likes and dislikes when it comes to artworks and then books, and places they have both visited. Alice notices from the clock on the wall almost an hour has slid by. *Not miss-spent,* she tells herself. *I'm gaining her trust.* There's a pause while Sarah goes to order soup for them both.

She returns and sits, then says softly, 'My sister was the creative one.' She looks uneasily at her hands, held together as if in prayer in front of her.

'Sylvia.'

'You remembered.' The tautness in her posture eases a little.

'It must have been awful, losing her like that,' says Alice with genuine feeling.

Sarah snaps her gaze upwards. 'You googled?'

'Went to the library.'

This appears to please Sarah. Even so, her tone is heavy, 'You know the Franklande family tragedy then.'

She sounds so forlorn Alice almost reaches over and touches those praying hands. Instead, the waitress bustles over with soup and rolls, glasses of water and cutlery. There are several minutes during which everything is set on the table, the used mugs are cleared and the two women take appreciative first spoonfuls of the mushroom and basil concoction.

Then Alice says softly, 'I . . . I truly don't know how you would cope with all that.'

Sarah puts down her spoon and butters a piece of bread which she then doesn't eat. 'You do, though, you just do, because you have to.'

Alice notices the use of 'you'. *More distancing than 'I'. Not owning it. Perhaps it's the only way.*

Sarah takes some more mouthfuls. 'I taught her to swim,' she says pensively. Then she continues more harshly: 'I ran away. I didn't come back. When it all happened. I couldn't afford . . . I should have done.' She pushes her half-finished meal away from her, tidying up crumbs with a napkin. 'Maybe I could have saved her.'

Alice flinches in the face of the other woman's guilt. She seeks to alleviate it. 'What about your brother? He was there.'

'Roland?' Sarah shakes her head. She seems to find it difficult to articulate what she wants to express about her brother. She stacks her mostly empty bowl on her empty plate, with her knife, spoon and glass. She says, 'He's not good at that type of thing.'

Alice slowly finishes her soup, wondering what direction to take the conversation in. Finally, she plumps for, 'What brought you back now?'

'Too late you mean,' says Sarah flatly. She sits back. 'Of course, the job. Always the job. I didn't come back before because of the job. After MIT, Leonard invited me to Arch-Tech, his US business, and I went.'

'How did you get to know Leonard Arch?' Alice is caught between her mission and wanting to dig deeper into this woman in front of her. This question appears an acceptable middle way.

'Leonard's an old friend of my brother's. Roland still acts as his accountant. They met at university in Leeds. Though Leonard famously didn't complete his business degree and his first business, the one before Arch-Tech, spectacularly bombed, he has become the most successful entrepreneur to come out of that university. Probably any university in the UK.'

The slight flattening of tone and screw of Sarah's lips suggests to Alice a not entirely harmonious relationship between Sarah and her boss. *Perhaps she rebuffed his advances one time?* Alice thinks. *Yet, she still works for him?*

'Look, I think I should be going.'

Alice is surprised at her own disappointment. 'OK,' she says slowly. 'I thought maybe another coffee? Or a walk?'

'No,' says Sarah with force. She puts on her brown wool jacket, and pulls out a scarlet knitted beret from its pocket.

'Sarah, I . . .' Alice begins to say. *I want to see you again,* her mind finishes.

The woman hesitates, beret clutched tightly in her hand. 'It's been, it's been nice, thank you.' Then she walks away.

'Another time?' Alice says softly to the empty banquette across the table.

Another minute and Sarah returns. 'It's been more than nice,' she says stiffly. 'I have really enjoyed this. Shall I . . . shall I call you?'

Alice gives her enthusiastic agreement.

'Good,' says Sarah before striding off.

Alice judges her 'yes' was a bit more eager than she intended. *It's only because I want to fulfil my mission,* she tells herself. She thinks about messaging Orson. Then decides to wait until she sees him to tell him she has confirmed at least some of his suspicions about ScarTek and Leonard Arch. Whether it is at the thought of this, or the thought of seeing Sarah again, Alice steps lightly out of the café and into the wintery spray being tossed across the pavement by the sea galloping up the beach.

Chapter 14

Donna's headache, which settled in after seeing Elizabeth yesterday, is still thrumming away, despite regular intakes of painkillers. Perhaps as a consequence, she is slightly nauseous. Plus she is bleeding again. She feels hollowed out. It is as if nothing of the self she recognises is left in this body any more.

With an effort she calls Jim. Sunday morning has become their time to talk on the phone. Just after Donna gets up and just before Jim goes off to play golf. This morning when he asks how she is, she tells him.

'I didn't think you sounded too good. I thought you were going to the doctor, get some of that HRT?' He sounds considerate.

'HRT isn't helpful until I go into the menopause. I am peri-menopausal.' How many times has she explained this to him? *At least he's trying,* she tells herself.

'Well get yourself to the GP, he must be able to do something.'

Donna grunts an agreement, knowing she's been putting it off. Why? Her cheeks begin to burn. She doesn't need to name the emotion. Embarrassment. It feels like a hook is twisting into the nether regions of her right eye. After yesterday, she had hoped to say something to Jim about what she had omitted to tell him – over all these years – concerning where she comes from. Instead, she lets Jim control the conversation. He tells her about a run-down canal warehouse in Birmingham he and Christopher have their eye on for redeveloping. It seems the project is moving forwards. And, from his voice, Donna can hear how pleased – how proud – her husband is to be working with their son. It recalls to her that, on many levels, their family does work.

After hearing him out, Donna reminds him of their other child. 'I went to see Elizabeth yesterday.'

'Yes, every other Saturday, I know the routine. How was she?'

'Good.' For once, this is more than a half truth. Before they parted, Elizabeth had said she thought she could really make a go of it this time. Donna now repeats this to Jim.

'Well we've heard that before.'

His dismissal clangs into the throb in her head. 'I really think she means it and could do it,' she says defensively.

Jim harrumphs. 'You're too soft on her, Donna, much too trusting.'

She wants to shove some evidence under his nose to prove him wrong, but can't find any, not from the last ten years.

He says he has to go or he'll be late for his game. 'Take care,' he says.

'Love you. Miss you,' she responds as he hangs up.

She is not sure he heard her. She is not sure she wants him to have heard her. *Solid.* The word she used to describe her marriage which Elizabeth echoed back to her. It now feels heavy. *Like as I spread my wings, it pulls me down.*

She dismisses the thought as quickly as it comes. Though

she doesn't want him to be, Donna has to admit Jim is right about Elizabeth. Their daughter has promised all sorts of things which have not materialised. Because of her addiction to drugs and alcohol. They've become the reason, the stem, the root, for all her bad behaviour and difficulties. *Yet why did she begin with them in the first place?* Donna pushes herself off the sofa and goes into the kitchen to replenish her cup of peppermint tea. It's a question she has circled often and never found an adequate response to. Yes, Elizabeth was always the one to jump in, try new things, she always wanted excitement. She wanted things to distract her from her doubts, her fears, her low moods. And once drugs take hold, it's harder to let go of them. But where did Elizabeth get her downward spirals from? Christopher never had the same plunges into gloom. How much has it to do with the way Elizabeth was brought up? *How much has it to do with me and Jim?* Donna stares out at the small square rear garden of her rented house through the small square window of its small square kitchen. *How much are we moulded by our upbringing? Why did I find it so easy to lie about where I came from? Did my lies somehow shape Elizabeth?*

Each thought elicits a half turn of the hook in her eye.

Then the doorbell adds its persecution. Donna glances at the clock on the wall. She's still in her PJs, under a fleecy dressing gown. She goes to the door full of apologies which she blurts out to her neighbour, Rose Short. On first meeting, five months ago, when Donna moved to Scarborough, she had not immediately taken to her neighbour. Donna thought Rose too opinionated and disapproving of those who are not. But over time, Rose has been a timely reminder to Donna of her younger – more active, more aware – days. She had known plenty of women like Rose then and had respected them. This respect has transferred itself onto Rose. Plus, there is no doubt, Rose is kind. Not only has she been attentive and caring (without being overly intrusive), she has also invited Donna to convivial evenings with her own circle of friends. Mostly women, mostly approaching or well over fifty years old, from diverse backgrounds, each with their own story to tell. They tended to do the minor double-take on realising Donna is a police officer rather than the bank teller they had taken her for.

This Sunday, Rose has turned up (on time, as usual), to take Donna for her first sea swim. Rose has assured her starting in the winter means it cannot get worse. After several months going regularly to the swimming pool, Donna has reclaimed her confidence in the water and she felt ready, despite the season. However, not today. Not today. Rose – a dynamo whose stature matches her surname, her hair in a long grey plaited tail – understands the situation with one swift glance. She pops to her house for some of her home-made concoction of motherwort, balm and mint. She instructs Donna once again to seek medical advice, while waving away her protests that it is only her 'time of life'. Then Rose tells her to go to bed and rest. She will be back later to check on her. Donna imagines this visit will be accompanied by some delicious vegetable stew, followed by a beetroot and chocolate cake, which is Donna's favourite. She takes a dose of Rose's treatment, before thankfully padding up to bed.

Donna sleeps. When she wakes the cramps have eased. The chisel is no longer biting its way into her temple. Donna moves as if she is made of glass and any jerky step would shatter her. She takes a shower and dresses, gradually regaining a modicum of robustness. She pauses by her bedroom window. Across the quiet crescent is a line of narrow brick dwellings, copies to the one she is standing in. Very different from the expansive detached villa sitting in the centre of its own gardens which she and Jim own. Yet she's happy here, the space is enough for just her. She has found she likes her time on her own, when everything within her domain is under her control, such a contrast to her frenetic work hours, and to living with Jim.

She turns on her laptop to check her personal emails. There are a couple from friends – *yes they are my friends, Elizabeth* – in Kenilworth wishing her a happy new year but not saying much else. Once she has replied to them, she turns to the internet, looking up the blog post Elizabeth had mentioned. *Why I'm No Longer Talking to White People About Race* by someone called Reni Eddo-Lodge. Reading it almost brings back her headache. She snaps her laptop closed. She stands, stretching. The house she has rented for her probationary year is at the rear of the town. When she took it, she did not care it was a long way from the beach. She did not consider it possible she would increasingly be drawn to the sea. Now, however, it is where she wants to go.

As she walks, she mulls over what she has just read. When Donna came to Britain in the 1980s, she dived into feminism. She took part in protests: against government cuts; reclaiming the night for women; and, yes, against racism. But didn't she always assume the experience of the black women she strode beside was the same as hers? Because they were women? Wasn't that enough? And what has she been doing these last few decades to not notice ideas changing? Married, having children, launching (late) into an absorbing career – were any of these excuses for being ignorant, thoughtless, heartless?

Her route takes her through an area of the town's old cemetery. Ivy and hebe bushes entangle with grey monuments. Urns and drapery. An angel with a broken wing. Mainly to distract herself from her increasingly troubling thoughts, Donna slows to read the inscriptions. A number list whole families, from month-old babies to adults, who 'fell asleep' or were 'enjoined with God' over a century. Others are mostly blank, the generations who came after having left the area or chosen cremation. A robin flits down from the dark green, low-slung branches of a yew to sit on a sculpted anchor and rattle out its territorial song. Donna notices more of these memorials, which are specifically for seafarers. She lingers over their epitaphs.

Finally, she takes the path which carries her into Peasholm Glen, alongside the little stream. The trees hang onto the precipitous slopes on either side. The trunks of the beech have the girth and texture of an elephant's leg, the canopy high above. In amongst the birch, the hawthorn, the holly, there are rare trees, the red oak with its crimson leaves, the butter-yellow tulip tree. However, at this time of year, apart from the evergreens, branches are bare. They are coppered and blackened by the damp. At the end of the glen is the park. There is the red and gold pagoda, the Edwardian idea of Chinese, topping the artificial mound at the centre of the lake. Its glassy surface is fussed up by the squabble of

Canada geese, mallards, moorhens and black-headed gulls. Donna's pace is quickening. Though pretty, this is tame. Round the corner, she is confronted by the turbulent sea.

She rests her elbows on the rusted rail at the edge of the promenade, the tart air scudding against her cheeks. The sound of the waves rumbles continuously. No inflection, even as one tumbles over, and another loses its balance as they race. They sloosh up arcs of froth in their wake. The sky is a jagged patchwork of greys. Abruptly the stitches give way and Donna is looking into another world. A region of blue skies. For a millisecond she imagines a golden beach and swaying palm trees. Then, as quickly, this dream world is closed off again. The sun, which must have been lighting it, becomes a white disc tightly fastened behind grey hessian.

She ponders over those graves for sailors – non-graves – for many had not been laid to rest in their home town. 'Drowned'; 'Lost at sea'. She's committed one to memory: 'No one to tell of the wreck/ but his cares are past/ as he is safely reached God's safe harbour at last.' *For a first mate aged thirty-three, the same as our Col Flither.* The anchor chains delicately fashioned from hard stone wrap around the memorials, weighting them down, holding them fast. Giving the grieving families something to grasp on to, Donna supposes, when their loved ones will never return. The blank spaces on some of the stones take on meaning. They are waiting. Waiting to give fathers, husbands, sons a homecoming. Of a sort. All at once, she understands something about Pat Flither which has been mystifying her. She turns for home satisfied that she has a new insight to bring to the case. She will tell Theo in the morning.

Chapter 15

'Back from the Dead?' Theo comes to Donna's desk to show her the headline on the local paper's website.

'The question mark says it all.' She scans through the article. 'I don't see anything new here, do you?' It isn't more than a regurgitation of the release from the force's press office coupled with the brief quote from Doug.

'No. The paper has hardly any journalists left – it doesn't have anyone to do any real investigative stuff.'

'No use to us, then.' Donna is reconsidering her thoughts from yesterday. They had seemed revelatory at the time. Now they appear too lacking in rigour to share with her DI.

'It might shake something loose.' He doesn't sound convinced. 'Are you busy, Donna?'

She considers what the right response might be. Would it be unprofessional to admit she is happy to find any excuse to get out of the office and avoid once again prompting dentists' receptionists who have yet to confirm whether Col Flither was a patient? On the other hand, saying she is busy might mean missing out on something more interesting.

Luckily, her DI's question is one of those the English don't need an answer to. He wants her to come with him to see Doug. 'I think he has more to tell us. And I need to get out into the fresh air, don't you?'

Another query which apparently requires no response. They make their way through the town centre and to the top of the cliffs where the vista opens up.

'There it is,' says Theo softly.

Today, 'it' – the sea – is a jagged jumble of slates, tipping this way and then that. The clouds are grey clods in the sky. Only a thin seam of pale blue settles uneasily on the horizon. Though it is not the quickest route, Theo leads them down the steps and along the foreshore by the harbour. From here it is up a steep hill. Donna notices a narrow passageway branching off, winding behind the fish and chip shops, the cafés and other businesses on the front. There is a blue plaque adorning the entrance of what is known as the Bolts. Donna pauses to read it. Then she scurries to catch up with Theo. Puffing at the climb, she reaches him as he pauses at a junction with an even more constricted residential street. A few paces on is a neat blue door with a sail boat as a knocker.

Doug is slow to come to the door. However, he is quick to invite them in and furnish them with tea and biscuits. He talks as he does so. Donna gathers that Doug's wife is a local councillor (currently out at some meeting) and a lifetime at sea has made him self sufficient. Now he is (unhappily) retired to 'dry dock', he is the one who keeps everything clean and tidy, who orders in supplies, caters. The biscuits are from a batch he turned out that morning. Donna can smell the vanilla essence and rubbed butter.

He sits. 'Right then, what's on your mind?'

Theo compliments the biscuits.

Doug inclines his head. 'You didn't happen here to taste m'wares. You're here to talk about Col. No doubt people have been giving their opinions.'

'The overriding one is that Col died eighteen months ago when the trawler went down.'

'The *Fiskeri-Marguerite*. It was a fine boat as it goes, but they should never have gone out in that weather. With all the tech on board, they think they can handle anything the sea cares to throw at them. They can't.'

'The *Fiskeri-Marguerite* went down all hands,' says Theo, his tone remaining gently conversational.

'Maybe yes, maybe no.' Doug takes a slurp of tea.

'If not, then where has Col been all this time?'

Doug hesitates. 'Col was never where he was supposed to be. We don't know where he's been, but he must have gone somewhere, otherwise he couldn't end up in the harbour like he did, could he?'

Donna feels the urge to laugh at this impeccable logic. She covers it with another melting mouthful of biscuit.

Doug continues, gesturing to the window. 'He'd have been somewhere out there, doing summat. He couldn't spend five minutes aground without feeling out of sorts. He had the opposite of sea sickness – he had land sickness.'

Theo says, 'You can put an end to the doubts by persuading Pat to give us something of Col's with his DNA on.'

'That's as maybe, there'll alus be some who want to believe their own theories.' Then he sighs heavily. 'I'll get the lass to speak to her sister, OK?' He straightens himself in his chair. 'Now, lad, our Pat is fretting over having a burial, it's not good having a body overground when it should be underground, if you get my meaning. I was hoping you could see your way to releasing him, to his mother.'

Donna sees again those gravestones, marking empty graves. Waiting for the lost.

Theo says, 'We won't be releasing Col's body until we know where he's been for the last eighteen months, what brought him back to Scarborough and how he died.'

Doug is clearly disconcerted.

Donna wonders again at Pat's motivations. She says: 'Don't you want to know all this too? Doesn't Mrs Flither? Don't you want to know the truth of what happened?'

Doug turns his attention to her. 'And you'll be able to tell me, will you, DC Morris? You'll be able to ferret out the truth?' He shakes his head, his jowls sagging further into his neck. 'Good luck to ye, that's all I have to say.' He takes another gulp of tea and puts his cup and saucer down with a rattle. 'I've been on the seas all m'life and I can tell ye, there's nowt more unfathomable than folks.'

Doug resides several streets up the slope from the harbour. They're sitting in the lounge at the rear of the house. It's an unfussy room, light painted with one framed print on one wall, of a lifeboat being launched. There's a bookcase and a small sideboard with family photos on the top. No TV. The window is large and beside it stands an impressive telescope.

'Good view,' Theo says.

'Aye, fair down to Flamborough. Have a look, lass, you're new around here, give you the lay of coast.'

Donna does as she is bid. Through the glass she can

see the hotchpotch of shops, food outlets, restaurants and amusement arcades which fringe the foreshore. The arms of the harbour sweep out around the yacht marina and the lighthouse stands at one end. It looks like a feeble lifebelt floating on the charcoal waves, rolling unchecked to the horizon. *And beyond? Germany,* Donna has worked out. *Indeed, this used to be called the German Ocean.*

As she is musing, Theo is getting on with their proper job. 'What time did you say you got home the evening of Saturday the fourth of January?'

'Around seven. Pat and Em came round.'

'What time did they leave?'

'Ten-ish.'

'Straight to bed?'

'Aye.' Doug stands slowly. 'Now, lad, I don't mean to be rude, but this chemo is knocking me for six. I'm off to the heads. Will you see yourself out?'

After he leaves, Theo comes to join Donna. 'What do you see?'

She points. From this vantage Doug can look down onto the Bolts. She repeats what she read on the blue plaque. Perhaps they were used as drains when the sea was high. Or maybe by fugitives from justice. And Doug has a good view down the length of them.

Chapter 16

As soon as she enters the police station, Donna can taste the crackle in the atmosphere, like the aftermath of a lightning strike. When she and her DI reach the incident room, they discover what has caused it. Harrie briskly intercepts them. The DCI is waiting in Theo's office.

Detective Chief Inspector Vaughn Sewell is standing by the window and stays posed there while telling the three of them to sit. He has been described (in Donna's hearing) as a silver fox. Not quite a George Clooney, the DCI has indeed a full head of dark hair rakishly threaded with grey. He starts by bestowing a charismatic beam on Donna, saying he's sorry he hasn't caught up with her until now . . .

It's not difficult, I'm mostly at one of your police stations.

. . . and he has heard good things about her from DI Akande. He smoothly carries on. It transpires he wants to talk about the penthouse party and it is soon clear why. He was a guest. The host was responsible for creating the luxuriously appointed apartment and owns several businesses on the foreshore.

'He is a . . .' The DCI pauses before supplying the word, 'friend'. A friend who is less than charmed by the request for his invitee list. 'He came to me with his qualms. Of course, I explained why he must hand it over. I have it here.' The DCI indicates the Manila folder he is holding. 'And I promised him it would be handled with the utmost discretion.'

What went on at this party? wonders Donna. *Drugs? Prostitutes? Surely not with the DCI there?*

As if hearing her question, Sewell is quick to give assurances that there was nothing at the party which would require police investigation.

'People just . . .' He taps the folder with a chubby finger. 'The people on this list are rightly defensive of their privacy when they have the rare opportunity to have a night off, out of the media gaze.'

Who were these people? Film stars?

'And . . .' The DCI pauses and glances out of the window. 'And I want to give you the heads up. There was an incident. It was quickly and properly dealt with. I wanted to be sure I told you about it.'

They wait for more details and when none come, Theo asks for them. Sewell expresses surprise that they need more than his guarantee that it was nothing of any importance. Theo is emphatic in assuring him they do.

Finally the DCI says: 'About eleven p.m. a young man gatecrashed the event and dumped rotting fish on the floor. I believe it was some kind of environmental protest. He was ejected.' Sewell sounds irritated, whether with the protester or with his own staff, Donna cannot tell. Sewell hands Theo the folder. 'As well as the guest list, there's a CD with the CCTV from the penthouse door. But the young man has his hoodie pulled up. For obvious reasons he did not want to be identified.'

'Did nobody recognise him?' Donna asks abruptly, then wonders if she has spoken out of turn.

Certainly, Sewell takes a moment before replying. 'He seemed to have a particular problem with Leonard Arch, the CEO of ScarTek. You'll have heard of him. An important investor in town, ScarTek provides a lot of employment. Leonard has assured me he had no idea who the young man was.' His phone chirrups and he checks the display. 'I have to go.'

Theo rises to his feet. 'We will need a full statement from you, sir.'

Sewell nods.

Theo continues, 'And we will be talking to the people on this list.'

'Of course,' says Sewell, his countenance congealing into unsmiling. 'As witnesses, not suspects.'

'At the moment, we're struggling to find any persons of interest. We can't rule anyone out.'

'I'm merely saying, Theo, be careful. Don't ruffle any feathers. These people have influence, perhaps only in North Yorkshire, but it's the pond we all live and work in.' Then Sewell's face relaxes, his bonhomie returns. 'I have confidence in the way you run your team, Theo. I know I can trust you all to use your good sense.' And with that brief homily he is gone.

Once DCI Vaughn Sewell reaches the garage and drives off, it is as if the whole building exhales. Theo makes himself and Harrie a strong coffee and Donna accepts a herbal tea. Too much caffeine will have her crippled with a headache again. She breathes in as much of the odour of the coffee as she can.

Theo reads through the list. 'The great and the good,' he says finally. 'Is it likely any of them would even know Col Flither, let alone kill him?'

'They might have seen something,' says Harrie. 'And what about this protester?'

Donna adds, 'It does put someone else out near the harbour around midnight who might have an issue with Col's job on trawlers.'

Theo nods. 'We'll start with Arch, then. I don't care what he's told his close personal acquaintance, the DCI, you two get off and interview him. And' – he smiles – 'be nice.'

ScarTek has a large compound on the cliffs north of Scarborough. It is in a slight dip, concealed from the road and from the casual traveller. A notice at the start of the track leading up to the main gate states very clearly: PRIVATE. NO ENTRY. ACCESS RESERVED FOR SCARTEK EMPLOYEES AND VISITORS. The perimeter fence is impressive. Every several metres CCTV cameras continuously survey the area. They look expensive. It reminds Donna of the security around the prisons Elizabeth has frequented. Then, unbidden, of another wall, several hundred miles away. And another lifetime.

She is driving, so has to refocus when brought to a halt at the gate kiosk. They called in advance. They show their ID, are given temporary badges and are let through. The narrow roadway takes them to a car park and from there notices point them to reception. There are plenty more signs telling them where they are not welcome. Most of the brick buildings are one storey. On the side furthest away are two hangar-type structures, one with a chimney through which smoke or steam vents into the cloudy sky.

The reception is furnished in pine with a dark carpet. They are told Mr Arch will be with them soon and to take a seat. Donna's gaze roams the walls. The framed photos are all of Leonard Arch in a variety of brightly coloured cravats shaking hands here with a politician, there with a celebrity chef, here with a comedian known for her environmental credentials. Arch has the same smile each time, curved lips minimally parted to show the tips of white teeth.

Finally, Arch's secretary arrives to take them through a pine door opened by a pass slung round her neck. They go down several corridors, with further pine doors closed on either side. There's little noise, murmurs of voices and the sound of a printer whirring. There's the smell of newly laid carpets. Leonard Arch's office is reached through his secretary's. It is the only one with a decorative door. It's made of a heavy wood carved with panels and whorls, with a sturdy brass handle at the centre. It opens onto an expanse of gold-coloured shagpile, at the extreme reaches of which is a copious desk.

Leonard Arch comes forward, his hand outstretched, his smile the same one as in the photos. He is shorter than Donna expects, rounder, with a chubby face. Those photos had been carefully choreographed. The grip of his hand is firm. He is wearing an open-necked shirt and grey trousers pleated at the waist. He has several computer screens on his desk and a couple of folders. Apart from that, any other paperwork or office paraphernalia must be in the cupboards which line the walls made to resemble mahogany panelling. Arch ushers Donna and Harrie to a suite of upholstered chairs around a glass coffee table which stand by a large window. There is grass and a flower bed, and a screen of trees beyond. The fence is still in evidence with its roving camera eyes.

Once refreshments have been offered, and refused, Leonard Arch asks, 'How can I help you two detectives?'

Donna has the impression he barely resisted using the word 'ladies' instead of 'detectives'. However, perhaps she is wrong.

He continues: 'My secretary said this has something to do with the poor man being fished out of the harbour the other week? The local radio said he had been identified, but I don't recall . . . ?'

'We believe him to be a local fisherman,' says Harrie. 'Colin Flither.'

'Only believe?' asks Arch. 'Or is that just police-speak?'

'Do you know Mr Flither?' asks Harrie. 'Or the Flither family?'

'I believe not,' says Arch.

The repetition of 'believe' puts Donna on alert and she sees Harrie has taken note.

She continues with questions about the penthouse party. When Arch arrived. When he left. Who he talked to. Donna recognises that while answering carefully, Arch is not giving away more than is strictly necessary. He relaxes in his chair. He ate at a country restaurant with the mayor, his wife and another local businessman before the party. Arch

103

was driven to Scarborough with the others by the mayor's wife at about ten p.m. Apart from her, Arch admits, the group had already had several bottles of wine. He describes the penthouse party itself as a boozy affair. At around two-thirty a.m., Arch took a taxi to his Whitby pied-à-terre and slept late into the Sunday afternoon.

'We understand there was a gatecrasher,' says Harrie. 'Can you tell us about him?'

'Some nonsense about sea pollution. He should never have got in. I heard the door security was duped. Well, they won't be used again in this town.'

'We understand he made straight for you.'

'No.' Arch appears to take a moment of consideration. 'No, I don't think I was his target. ScarTek has an excellent environmental record.'

'Did you recognise him?'

Shake of the head.

'Could you describe him?'

Again, the slight pause. 'I imagine you would say he was of medium height, well built. He had the hood on his top up, partly covering his face. Ah, you know, Detective Shilling . . .' He gives an ingratiating smile. 'I'd been drinking several hours by then. I would not make what you might call the most reliable of witnesses.'

'Did he say anything?'

'Something about us all being to blame for the climate crisis.'

'Nothing specifically to you?'

'Not that I recall.'

Donna can't place his accent, except it has a rather

studied quality. She asks: 'Did you leave the party at any point? Or go onto the balcony?'

'I may have gone onto the balcony to admire the view. Our host was keen we all got the full experience.'

'Did you notice anything?'

Arch appears to ruminate, then says: 'The harbour, some boats, there were lights on the yachts. They do a display every year.'

'I meant anything suspicious.'

'Define suspicious.' Maybe he has grown weary of the interview or he can't help himself. He offers up a winning smile.

Donna isn't won over. 'Anything, anything at all.'

'It was a Saturday night, DC Morris, there were groups of people hanging around, going in and out of the pubs, having fish and chips. The usual.'

'How about in the early hours, when you left?'

'It was quieter, but there were still some lads milling about. I didn't take much notice. The taxi came right up to the door.'

Harrie asks about the movements of the other guests at the party. Arch merely shrugs, saying people came and went. He didn't keep tabs on everyone. He looks pointedly at the huge, gold-coloured Rolex on his wrist, says he has a meeting.

Donna exchanges a glance with her detective sergeant. As they both stand, Harrie thanks Arch for his cooperation, while emphasising they may be back with further questions.

He remains seated, picking at a chord on the arm of his chair. 'You're pretty sure this Col Flither was killed on the Saturday night?'

'It's one possibility we're looking at,' replies Harrie.

'It'll be a pub brawl, then. Somebody getting heated, taking a pop. Now.' He waves his hand towards the door of his office, as if shooing hens from under his feet. 'My secretary will see you out.'

During their walk to the door, Donna feels Leonard Arch's gaze on her back, just as the cameras will track them to her car.

Chapter 17

Though it's only early evening, Alice wakes Fareeha. She looks heavy and weary as she moves around the flat fixing them both peppermint tea and sandwiches. Alice isn't feeling too bright herself after a shift waitressing. She sinks thankfully into Fareeha's pliant sofa and stretches her aching legs along it.

'You wouldn't have thought we'd just come out of a season of excess consumption,' she says, 'the way people were putting it away today.' Her friend brings over a plate and mug. Alice can see she hasn't heard her properly. 'What's up?'

Fareeha sits in one of the armchairs and takes several mouthfuls before answering. 'I'm going home, to Mum and Dad's.'

Nooo! Alice catches the exclamation before it is articulated. She substitutes it with a shaky, 'Oh?'

Fareeha puts down her half-eaten snack and curls herself up, clasping her cup. 'I can't stay here. I can't afford to stay here, not unless I work twelve hours a day. And I just haven't the energy to start again somewhere else. I'm so tired.' Her expression is one of defeat. 'And, oh Alice, I just want to be cared for. You know what I mean?'

I'd care for you, thinks Alice. But she does get what

Fareeha means. When Alice goes to her parents' organic smallholding on the borders of Wales, it's like entering a warm nest. And for all the differences of opinions Fareeha has with her dad, she feels the same.

She carries on talking to a spot in the corner of the room about how it'll be easier to be at home once the baby comes and how she wants her little one to be surrounded by cousins, like she was. Finally, Fareeha's pinkened gaze comes to rest on Alice. 'You do understand, Alice?'

Alice nods vigorously. She doesn't lack understanding. She just wishes it wasn't so.

'You'll come and visit,' says Fareeha quickly, rubbing at her eyes. Her tone wavers between convivial and brittle. 'Not visit, stay, for as long as you like. I'll expect it. And we'll be in touch all the time.'

They both know it won't be the same.

However, Alice goes along with the hatching of plans for her to be shown the many delights of Bradford and the surrounding area. It even cheers her. For a while. She finishes her sandwiches and Fareeha brings over cake. She's saying she won't stop campaigning. 'I've got more reason to now than ever.'

Alice thinks maybe no sleep, changing nappies and feeding could slow her friend down more than a little. The realities of motherhood will also mean, Alice expects, that she will have to find a way of slipping into the cracks in between.

'Don't look sad, Alice,' says Fareeha. 'You'll start me off again.'

'Oh, honey,' says Alice quickly. 'I'm not sad, just

exhausted. I didn't get to sit down in eight hours. When are you going?' She manages to keep her voice conversational.

'I have to give a month's notice, so will have to pay until end of Feb, I suppose. Unless I can find someone to take it over for me?'

'Don't look at me,' says Alice. 'I'm happy upstairs. But I'll ask around for you and we can put it out on Facebook and WhatsApp.'

'I'll tell Mum tomorrow.'

She told me first. This mollifies Alice a little.

'She'll probably want to get in the car and come and pick me up there and then. But, I don't know, I want a bit of time, you know, to say goodbye properly.'

'Yes.' Would a short or long goodbye be worse? Alice cannot tell. 'I'll miss you. Lots.'

'I'll miss you too.' Fareeha sits forward.

'And it's for the best,' says Alice with resolve, more for herself than for Fareeha.

Fareeha will be fine, cocooned within her family, reconnecting with her old friends, becoming a mother. Alice suddenly feels chilled. And more weary than she thinks is possible. Slowly, she picks up crockery and cutlery. When Fareeha tells her to leave it by the sink, Alice is pleased to do so. She says she will go up now. Fareeha protests that Alice hasn't told her about her day, about her news. She wants Alice to sit and talk for a while. Alice shakes her head, though she still manages to drag up a brief tale of a woman wanting a saucer of milk which she fed to a cat Alice had thought was some kind of hairy beret on the chair next to her. It's not one of her funniest anecdotes, yet it does the trick.

109

'Did she come in wearing it on her head?' asks Fareeha, smiling.

Alice laughs. 'It was in her wheelie basket I think. I didn't notice it until she offered it the milk and a little pink tongue poked out. Gave me quite a turn. Now, I am shattered and I need a shower before I fall into bed.' She pauses on her way out. 'You will tell me as soon as you've decided – when you're going, I mean?'

'Of course.' Fareeha comes over and gives her a big hug.

Alice slowly climbs the stairs to her rooms. Since Saturday, she has been bubbling to tell her friend about meeting with Sarah, but every time she has come to the brink, the words have dried in her mouth. It is strange. She is not used to keeping things from Fareeha. However, she still can't quite get her encounter with Sarah straight in her mind and doesn't want to submit it to Fareeha's forensic questioning. If it had clearly been a strike for the cause, then it would be easy. Only there's the lingering concern that she enjoyed Sarah's company a little too much. And Fareeha would sniff this out. No doubt. *Anyway.* Alice jabs her key into the lock. *There's been nothing from Ms Franklande. She evidently does not feel the same.*

Chapter 18

There are times when Donna's inclination to be direct – blunt, as others might say – pays dividends. This morning, on her way into work, she had visited all the dentists who had not responded. She had cajoled, waited and then moved onto forthright. It took her to mid-morning to get a confirmed answer to her query. She finds she is not particularly shocked. She was already working on a fifty-fifty probability. She opts for a direct approach with her DI as well. When she delivers her conclusion to him in his office, he sounds more annoyed than amazed.

'Get them in. If they've been wasting our time for the thrill of it, I'll charge them, grieving mother and terminal illness notwithstanding.'

Donna pauses, wondering whether this is the moment to share her speculations brought on by the gravestones. Theo's 'Sometime today would be good, Donna,' suggests not.

Donna brings Pat Flither and Doug Prichard into the interview room. The high secured windows are narrow grey oblongs, the January sun having made its brief appearance before dipping behind Oliver's Mount. There is a smell of bleach in the close atmosphere. There is a table with a scarred top and four hard-back chairs. Theo is leaning against one of the walls. It has been painted a matt grey-pinky colour, which is apparently soothing. It does not seem to be working on him.

They had discussed the possibility of a fight, or at least a few 'no comments', but Pat is disarmingly honest: 'It could have been him. Why not? I wanted it to be him. Come home to me.'

With the four of them in there, it is more than a little warm. Even so, Pat has refused to relinquish her thick coat. At least it hangs open now, revealing a rather pretty cream blouse with a ruffle across her shelf-like chest. She's leaning her square chin into her doughy fingers, lids closed tight over her eyes. Doug, his cheeks cherry red, rubs a hand over his scalp and then brings it down onto his sister-in-law's shoulder.

He says, 'It was the lad, the lad who put it into her mind.'

'What lad?' Theo asks sharply.

'Yorn lad, what's his name?' He looks at Pat's shuttered face, then sighs. 'Brian, a DC I think he said he was.'

'DC Brian Chesters?' Donna asks tentatively. *What's he been up to now?*

'Aye.'

Theo takes a seat, says more conversationally, 'Please tell us exactly what happened, Mr Prichard.'

'It was him who came round to see me, said you'd found Col, in the harbour. I said, no lad, Col's been missing these eighteen months, lost off the Faroes, least-ways it was what we were told. Nothing's official, like, have to wait seven years without a body.' He scrapes his scalp again, and tiny flakes of skin lift into the fuggy air. 'Though our lass says there could be summat we could do through the courts, only

Pat she's reluctant. Keeps saying, maybe he'll come back.' He shakes his head. 'She needed to see him, his body, before she could accept it proper.'

'So to be clear, DC Chesters came to you?' Donna asks quietly.

'Aye.'

'When was this?'

'The evening afore you lot came round to see us.'

'Wednesday the eighth of January?'

'Aye, that'd be about right.'

'And what did he say?'

'He said the body from the harbour was Col's.'

Theo leans forward. 'Are you sure those were his exact words?'

Doug takes a moment to consider. 'No, mebs it was more like, could be Col's.'

Donna lets out her breath. *An innocent mistake? Better than leading a witness.*

Doug continues, 'It was the tatt which got her, the porpoise on his arm.'

'It was a vaquita, very specifically,' Theo mutters to himself.

'She wanted to see him,' Doug finishes, as if he's not heard Theo. Perhaps he hasn't.

'And you?' Donna asks.

'I didn't look, love, not proper. I've seen dead bodies afore. Two. Me dad – he died peaceful in his bed. And me cousin – he'd got caught in a squall when it blew up, wasn't paying enough attention and got heaved over. They pulled him out not six hours later. I know what a drowned man looks like. Don't need to see another. 'Sides this' – he rubs his belly – 'is making me more squeamish than I used to be.'

'You knew, though,' says Theo. 'You knew it wasn't Col.'

Doug looks from Donna to Theo, those navy eyes as untroubled as a flat sea. 'I did not, lad. I didn't look proper. It was Pat who was doing the identifying and she saw what she wanted to see.'

Pat suddenly lunges forwards, her fingers grasping at the soft wool of Theo's jacket sleeve. 'You're sure it's not him? You're sure it's not Col?' Her eyes are inflamed, pink cracks spinning out from the iris.

'We are, Mrs Flither.' He pats her hand. 'DC Morris here has corroborated it with Col's dentist.'

'He never went,' Pat spits out in Donna's direction.

'Not for a while, it's true,' says Donna easily. 'But the dentist assured me the formation of the jaw and the teeth within it do not change that significantly, especially in adulthood. Col had had several of his wisdom teeth out.'

'Aye he got an abscess,' Doug agrees gloomily. 'Left getting it looked at and had to get a fair few of his teeth pulled.'

'Our deceased has a full set.'

Pat releases her grip on Theo and sits back.

Donna takes out the photo of the vaquita tattoo. 'You are sure you don't recognise this, Mrs Flither? Please take a good look.'

She doesn't. However, Doug moves uneasily in his seat.

Donna turns her gaze on him. 'You, Mr Prichard, you recognise this?'

He hesitates, scraping the tattered skin on his scalp again. Then he nods. 'Aye, love. I do.'

114

Chapter 19

Theo decides not to charge Pat or Doug. He allows them to leave with a stern warning. It would have winded Donna to be on the receiving end of it, however, Pat Flither exits with her chin in the air, followed by a more downcast Doug.

Theo's ire is now focused on Brian Chesters. 'What was he thinking?' He is pacing the short distance between the door of the interview room and its end wall. He says, with a hint of chagrin, 'He was a different DC when I first met him, enthusiastic, a bit too bouncing at times, but he could be relied on to put the work in.'

'Perhaps it wasn't as Doug said, not exactly,' offers Donna. 'Doug is obviously desperate to get Pat some peace and we've seen how frantic she is.'

Theo halts as if considering this. 'Perhaps. We can all make mistakes.' It's clear he'd prefer to believe the best of his DC. This may be why his tone is more measured when they find Brian in an otherwise empty CID office.

'Doug's lying.' Chesters's defence of himself is robust. He is sitting back in his chair, arms crossed. 'You don't think I know the dangers of leading a witness?'

Theo sighs. 'OK let's suppose Mr Prichard and Mrs Flither did get the wrong end of the stick. What I don't understand is why you went to them in the first place, without running it by Harrie or me?'

Tension delineates Brian's jaw, though, when he speaks, his tone is even. 'You'd both gone. I was using my initiative. I know you're always encouraging us to do that.' His attempted grin is contorted. 'I thought you'd be pleased, to have a name. I didn't expect the old bat to identify the body as her son if it wasn't.'

'Pat Flither or Mrs Flither, Detective Constable,' Theo says tersely.

Donna wishes she could leave them to it, without calling attention to herself.

Theo continues: 'But why go to Doug in the first place? What alerted you?'

'Everyone knows Col. I remembered the porpoise on his arm.'

'Only it wasn't a porpoise.'

'So I forgot the name of it.'

'You'd have remembered it if you'd taken notes. Or even bothered to take the photo,' snaps Theo. 'And if you had you'd have got a correct ID off Doug.'

For the first time, Chesters looks a smidge nonplussed. 'What d'you mean?'

'I've got to ring the DCI. Donna, you tell him. At least you seem to understand the rudiments of police work.' He strides away.

She wishes he hadn't left her with the task, or the epithet. Brian has scalpels for eyes. Donna feels overheated and as if her face has turned a hue of raspberry. She forces herself to remain calm and say, 'Doug named our deceased as

Orson Reed.' Then it comes to her, where she'd heard the name before.

Chapter 20

'So we start at the beginning.'

Theo's tone is expressionless. It is greeted without a murmur. Everyone knows what it means to recommence a case from zero again. They are all studiously not looking in Brian's direction. Donna sneaks a glance. His head is down, his notebook is open, pen in hand. Without comment he acquiesces to reviewing every scrap of CCTV footage once more. Donna thinks that perhaps a night's reflection has made him realise how lucky he is Theo hasn't taken any more punitive steps than giving him this shedload of grunt work.

Harrie is filling in what they have already gleaned about Orson Reed. Fortunately, he lived a lot of his life online, plus there's what Doug told them about his work with the fishing community. 'An' that's all I know, DC Morris,' Doug had said. Donna didn't believe him.

She turns her attention to the summary Harrie is giving. Orson Reed finished his MSc in marine biology at the Scarborough campus of Hull University in 2006 and set about organising a group he named 'Citizen Action Rebellion, Planet Emergency', or CARPE. Over the years, he's been involved in a great deal of direct action. Preventing a road from going through ancient woodland. Tackling supermarkets on single-use plastic packaging and the clothes industry on waste and the use of sweatshop labour. Confronting food companies on their use of palm oil grown in areas cleared of rainforest. Campaigning against proposed fracking sites. 'Interesting he isn't on any police database,' Harrie concludes.

'Perhaps he stayed this side of legal,' says Theo.

'Or he made sure we didn't catch him doing the illegal stuff,' says Harrie. She continues with more recent and local activities. He initiated a project with the local fishing boat crews to retrieve 'ghost gear'. This is fishing equipment lost accidentally or abandoned deliberately, which makes up 10 per cent of marine litter. He also launched a campaign concerned with pollution around the bays at Scarborough, including the public shaming of the local water company and council.

'You're saying the stabbing is to do with his environmental activities?' someone asks.

'We're not going to jump to any conclusions,' responds Harrie. 'The use of a knife suggests a more personal issue. We need to know more, especially what Mr Reed did not reveal on social media. A CSI team has been at his caravan where he's been living. And, yes, we already have DNA corroboration for the ID of our deceased.' She allows herself a grim smile. 'His caravan was pitched on the Gosawk Farm.' She nods at a few of the responses. 'Many of us had a few dealings with old Mr Gosawk due to his crusade against walkers. It turned out to be caused by the onset of dementia and he's now in a home. His daughter, Viv, came back to run the farm. She says she last saw Orson Saturday the fourth of January. This fits with the timeline we are working on.

We have the murder weapon. The knife found in the dump-ster has been wiped clean, but small drops of our deceased's blood were found under the edge of the handle, along with a DNA result which does not match Mr Reed, nor has given us any hits on our databases. This could prove useful once we have a suspect. The knife is what Prof Jayasundera describes as a chef's knife, of good quality, possibly a professional's.'

She pauses to look at her notes. 'The prof is still con-cerned about the presence of some kind of sleeping tablet in our deceased's bloodstream. Without knowing what he was taking, we can't do any further confirmative tests. Finally, there is the disturbance at the penthouse party. Was Mr Reed our gatecrasher? We're assuming yes, but we need this substantiated.' She finishes by doling out tasks. There are, she says, a lot of people to talk to, including Orson's friends, colleagues and adversaries. His parents are being informed by the Foreign Office as they live in Dubai. Then there are the witnesses from the Kiss Me Hardy, the harbour and the penthouse party to be interviewed, or re-interviewed in some cases, with the new ID and photo. Technical forensics will also be digging deeper into his various online accounts and trying to trace a phone account. Currently, there's no sign of a computer. 'That's it,' says Harrie, glancing at Theo. He nods.

The room bursts with pent-up energy. Now, at last, they are on the right track. Donna knows it is this thought which is re-vitalising her and her colleagues.

Alice says they can come and see her in her studio if they want. It is housed in what was once a summer villa for the aristocracy, the twin of the art gallery, which stands beside it on the Crescent. Harrie says it is close by and they will walk. Maybe she had engineered this interlude to talk about Brian. Or maybe it all just tumbles out. She can't understand how he could have got it so wrong. 'He didn't use to be slap-dash,' she says. 'We started together, you know, in CID. 2002. It took a while. I had my degree and initially he was pretty scathing. *Very* scathing.'

'Jealous?'

'Yeah, maybe. I was impressed by the range of jobs he'd done. He'd worked at the hospital, trained as a paramedic. I told him he had skills I didn't. And he'd been a carer for his dad for years. Brian lacked confidence, I think, and covered it with this daft bravado. Yeah, it took a while, but we became friends.' She's dressed in a thick waterproof jacket, black like her trouser suit underneath. Her sharp cheekbones are blushered pink. A loop of blonde hair slides across one of them until Harrie tucks it away into the severe bun on the back of her head. She carries on more softly, 'He wasn't always the quickest off the blocks. He was a grafter, a solid grafter. He's changed.'

'When? When did he start to change?'

Harrie's brow furrows. 'He seemed to crash, right after he failed his first sergeant exams. We both took them together in March 2012. Right after Theo got DI, I got the promotion. Yeah, that's no surprise. I'd outdone him again. But then, you know, he did pull himself back up again.'

'Until he failed them a second time, last year.'

'You were here for that, weren't you? It wasn't pretty.' Harrie hesitates before continuing. 'I wonder if he's in trouble. You've

121

noticed his new clothes and those daft two-tone shoes? He's got a new car too. And not some second-hand jalopy, neither. An Audi, one of those small, sporty ones. Said it was on the tick. Perhaps he's in debt, in over his head?'

'Why don't you ask him?'

'He doesn't talk to me any more.' She sounds genuinely despondent. 'He could be bloody irritating with his chatter. Now I miss it.'

They arrive at the resplendent gateposts of wind-chewed sandstone. A notice announces it as a creative industries centre, saying it was once the home of writers Edith, Osbert and Sacheverell Sitwell. The reception is substantial with a finely tiled floor and hung with original paintings. Directed along a corridor to some lifts, Donna sees into what was an expansive conservatory. It has been transformed into a gallery. The studios are 'below stairs', where the floors are flagged and ceilings lower. They find Alice in a large oblong room. The end wall has windows overlooking a grassy slope. The remaining walls are lined with cupboards. There are several work benches. One holds ceramics in different stages of development, another a small printing press. The air smells of a mix of clay and inks.

Alice sits at a third table. She has been working on a computer and has various notebooks and sketchbooks open. She indicates Donna and Harrie should grab a seat from the ill-assorted assembly of chairs which dot the room. Donna finds herself in a camping chair made of a stripy fabric. It gives rather too much as she sits. Harrie perches on a stool daubed with paint. Alice is gabbling (perhaps from nerves) an explanation about how she's lucky to get the use of the studio space for free because she sits on reception sometimes and how she's been able to set up a darkroom. She indicates a shanty-built structure in the corner covered over with carpet underlay.

'Digital's great, but there's nothing like real film, is there? And I'm experimenting with natural sources of chemicals, like seaweed,' she says, glancing from one to the other with an eager smile which soon dissolves. 'You look serious. Is it about Ian? He's not . . . I mean, he's OK, right?'

Harrie says gently, 'It's not about Ian Renshawe, Ms Miller.'

'Alice,' she breathes out.

'Alice. It's Orson Reed,' says Harrie.

'What's happened?' Something defensive comes into Alice's features.

'I am very sorry to have to inform you, Mr Reed has been found dead.'

Shock floods Alice's face. 'What? How? No, no, you can't be right. When?'

'His body was found on Tuesday the seventh of January.'

Alice repeats 'no' several times, as puzzlement brings tucks to her smooth brow. Then she grins. 'Oh no, you have got it wrong. You see he WhatsApped me and Fareeha on Thursday. Yes, it was Thursday the ninth.' She grabs her phone from the surface near her and starts scrolling. 'See? See?' She holds it out.

Donna is the closest to her and takes it. 'It appears to be from him,' she confirms. 'We'll have to take this to have it investigated.'

'You're taking my phone?' The disbelief has returned to Alice's demeanour and tone. 'Can you do that?'

'We could get a warrant,' explains Donna. 'It would be easier if you would give us permission?'

'I'm not sure I want to.' Alice's hands twist against each other in her lap.

'You do want us to find out what happened to Mr Reed, don't you?' says Donna.

'Nothing has,' responds Alice, rallying a little. 'He's not the person you've found.'

'I'm afraid he is,' says Harrie firmly. 'We have matched DNA.'

There's a pause before Alice speaks again. They can hear the chatter and laugh from a couple of people passing in the corridor, then a stray piano playing as a door is opened and closed. Again, Alice says Harrie and Donna are wrong, however, she's fast losing conviction. She begins to sag, like some of the slumped pots waiting to be painted on the nearby worktop.

Harrie pulls out the photo of the vaquita tattoo. 'Do you recognise this?'

'Someone else could have one like that, couldn't they?' asks Alice, a plea in her voice.

'Alice,' says Donna, as if she is coaxing a frightened child. 'We have DNA. There is no doubt. We are very sorry.'

'No, no,' Alice mutters, shaking her head, crossing her arms. Then eventually she is still. 'Poor Orson. How did it happen?'

'That's what we want to find out,' says Harrie, sounding businesslike. 'All we know at the moment is that he was stabbed and ended up off the harbour wall.'

'Stabbed? Harbour wall? How, how is it possible?' Alice narrows her eyes, which are becoming glassy. She searches in her dungaree pockets and finds a tissue to dab at them.

'Tell me,' says Donna quietly. 'Tell me about Orson.' It's a technique she has adopted from Theo. It works, to a certain extent, on Alice.

The friendship between her and Orson is obvious. Equally obvious is that she is wary of giving too much away about Orson's activities. They do not learn much more about them than was already in the public domain. Harrie asks about friends. Alice names herself and Fareeha and a few others who are already on the list for interview from the CARPE social media pages.

'How about lovers?' Harrie asks. They've also established the relationship Viv Gosawk had with their victim.

Alice's hands clasp each other. Her shoulders hunch. 'Orson has, had . . .' She falters and then continues. 'He has lots of friends.'

'No one special?' asks Donna.

'We're all special,' says Alice with certainty.

'How about enemies?' asks Harrie. 'Threats?'

There's a glimmer of a smile as Alice replies: 'Threats aplenty on social media. Solicitors' letters. But, I mean, to actually stab someone, it's a whole different level, isn't it?' The seriousness of it strikes her forcibly again and her creamy skin blanches. She rocks slightly.

Donna wonders if she is about to faint. She suggests a break and a tea. Alice accepts gratefully, indicating the kettle on the metal Belfast sink by the windows. While she

125

is waiting for it to boil, Donna opens one of the panes. The breeze is chill and reviving. It and the tea bring some colour to Alice's face.

Donna asks her about Ian Renshawe. 'You didn't mention him when you were talking about friends.'

Alice considers this. 'No, I suppose not. They came to know each other through Fareeha and they got along. Orson could get along with most people.'

'Ian not so much?'

'He was a bit stand-offish, I suppose, and away quite a lot. He'd come along, to demos and the like, but he wouldn't want to be at the forefront.'

'And he left Scarborough Saturday morning?'

'Yes, yes, as far as I know.' There's a pause, the confusion twisting into the flesh on her round face. 'Oh but, you can't be thinking, Ian wouldn't, he'd never . . . would he?' She has dark brown irises; they look like large chocolate buttons as her eyes widen.

Donna lets the question go unanswered. She points at Alice's laptop. Did Orson have a computer? Alice shakes her head; he did everything on his phone. Donna asks about Orson taking sleeping tablets. Alice's negative response is accompanied by surprise.

'Orson never had any problem sleeping,' she says, almost with amusement. 'Are you sure, sure it's him?'

'Yes,' says Harrie decisively, and then asks where the younger woman was on the night of Saturday 4 January.

'Working,' she replies, sounding distracted. 'Um, I was waitressing at a party at that new penthouse they've built on the harbour. Oh.' Another pause, her gaze drops to her lap.

'Don't tell me I was serving drinks and canapés to stuffed shirts when Orson was being – being – killed. Fuck!'

The exclamation at the end hits Donna with force. It also injects a stiffness into Alice's manner, a certain fierceness into her expression. Plus there's something else, a guardedness. She's had a realisation she's holding back on. Which is possibly why her initial description of the party is vague. Until Harrie says, 'We know about the incident with the rotten fish, Alice. Was the gatecrasher Mr Reed?'

Alice says no, even as she nods her head. She looks more miserable.

'Did you know what he was going to do?' asks Harrie.

Again the denial out of her mouth, while her head does the opposite. Maybe she realises, as she says, 'I mean he'd suggested it, as something we could do together, but I dissuaded him.' She glances away. 'I couldn't afford to lose the job and, really, it was hardly more than a gnat's bite on a rhino's arse. Not worth it.'

'What happened?'

'I don't know, exactly.' Alice continues to talk to the view through the window. 'I'd just grabbed a mo to go for a wee. When I got back, I was stuck behind everyone else. Orson had emptied one box of rotten fish onto the floor and was giving his speech about capitalism and climate change. Of course, he was absolutely right in what he was saying, but no one there gave a fuck.' She turns back. 'He was filming it all, you see, he was going to use it on CARPE's media platforms. He had his body cam on.'

'Do you think anyone else noticed?'

She shrugs. 'It never got uploaded anyway, did it?'

'What about the other box?' asks Donna. She can feel herself easing forward, as if watching for the bob of the float on a line she has cast.

Alice looks at her. 'What?'

'You said Orson emptied one box. That suggests there was another?'

'Yes.' She halts, licks her lips and clamps them into a flat line. Then she says: 'Oh well, I guess you'll get to find out, anyhow. He tried to launch that one at the cravat-wearing gnome, Leonard Arch. Orson called him a bastard and said he was going to bring him down.'

Which Arch failed to mention.

'Sounds like a threat,' says Harrie. 'What do you think he meant by that?'

'Oh, Orson has a file yay thick on ScarTek. Polluting the seas around here. Lobbying for licences for fracking companies, so ScarTek can supply the chemicals. Professor Cullen . . .' She runs out of steam.

'Who is Professor Cullen?' asks Donna.

'Orson's tutor from uni. They became friends after Orson graduated. The professor produced a report into the water quality off the Scarborough coast. Orson said Arch had put pressure on Cullen to take out the sections which would have damned ScarTek.'

'How?' asks Harrie.

Alice shrugs.

'We will have to talk to him.'

'You can't, he's dead.' Alice's tone is strangled. 'He committed suicide last year.'

'Where's the file?' asks Donna.

128

'What?' Alice glances up.

'The file Orson had on ScarTek?'

Alice taps her temple. 'I meant in his head, on his phone. Not a literal file.' Her head tips forward. 'Look, could we carry this on some other time? Orson's dead, I'm finding it kinda hard to keep thinking straight.'

'Just a bit longer, Alice,' says Harrie. 'A few things more, if you don't mind?' When the younger woman doesn't object, Harrie goes on. 'What happened after Mr Reed confronted Leonard Arch?'

'This big guy grabbed him, think he said he was part of you lot—'

The DCI?

'And, of course, security piled in. It was over in a moment. Orson was thrown out.'

'And afterwards?' Harrie prompts.

Alice shrugs. 'Some people left, I guess the more sober. Your mate stayed and Arch did too. Right through to when it ended. Two a.m. I didn't get home till half past three, with all the cleaning up.'

'Did you see Leonard Arch leave the party after Mr Reed was ejected?' asks Harrie.

This time Alice gives a very definite shake of her head. 'More's the pity. Couldn't keep his hands to himself, the bastard.'

'And how did you get home?' Harrie is checking Alice's alibi. They still can't be certain when Orson died.

Alice does not indicate she has noticed. 'Taxi. The one saving grace of the job. That and the money.' Gloom descends on her young face and weights her shoulders.

Harrie and Donna share an unspoken agreement: *That's enough. For now.*

'If you think of anything,' says Harrie, handing over her card, 'give us a call.' She stands and Donna follows suit.

'Um.' Alice gathers herself before saying resolutely: 'I don't want you taking my phone, my whole life is on it. I'll bring it in whenever you want for you to do what you need to do, but I won't hand it over for you to keep.'

Harrie nods slowly. 'OK, I'll get one of our tech officers to arrange it with you.' She indicates to Donna to hand over the phone, then adds: 'You do know you can't delete anything permanently? We will always be able to retrieve it.'

Alice gives no response, merely takes her device and pockets it quickly.

Donna cannot tell whether deletion was on the young woman's mind or whether she really could not imagine existing without her phone.

By the time they have walked over to Fareeha Gopal's apartment, Alice has evidently used her mobile for at least one thing: to let her friend know the essentials of what the two police officers on her doorstep want to talk about.

Chapter 21

Alice is glad of the sharp air and the muddy path as she cycles the old railway track. They mean her mind is occupied in keeping her upright. Otherwise she worries she might become overwhelmed with unhappy thoughts, brutal images and questions which have no answers. She arrives at Gosawk Farm. She had hoped to sit beside Orson's caravan. Or even in it, having persuaded Viv to relinquish a key. Alice believed she would feel Orson close again and this might bring her some respite. She had not bargained on the police cordon, the PC keeping watch and the person in the white forensic suit she can see through the window. She had not bargained on them having taking possession of Orson's space. Of having polluted it. For her, at least.

She chains up her bike and takes the track which Orson had shown her. It leads up over a shoulder of land planted with dark green brassica. Alice can smell the blend of pepper and hot metal coming off them. She puffs slightly at the rise. She ducks her head against the increasing salt-laden gusts. She arrives at the cliff top and slumps down onto the seat set there. The tangle of bramble and stunted hawthorn form a thin edging for the waterscape of shifting tinctures of greys and muted iolite under a bruised sky. Orson sat here on his penultimate morning. It was here he had taken and posted

131

the photo of the robin resting on a strand of hedge pointing to the heavens like a finger. Alice flattens her hands against the slats of the bench as if she might feel again the warmth of her friend. As if he might have left it there to comfort her.

Yes, she is used to the death which comes with keeping animals on a smallholding. Yes, both her grandfathers have died, plus an aunt, taken, as they said, before her time by cancer. But this death, Orson's death, is of a different complexity. Not only was he too young, at thirty-three, two years older than her, but he was also brim-full of vitality. His energy swept everyone along. His energy carried Alice through. Then there is the manner of his passing. A stabbing. A murder. It's incomprehensible.

Her tormenting contemplation on Orson becomes entwined with thoughts about Sylvia. Dead even younger. And by her own volition. Alice tries to imagine a family environment which would push a girl to drown herself. It must have been truly awful. And where was Roland? Sarah is still beating herself up about not being around, but Roland was there and apparently did nothing. Alice thinks of her own brother, younger by several years, yet she could always go to him with troubles. And he comes to her. *Doesn't he?* The spike of doubt jabs deep. Takes her breath away. Orson had become like a brother to her. Had she let him come between her and her own sibling? She promises herself to ring him as soon as she gets home.

She turns away from the waves which had devoured both Sylvia and Orson. She wants to feel anchored. Only the land undulates as it rises to the moors. Fields of raw jade interwoven with slashes of brown, stretches of leafless hedges and clumps of skeleton trees. Alice grips the damp wood of the bench as a life raft. She is unsure whether she believes in a spirit after death. The body, she is certain, returns to a kind of cosmic recycling machine. She anticipates her cells will become part of a silver birch or a rowan. But a soul? There's a thing she's never quite come to a conclusion on. Orson was a non-spirit man. She hopes he was wrong. Since, if ever there is a time when she needs him, it is now. To discuss what she can and cannot tell the police. To reassure her he didn't hold their last argument against her. She tells herself it wasn't serious, not in the scheme of things. They'd had fallings out before. They had always made up. *Only this time, it can't happen.* This thought brings an excoriating sob up her throat.

Orson never coming back. Orson never to tease her again, never to laugh at her jokes, never to hold her in his enveloping hug. *Never, never, never.* 'People are dying,' he said the last time she saw him. She thought he meant in general – people are dying because of climate change. Now she wonders: did he mean specific people? Professor Cullen? Himself? She holds herself tight. Did he know what was going to happen? *And I let him walk away, angry.* She drops her face into her hands.

Chapter 22

Donna and Harrie discuss the interview with Fareeha Gopal as they walk towards town along the Esplanade. Both are wrapped against the maul of the wind blowing in from Siberia. It smells of snow. Donna can see the grey pinstripes of sleet hanging across the entrance to the bay. They interrupted Fareeha in packing glasses and ornaments into a cardboard box. 'I don't know how I accumulated all this stuff,' she said. 'It's all going to the charity shop.' Donna wonders whether there were gifts from Ian Renshawe in amongst the 'stuff'. She and Harrie consider if it is significant that Fareeha is preparing to leave shortly after her lover quit the town. Is she following him? Is his disappearance on the same day as Orson's murder more than a coincidence? The ANPR is now rated 'urgent'.

Fareeha didn't add much to what they already know about Orson Reed. Her tone was less adoring than Alice's. Orson's heart was in the right place, he was good at getting people riled up and organised. And he was even better at making himself the centre of attention. When it suited him. This was the general gist. However, neither Donna nor Harrie detected any real rancour. Not enough to lead to murder. Though a question mark has to remain. They both know that people are motivated to kill for a whole mix of emotions.

And some are very good at concealing what they are feeling.

They checked Fareeha's whereabouts on the evening and night of Saturday 4 January. She had been alone, though she had spoken separately on WhatsApp video calls to her mother, her sister and one of her bookkeeping clients. Watching Fareeha drag herself around her flat, both Harrie and Donna agree they find it hard to envisage her being able to confront and kill the fit Orson on the harbour.

They cross the dainty Spa Bridge. Harrie peels off left towards the police station. Donna turns the other way.

'Where are you going?' asks Harrie.

'The barmaid at the Kiss Me said she would speak to me before her shift starts.'

'OK.'

'It's Nicky Fletcher.'

'Oh.' Harrie halts. Her mouth flattens. 'Give her my love,' she says, setting off once more.

Nicky Fletcher. Not two months ago she was one of their own. In her twenties, at the beginning of her career, she suddenly left. She let on to Donna about an aggressive sexual advance which turned to bullying when rejected. She refused to bring a complaint. In all probability the perpetrator was – the increasingly wayward – DC Brian Chesters.

Nicky appears relatively upbeat in speaking to Donna. Her police training makes her a good witness. And she has spoken to Orson Reed on several occasions when he was in for a drink. He was a good laugh. Always up for the karaoke. Yes he sometimes got into heated discussions with a few of the locals. It never got physical. Not on the premises, anyway. She reluctantly gives a couple of names while insisting it was more robust joshing than anything else.

Donna asks her about Saturday 4 January. It had been busy and raucous. Even so, Nicky is able to say with some certainty that Orson came in around eight or eight-fifteen. She considers for a moment, then says he did appear out of sorts. He drank his first pint real quick. He was more steady with his second. He began to join in with the conversations around him. Loosen up a little. Nicky is pretty certain Orson only had the two drinks and wasn't drunk when he left around eleven p.m. Someone called out that he should stay for the next song, it was his favourite. He said he had an appointment. Then he left. Nicky doesn't remember him carrying any boxes, though he had a backpack. Nor did anyone immediately follow him. She thinks he turned towards the harbour, though can't be sure. There was some wise-cracking about what kind of appointment Orson might have arranged for eleven p.m. at the harbour. Then he got forgotten as the beer and whisky flowed.

As Donna is about to leave, Nicky says: 'Stay for a drink. On the house. You're going off duty now, right?'

Donna is intending to, and would rather be off home. She is flagging. Wants – needs – a shower, to eat and to put her feet up. However, something in Nicky's expression – part jolly, part beseeching – means she agrees to an apple juice. Nicky returns with two, both jazzed up with slices of lemon and lime, a cocktail umbrella in each. The younger woman was always on the plump side, however (she now confirms), she's taken up running and is looking fitter. Her face retains

136

an appealing cherubic rotundness. She asks Donna how she is and after Trev and a few of her other colleagues. There's a wistfulness in her voice.

After responding to her enquiries, Donna asks: 'Won't you think of coming back, Nicky? You'd be welcomed in two wriggles of a lamb's tale.'

Nicky shakes her head. She says quietly: 'You're very kind Donna. You always were kind to me. But I've shown I'm not up to it. I'm not strong enough.'

'It isn't about strength, this work. There're other qualities which are important: smartness, being able to get people to talk, being able to calm situations.'

Nicky smiles. 'Yeah, that comes in useful here too.'

'Anyway, it's not about toughing it out. We all need a bit of encouragement sometimes.'

'Maybe. Anyhow, I've shown too much vulnerability. I couldn't come back from that.' Nicky takes a swallow of drink, then says, 'I'm signed up to college, care worker training.'

Donna toasts this future. Nicky will surely do well at it. But she would have been a good police officer.

'My uncle is pleased,' Nicky says, with a sardonic turn of her mouth.

The uncle who Nicky had intended to emulate, to make proud, by following onto the force, despite his conviction that it wasn't for 'lassies'. The uncle who belonged to the old days. Donna says her goodbyes and wraps herself up for the walk home. She reflects on Nicky's experience. They suggest those days are not as bygone as she would like to think they are.

Chapter 23

She considers ignoring the email, even binning it. Not only is she not in the mood to socialise, there is also something in the tone, as if Sarah thinks she is doing Alice the favour. Though, Alice supposes, she did set up the conceit this way when they first met. Only eight days ago. How things have changed. Then Alice felt like a warrior princess going into battle for Orson and what they both believed in. Now there is no Orson. Her finger hovers over the delete. Yet, there are still their shared beliefs: the overwhelming importance of the natural environment and the need to protect it against wilful or thoughtless destruction by humans. Orson would not want her to give up on this. He would want her to be even more dedicated to it. And, if he had made enemies at ScarTek – enough to see him killed (which, quite frankly, is still surreal) – then maybe she can learn something useful from cultivating a friendship with Sarah? She pictures herself re-buckling up her armour. For Orson. She taps on 'reply'.

She has reason to revisit her impulse when she sees Sarah waiting for her in a booth in the bar at the Spa. For a moment, she allows herself to acknowledge she finds the other woman attractive. If there is a heaven, Alice thinks,

Orson would be sitting on his cloud and laughing. Not that he ever hesitated to mix business with pleasure when it suited him. And pleasure always suited him.

The bar is a wide open space with doors and windows fronting onto the spitting and rolling sea. The servery is in the centre. The plaid-covered booths are along the rear wall. As Alice approaches, Sarah stands, almost knocking her glass of red wine over. Her nervousness comes through in her disjointed greeting. Is this OK? Would Alice prefer a sea view? Not that anything can be seen as its dark outside. What does she want to drink? Is that a blush creeping across the white skin of Sarah's cheeks as she says it's good to see Alice again?

Alice unwinds her long red scarf and takes off her yellow mac. Underneath she has on one of her charity shop finds: a damson-coloured velvet dress which flows seductively across her hips. She has a similar-coloured ribbon wound round her short dark hair, only its burgundy dipped tips showing. The inordinate amount of time it had taken her to decide on an outfit should have told her something. Sarah is in jeans with (if the drape is anything to go by) a silk blouse, plus a chip of diamond in each ear and on a chain around her neck. At Alice's request, she orders a local craft beer from a passing waiter. Her delivery makes the portly man unconsciously come out of his slouch.

It takes a while for the drink to arrive. Alice suddenly realises she won't know how to respond if she is asked anything about how she is or what she has been doing. Can she lie convincingly enough? Does she want to? To avoid this happening, she plies Sarah with questions about her day. Sarah ceases to fiddle with her wine glass. She seems to relax in answering. Her work appears to be a mix of managing staff, of reviewing data and of meetings.

'So you don't do the actual experiments?' asks Alice, finding she honestly wants to know more about the woman she is with.

'I have the overview of what my colleagues are doing. I rarely pick up a pipette, these days, or look down a microscope. I do miss being more hands on.' Her mouth gives its appealing lopsided grin.

'Do you sometimes sneak in to fiddle about with the test tubes, when no one is looking?'

'Well, that would cause havoc with our results,' says Sarah. Then her poker face disintegrates and she laughs. 'Don't tell anyone – I have my own set at home to play with.'

Alice isn't entirely sure whether she is joking.

With the arrival of the beer, Sarah turns to Alice. 'Enough about me. What about you?'

'I don't think I've wielded a pipette since my GCSEs.' She knows her attempt at keeping things light is falling flat. She should not have come. She is in no condition to maintain a polite conversation, let alone do any detective work. *What was I thinking?* She must keep the spotlight away from her for as long as possible. She takes a few sips of her drink, then asks, 'How did it feel to come back?'

Sarah pauses before responding. 'I never thought I would, after everything.'

'No.' Alice forges on. 'It doesn't sound like an easy childhood.'

'You did read the newspaper articles, huh?' A long gulp

of wine. 'My dad . . . my dad, he was what you might call a jack-the-lad. He was always getting us kids things – bikes, games, furniture for our bedrooms – and then it would disappear again. We learned not to mention it. As we got older, of course, we worked out it had gone to pay off bills, or debts.' Another swallow from her glass. She puts it down, then says firmly, her gaze on the table: 'No. No. As a dad he was fun, he was exciting, when he was there, but he wasn't, he wasn't a very nice man, to Mum anyway.'

'And you had to pick up the pieces?'

'For Sylvia, yes. Roland is older, he looked after himself. Sometimes he looked after Mum, took her to hospital once, or maybe twice, when it was really bad. I often wondered why she didn't leave. I think she tried. We went to stay with Mum's sister, in Hessle, you know, in Hull? But it was like she couldn't cope without him, she fell apart.' She half smiles her quirky lopsided smile. 'Those six months with our aunt were probably the most stable we had. I remember she would take us three kids off to Spurn Point. Give our mum a break, she said. She loved birdwatching. It was the wildest place we had ever been; we were used to the boating lake in Peasholm.' She gasps a kind of laugh.

Alice grins. 'I went to Spurn Point to do some photographing. It's certainly a mysterious place. Lonely.'

'Yes, Sylvia took to it. Me and Roland, not so much. Roland was going through his "I'm too cool for family" teenage thing. He was – is – good at splitting himself off. Mum, well, I think, she just made him angry.'

'And you?'

'Was I angry? I left, didn't I? I get it now – more than

141

I did, anyway – he controlled her, she couldn't conceive of a way out.'

They both take a moment to reflect on this, Alice sipping at her beer. She feels weary.

'Look,' says Sarah. 'I'm sorry. I have upset you. I didn't mean to . . .'

Alice shakes her head. 'It's not anything you've said. I mean, it's tragic, your story, but it's not that.' She can't work out how to go on.

'Has something happened? Tell me.' Sarah's tone is gentle, her gaze has intensified.

Alice takes a breath; she is about to divert the conversation again. Then she says, 'A friend, a friend of mine, he's dead.' Her words are forlorn. Tears are threatening. Then one breaks free and dribbles down her nose.

'Oh, here.' Sarah searches in her bag and finds a cotton handkerchief. 'It's clean.'

Alice takes it. It is soft to the touch. *Who carries a handkerchief any more?* Ridiculously, it reminds her of her gran, who always does. The temptation to fold her arms on the table, lay her head down and weep increases. 'I'm sorry.'

'No, no, don't be. It's awful to lose someone you are fond of. It's like being scraped out hollow.'

Sylvia. Phil and June Franklande. Perhaps others. Sarah knows what she is talking about. 'Yes, it is.' Alice wipes her eyes. 'Maybe I shouldn't have come.'

'If you want to go, I'll get you a taxi. No problem. We can do this another time. But . . .' She hesitates. 'No, of course, you'll want to go home.' She's delving into her bag for her mobile.

'But?'

Sarah pauses. 'Well, if you want to stay, I can listen.' She's staring down at her fingers.

Yes. No! Yes. Alice can't decide. She watches Sarah begin to tap on her phone, then get through to the taxi firm, before Alice says: 'No, wait. I'll stay for a bit. I'd like to.'

After ending the call, Sarah says, 'Tell me about your friend.'

At first Alice struggles to find the right words. She wants to talk about Orson, yes, but this is Sarah Franklande, employee of ScarTek. The fine line Alice is walking keeps tripping her up. Eventually, she manages to get out several comprehensible sentences about Orson's fun personality – does she even say 'larking about'? – about his kindness and about his commitment to environmental action, before running out of steam.

After a moment, Sarah says, 'Orson sounds like a good bloke, a good friend.'

And yet we were both so angry with each other the last time. Alice stows the thought. *We'd have come back from it, if he hadn't been . . .* She pushes herself. *This is your chance to pull something useful out of this mess.* 'You didn't know him, then?'

Another pause, this one a bit longer. Is there more guardedness in Sarah's features as she responds? 'I am not aware of knowing him. Should I have done?'

'Orson knew lots of people,' says Alice quickly. She takes a couple of gulps of her beer. It's citrusy and hoppy. Orson would have loved it.

Sarah is once again toying with her wine glass, which

is now empty. 'You and Orson,' she says slowly, 'were colleagues when it came to the environmental work?'

Alice nods.

'I can see it's very important to you.' Sarah has ceased to look at Alice.

'Isn't it to everybody?' says Alice in a rush. 'Shouldn't it be? Once our natural environment begins to deteriorate, we humans will have had it. We're already more than halfway to where it'll be completely fucked up. Climate change isn't a theory any more.'

'It came into my PhD in 1995.'

This is a surprise. 'A denier?'

'Of course not.' Sarah sounds mildly offended. 'The evidence was there even then. It was indisputable.'

'Larch-Tek was supplying the fracking industry.'

'We were trying to clean the industry up, modify the chemicals they were using.'

'It's still a fossil fuel.' Alice leans in.

'There has to be a bridge energy. Renewables weren't producing enough. Still aren't.'

Oh Sarah. Alice feels the disappointment pooling into her stomach like acid. 'They would if we turned down our consumption and stopped measuring economic success by growth.'

'And people's jobs?'

'There'll always be plenty of jobs, cleaning up the mess we've made, innovating, repairing, food production, caring for others. We're always so UK-centric. Looking internationally, there are people dying.' She pauses for a breath and continues more soberly. 'I suppose you see nuclear as

144

a bridge energy as well?' It's as if she's thrown down her gauntlet on the table top.

'I follow the science.' Sarah raises her chin an inch.

The two women stare at each other. Alice is telling herself off for ever thinking kindly of Sarah. *Why did I bother coming? Why did I fucking bother?* She controls her urge to spit out her retort.

'Do you indeed? Which is why you feel OK about ignoring ScarTek's fouling of the seas around here. Sodium hypochlorite and polymeric carbohydrate coming out of your waste pipes.'

'Bleach and starch—'

'Starch which encourages blooms of mutant algae—'

'Non-native algae.'

'Which fucks up the Ph level, impeding filter feeders – worms, molluscs – and their role in keeping the water clean, meaning Scarborough's blue flag status is endangered.'

'There was an issue with a product we were producing for a potato-processing company. It's been dealt with.'

'Yeah, by building an extension to your outfall pipe out beyond the jurisdiction of the Environment Agency. Thus avoiding fines, bad publicity, withdrawal of investors. Maybe further investigations and even civil or criminal court actions.'

Sarah's light blue eyes narrow; they blink one too many times. 'The Cullen Report exonerated ScarTek,' she says firmly.

Alice is on a roll and doesn't think before blurting out: 'No it didn't. I saw it before it was redacted. Orson had a copy.' The split second after, she regrets it, not least because Orson swore her to secrecy. But also because of the hardening in Sarah's face. It's impossible to read. Angry? Defensive? Scared? Something has closed down in her.

A duet has begun a set in the bar. The melodious notes of a Celtic harp and guitar float over the chink of others eating and drinking. Finally Sarah says in a neutral tone, 'Why would Professor Cullen change his report?'

He was got at, had been Orson's verdict. Alice does not repeat it. She takes another swallow of beer. *What does Sarah already know?* She cannot tell. However, she's said too much, of that she is certain.

Then Sarah seems to soften again. She puts her hands on the table, as if they are reaching out to Alice's. 'As I am sure you have already learned from Google, I came to ScarTek last November, after the Cullen Report and after the professor's unfortunate, um, demise.'

Suicide. You can't even acknowledge it!

'However, I am well aware of its findings, its published findings, and I only agreed to come if I was allowed to review and overhaul where necessary all of ScarTek's procedures. Leonard agreed to this; indeed, he welcomed it.'

Leonard. The easy way she says his name tastes rotten in Alice's mouth. All at once she wishes she was at home, in her attic refuge, listening to some Joni Mitchell and crying. Yes, she needs to cry. 'Good luck to you,' she says stiffly. She begins to put on her outdoor things.

'Alice, I . . .' For a moment, Sarah's palm touches Alice's forearm.

Alice feels it like an electrical charge. *I don't want this woman,* she snaps at herself as she quickly stands. 'Thanks for the drink.'

146

'Let me, let me get you a taxi.'

'No thanks, I'd rather walk.'

'OK.' Sarah sounds dejected.

Alice tells herself she doesn't care. She sweeps out of the bar with what she hopes is dignity and aplomb.

Chapter 24

Donna knows she cannot protest, though she wants to. DC Brian Chesters is the last person she wants to work with. She can see from his demeanour, the feeling is mutual. However, Donna does not want to spoil the rapport she has been building with Harrie by refusing her instructions. In any case, *I'm a probationer, I do what I am told.* She assumes Brian has his own reasons for acquiescing without a murmur when the DS hands out the day's tasks.

Making friends with Donna does not seem to be amongst them. He insists they are going to drive to the harbour, though she would rather walk. And he lets his impatience show when she says she needs a moment before they leave.

'My mum got right mardy when she hit fifty,' he says, once they are in the car and he is manoeuvring out of the garage. 'Dad said it was the change and to ignore her.'

Donna feels an instant kinship with Mrs Chesters.

'Is that what's bothering you, Donna? The change?'

Donna's insides shrivel, leaving a sense of fragile hollowness. She tells herself to toughen up. Then she recalls what Harrie said about Brian being a carer. Immediately she wants to know more. 'Your parents live in Scarborough?' Curiosity. It was one of her least appealing qualities according to her husband.

'Yeah.' As usual, Brian is driving too fast. He carries on, even as the traffic light turns from amber to red.

Donna's right foot slams to the floor. 'What do they do?' She keeps her voice as steady as she can manage.

'They bought a B'n'B over here, when Dad got ill. Emphysema. Probably from all the asbestos he handled. He was a builder.'

He takes a corner sharply and Donna clutches the handle in the door.

'Don't you like my driving, Donna?' Brian says, slamming on the brakes, because this time the traffic light is most definitely red. 'I've done my advanced course and HSDT.'

High Speed Driver Training. She was very proud when she passed hers. 'So have I.'

'Really?' He moves off swiftly when the lights change. 'I wouldn't have thought they'd bother with you being that bit older.'

Fury begins to overpower shame, as well as, inconveniently, heating her up. 'How's your dad doing now?'

'He's dead, Donna. March twenty-fourth 2012. Sixty-seven years old. He'd have liked to see me a detective sergeant, but it wasn't to be.' As he swerves the car into a parking space on the fishing pier, he says, 'You're a sour kraut . . .'

At least, Donna thinks he does. Brian is an expert mutterer and she's distracted by bracing herself for impact.

He slams on the brakes and faces her: 'How about your mooter and farter?' The twist of his mouth suggests he is trying not to laugh at his own joke, before his expression settles into studiously bored.

For a moment, his verbal poking renders her wordless. She wants to hit back. Her usual response, they died when she was young, would probably have done it. But as her spurt of anger is replaced by sadness – *what about them, Donna?* – the truth slips out: 'I don't know.'

He can't keep surprise from his countenance. 'How come?' He sounds almost as if he cares about the answer.

'Lost touch,' she says quickly, throwing open the door and heaving herself out.

Brian takes his time to exit the car, but once they are on the way to the harbour, he is brisk. 'Watch and learn, DC Morris,' he says. 'I'll lead on the questioning. Terry Prichard is a bottom ender and they're a shifty bunch. Doug's nephew. Not that they've spoken for decades. Summat to do with a boat purchase way back when.'

They reach the wharf where several boats are tied up. They halt by a small vessel, marked with the local moniker 'SH'. A man is standing bent over in the stern, working on the fixings on the engine, his neck as thick and knotted as a ship's rope. Eventually, after Brian has called down to him several times, he turns his head. Terry Prichard agrees they can come aboard, with a grunt and a curt nod. Despite his two-tone shoes, more suited to the city, Brian confidently swings himself onto the ladder hanging parallel to the harbour wall and descends to the deck. Donna follows with more trepidation. She finds the rungs are slippery, her nose is inches away from green slime and, when she reaches it, the deck is far from steady. She grasps at the wooden rail around the edge of the boat and brings herself to lean against it with an ungainly stride.

Both men are watching her, mainly with amusement, though Terry shows a hint of concern. After rubbing his on a dirty towel, Terry shakes their hands. His are large and calloused. He grins widely. 'One of them screws sheared off when we were out last night, nearly lost the casing. Pieces of shit. Never buy nothing from a man in a pub with a squinty eye.'

Donna is pretty sure she's being teased. Terry is a respected fisherman, he wouldn't risk his crew, let alone his boat, for the sake of saving a few pennies. She says, 'Thanks for seeing us, Mr Prichard.'

'Terry. Want a brew?' He goes the few steps to the prow, into the tiny wooden cabin and busies himself. The *Lucy May* is tied up, her nose against the arse of one of the big trawlers. Donna recognises the 'PD' denoting it is in from Peterhead. From this angle the immensity of the trawling gear, its cogs and chains, is clear. It reaches up above the *Lucy May*, a shark's jaw about to snap shut. The smell of fish gone bad mostly comes from this direction, mingling with diesel and machine oil.

'Here you go.' Terry hands over tan-coloured milky liquid in chipped and stained mugs. Donna takes a mouthful from hers. Highly sugared. Even so, she swallows it down. She has a flash of memory. In her childhood, tea was used as a balm for all sorts of ills, especially tea with too much sugar. When it was available. She carefully rests her cup on the top of a storage locker by her feet and takes hold of the handrail again, her fingers gripping on.

'First time on a boat?' asks Terry. 'You'll get used to it. Widen your stance a bit. Relax into it.' He demonstrates, legs set apart and bending slightly at the knee.

Donna nods with more certainty than she feels. The movement under her feet is slight and yet is making her light-headed.

'DC Morris will be taking notes,' says Brian pointedly. He watches with a smirk as she gingerly lets go of her perch, leans over and extracts her notepad and pen from her bag.

She is thankful she manages to straighten, finding sufficient balance to get on with the task assigned to her, without making too much of a fool of herself. She had wondered whether they'd be prising answers out of Terry like whelks from their shells. However, he starts straight in.

'You'll be wanting to know about Orson, right enough, poor sod.' His voice is gravelly, and there's a genuine sadness in his demeanour. 'I introduced him to the folks round here. There were those who didn't like what he had to say. Said what did he know? Over us. The sea has been our business for centuries. But I said mistakes have been made, people have got greedy, careless. And I reckon it's allus worth listening to thems who have researched, done some thinking. Not that we're the worst offenders.' He flicks a glance forwards, towards the trawler, then upwards, as if it would leap the castle mound to the cliffs beyond North Bay. 'I liked Orson. He was above board,' Terry says simply. 'I was the first to go for his ghost gear project.'

The day is not as grey as it has been of late, the clouds are higher and there's a smattering of blue between them. However, there's a sharp wind. The water slops against the little boat as it moves it up and down. Donna tries Terry's trick. She imagines she looks ridiculous, her knees bending like an amateur ballerina. But it works. She feels less unsteady.

'How about those who didn't like him?' asks Brian. 'Get into some fights?'

'Aye, happen he did. Verbal, not fists. Not that I saw, any road.'

'Still, we need names,' insists Brian.

Terry's chin sinks forward, as if he is captivated by the tea in the mug held tight to his broad chest.

'Terry, names?' says Brian sharply.

'Dick Tover. Him and Orson had a scrap about a month back.'

'And his mate Zeb whatsisname?' asks Brian.

'Aye, mebbe.' Terry pauses before going on. 'But you're looking starboard when you should be headed port.'

'Being enigmatic doesn't suit you, Terry,' says Brian. 'Tell it to me straight.'

Terry laughs at this. 'Aye, I'll tell it to you straight, Brian Chesters. I met Orson Reed at the Weighed Anchor.'

There's a definite visceral reaction in Brian, a bristling. Donna senses it. Perhaps Terry does, too, as he turns to her.

'You're new around here, ain't ya? The Weighed Anchor is the place for us queers.' His stare does not waver, though Donna gets the impression of a discomfort crawling under his skin. She smiles encouragingly. He continues. 'Used to think of it as a safe place until what happened to Neal. Neal Williams.'

'What happened to Mr Williams?' Donna asks softly, matching her tone to his.

'Got beaten up, didn't he? Happen the same bloke got Orson.'

'Who was the perpetrator?'

Terry shrugs. 'Never got caught. Your lot didn't bother.' His voice has gone rusty.

Donna is about to dig for more information when Brian cuts in. 'Did you and Orson have a relationship?' When she looks at him, she sees his expression is as harsh as his tone.

Terry shakes his head. 'Not for want of trying, on my part,' he says quietly, a flimsy smile appearing, then flattening. 'But he was interested elsewhere.'

'Where?' Brian asks sharply.

'Tony Prichard.' Terry takes a gulp of tea and looks up. There's challenge in his glance and his tone. 'That would be my cousin – that's who you need to be asking about Orson.'

'Doug's youngest?'

'He'd never said, did he?' He puts his mug down in the wheelhouse with a definitive thump. He continues, his voice growing more strident: 'You won't find Tony hereabouts. Long gone. Last seen Saturday fourth January. Chef-ing on a container ship out of Teesside. Yeah, then Orson turns up in the harbour Tuesday following. Thems Longwestgate Prichards think they can lord it ova all of us. Got yous caught in their creel. Thinks naebody dursn't say nowt. But Orson didn't deserve to have a knife stuck in him and get tossed in the harbour like he's nowt but a clarty long tail.'

A trawler chugs into the harbour, causing a wash which carries the *Lucy May* upwards. Then she drops and Donna's stomach goes with it. She yelps, her hands once again hooking themselves onto the rail.

Terry lets out a harsh spurt of laughter. 'I'll have to renew that bit of gunnel, Detective Constable, by the time you're done.' It's as if the tension in him had to be released – in tears or laughter – and now it has been, he's glad it was the latter. 'I'm telling you, it's Tony Prichard ye wants. Now if we're done? I ain't got time to be faffing around with yous lot all day.'

Brian nods curtly and quickly starts up the ladder that will take them up to the wharf.

Nonplussed, Donna says how grateful they are for Terry's time (thinking, *though my colleague is hardly showing it*). Then she asks where he was on the first Saturday in January. His explanation is succinct – a trip to a bowling alley and then a stay over with friends in York – and verifiable. She closes her notebook and – feeling Terry watching her – hopes her departure from the *Lucy May* is not as ungainly as it feels. Once on firmer ground, it takes a moment for her feet to feel settled on the stone and for her head to reaffix to her neck.

'Come on,' says Brian roughly. 'I told you I was taking the lead on this interview.' He walks off.

'And you did,' she says as she catches him up. 'Do you know about the assault on Neal Williams?'

'Never reported.'

How can he know?

Chesters continues. 'No, Tony Prichard's our man. Orson's lover, a chef, and hightails out of town once he's done the deed. All of which his old man forgot to mention.'

'Could be a bottom enders' feud speaking?' says Donna, thinking aloud.

They've reached the car. Brian unlocks it. The beep of the electronic mechanism masks what he says next.

Donna is sure it is something along the lines of, *a stabbing, it's just the MO one of them queers would choose*. He gets in.

Donna opens the door on her side of the car. 'What did you say?'

'You coming?' Brian asks roughly, firing up the engine.

Donna doesn't move. 'I asked, what did you say?'

'Walk, then.' He leans over, pulls the door shut and screeches away.

For a moment, Donna is stuck in her own disbelief. Then she stomps quickly to the railings at the edge of the pier, her fists clenched. She lets go of her impotency with a loud, discordant, '*Scheiße.*' The slop of the grey-green sea, and the preening seagulls sitting on it, are bothered not a jot.

Chapter 25

Donna forces herself up through thick, damp layers of sleep. She realises at one and the same time: her alarm clock went off ten minutes ago and is giving out increasingly forlorn intermittent beeps; plus the ringing is from her mobile. She grasps it and squeaks a greeting. It is her DI. It takes a moment for her to catch up with what he is saying. He had trouble starting his car this morning and has had to have it taken to the garage. The only unmarked police car available is the one everyone avoids as it smells as if there is something putrefying in the heater and complains at being asked to go above thirty miles an hour. Donna agrees to taking her car and to picking up Theo at the station in thirty minutes, before she recalls what the plans for today are. When she does, she rolls slowly out of bed and pads into the bathroom.

After her altercation with Brian yesterday, plus her time spent updating the case logs and on follow-up phone calls and finally the late afternoon briefing, Donna's head began to ache. She fell into bed by nine p.m., slept soundly for several hours, before being awake for most of the rest of the night. The face which she sees in the mirror is pale and saggy. The headache-demon is gouging at her temple with a pickaxe. Her menstrual bleeding is profuse. She wonders if she should get back to Theo, tell him she is sick and that he should get someone else to accompany him. Then she remembers her conversation with Nicky. *I am not ill, these are natural bodily functions*, she tells herself. *I might never be as strong as Theo or Harrie, but I am resilient.*

She is feeling moderately more in control by the time she drives to the station. Grimly thinking she is probably keeping paracetamol manufacturers in business, she's taken as many painkillers as she can stomach, then scurried round and packed an emergency kit for the day, including a change of clothes. Though it has made her ten minutes late, it eases her anxiety. Theo doesn't comment on her tardiness. He bounces into the passenger seat. As they climb the ranks, some officers enjoy more time in a warm office. Not Theo. *Yes*, thinks Donna, *it's good to be going somewhere, following a lead.*

They take the coast road south. The land becomes flat. The partly flooded pastures are the domain of geese and ducks. Then there are the fields of wind turbines – monumental white irises stark against the washed-out sky. As she drives, Donna relaxes more, listening to Theo run through the particulars of the case. At yesterday's briefing, he praised everyone's hard work. He made particular mention of Brian's review of the CCTV. He had apparently been working late to get it done. Donna has told no one how he acted towards her. She is beginning to question her own version of it. Had she heard right? In any case, Brian would contest it, say it was just banter. Also, though she is sure Harrie or Theo would offer her a sympathetic ear, she doesn't want

Chesters thinking she can't stand up for herself. And Theo appeared exuberant when applauding his errant DC, as if the report was proof Brian is back in the fold.

There's no denying that, because of it, they now have a good timeline for Orson's movements. He left Gosawk Farm at around four-thirty p.m., walking the hour into town as he normally did. He had a dish of rice and dahl at an Indian café, where he is not an infrequent customer. He left there at seven p.m., turning up at the Kiss Me Hardy at around eight or eight-fifteen. An hour or hour and fifteen to cross town seems a bit long. Did he meet someone along the way? Or merely take the scenic route? He leaves the pub at eleven p.m. He is seen by a camera on the fishing pier going towards the harbour. He stages his protest at the penthouse party and leaves there around eleven-thirty. He is not picked up by the fishing pier camera again and the one which would have caught him further along towards the harbour wall has been vandalised. Brian checked routes Orson might have taken – and there are many – to leave the waterfront area. There are no more sightings of Orson Reed. The presumption has to be that he met his killer not long after he left the penthouse. By accident or design is not clear. At the Kiss Me Hardy, he said he had an appointment. Perhaps he meant the party. Nothing from tech forensics up to this point has unearthed an arrangement for that Saturday night, though without an actual phone their work is slow. Plus Orson appears to have been a fan of the encrypted WhatsApp.

Now for persons of interest. Donna quickly struck Dick Tover and his mate Zeb Unwin off the list. Dick was in Hull at a family gathering on his wife's side and Zeb was doing his stint as a volunteer firefighter. Other officers had similarly checked on names given by Nicky. Then there's Tony Prichard. He joined his ship at nine a.m. on Sunday 5 January. They still need to talk to him, pin down his movements for the Saturday and ascertain what his relationship with Orson really was. Harrie and Brian are working on that today.

'What about Viv Gosawk?' says Donna. She slows down behind a tractor throwing up mud from its gargantuan tyres. 'I thought initially we had her fixed as Orson's girlfriend.'

'Perhaps that was the problem for Tony.'

'Or Viv.' *Or others?* Donna remembers Alice saying, 'He has lots of friends.'

'She says she didn't move from the farm on that night. One of her neighbours walking his dog puts her there at ten p.m. And she didn't run away to sea. We still can't rule out a chance meeting and a brawl. Tover and Unwin were probably not the only people who had problems with Orson's views or ways of working.'

'Don't the WhatsApp messages to Fareeha and Alice suggest something more thought-through? With the killer taking Orson's phone and deciding to use it to delay his friends from looking for him?'

Theo agrees, then says, 'We're waiting on ANPR for Ian Renshawe, aren't we? What's the delay? Can you chase it up?'

Donna nods, wishing she wasn't driving and had a notepad so she could jot this task down. Unhappily, she can no longer rely on her memory. 'What do you think about Neal Williams, the man Terry said had been beaten up . . .' The reason for the assault becomes stuck to her tongue.

'Because he is gay,' says Theo coolly. 'You can say it, Donna, I won't be offended. I saw you'd added it to the log.'

She feels mildly foolish at her reticence. No one gets to be DI without coming across violence prompted by every conceivable motivation.

'Do you think it significant?' Theo asks, unaware of her discomfort or ignoring it.

'It was never reported.' *And Brian knew, as soon as it was mentioned?* The puzzlement returns, though she doesn't air it.

'See what you can find out about it. And I've a favour to ask you. Orson's parents are flying into the UK as we speak. I'm due to see them tomorrow morning. I'd like you along, if you are up for it? I know it'll be overtime for you.'

Her visits to Elizabeth are once a fortnight, which means not this weekend. Seeing her daughter would be the only reason to refuse Theo such a direct and gratifying request. Though she suspects it's her maternal presence which is being sought, not necessarily her sharp detective's mind.

Feeling the urge to prove herself, she says, 'I'm wondering how Orson's environmental work plays into the relationship with his mum, given her job with an oil company.'

'More of a conglomerate, as I understand it. It must have made for interesting conversations over Christmas dinner.'

Donna knows all about them. 'Maybe that's why he didn't go to Dubai for the festivities.'

'Probably wouldn't hold with the flying, either,' says Theo. 'Even with his, shall we say, complex personal life, we shouldn't lose sight of Orson Reed's activism.'

Hence their mission today. One thing tech forensics has

161

unearthed is an email account for Orson and in it they've found an exchange with his supervisor from university, Professor Zavier Cullen. It didn't take long to discover he was the author of the Cullen Report into water quality in the two Scarborough bays. And further, that he had committed suicide a couple of months after it was published at the beginning of July last year. Orson Reed had spoken to the Humberside police at that time, saying Professor Cullen would never have committed suicide and they should be investigating a murder. Now Orson himself is dead.

The flat drowned land. The wedge of dun stratus above. The increasingly narrow and winding road. By the time they've been going for two hours, Donna is wondering if their destination is at the ends of the earth. Then she takes the turn advised by the satnav down a sand-strewn track which halts at a barrier. Beyond there are only mud-coloured dunes. Donna pulls into a small parking bay and steps out of the car. The roaring of waves, the screech of gulls and the slam of grit-laden wind assaults her. Maybe this really is the very terminus of solid ground.

'DC Morris? DI Akande?' A young man is approaching them. 'I'm DS Gus Spinelli.' He is dressed in an olive-green jacket, which would probably (Donna judges) withstand an ascent of Everest, and a thick beanie drawn low across his brows. There's not much to see of him apart from several lustrous dark curls escaping his hat and a tanned complexion. 'Welcome to Spurn Point,' he continues genially, shaking their hands. 'You must need a coffee after the drive. There's a visitor centre with a café over this way.'

Donna is relieved. The wooden building sitting on stilts is down a path sheltered by bushes. They enter a large open space with a wall of windows. It is set at an angle, like the plane of a triangle, so Donna feels as if the churning clouds are toppling in on her. There are a few people around. Two young women with small children are pointing through the windows while referring to explanation boards. At the café tables sit a clutch of adults – two couples and a group of three men. They have divested themselves of their outer coats and hats. The three men are discussing their cameras, which have lenses the size of telescopes. After giving her order to Theo for a decaf coffee and teacake with butter, Donna rushes to the toilets. It takes her a while to tidy herself up. On her return, she finds Theo and Gus in an easy conversation about cycling routes they have done. As she sits she has the impression she is intruding. However, they quickly turn to the matter in hand. Though she is the only one to do so, she is glad she has ordered some food. *Why am I so ravenous?* She munches on – the butter deliciously salty – as she listens to Gus talk about Professor Zavier Cullen and his untimely death.

At forty-eight years of age, Professor Cullen had been a long-standing member, indeed one of the founding members, of the Marine and Environmental Sciences Department at Hull University. He had a relatively distinguished academic career, talking at conferences and publishing papers and a book on the health of the seas along the Dogger Bank, especially where it interacts with the changing contours of Spurn Point. Professor Cullen didn't come onto the police's radar until his body was discovered about four months ago, mid-morning on Wednesday 18 September 2013. He was found in his car by two of the rangers who volunteer with the nature sanctuary. He must have arrived at some point during the night, or staff would have noticed him the previous day. He had drunk a quantity of alcohol, taken some prescription sleeping tablets, attempted to cut his wrists and (what killed him) run a pipe from the exhaust into the car.

'Carbon monoxide poisoning,' Donna says, wiping her fingers on a napkin.

Gus nods. 'We weren't in much doubt that it was suicide.'

'Because of his investigation into sea pollution?' asks Theo.

'No. After having a clean sheet for over twenty years, Professor Cullen had had an affair with one of his students. His wife was on the verge of leaving him and, if it became public, he'd likely lose his job. He had left notes for his wife and his student, asking them to forgive him. They read like suicide notes.'

'So it was Orson Reed who brought up Cullen's report with you?'

'Yes. We obviously knew about it. We were told it had been accepted by all the stakeholders – the borough council, the water authority, the environmental agency, ScarTek—'

'ScarTek?' interrupts Theo.

'Yes, as a business, the only business in the area, which has an outflow pipe into the bay at Scarborough, Professor Cullen had a look at them.'

'What were the findings of the report?' asks Donna.

'Inconclusive, apparently. I can't say I read it all.' Gus smiles; he has a warm smile and the skin crinkles around his green eyes as he does so. Now he is out of his outdoor gear, Donna can see he is not a big man; he is around the same stature as her DI and, like him, toned. Gus is perhaps a few years younger than Theo. His hair is vibrantly curly. This and his colouring make her think of the Mediterranean. Gus continues, referring to a notebook: 'There appeared to be several possible sources of pollution including: the more frequent overflowing of storm drains because of changes in the weather; run-off from agricultural land; a mainly Edwardian water-treatment system; more people owning pet dogs and not clearing up after them; plastic and other waste from visitors to the beach; increased numbers of herring gulls attracted by food waste left by said visitors. The local and water authorities have started to take action to address these.'

'Nothing about ScarTek then?' asks Theo.

Gus shakes his head. 'I believe they agreed to voluntarily review their processes, but they weren't specifically mentioned in the recommendations section. Is ScarTek of interest in your current case?'

'Only because its owner, Leonard Arch, was at a party near the harbour when our victim was killed.'

'As was our DCI,' says Donna.

Theo says, 'Well observed, Donna.'

She worries she has been too direct again. She is relieved when he chuckles and Gus grins. She feels welcomed back into the fold. 'Though Orson particularly targeted Arch. Called him a bastard and said he had enough to bring him down, if I recall rightly.'

Theo nods. 'We have to talk to him again. You tried to reach him yesterday, didn't you?'

'He was unavailable. I only got as far as one of the managers, a Sarah Franklande. I asked her about Orson. She said she had heard of him due to his activism, but was not aware of him being in touch with the company. I'll keep trying.'

Theo turns to Gus and asks at what point did Orson contact Humberside about Professor Cullen.

'After the inquest.'

'Basically when you thought the case was closed?'

He nods. 'I only spoke to him once, over the phone. One of my colleagues took his statement, but I got the impression he had been hoping not to have to say anything, that we'd come across something in our investigations.'

'Something?'

'Mr Reed said the report had been redacted – Professor Cullen had changed it under pressure. He thought we would find the unedited versions amongst his things and start to make connections. Only we didn't. There's a wood burner in the Cullens' house. Mrs Cullen didn't notice anything specific, but a lot of paper could have gone through that and not left a trace.'

'What about digital versions?'

'Professor ran over his phone, laptop and memory stick before killing himself. They were smashed beyond repair. I've always thought he might have been meaning to throw them into the sea and then couldn't bring himself to do so because he would be polluting it. The assumption was he did this to hide evidence of his affair. Our tech boys haven't found anything in his personal or university email accounts. If he did write a different version of the report, he didn't pass it around much.'

'Maybe only to Orson Reed,' says Donna.

They all consider this in silence for a moment. Then Theo asks, 'What exactly did Orson say?'

'You've read his statement. He was very cagey with both me and my colleague. Just that we should look more closely at Professor Cullen's death and that he had been killed because of his report.'

'He didn't mention ScarTek or Leonard Arch?'

'He did not.' Gus breaks another brief interlude of quiet between them with the suggestion that he take them to see where Professor Cullen was found. 'I've commandeered one of the reserve's four-by-fours.' It seems to re-energise him.

Luckily, this time the men need to use the facilities, so Donna can slope off too. She is the last to arrive at the jeep-type vehicle, which has driven through the now-opened barrier. Theo and Gus are already in the front, once again companionably talking. She clambers into the back. Gus sets off. Immediately they are in a rugged terrain, the road-way a rutted track of sand, hemmed in by dunes up to seven or eight foot in height. Then, all of a sudden, these fall away and they are on a narrow strand, water the colour and consistency of mercury flowing up the shallow shelving beach. Above, the clouds are rising like enormous whips of charcoal cream to be licked by a giant. White rags carried by the wind resolve themselves into gulls Donna recognises as herring, little and black-headed. They waver on the updraught and then fold wings to land. A tree trunk flayed of its bark appears as the skeletal remains of a creature which might have heaved itself onto the sand with the notion of finding safety.

The four-by-four rocks at increasingly severe angles. Donna grasps at a leather strap helpfully hanging by the window. 'How on earth did Professor Cullen drive out here in his car?' she asks.

The conversation up front ceases. From the words she's grasped, it's been about music and local bands. She is asked to repeat herself, the noise of the engine and the buffet of the wind making her hard to hear.

Gus chuckles as he responds, 'This was a road up until December last year, then a storm whipped it away.' He goes on to explain about the RNLI community which used to live down the end of peninsular. The families have had to move out. Only those on duty stay during their shifts. 'The children couldn't get to school. It's why Spurn Point is so special: its coastline is constantly altering.'

Donna gazes through the rear window and wonders if the remaining narrow spit of land might be gone by the time they want to leave.

They re-join a road of sorts on a broader stretch of land and come to a lighthouse perched safely away from the encroaching waves – more clues to the nomadic coastline. It was in the lee of this building that Professor Cullen was found. Of course, there is not much to see in terms of evidence now, the land having been scraped on numerous occasions by gales and rain. And, as Gus admits, by the time forensics got down here on 18 September, beyond the car itself, the crime scene was very difficult to interpret.

'I suppose someone could have come and hooked up the pipe, say, if Professor Cullen was already unconscious from the pills and loss of blood.'

Theo lets his gaze travel around the horizon. 'There's no way of telling if someone comes onto Spurn Point?'

Gus shakes his head. 'Not with a hundred per cent certainty. CCTV and ANPR stop several miles up the road.' His features take on a glummer cast. 'To be honest, we weren't looking for anyone else. And when Mr Reed brought up the possibility, he didn't give us enough to go on.'

'Where were Professor Cullen's laptop et cetera?' asks Donna. She's been looking at the gravelly ground around the base of the lighthouse.

'Over there, about where you are standing,' says Gus.

'And where was his car?'

'Um . . .' Gus takes a moment to consider. 'Yes, more over my way.'

'So he drove over his stuff here and then parked up over there?'

'I guess so. I imagine he wanted to check it was done properly.'

'Yes.' She pauses before saying slowly, 'Or another vehicle could have done it?'

'It's a possibility.' He looks a tad more disconcerted.

No one, Donna says to herself, *especially a conscientious officer like DS Spinelli, likes to think their investigation might have fallen short.*

Gus reminds them of the tides and they all pile into the four-by-four, the lads, as Donna is now thinking of them, upfront and chatting easily. She is glad not to be asked to contribute. She is beginning to feel scoured out, as if the Spurn Point grit-laden gusts have gone through her rather than round her. Despite having taken further painkillers, the headache-demon is beginning to gouge down the right flank of her face. She wonders how she is going to manage the drive to Scarborough. She closes her eyes and breathes deeply and evenly. The jerking and keeling is replaced by a sense of floating, as if she is drifting on a lilo on a lake, perfectly smooth and warmed by the sun. Then she is suddenly heaved off the inflatable and she finds herself awake and practically falling into her DI's arms as he opens the door for her. The hanging handle is once again useful for her to grip and then to aid her to exit the vehicle with some poise. Theo does not appear to notice. He is saying his goodbyes to DS Gus Spinelli, who also dips in to give Donna's hand a shake, before he locks up the car and saunters away. Donna notices her DI's gaze linger on the receding Gus for a smidge longer than would be usual. Then Theo turns to her. She says all in a rush that she needs to go into the centre to use the toilets.

'Are you OK, Donna? You're looking rather pale. Would you rather I drove back? You drove here so it would only be fair.'

Her right eye now feels as if it is constantly in spasm. The headache-demon has pushed a needle through it. If it wouldn't have been unseemly, Donna could have hugged her DI for his offer and also for making it seem like a reasonable proposition.

'Yes,' she croaks, before grabbing her bag from her car and dashing off.

Chapter 26

Donna wakes to find them stopped at the edge of the road as dusk is inexorably folding into evening. 'What?' she says. 'Where are we?'

'Still in Humberside,' responds Theo. 'Unfortunately.'

A flicker in the dark makes her glance back. Behind them, there is a police car, its lights flashing. One of the officers strides towards them. He is young and rangy. As he thrusts his face at Theo's window, Donna can see the PC's skin is pasty with a dapple of acne scars on the chin, given an alien glaze by the intermittent blue illumination.

Theo rolls down his window halfway and asks why they have been stopped.

The traffic cop trots out the usual explanation: 'Reason to believe an offence has been committed.' He demands to see Theo's driving licence.

Theo asks: 'What offence? What reason?' as he stretches into the back of the car for his jacket.

In this moment, the officer gets edgy. He practically shouts, 'What are you doing?'

'I'm just getting my ID,' says Theo his tone steady. 'I am Det—'

'Step out of the car, sir,' says the traffic cop.

Donna cannot grasp what is going on. It is almost as if

171

she is watching some sci-fi film. Perhaps she is still asleep and this is a nightmare. The blast of chill air as the officer wrenches open Theo's door slaps her in the face. 'What's going on?' She blurts out. 'Do you know who this is?'

'Get out of the car,' the PC repeats more emphatically. 'Can you prove this is your car?'

'No,' screeches Donna. 'Because it's mine!'

Either the officer doesn't hear or isn't interested.

As he gets out of the car, Theo keeps his voice level, saying he can explain, he has his ID in his jacket. The officer grasps at his arm.

Donna knows she must move and somehow make this stop, yet she feels slow and stupid. Minutes are being pulled apart like sticky gum. She pushes her own door open, finds it impeded by a hedge and her feet tangled in the straps of her bag. She finally makes an ungainly exit and rushes round to the front of the car. The traffic cop has turned Theo against the bonnet, telling him not to resist arrest.

Arrest?

Donna pulls her warrant card out of her bag and shoves it into the officer's face. She screams: 'I am DC Donna Morris, this is DI Theo Akande and we are both from Scarborough nick!'

The officer steps away from Theo, his hands raised as if Donna has a gun on him. He immediately begins to stutter an apology: 'Sorry, um, ma'am, sir. I was only doing my job.'

'Well not fucking well enough,' says Donna loudly.

Meanwhile his colleague has leapt out of the squad car carrying confirmation that the car is registered to DC Donna Morris, currently a probationer at their sister force.

Both officers now look towards Theo. He stands leaning against the car, his arms crossed.

For a split second it is as if everyone is holding their breath.

Then Theo says, 'Now, will you explain to me the "just cause"?'

Donna can hear the anger rumbling below the words, can see it making his features hard edged. She's not sure the others would be as attuned.

The officer who had made the first approach steps back. He also folds his arms. He glares at his feet.

His colleague begins an explanation of sorts: 'We're checking for uninsured drivers and stolen vehicles, we saw this car being driven by a . . .' He pauses. He glances away. 'By a man.'

'Has it been reported stolen?' asks Theo.

'I was, I was doing the full checks, as, er um . . .'

'As your colleague here decided to jump in,' says Theo. 'What have you got to say for yourself?' He directs this question at the other officer.

After a moment, he drops his arms and opens the palms to Theo. 'An honest mistake, sir.' The word 'sir' is now soaked in deference rather than disdain. 'Yes, I admit, I was a bit quick off the blocks, but we've had gangs using this route with stolen vehicles, haven't we?' He looks over at his companion for confirmation. It is given without much conviction. 'And we've had them driving off at speed – dangerous speed – when stopped. It would have been a risk to other road users, yes.' He seems to have relaxed a little, having hopped onto this tenuous excuse. 'These are tricky roads around here, sir, we don't want people driving them at speed.'

'Was I breaking the speed limit?' asks Theo.

'No sir, of course not, but what I'm saying is, if you had been a TWOC, then you might have been tempted to.' His voice peters out and he takes another glance at his boots.

His colleague jumps in with further apologies. 'No harm done, eh,' he says with desperation. 'We can all get on our way. I am sure you are eager to get to Scarborough.'

With all the adrenalin draining away from her, the exhaustion is beginning to creep in once more, and Donna is feeling the cold. In all honesty, she would be grateful to get back in the car. However, she forces herself to stay standing full-square and focused. No way is she going to let her DI down.

He pushes himself upright. 'Warrant cards, come on both of you. Donna, please take a photo of each, plus the licence plate of their car. Don't think,' he says firmly to the officers, 'I won't take this further.'

Donna does as requested. The two officers hold out hands to be shaken. They are not taken. With further apologies, they return to their car, do a U-turn and drive away.

They leave behind them a void. Not a silence. The wind through the pines sounds like the sea off Spurn Point. A pheasant clatters out of the undergrowth, puts a foot on the tarmac, thinks better of it and bustles back through the hedge. No. It's an abyss. Over which Donna doesn't know how to step. She is frozen. With disbelief. With – yes, she can feel the shake in her legs – with alarm.

'That was fucking awful,' she says, after what appears to be an age.

'Are you OK?' asks Theo.

Somewhere at the back of her brain she is aware this is the wrong way round, yet another part of her is grateful for his concern. 'Did that really happen?'

'I guess it's the first time for you.'

'Being pulled over? Well, yes.' She feels slightly sick. *Is it for him?* She desperately wants to find the right thing to say and yet her tongue feels stuck to the roof of her clamped mouth.

'Let's go,' Theo says abruptly.

Once they are back on the road again, Donna imagines the two white traffic officers turning the whole incident into a good joke or into another reason to distrust a black man. They would be at least discussing it. Normalising it. Not like her and Theo. She does her best to marshal her breathing and her thoughts. 'We'll make a complaint,' she says with determination.

'Will we?'

'You said, back there . . .' She is making him more angry when she only wants to show her support. She is out of kilter. Not sure which is the right way up.

'Of course I did. But don't you think it is my call? It's not as if you have anything to lose.'

What does he mean? I'm a woman. I'm an older woman. I'm a probationer. Crossness is beginning to win. *I have plenty to lose.* 'Because I'm white,' she says dully, not truly believing it.

'Of course because you are white.'

Well there's nothing more to be said, then. She folds her hands into her lap and stares out the window.

Nothing more is said.

Chapter 27

Donna spends most of the early hours turning over the incident with the traffic officers the previous evening. Or, rather, the discussion with Theo afterwards. She starts off thinking he could have handled it better. However, her prickliness over that begins to resolve itself into embarrassment at her own behaviour. *Why couldn't I work out what to say to him?* she thinks as she sips her peppermint tea, curled up on her sofa in the semi-darkness. *I only wanted to show him I was on his side. He must get that. Doesn't he?* The notion that he might not makes her retreat under the blanket. The urge to phone him and explain herself is almost uncontainable. She's only stopped by her daughter's words coming back to her: *it's always worse for the person of colour.* And by the time on the clock. She turns over to try and get comfortable. *Maybe he's right – if he sticks his head above the parapet, it will go badly for him.* She decides she will find a moment to talk with him, honestly apologise and meanwhile show him her commitment through her work.

She manages a doze before having to get ready for the appointment with Orson's parents. On checking her phone she finds a response from Leonard Arch. He is available later today. She hopes this will please Theo.

When they meet outside one of the upmarket B&Bs on

South Cliff, DI Akande is particularly brisk. Though agreeing to it, he expresses neither pleasure nor displeasure at having the opportunity to speak with Arch. Donna feels she still has ground to make up.

The B&B owner takes them into the lounge, a high-ceilinged room which has a tiled fireplace and a large bay window giving onto a carefully tended garden. Ursula and Roger Reed are waiting for them. Ursula's sandy features and pastel-blue eyes echo those Donna has seen in Orson's photo, while it is his father who has his well-built physical presence. Both look tired. Sad. Roger Reed appears crushed, slumped downwards in his armchair. He is wearing a white shirt, which could do with an iron, and jeans. For Donna, on meeting his parents, Orson Reed becomes more than a victim. He becomes more than the man, more than the activist. He becomes a son.

As Theo begins with some open questions about Orson, it is Ursula who talks. Her spine is straight, her hands clutch each other on her lap. She is wearing a taupe-coloured dress which comes to her shins and an equally long brown cardigan. She describes an indulged childhood for her son, the family moving every few years for his mother's job, from one exotic location to another. 'I did worry about him not being able to hold onto friends,' says Mrs Reed. 'But he's always made friends easily, very easily.' She swallows, her fingers go to her throat as if there is a constriction there. 'It's made him good with change, he enjoys being peripatetic. And loves nature, he loved the nature wherever we were.'

Donna notices Orson has not gone into the past tense.

Her heart contracts for this mother who has lost her child.

'We knew this would happen,' Roger blurts out, his voice rough.

'No we didn't, darling,' says Ursula, gazing over at him, her face soft with pity. She turns to Theo. 'We knew he got into scrapes, got into conflict with people; it was inevitable with what he was trying to do. But nothing like this.' Disbelief washes into her eyes, which become liquid. She dabs at them with the handkerchief she retrieves from a pocket in her cardigan.

'Was there anything specific, recently?' asks Theo gently.

Ursula shakes her head, still trying to stem the tide dribbling down her cheeks.

Roger rouses himself again. 'We didn't really talk any more.'

'Yes we did,' says his wife sharply. 'Every month.'

'We didn't say anything, though, did we? Not beyond the usual.' His chin has sunk into his neck, causing the flesh to bulge out. His nose is a bulbous beacon in the middle of his white face.

Donna speculates about the amount of alcohol Orson Reed's father consumes.

Roger continues, 'If our son was in trouble, we'd be the last people to know.'

Donna's sympathies transfer to the father. How often has she thought this about Elizabeth?

'Oh no.' The words escape with a breath from Ursula.

'It's true.' Roger sounds cross. 'He couldn't agree with what you do for a living, with our lifestyle, and that was the end of it.'

'We still loved each other,' Ursula says faintly, blowing her nose.

'I'm not talking about love, Ursula. The detective inspector here doesn't want to know about love, he wants to know who killed our son.'

Donna supposes her gender has rendered her invisible. Unconsciously she shifts in her seat, to reassert her existence.

Roger Reed doesn't notice; he's continuing with his own thought. 'And so do I.' He glances at his watch. 'Could do with a drink, a proper one.'

'It's too early, darling.' Now the situation is reversed. Ursula has caved in and Roger is all energy, a fiery, caustic energy. He has none of the poise of his wife.

Donna wonders what Roger Reed does all day. Theo had mentioned a portfolio of shares. Does Roger win or lose on the lottery of the stock market? Maybe his alcohol intake is somehow regulated by how much he feels diminished by his wife's success. Then Jim comes to mind. Jim has his property business, he seems content with what he achieves. But he's not exactly encouraging of her own advancement outside the home.

She brings herself back to the present and asks, 'Could you think of anyone, Mr Reed, who would want to kill your son?'

Roger tries not to look surprised at the female police officer speaking. 'Any number of people, DC, um . . . ah. It'll be to do with his work, no doubt. Ursula, can you go and see if our genial hosts could rustle up a tot of brandy?'

She shakes her head, mutters, 'At least wait until midday, darling.'

179

Red pigmentation seeps down from his nose into his double chins. 'I'll do it, then.'

'Mr Reed,' says Theo quickly. 'Just a few more questions?'

The older man slouches into his chair.

Theo nods at Donna and she continues: 'How about his personal life? Could that have caused conflict?'

There's a silence as the parents glance at each other. Ursula appears to steel herself. Unconsciously echoing Alice, she says: 'Orson, has lots of friends. He is, um, he was bisexual polyamorous.'

Roger growls underneath, 'Philandering.'

Ursula continues with fortitude. 'Some people found that hard to understand, but he is, Orson is just, oh, he is just so full of love.'

'Yes, yes,' bursts in Roger. 'He liked to spread it around. We had other terms for it in my youth.'

'Did Orson ever mention Tony Prichard?' asks Theo.

The Reed parents exchange a look, as if checking out what the other person knows. They both shake their heads.

'Was this person special to Orson?' asks Ursula quietly.

'We believe Orson and Tony were in a relationship.'

Roger mutters, 'We didn't say anything to each other', while his wife says more brightly, 'I'd like to meet this person.'

'Unfortunately, Tony Prichard has left Scarborough,' says Theo.

Roger erupts to his feet. 'There you are, then. The guilty always run. Are we done?' He doesn't wait for an answer before trudging wearily out the room.

Chapter 28

Donna and Theo have enough time to grab a sandwich and a drink before their appointment with Leonard Arch. Despite the chill, they eat sitting on a bench sequestered into a little Edwardian wooden shelter on top of the cliffs in the northern reaches of Whitby. Across the harbour, the abbey ruins are skeletal. Below them mica blades rip through the sea. In their wake, the fragile spindrift spurts from the raw edges.

Conversation is perfunctory. Donna is rehearsing ways to make it as easy as it has been in the past. She takes her final mouthful of egg mayonnaise and a slug of warming lemon and ginger tea. She brushes down her chest and her skirt. She hopes she does not have cress caught in her teeth as she turns to Theo.

'Look,' she says, more abruptly than she means to, 'do you want to talk about what happened last night?'

Theo continues to stare over the waves, chews and swallows, before responding, 'Do you?'

'I want, I want . . .' *I want not to be in the wrong.* She gathers herself: 'I want to say sorry. Of course what happens next is up to you. I do get it.'

He looks at her. 'Do you?'

Yes! She swallows down her nervous energy. 'Probably not. But I am open to trying.'

As he squashes up the litter from his lunch, he says: 'I grew up in Birmingham. I worked as a DC in Manchester. Cities built on wealth accumulated from exploitation, especially of the black body.' He glances around. 'I guess some of these charming terraces were funded by the same. Though perhaps the whales suffered more.' He pauses. 'It's not that I want to think about this all the time, it's just that I don't have a choice not to.'

'And I do.' *It's not my fault,* she wants to throw back at him. She doesn't. Instead, she holds out her hands for the screwed-up paper bag and cup he is slowly crushing into oblivion.

When she returns from the bin and the public loos, he stands. 'Ready?' He smiles.

She realises it is the first time this morning he has granted her one. She realises this is unusual.

Leonard Arch has several abodes. London, San Francisco, Puerto Banús and here in Whitby. It is not his most valuable property by a long chalk, but it is one of the most expensive by square metre he could have bought in the area. His is on the top floor of a newly built cluster of exclusive apartments with sea views and a gated communal garden. As they wait to be admitted, Theo tells Donna he has looked at the specs: there is an infinity and an exercise pool on the roof.

She glances up. 'I hope his ceiling is adequately water-proofed,' she says and is rewarded by her DI's chuckle.

Arch answers the video entry phone and buzzes them through. There is a similar security system to get them through the front door. They both agree to take the carpeted

182

stairs rather than the lift and arrive at the third floor. Here they have to wait in a little lobby with two doors, presumably to two different flats. Donna searches out and finds the little cameras in the corners of the ceilings. After a second or two, they are let through one door into Leonard Arch's pad. They are in a large room with a wall of windows giving onto a balcony. The first thing which impacts Donna is the sweeping view across the bay with the abbey visible to one side. The second thing she notices is that everything is high-end and the place appears hardly used. Not a smear nor lingering mug ring. No misplaced magazine nor phone charger. No odour beyond cleaning fluid. No ornaments. The only image on the walls is a portrait of Arch, rather abstract and in thick oils.

The man himself is playing the genial host, asking after their journey over and offering refreshments. With porcelain mugs of coffee in hand, they sit by the panoramic vista in capacious arm chairs, while Arch sits sideways on the chaise long, his feet planted on the parquet.

He smiles at Donna. 'Good to see you again DC Morris, and so soon after the last time. What can I do for you today?'

'We're still investigating the murder which took place on Saturday, the fourth of January or the early hours of Sunday, the fifth of January. Our victim was Orson Reed.'

'And you can be certain of that now, can you?' Arch asks, a slight twitch upwards of his mouth. 'I understand there was some doubt before.'

Doubt. An interesting word. Beyond reasonable doubt.

Donna responds, 'Yes we can.'

'And of the date?'

'Yes.'

'Then I don't know how I can help you. I've already said I was at the party and was brought back here by taxi. All perfectly verifiable.'

'Did you know Orson Reed?'

He pauses, as if giving this some thought. 'I believe not. Should I?'

Donna says: 'Mr Reed targeted you at the penthouse. Called you a bastard.'

'Oh, that.' Arch throws an arm over the back of the sofa while leaning back. 'He was tossing insults around along with the fish.'

'He knew who you were.'

'Who I am and what I look like is hardly secret.'

'He said he had enough to bring you down. What did he mean by that?'

'I have no idea. An idle threat.'

'A threat nonetheless.'

'An empty one.'

'You have never had any contact with Orson Reed before that Saturday?'

'Not that I am aware of.'

A politician's answer. Tension has crept into her posture, forcing her tightly forwards. She eases back. 'Could you have had communication with him and not been aware of it?'

He shrugs. 'I meet lots of people, talk to lots of people, exchange emails with lots of people. I can't be expected to remember all of them. If I have had any dealings with Mr Reed, they were not significant.'

There's a pause. She glances over at Theo, for him to take over. She is sapped of energy.

He asks about Professor Zavier Cullen. 'What about your dealings with him? Were they significant?'

Arch does not immediately respond. His eyes move to the view. 'They were cordial and professional. I had a lot of respect for Professor Cullen. I was sad to hear about his death. A personal issue, I understand.'

'He did not mention ScarTek in the recommendations of his final report?'

'Why would he? We have an exemplary record.'

'How about in an earlier version of his report?'

'Was there one? I didn't know about one.' He brings his gaze back to Theo.

When asked where he was on 17 and 19 September last year he has to refer to the calendar on his phone. Donna itches to take a look at what else is stored there. But they have no grounds for a warrant. Finally he says he was enjoying some R&R in Puerto Banús. He gives them his flight numbers and his favourite bar and restaurant to check with.

'I'm sorry I can't help you more,' he finishes. He means it as their cue to leave.

'Do you think he was lying?' asks Donna as Theo drives them out of Whitby.

Theo shrugs. 'He was certainly very careful with his answers.'

'Allowing him to claim lapses in memory at a later date if necessary?'

'Exactly.'

'Bit of a waste of time then.' She feels her disgruntlement.

'Not entirely. You and I got to talk.'

185

She grins to herself as she stares out the window. They are at the turn-off where she would take the moor's road to HMP North Yorkshire. Unconsciously, her gaze lingers in the direction of the prison.

Perhaps he notices. Perhaps he somehow catches her thoughts. Perhaps he is merely interested. Whatever, he asks about Elizabeth. Donna tells him that her daughter is doing OK. Then she thinks about Ursula and Roger Reed. *We don't talk any more.* She knows what it means to exchange words, sentences, without anything actually being said. *But me and Elizabeth do talk. Now.* She reassures herself.

'She's keeping her nose clean for her parole board. At least I hope she is.' If there's one thing which can be relied upon, it is that Elizabeth will be impelled to act by her emotion. 'Heart over head, that's my girl. And not always in a good way.'

They are following the road that links the two coastal towns. It loops around the tussocks and dales, which are covered over with dormant bracken and heather, a jumble of black, brown and dull amber. There's something confessional about sitting side by side in a car and Donna's minor confidence appears to encourage Theo into opening up. Some of what he says, Donna already knows. His father came over from Nigeria after his own parents died in a car crash. Possibly caused by (this bit is new to Donna) faulty servicing by a mechanic wanting to make a quick buck. Kayin Akande – who chose Kevin as an alternative name, to 'make things easier' – joined two brothers already settled in Birmingham. He went to college and became an engineer. Theo's mum, Maria-Luisa, was a nurse, originally from

Cardiff. Her family, generations back, had come to work in the town's docks from the Cape Verde islands.

'Do you visit Nigeria much?' asks Donna.

'As kids we went a few times. We went to Cardiff every year. Looking back, I think Dad was reluctant. Maybe he found it difficult. Or maybe it was something to do with wanting us to feel rooted here. Not sure. These days my eldest sister goes pretty much annually.' Theo has two sisters. Both older, the eldest a whizz in the City, the other a nurse.

'And you?'

'Not so much.' He pauses, then almost chuckles. 'In this country, it's my skin colour which is a problem. In Nigeria it's who I love.' He negotiates a hairpin bend and a cyclist struggling up an incline before continuing. 'Both our parents gave us the confidence to have faith in ourselves. For my mum, I'm not saying it was easy, or even is easy still, sometimes, the language people can use. I am glad she is not on social media. But she never had any question over her Black-Britishness. She knew to her soul she belonged in this country. She likes to turn on the Welsh accent or better still speak Welsh, just to confuse people.' This brings a grin to his face. 'For my dad it is different. Having confidence in himself in this country was not a given. Perhaps in any country. His childhood was tough, there was violence – not in the home, in the society. My dad was young to be an orphan. The 1970s and 80s were not an easy time to be a black man in England. I was still a kid. I got the bullying and the racist comments. But dad, he met the real aggression.'

'There were the Handsworth riots, right?' She was new to the UK. Friends of hers had taken her to a march through London after children died in a fire. *Thirteen dead and nothing said,* she recalls the chants. But she hadn't really understood what it was all about. She was still learning how to be. And when she met Jim a year later, she remoulded herself once again, into wife and mother.

'Riots, yes, I guess you could call them that. Or the response to years of police brutality and prejudice. You cannot imagine the scars that leaves.'

She can, to a certain extent. She hasn't shared with her DI exactly why she fled her homeland in her late teens.

He continues: 'Dad was . . . Dad was so disappointed in this country. He had taken it into his heart and he believed it would take him into its own. He wanted to believe it would . . . had. He joined some of the demonstrations. Went to London for one after the New Cross fire in January 1981—'

That was it!

'I'm not sure he was entirely comfortable. I think he felt his experience was . . . had to be . . . different from people who had come from the Caribbean. His ancestors had never been enslaved.'

'How did he feel about you joining the force?'

'He was proud, you know. Scared, too, I guess, though he didn't exactly express it. Like me, he had faith things could change. And they have.'

'Not enough,' Donna says softly, thinking about what had happened the evening before.

'No, not enough. Not nearly enough.'

188

Chapter 29

Alice nestles down in her bed. She worked all day yesterday. She's not working today, Sunday. She's been reading *Flight Behaviour* by Barbara Kingsolver – borrowed from Orson (now never to be given back). However, soon she will have to come out of her warm nest and go to the bathroom and then replenish her tea. The clouds belch another clatter of sleet onto the skylight. *I will go somewhere warm,* she thinks. *Once Fareeha leaves, I have nothing to keep me here.* Her mind supplies the question she is trying to ignore, *What about Sarah?* She shakes her head, while forcing herself out into the chilly air. *No. There's nothing there for you, Alice,* she tells herself.

As she goes about her bedsit, she makes her plans. She will stay with her parents for a few weeks then go off to France and down to Spain or Italy, using her parents' network of organic smallholders and bar work to sustain her. On her return from the bathroom to the wardrobe, she practically falls over the two box files, brought up by Fareeha the previous afternoon. The Citizen Action Rebellion, Planet Emergency box files. She had considered delaying sorting them for a while, but now she is thinking of travelling, and soon, she decides not to put it off. She dresses in joggers and a thick Gansey-style sweater she had knitted. She gets another mug of fruit tea and sits on a cushion on the floor, propped up by the bed. She wonders if Orson's parents will appear at some point. From Orson's descriptions she doesn't think she will like them very much. On the other hand, maybe they would want – and legally have a right to – some of this stuff? One box is mainly CARPE meeting minutes, leaflets and newsletters. After scanning them, she decides to keep one copy of each leaflet and newsletter and to dump the rest. Under all the paperwork – *useless now*; she sighs at the waste of trees – there is a mobile phone. It is clunky and cheap. She thinks maybe it is the one Orson bought for them to take to demos and actions, the only phone numbers on it being for sympathetic solicitors. She tries switching it on. The battery needs recharging and the lead she has doesn't fit. Not knowing what else to do for now, she places it on a shelf.

She sits down to sort the other box. It is less ordered, with a muddle of articles, information sheets from various environmental organisations and other bits of paper. She begins to separate out things to keep from things to throw. The latter stack grows faster. She finds a photo she took at a demo of Orson and Fareeha. It had made its way into the *Guardian*. She gazes at it for a moment. Fareeha looks so . . . so? So un-pregnant. And Orson? Just so alive. She puts it on the to-save pile.

Further down she pulls out a beer mat with a load of figures on it. She recognises them. '8 million tons': the amount of plastic entering the oceans every year. '1.6 million km^2': the size of the garbage patch in the Pacific. '60 per cent': the contribution made by animal farming to the greenhouse gas emissions of agriculture as a whole. The handwriting is Orson's. It's quick and flowing. She can imagine him speaking as he writes, fluently, passionately, explaining something to somebody he's met in the pub. The beer mat goes with her photo.

There's a page torn from a book. A poem Orson thought worth holding onto. Alice reads some of the words:

> The world changes
> after a storm
> trees become bonsai
> telegraph poles fence tops.
> The old lady oak
> in her pleated serge cloak
> has a mirror now
> to gaze at herself in
> and weep
> for her once straight spine
> is crooked, her arms bent
> too heavy
> to embrace the sky.

It's a poet Alice doesn't know, Eta Snave. But Orson liked it, meaning Alice cannot throw it away. She reads on:

> Sheep stare warily
> at the creep of water.
> Ducks rejoice
> at new possibilities.
> Their view is forever altered.
> Oak, sky, sheep, duck watch the waters recede
> their field no longer – quite – as they recall it.

She smiles a little. Did Orson see himself as a duck? Always ready to leap in. *I feel like the oak,* she thinks. *Weeping, crooked, everything too heavy.* She sits back. She pulls her knees to her chest, resting her forehead on them. *And everything will be forever altered.* She finds she cannot move for a while. She doesn't cry. It's as if her tears have frozen her insides.

Eventually thoughts of Orson's get up and go help her to do the same. She shoves everything to be discarded into a bag to go to the recycling. She bundles together the bits she is keeping and puts them beside the phone. She can donate the box files to a charity shop. As she picks one of them up, she realises there is still a further cardboard wallet jammed into the bottom of it. She pulls it out, opens it and begins to read. It is the Cullen Report. She leafs through to the findings and recommendations. Yes, it is the non-expurgated one. She sits on the edge of her bed. What to do with it? She has an impulse to thrust it under Sarah's nose and shout, 'There, I told you so!' But is that what Orson would want her to do? She is desperate to do the right thing. Orson was convinced someone had got at his former tutor and that someone came from ScarTek. *People are dying.* Professor Cullen. Then Orson. The report's binding suddenly feels like it might singe her fingers. She throws it with all her might in the direction of the recycling bag. It lands with a satisfying thwack.

Chapter 30

Scheiße! As soon as Theo comes into the CID room halfway through Monday morning to ask her about the follow-up on the ANPR for Ian Renshawe, she remembers she hasn't done it.

She has been musing on her conversation with Rose the previous day. As someone involved in the local environmental scene, Rose had been on the list of people to be questioned about Orson. As she is Donna's neighbour, a PC had taken Rose's statement. Donna would not have brought it up, only Rose was eager to speak about it. She had brought around her delicious homemade lemon cake. Donna accepted it as compensation for having to hear, on her day off, Rose's thoughts on the investigation.

Rose had only met Orson once. She had found him personable enough – though his methods were not universally approved of by everybody in the green movement. Some saw him as divisive, too quick to move from direct action to criminal damage, believing the energy that underpins a protest determines the society which will develop from it. 'The more aggressive the energy, the more aggressive the results,' Rose said. 'It's why Gandhi and Martin Luther King preached nonviolence.' When Theo approached her, Donna was pondering this. Orson had escaped arrest and had not been charged with any offence, so she questions the definition of criminal damage being used. On the other hand, could such conflicts have led to an argument with a fatal result? Now her thoughts snap to the present and her failure.

'Sorry,' she says. 'I'll get onto it.'

'Don't bother. DCI Sewell wants to talk to us both about it. He'll be on a video call in my office. Now.'

Donna guesses from his curtness, Theo isn't impressed by her lapse in memory. She grabs her notebook and follows him.

She has to sit at the same side of the desk as Theo for them both to see DCI Sewell on the screen, and be seen by him. After her blunder, she doesn't feel entirely comfortable with the proximity. Especially as Theo is not his habitual relaxed self.

Sewell comes quickly to what is undoubtedly the matter at the top of his agenda: Donna's interview with Fareeha Gopal about Ian Renshawe not being where he was expected to be and Donna's subsequent opening of a misper's file along with the ANPR request. Sewell's conclusion, that Donna should close the logs down with 'No Further Action', surprises her. By Theo's slight lean forward, Donna supposes he wasn't anticipating this, either.

'I'm sorry, sir,' says Donna. 'Just to be clear, you want the misper case for Ian Renshawe NFA-ed, even though we still don't know where he is and we want to talk to him about our murder victim, Orson Reed?'

'Yes.'

'Why?'

DCI gives one of his genial smiles. 'It's on a need to know basis, DC Morris. I merely want to be assured none of this has gone any further than Scarborough CID and traffic?'

'Well . . .' For a moment Donna hesitates over what to say next. 'I did suggest to Ms Gopal she contact the Salvation Army and use her social media channels. I don't know if she did.'

'Ah.' He pauses. Then he says: 'You had better get onto the Sally Army and have any posts removed. I don't suppose we can do anything about Ms Gopal's social media.' He seems to be giving this serious consideration.

Into the lull, Theo says: 'I think you can be a bit more open with us, sir. After all, we are in the middle of a murder case and Ian Renshawe is a person of interest.' Though his tone is polite, Donna can sense the tautness he is holding.

'No, Theo, Ian Renshawe is definitely not a person of interest. Shall we move on? Could you update me about Tony Prichard, who must be your main suspect.'

While Theo takes a breath – either to steady himself or as he considers what to say next – Donna asks quickly, 'What about Fareeha Gopal?'

'What about her?' asks Sewell, his features a study of disinterest.

'She's carrying Ian Renshawe's child. She is in her last trimester.'

Sewell's face loses its composure, for just a second or two. He pushes his lips together. They are rather full; it is almost as if he is pouting. 'This was not in your report.'

'I'm sorry, I wasn't aware it was something which should go onto a misper's log. What about Fareeha Gopal's right to privacy?' Not to mention Ian Renshawe's disappearance not being very significant to the police. Until now.

'I will take advice,' says Sewell. 'Currently, my instructions to Scarborough CID are that no one from the force approaches Ms Gopal without running it past me first. And the other woman who came in with her?'

'Alice Millson.'

'Yes, any follow-up with them on the murder investigation will need my express permission. Understood?'

Donna glances at Theo. He has gone very still. His face is a stony cast. After what feels like an age, he says, 'Your instructions have been received, sir.'

The smile, slightly less shiny, is back. Sewell says: 'Good. Now where are you with Prichard?'

With a delivery more robotic than his usual, Theo explains that DS Shilling and DC Chesters had spent Friday attempting to speak to Tony Prichard. They had failed.

'Don't tell me they don't have satellite phones on these container ships,' says Sewell.

'They do indeed, sir. However, Tony Prichard has up to now refused to speak to any of my officers. He has delivered a statement via his captain that he knows nothing about the death of Orson Reed, but nothing more.'

'So get a warrant. And if he doesn't comply, get the coastguard involved.'

'He's well outside their jurisdiction now, sir. Plus his ship has a Venezuelan flag. The UK has no treaty with them for extradition nor any procedure for police cooperation.'

Sewell looks displeased, but less displeased than when he was told Fareeha Gopal was pregnant by Ian Renshawe.

'What does his father say?'

'Doug Prichard has been unreachable. He's been in a hospital in Hull receiving treatment. His wife is with him.'

'That might be too convenient,' says Sewell with a sigh. 'What did your predecessor used to say? "If it smells like pig, you're probably in Malton bacon factory." It smells like Tony Prichard is your man. A lovers' tiff after all. OK, you can't do more for the moment. We can't risk losing any goodwill you might have with the Bottom Enders if you push Doug Prichard. They'll close ranks and Tony will suddenly find himself with a pub-load of alibis.' Sewell sounds fatigued. 'We'll have to wait until Doug is well enough, or ready, to talk.'

The DCI finishes the call quickly after this, suddenly finding himself in a hurry for another meeting.

When Sewell disappears from the screen, Donna feels herself deflate. Her immediate thoughts are for Fareeha. *What type of man had she got herself caught up with?*

Theo stands up and paces smartly to the window and then to the kettle, offers her a tea which she accepts.

'What was all that about?' he says finally. His voice more its usual warm timbre.

Whatever else it has done, the debacle with the DCI has swept Donna's slipup out of court. She is relieved. 'I don't know.'

'Nor do I.' As the kettle clicks off he busies himself with making the drinks. He brings them over and sits again. 'And I don't like not knowing, especially when I am senior investigating officer. DCI Sewell might say with certainty that Tony Prichard is our man, then he warns us to be careful when talking to people who were at the penthouse party and now he tells us to wipe our memory banks of Ian Renshawe.'

'Do you think he's right about Doug hiding from us?'

Theo shrugs.

Donna is thinking about Doug with his telescope perched above the harbour and the Bolts. Doug had said he was in bed by ten. But then he'd been more than economical with the truth before. She is about to share this observation with her DI, when Harrie opens the door. A call has come in. Another body.

Chapter 31

The young woman is seated on the ground in the doorway of a beach hut. She is wrapped in a blanket, her knees up to her chest, with a bobble hat pulled low over her brow. She could be sleeping. This is undoubtedly why it took a passer-by until his second perambulation of the day – exercising a neighbour's dog – to approach her. The dog went up to her and started barking. When she did not react, the walker investigated. Putting his hand on her shoulder, he found she was set in her position; touching the skin on her face, he felt its chill. A member of the local mountain rescue team, he recognised someone who had been dead for several hours. Even so, he checked for vital signs as much as he could without overly disturbing the body. Then he stepped away, called the dog to heel and phoned the police.

All this Donna and Harrie learn from the PC who was first on the scene. They are in a raised alcove. It is off the main path which meanders, above the beach, from the Spa to what had once been a seawater lido. This is now covered over with tarmac and a rather forlorn mound of grass. Donna has taken many a daily constitutional this way, past these long-abandoned huts. Frequently broken into by people looking for a warm place to sleep, their once vibrantly painted fronts are patched with bland plywood. Everywhere is dripping. Behind the huts, radioactive-green slime spurts down the walls from the overhanging cliffs above. The concrete under Donna's feet is slippy. The now retreating sea has recently burped up bladderwrack, plus a peculiar assemblage. It takes Donna a couple of seconds to work out it is half of a large battered plastic container with rope wrapped round it. Attached to this is a string tied to a deflated balloon. Donna can still read the numerical seven outlined in gold. Hung by the string is a bundle of bones and grey feathers, the remains of an unfortunate seabird. In this dreary recess, the brightness of the crime scene manager's white tent is incongruous.

As Donna and Harrie approach it, the CSM, Ethan Buckle, exits. He hands over several evidence bags to Harrie.

'Our deceased is Sylvia Franklande,' he says. 'It looks like blunt force trauma. Maybe a bit of wood found hereabouts. There's planks been brought in on the tide or prised off these huts when they've been broken into. She was killed sometime between about six o'clock last night and six this morning.'

Harrie gives him a quizzical look. It's unusual for them to have so much information so immediately.

He nods to the bags. 'We've a purse with money, a student card and a credit card. Plus, we've got a train ticket for her. She arrived from Hull yesterday on the seventeen thirty-four. It would have taken her twenty minutes or so to get down here. I expect, though, she wasn't killed until a bit later. There's still some passage of walkers and runners along here in the early evening. Then our witness first noticed her when he took his walk at six this morning. She had a return ticket. She wasn't meaning to stay. No phone. But this.' He indicates one of the bags.

Donna leans in. Faded photos, creased with age. They had been taken in an old-fashioned photo booth. They show two teenaged girls, their faces squashed into the column of frames. Only two images remain. There would have been four. *Who has the other two?* The girls are giggling. One is mousy haired, one dark haired. Harrie turns the evidence bag over. On the reverse side of one photo is the date: 06.01.1994.

Ethan Buckle leads Donna and Harrie to his domain. Inside Sylvia is now curled on her side. The removal of her hat has revealed the ugly, gaping gash across the rear of her skull. Her hair is dark and shiny with the wet and the blood. Her features are elfin. She isn't tall. She doesn't look particularly robust. A gold earring nestles on her earlobe, a gold chain is visible around her narrow neck, a thin gold bangle around her bony wrist. The eyes are brown. They stare inertly towards Donna's boots.

They look out with vitality from the photo, recouped from Sylvia Franklande's student card, and now gracing one side of the interactive board in the CID section. The room is rammed, despite it being early evening. A second murder on their patch, this time a young woman, someone who was supposed to be already dead. Most officers are shocked, a few are intrigued, enough to want to be at the briefing. On the other side of the board is the photo of Orson Reed. The question everyone is asking themselves is: could there be a link?

Harrie remains methodical. She runs through what the CSM said, adding that Professor Jayasundera will report the following day. Meanwhile, it seems they already have a lot to go on. Old hands, such as PC Trench, and those who are local, know the name Franklande, or, at least, have winkled it out of their memory. A man who shoots his wife and then himself, even twenty years ago, is something which never quite goes beyond recall. Then his fourteen-year-old daughter, who found the bodies, apparently committed suicide.

Someone whispers, 'Another "back from the dead". We'll have Lazarus walking in next.'

Whether she hears the comment or not, Harrie responds to the substantive point: 'The coroner investigated and ruled there was enough evidence to reasonably believe she had committed suicide. There was her general emotional state, her note, her clothes on the beach. We didn't have as much CCTV evidence in 1994, but Sylvia wasn't seen in the town after she purportedly walked into the sea. The case was closed.' She looks down at her notes before continuing: 'Trev spoke to a Miriam Toogood, best friends with Sylvia from school; the following information comes from her. After her parents' funeral, Sylvia went to Leeds to stay with her brother, Roland. Only it didn't work out. Sylvia told him she wanted to live with the Toogoods and that they had agreed. In fact she hadn't mentioned anything to them.'

'They'd have taken her,' Trevor Trench adds. 'Miriam wanted us to know that.'

Harrie nods. 'Roland Franklande sent his sister off to Scarborough with a purse full of cash to cover her board. She then staged her own drowning and used the money to take a coach to London. Luckily she sat next to a young woman who basically took her under her wing for the subsequent years. Once Sylvia turned sixteen, she got back in touch with Miriam, told her what she had done and swore her to secrecy. A vow Miriam has maintained, even from close family.'

'Sylvia didn't change her name through all this?' asks someone from the back.

Harrie shakes her head. 'As a fourteen-year-old, she wouldn't have been able to without her brother's consent. Miriam said Sylvia had thought about it later on, but felt there was no need. She had built her life in London. She spent thirteen years there. She studied a bit, she found office-based work, she got on with her life. Then about seven years ago she moved to a job at Hull University. Her current address is a shared house in North Ferriby. That's ten miles west of Hull, for those of you who don't know. Means we'll be liaising with the Humberside force.' Harrie pauses for Theo to add that he's been in touch with DS Spinelli.

Is Donna imagining the brightening in his features?

Harrie resumes with what needs to be done. She and Donna will visit the sister, Sarah, this evening.

Donna thinks about the poised, rather imperious voice on the phone the other afternoon. She has more than a minor qualm about knowing she is going to drop a ruddy big rock into Sarah's composure. Donna pulls *Still waters run deep* from her collection of English idioms.

Harrie continues to list tasks. DC Chesters will contact Roland Franklande. There are the usual follow-ups at the train station, questioning users of the footpath between

Spa and beach huts, gathering CCTV where possible, to pin down a decent timeline. There're phone records to be requested and social media accounts to be identified. 'Nothing has immediately come up, but I can't believe a woman of Sylvia's age didn't have any,' says Harrie. 'They'll be there somewhere.' She checks her notes. She wants Donna to re-look at the original Franklande case. And finally, finally, Harrie comes to the question mark over the link with their other murder. 'Sarah Franklande, she works for ScarTek. Orson Reed's activism may have brought him in contact with ScarTek.' She says it in a deadpan tone, as if to forestall the buzz which starts up anyway.

Theo stands and all attention goes to him. 'Two murders in our town in such a short space of time is unusual. We all know that. The DCI is concerned with rumours starting up about a serial killer fuelled by lurid press headlines. He wants quick results. We all want quick results. But that doesn't mean we jump to conclusions nor do shoddy work. I trust everyone to keep an open mind on this. We have two young people dead; we owe it to them and their loved ones to find out what really happened to them. Let's get to it.'

As officers begin to move, Brian can be heard saying as if ruminating to himself, 'Didn't Sarah Franklande move back to Scarborough end of last year? And within months, we have two murders where her name comes up.'

Not to mention her parents. Also dead, thinks Donna, expecting others are doing the same.

Chapter 32

Sarah Franklande lives in one of the terraced streets spreading out from the Cinder Track. They were constructed in the nineteenth century for railway workers. Sarah's was probably built for an engineer, with its miniature bay window and patch of lawn with borders at the front. There's not much delay between Harrie pushing on the bell and Sarah opening the door wide. Statuesque is the first word to come to Donna's mind. Sarah is probably five feet seven or eight. She is wearing grey joggers, a navy rollneck and cardi. Her light-brown hair hangs to her broad shoulders. Her face is fuller than her sister's. It has acquired a few more creases and shadows over the passage of twenty years. Nor is Sarah giggling. Indeed, her mouth with its slight droop to the left doesn't look as if it could giggle any more. Nevertheless, Donna recognises Sarah as the other teenager in the photos found with Sylvia. Sarah listens to Harrie's introductions and lets them in without comment. She leads them into a small hall – polished floorboards and cream painted – then into the lounge. There's a Victorian-era mantelpiece and grate in the wall opposite the door. There's a sofa, an easy chair and a low table. There are a few books piled up on the floor by the fireplace, as if waiting for shelves. There are no ornaments, photographs or pictures. Sarah takes the chair and indicates Harrie and Donna should sit on the sofa. Then she waits.

The sofa is not large. Donna ponders asking for another chair.

Harrie sits forwards. 'I am very sorry Ms Franklande, we have some difficult news.'

Sarah does not react. She has her hands neatly folded in her lap.

Harrie goes on, 'Your sister was found today—'

'Found?' Sarah jumps in. It's as if a spasm goes through her body. Her fingers grip each other. 'How is that possible? She died—'

'Sylvia died sometime between late yesterday evening and early this morning.'

'No!' She says it emphatically. 'It can't be.' Her face muscles clinch, bringing a deep fork between her eyebrows. That slumping corner of her mouth twitches.

'We are very sorry for your loss,' says Harrie.

Sarah flaps her hand as if there is an annoying insect near. 'Tell me. Tell me what has happened.'

'Obviously we are still investigating. What I can say is that Sylvia was found this morning by some beach huts in South Bay, Scarborough. I am sorry we have to tell you: Sylvia was killed.'

For a moment, Sarah is still. 'No, no, no,' she says softly. 'That cannot be. She killed herself.' Only her eyelids move, to blink, several times. Donna notices the eyes are blue, not brown like her sister's; a very pale blue which is becoming liquid.

Then with what appears a supreme effort, Sarah stands

up, wobbles and clutches at the mantelpiece. 'I didn't offer you any refreshments. Do you want some tea?'

Donna levers herself up. 'You sit, Ms Franklande.'

'Sarah. Didn't we speak . . . ?' She crumples back down.

'We spoke on the phone, last Thursday evening, about Orson Reed. Can I get you something to drink?'

'Yes, Orson. He's dead too.'

Donna clocks this. She hadn't told Sarah Orson was dead. She had said her questions were for an unspecified investigation. But then, information about Orson's murder had been released to the local news.

Sarah gives instructions for getting to the kitchen, for finding gin and a mixer for herself and for making tea if the others want it. Donna goes through to the back of the house and does as she is bid. As she waits for the kettle to boil, her gaze idly shifts to the little table taking up most of the floor space. It appears as if Sarah had been at her laptop (now gone to standby) when she was interrupted. By its side is a quantity of A4 paper, bound in a faded cardboard cover. *Pollution in the North and South Bays of Scarborough, North Yorkshire*, Donna reads. *A report. April 2013. Professor Zavier Cullen.* There is a bookmark holding a place some way in. The kettle clicks off and Donna busies herself. She returns to the lounge first with a chair, then with the drinks. She has poured herself a glass of water. Harrie has a coffee. Donna can't risk it this late in the evening. She sniffs the aroma as she hands it over to her colleague. *Is caffeine-envy a thing?*

It seems Harrie has been parrying questions from Sarah about her sister's death. Sarah takes a gulp from her glass, puts it on the floor and sinks into the chair.

'You've told me everything you can't tell me about how Sylv died and where she's been for the last twenty years. So tell me what you want from me.'

'Perhaps you could tell us something about Sylvia?' Donna asks.

'Something?' Sarah's gaze moves to Donna.

She feels pricked by it.

'What kind of something?'

'Anything you can tell us will be useful,' Donna says firmly.

'Will it?' Sarah glances to the upper corners of the room. She takes a deep breath. 'Sylvia Franklande, born 3rd March 1980, Scarborough. Dad, Philip, liked to be known as Phil. Mum, June. Sister, Sarah, six years older. Brother, Roland, eight years older.' She takes up her glass for another sip, then puts it down again. 'We Franklandes lived in Peasholm Crescent. Mum came from Hessle. Except for her sister, none of her family would have anything to do with us, because of Dad. He was from Bradford. He didn't keep in touch with his folks much, either. Our family, we were a little island, set adrift, a bit of an oddity in this town, where everyone's got their neb in each other's trouble.' The local accent reasserts itself as she goes on. She begins to wind a strand of hair around her index finger. A strangely adolescent pose. She speaks about what sounds like an ordinary childhood. Donna assumes, given what happened, this is a varnished version of a truth. Roland leaves at eighteen to go to Leeds to go to university and then train to be an accountant. Sarah stays to do her degree and MSc. To look after Sylvia. It's unspoken, however, Donna can hear it in the cracks appearing in her tale and her voice. Another swig of gin and Sarah sits a little straighter, says as if by rote: 'You know the rest. It's all in your files. Dad shoots Mum and then himself. Sylvia commits suicide. Only now you're telling me she didn't?' This realisation once again appears to strike her forcibly, her body crunches over a bit.

'When did you last see her?' asks Donna.

'See her?' She takes a moment to mull this question over. 'I left to go travelling in September 1993. She came to see me off at the station.' She stops twirling her hair and gives it a tug.

Donna is about to leap forward to stop her, surprised at the ferocity of it. It is over in a split second.

'And what about talk to her?' asks Harrie.

She shrugs. 'I sent a few postcards. I didn't ring home much. You didn't then. No mobiles.' She looks down.

'You had no idea she was coming to Scarborough last night?'

'Last night? . . . No.' Her features pinch. The edge of her mouth jerks.

'Where were you last night?'

'Here. Alone. I left work about six o'clock. After that I was alone.'

Harrie glances at Donna. She wonders whether to leave it at that. Sarah is bereaved. More questions could be asked later. On the other hand, there is always something to be gained for asking in the moment, before people have had time to think through a narrative. She decides to forge on. 'Just a couple of more things, Ms Franklande.' It seems easier to keep the distance, rather than resort to first names. 'I happened to see you have the Cullen Report on your kitchen table. Is it the unedited version or the final one?'

Sarah looks confused; she sounds cross: 'What has this to do with Sylvia?'

Donna waits.

Sarah sighs. 'I arrived at ScarTek after the Cullen Report was published. I am merely catching up with some reading. It is the version I received at work. Anything else?'

'One more question: where were you when your parents died?

'Granada, Spain. It'll be in your files. Now would you mind, could we talk further at another time?' She stands.

Harrie asks whether there is anyone they can call for Sarah. She shakes her head, saying she will talk to her brother. Then she briskly thanks them for their visit and bustles them out. Walking down the garden path, Donna realises there are things which don't add up in at least one of Sarah's answers.

Chapter 33

What am I doing here? Alice and Fareeha once spent a drunken evening comparing 'worst relationship decisions ever' stories. Alice had 'won' the unspoken competition by a mile. Even though she did not reveal the half of it. However, with the morning hangover, she did make a vow to be less biddable, less 'nice' (the verdict Fareeha used as a criticism). Alice swore to say 'no' more often. *And here I am,* she thinks crossly. Cross with Sarah for making the request. Cross with herself for giving in. *Again!* Initially she had made the excuse to herself that it would be an opportunity to check Sarah had received the Cullen Report. Alice had dropped it off at ScarTek reception marked personal and confidential, hoping this meant only Sarah would open it. In reality, Alice could have asked this over the phone and then said no, she would not come round. Ten-thirty was way too late. Doesn't Sarah have anyone else to call on? But then the treacherous thoughts, *She wants me, no one else. And I want her.* She'll just have to notch it up as another disastrous relationship decision, she decides. She changes out of her PJs into a long-sleeved T-shirt, her dungarees, pullover, scarf, her purple Docs and her yellow raincoat. She does not allow herself to ponder over her choice of outfit. *Take me as she finds me,* she thinks, as if regaining a modicum of control.

She thinks about turning back several times on her stomp through the damp night. The waning moon hangs in the sky, a luminescent pregnant belly escaping the folds of a dark cloak. Alice pauses for a moment to admire it. She feels as if she could reach out and run her fingers across the whorls and ridges on its pale surface. She recalls being fascinated by her mother's swollen abdomen when she was carrying Alice's younger brother. Alice had rested her head on the warm domed surface and felt the movement under the skin. It was the beginning of the strong bond which still exists today. Perhaps Sarah did the same when Sylvia was growing inside June's womb. And now Sylvia is dead. *Really dead.* Alice cannot imagine how she would survive this re-traumatisation. She hurries on. She has another moment of hesitation as she goes through the gate.

However, Sarah has already opened the front door. 'Thank you, thank you so much for coming,' she mumbles as she ushers Alice into the narrow hallway. 'I didn't know who else to ask. I wanted to . . . I mean . . . didn't know who else I wanted to ask.'

The two women find themselves facing each other in the confined space. It's almost as if the walls are conspiring to initiate the embrace. To Alice it feels natural to wind her arms around Sarah, while Sarah's hug pulls her in. Alice tips her head and Sarah's face dips down. They kiss gently on the lips. The awkwardness begins when they pull apart. Which they eventually do. Sarah is instantly intent on getting Alice into the lounge and offering drinks. Against her better judgement, Alice accepts a gin. When Sarah disappears off to fetch it, Alice sits down on the sofa. She notices the sparseness of the room's decoration. *Either Sarah is into minimalism. Or she's not planning on staying.*

She comes back with a tray which she sets on the table. There are two gin and tonics with slices of lime and a bowl of salted snacks. Sarah takes her glass and retreats to the easy chair, tucking her feet under her. She holds her drink in hands clenched across her chest like a padlocked barrier. Her parchment face is blotched with red, especially around her eyes.

'I'm sorry,' she says stiffly. 'I shouldn't have asked you to come.' She adds quickly, 'Here.' The blotches are joined by a blush.

Alice sips her gin. It's sharp and strong. She puts it on the tray. *I could – I should – walk out now,* she counsels herself. She doesn't move. 'Tell me,' she says.

'I don't know much. They wouldn't tell me anything. Just that . . . Sylvia . . . she's dead . . . killed—'

'Killed?' To Alice this is like a blow to the thorax. It almost cuts off the oxygen to her lungs.

Sarah nods. 'They found her body, by some beach huts on South Bay.'

Alice struggles to bring some calm into her body, remembering a soothing mantra she uses while practising yoga. After a second or so, she finds she can say, relatively steadily, 'Tell me about Sylvia, then.'

Perhaps it is the lateness of the hour, or the amount of gin Sarah has consumed (which, Alice starts to realise, is not minimal) or the way the light from the one standard lamp casts shadows. Whatever it is, slowly, slowly, Sarah begins to open up.

First come the happier – maybe more acceptable – rec-ollections. Such as the day one March, when Sylvia would have been seven or eight, on a treat from their dad for her birthday. Belated, as usual – one or two weeks – but who was counting? The weather was bright, if chilled. The dragon boats on the lake were still tied up out of school holidays. But Dad knew someone who knew someone and there was one set free, just for them. Dad and Sarah took turns pedal-ling, Sylvia squealing with delight. Roland was off with his mates. Where was their mum? Sarah cannot recall. 'Maybe she had a headache,' she suggests.

As time flows around them like a river skimming rocks, Sarah's features and voice lose any attempt at lightness. There was the night – no, nights plural – when Sylvia would sneak across their shared room and into Sarah's bed. Sarah would wrap them up in her bedclothes. Downstairs there would be a man's raised voice and thudding, followed by the front door slamming. Sylvia would be afraid. Sarah not. She knew they were safe; her daddy wouldn't harm her, them. Anyway, she reasoned, this was not her daddy, he had mor-phed into this other daddy. Perhaps he had taken a potion? When she discovered the story of Dr Jekyll and Mr Hyde it all made sense to her. Still, she would take her sister in her arms and hold her until she slept. Then she would leave her in bed and go to her mother: cleaning cuts; dabbing arnica where bruising was going to appear; administering aspirin with a shot of whisky. Sarah could not abide the stuff herself when she started to sample alcohol. She'd tidy up – righting furniture; throwing away broken crockery and glass. Finally she would put her mother to bed and wait, holding her

214

hand, until she too was asleep. A couple of times she'd see things were worse than usual and wake Roland (who apparently had adapted himself to sleeping through everything). They'd get their mother to hospital in a taxi. He'd go with their mother. Sarah would stay with Sylvia who, this time, wouldn't be comforted. Sarah would feel herself becoming tense, then angry, force herself to walk away rather than slap her sister. Tears – she always hated having to deal with them.

She is crying now, even as she says this. Alice feels the pull. She finds she cannot resist. She goes over. Sarah has her knees up to her chest, has closed herself in like a clam. Alice untangles her. She takes her back to the sofa where she sits, Sarah curled up by her side, her head in Alice's lap. From that position, her voice sounds even more distant, as if it is coming from another realm. She remembers afternoons, hot afternoons, sticky with fizzy orange juice. Her father would whizz her around and then throw her up in the air. For a short breathless moment, she could see the march of semis down the hill to where the lake in the park glinted blue through the trees. She could see the pattern of brown fences and square lawns repeating. She could see the line of crawling cars and the snorting buses on their way to the beach. She could see her mother sitting on a garden chair. 'And she looked so small, Alice, so insignificant.' Then finally Sarah would be falling. She would squeeze her eyes shut, clamp her jaw together, her stomach muscles contracted uneasily, her oesophagus burned. 'My brain would be shouting, what if he doesn't catch me? But he always did, Alice, he always caught me.'

'"She's just like her father." I used to hear them, Alice,' she says. 'They were talking to my mother, but they meant me. There was a little gang of us, neighbourhood kids. Mum would get them round, when things were going OK. And I'd have them organised. Playing tag and grandma's footsteps. Setting up long, convoluted scenarios. Ordering the other kids into roles – spies and Indians and spacemen. Always men. And the mothers would say, "Oh June, she's just like Phil."' Sarah takes on a rather breathy, high-pitched tone. She pauses before saying: 'And I was proud. Because being just like my father meant being strong, being someone who people liked, being someone who made people laugh. It felt good to be just like my father.' She sounds angry.

Alice strokes her cheek. 'I'm sure you're nothing like him,' she says softly.

Sarah sits up suddenly, knocking away Alice's fingers. 'You know nothing about me.' She stands, rather unsteadily. She says she has to go to the bathroom.

Left alone, Alice gives herself a good shake. She sees from her phone that it is nearly midnight. She should go. Yet she stays where she is. Sarah is away long enough for Alice to wonder if she has forgotten her and gone to bed. Or perhaps fallen? *Was she drunk enough?* Alice creeps out into the hall at the same moment that Sarah descends the stairs. Once again their close proximity charges the atmosphere. This time Alice resists it. She grabs her scarf and coat from the banister.

'You're going?'

Alice can't tell if Sarah is sad or relieved. Alice puts on her outdoor gear. She nods. 'It's late.'

'Of course.'

Still, the moment could go either way. Alice recognises this. She reiterates her vow, *No more bad relationship decisions.* She hurries towards the door.

'I need to go to the crematorium, for my parents. It's the anniversary,' Sarah says in a rush. Then, sounding totally wretched, 'Would you, I mean I know it's a lot to ask, but would you mind—'

'Why don't you ask Roland?' Alice says roughly.

'I want you.'

The force of Sarah's desire in those three words hits Alice. It confuses her.

'Maybe. Give me a ring,' she says.

She has the sense that Sarah might hold her there if she said no straight out. She forces herself to exit and go along the path. Not slowing her pace until she is well on her way down the street. Only then, under the glare of the moon – as white as a scraped bone – does she admit to having considered – nay, craved – relinquishing herself to Sarah Franklande.

Chapter 34

Donna is gratified to find that, despite the workload, she is sleeping and has not been slayed by a headache. Plus she has stopped bleeding. *Maybe this is it, I've tipped into menopause,* she thinks cheerfully. This Tuesday morning, she is in early. She is following up on Terry Prichard's account of his friend, Neal Williams, being beaten up because of his sexuality. She has spoken to Terry again and, despite his bold assertions, his grasp of the detail was sketchy. He thought the attack took place in a snicket near the Weighed Anchor two years ago, March or April 2012. Not surprisingly, Neal was pretty shaken up, eventually leaving Scarborough for Leeds in the summer of 2013, giving up his job – at ScarTek. Donna had pressed Terry, but he was certain: Neal Williams had worked at ScarTek. *Significant? Lots of people work at ScarTek. That's the whole point. It's why everyone is pussy-footing around Leonard Arch.* Donna searched for and did not find a police report of the assault. Nor did Neal Williams present himself at hospital. She hasn't been able to track down a GP for him. But she did find a postal address in Leeds for Neal himself through council tax records. A PC from the local nick has made first contact, giving Donna an email address. She sends off a message asking if Neal will agree to meet with her.

She tells Theo of her success as he drives them to North Ferriby. Back into Humberside territory. Neither mentions how their last trip ended as they once again cross the border. For Donna, it is easier not to.

Instead, they talk about some of the information their colleagues have already garnered and entered on the case log. Either witnesses or CCTV attest to Sylvia's time in Scarborough on Sunday evening. Her arrival by train. Her forty-five minutes sitting in a nearby greasy spoon over a Diet Coke and teacake (which she left half eaten). Was she waiting for someone or waiting for time to pass? The owner of the café thought her preoccupied and said she checked her phone often. But then what young person doesn't? Afterwards Sylvia walked down the High Street before taking the Spa Bridge over to the foreshore path. Her stride was resolute. She knew her way. Why wouldn't she? This is her childhood home town. The footage didn't capture her face, bundled up as she is in coat and bobble hat. After the Spa complex, she was lost to cameras. A dog walker has come forward. There was a young woman hanging around the former lido. When shown a photo of Sylvia, he couldn't be sure it was her. This was about seven-thirty p.m. He hadn't noticed anyone else. No other sighting of Sylvia has materialised.

'She must have been expecting someone,' says Donna. 'No one would choose to linger down there on a January night. I love walking those paths, but after dark it becomes a whole different kettle of kippers.' She sees Theo's smile. 'What?'

He shakes his head, 'I just enjoy your use of language. You're right, though, there's no lighting. With the weather we've been having, there wouldn't have been a moon. It's a lonely place.'

'Unless you're up to no good. It's a well-known place for getting and taking drugs.'

'Sylvia isn't on our system. Doesn't mean she wasn't taking recreationally, of course. We'll check it out with her housemates.' After a pause, he carries on. 'Sylvia met her killer down there. He or she must have arrived somehow. Either from town or down through the gardens or from the Holbeck car park on the cliff. All CCTV stops well short of the old South Bay pool.'

'Or it was someone who lives in the gardens. A rough sleeper.'

'It's possible. Though a lot of the regulars take up offers of hostel accommodation when the temperature hits zero. I've been thinking about the blanket. Sylvia didn't bring it with her.'

'And the way it was tucked round her suggests some compassion for our victim. Rough sleepers aren't beyond remorse.' Donna feels defensive, despite knowing it took a long time for Elizabeth to face her guilt.

'Not so much when drug addled. Anyway, apart from Sylvia's blood, the blanket was clean. And expensive.'

Donna stares out of the window at the flattened land. The sea nibbling at the bottom of crumbling cliffs is a distant memory. The morning is bright, the sun is in a strigilled sky, the blue achingly brilliant. She and Theo sweep through another village lined up on either side of the road, its church spire pricking the underside of the heavens. *Sarah spent years caring for her sister, protecting her.*

As if reading her thoughts, Theo asks her about impressions of Sarah from the previous evening. Was her shock at Sylvia's death authentic?

'Yes. Maybe. I suppose, they might have met, argued, Sarah hit out and she left not knowing how much damage she had done.'

'After wrapping her in a blanket?'

'It doesn't sound entirely plausible. It's not impossible, I guess. Did Brian speak to Roland?'

'He did and has already turned in the report.' Theo does not keep the modicum of surprise out of his voice. 'Roland was in Leeds where he lives with his partner and her children.'

'In a different town. With an alibi.' *Unlike Sarah.*

'Perhaps today will throw up some other persons of interest,' says Theo. The satnav indicates they are approaching their destination. 'Did I say DS Spinelli is meeting us at the house?' He did. He continues before Donna responds. 'He's a good bloke, isn't he?'

Does he want an answer? Donna turns this over before finally saying, 'I liked him.'

For the first time this morning she takes in what Theo is wearing. Always dapper, he usually wears a suit and tie when working. Today, it's a smart pair of black chinos with a rose-tinted open-necked shirt which match the frames of his glasses. His wool knee-length coat is on the back seat.

'Me too,' he says softly, so softly Donna isn't sure she has heard him right.

They arrive at a neat crescent of semi-detached houses.

221

Built of brick in the 1970s to echo some of the attributes of the older cottages in the town, they have steeply pitched tiled roofs with fancy carved wooden trim and Dutch-barn gable ends. Theo pulls up by one with an extensive dormer window. Gus is standing outside it. He is wearing jeans and a leather jacket which even Donna recognises as designer. He greets them both warmly. However, Donna senses an added enthusiasm when he turns from her to her DI. It reminds her of Christopher when he was first getting to know the woman who is now his wife.

Gus, though, has quickly moved onto business. Sylvia shared this house with two other young women. It is owned by one of the women's parents, who bought it rather than shell out on university accommodation for her. She has the extension into the attic, while Sylvia and the other woman rent on the middle floor, and they all share lounge and kitchen downstairs, and a small garden. This much he has gleaned from a land registry search and over the phone when he set up this visit. He also emailed Sylvia's photo to Mavis Lewis, the daughter of the house owners. She has confirmed their deceased's ID.

Mavis now opens the door to them. Dressed casually and probably in her mid-twenties, Mavis Lewis is of average build. Her skin is a rich brown colour, her black hair a mix of braids and weaves meeting in a bun at the back of her head. She takes them into the downstairs through-room, lounge at the front, kitchen/diner at the other end. Mavis indicates they can sit on the generous sofa and two easy chairs. She offers them refreshments then busies herself making coffee and getting Donna a glass of water. On her return, Mavis plonks herself on a large floor cushion. Her feet pop out of their crocs, revealing each toenail painted in shades of glittering red.

'I can't believe it,' she says. 'It's not true, is it? About Sylvia? She can't be dead. I only spoke to her forty-eight hours ago. I suppose that's a stupid thing to say. Anyone can die and it doesn't have to take long.' Her youth and natural bounce fight with the aberration of grief. Her features do not quite know what to do. However, Donna notices pink at the corners of Mavis's eyes and around her nostrils.

'I am very sorry, Ms Lewis,' says Theo gently.

'Mavis, Mavis is fine,' she says, taking out a tissue to wipe her nose with. 'What happened?'

'I am sorry to have to inform you, Sylvia was killed.'

Mavis nods, 'Yes obviously she was killed, I mean she wasn't old enough to fall down dead, right? What was it, some fucking arsehole driving too fast?' Then the true meaning of Theo's statement appears to dawn on her. Her eyes open wide. 'What do you mean killed? Deliberate?' She shakes her head. 'Can't be. No one would kill Sylv, everyone loved her, no one would actually set out to harm her. It must have been an accident. Must have been.'

Theo admits to this being a possibility. He then asks Mavis to tell them about her friend. It takes a while for her to collect her thoughts into some coherence, though eventually she does pretty well. She says she is studying to be a solicitor, first year of her post-grad legal practice course. It is probably why she manages to marshal what she has to tell them into a narrative. She met Sylvia Franklande four years previously, when Mavis was in the first year of her law degree. Mavis needed to find another person to share the house and Sylvia was in a bedsit she hated. Plus the two women found they had a mutual fondness for obscure art house films, especially French ones. The other person sharing the house has changed each year – the current incumbent, a first year masters student, is away in the US on a month-long research trip – but Mavis and Sylvia have become firm friends. The ten-year age gap between them has made no difference.

Sylvia started a part-time degree in ceramics a year after Mavis met her. Keeping her post in the university's admissions office gave her cut price fees. Sylvia was good at her job, well liked and was becoming an exceptional ceramicist. 'This is one of hers.' Mavis touches a delicately fluted vase standing on the floor beside her. It is decorated in blue and green, capturing the movement of water. It contains several long-stemmed flowers sculpted, Donna now realises, from porcelain. Mavis has run out of steam. She pulls her knees up and rests her chin on them. She gazes at the carpet.

Theo prompts her with questions regarding how much she knows about Sylvia's family life. Not much, it seems. Sylvia didn't like to speak about the past. 'I think her parents were dead,' Mavis says, not looking up. 'She had a brother. He helped with the rent.'

This causes a slight reaction from Theo. Donna cannot interpret it. She asks about relationships, boy – or girl – friends.

'That would be the hound,' says Mavis. She stands and offers more drinks. When the others refuse, she saunters to the kitchen to boil the kettle, saying she needs a tea. As she does so, she continues: 'Sebastian Hound. Heard of him? Photographer to the stars, or he was once. Still dines out on it. Sylv attended a short course he was running and they got it together.' She returns with her drink. 'Sylvia's.' She indicates the mug. It has numbers on it. 'She'd count when she was nervous. I bought this for her. She loves . . . loved it. Always used it.' She sounds glum.

Donna can smell the peppermint of the tea. She prompts, 'Sounds like you don't approve of the relationship with Mr Hound?'

Mavis shrugs. 'The hound's a snake. But she had to keep going back to him. It's like an addiction. You know?' She glances up quizzically. She holds the mug to her chest. She continues: 'Sometimes he wants her, then he doesn't, then he does. And there's always other women.'

'What about Sylvia? Does she see other people?'

She shakes her head. 'Are you joking? The hound doesn't like her seeing her friends. He's so controlling. And he gets violent, sometimes.'

'Has he hit her?'

'It's more, you know, what you'd call psychological, emotional control. Then he smashed her pots the week before last. Just went in the studio at uni and threw two of them on the floor.'

'Why?'

'Didn't need a reason. He was pissed over something. Probably not even to do with Sylv. That really got to her. He could jerk her around all he liked, but smash her pots? She was incandescent. I thought, that's it, at last. She went over last Monday night, said she was going to tell him. I said dump him by text for Christ sake. But she said she had stuff at his house she needed to retrieve. I said, stuff? You can fucking live without stuff, girl.' Mavis's features are grim. 'I should have stopped her. Tied her up. Locked her in.'

'What happened?'

'I don't know exactly. She said she would only be an hour. I was doing an essay and it was midnight before I thought about it and she wasn't back. She comes in maybe thirty minutes later? Just as I was thinking of alerting you lot. She seemed OK, physically I mean, intact. She wouldn't answer my questions, not properly. Said yes it was all over with Sebastian, but wouldn't say more. She gets like that some-times – private, cagey. It's not good to push. We were both tired. So we went to bed.' She pauses, takes a sip of tea, star-ing down. 'Last week was busy for me, the essay and then some exams. I guess we just let the topic drop. 'Till we had proper time, you know, to discuss. Saturday we did chores 'n' stuff. I was thinking I might ask her what happened with the hound on Sunday. But it wasn't to be. I had a long lie in, then a good soak in the bath. I only get those at the week-end. I came down, I don't know, after midday I guess. She was in the kitchen.' Mavis jerks her head towards the back of the house. 'Filling up her water bottle. She seemed OK. She said she was off out, going into Hull. She gave me a hug and she was outta here. Shit.' Mavis puts down her mug, liquid slops onto the carpet as she does so. She curls up tighter and puts her hands to her face. Through her sobs, she moans: 'It was the last time I saw her. If I'd known, if only I'd known, I'd have held her so close she couldn't breathe, I wouldn't have let her go. Why did I let her go?'

Donna has the urge to wrap her arms around Mavis, tell her not to blame herself. In her twenties, Elizabeth was not hug-able, not even approachable. For a moment, Mavis is the Elizabeth who never was.

Finally, Mavis draws in a deep gulp of oxygen, refinds the tissue and starts to compose herself. 'What else do you need to know?'

Theo asks, 'She definitely said Hull, not Scarborough?'

'Yeah, but from here you have to go to Hull for the train to Scarborough.'

'She didn't say why she was going out?'

Mavis shakes her head. 'And she went to Scarborough, you say?' She glances up. 'That's weird. Sylv never wanted to go there. I went there once with some other mates, rained all day, we had some fish and chips, then came home. Sylv said she wasn't interested. We'd go to York or Sheff or London together, but never Scarborough.' Another moment's thought. 'Though the hound's exhibition was in Scarborough.'

'It's where she grew up,' says Donna.

'Is it? She never said.' Mavis appears to contemplate this, and, perhaps, the other things she didn't know about her friend. This thought might be hanging over her as she responds to Theo's question about drugs, though she shakes her head emphatically and, with a smile, says a half a pint was Sylvia's limit.

Gus then asks, 'Could we ask where you were Sunday evening?'

'What? Why?' she says. Then she collects herself. 'Oh yeah, I get you. At film club, which Sylv was supposed to be at too. I can give you numbers for ten other people who were there with me.' Then she stands quickly in one fluid movement. 'You'll want to see her room, right?'

Gus joins the others as they get to their feet, and asks, 'Where does Sebastian Hound live?'

'Oh, just round the corner. Don't know his address but I can describe how to get there.'

They all follow her up the stairs. Donna hears Gus suggesting to Theo that he (Gus) is left to search Sylvia's room while Donna and Theo tackle 'the hound'. This meets with approval, though Theo says he wants a quick glance round the space Sylvia called home for the last several years. Donna is glad. It will help her build a better picture of the young woman. Plus it seems to have been a place where Sylvia was happy. An antidote to the last time Donna saw her, scrunched up in the dank doorway of a dilapidated beach hut.

They troop into the bedroom at the front of the house. By the window is a large desk. On its surface is the ubiquitous laptop, along with sketchpads, notebooks, pencils, crayons and art books, which are also piled on a bookshelf, on the floor and in storage boxes. To the other side of the room are a wardrobe and a double bed. Above this, is a large-format print of a black and white photograph. Donna recognises it immediately. The rotund form of the lighthouse surrounded by the blasted landscape of Spurn Point. The lighthouse where Professor Cullen's body was found. She notices Theo has clocked it as well.

He asks Mavis about it. Sylvia took it as part of the project she did during the course led by Sebastian Hound. Theo asks Mavis if she knows Orson Reed or Professor Zavier Cullen.

'Orson Reed, no. Isn't that Cullen guy the prof from uni who killed himself after he got caught out with one of his students? It was all over campus. What have they got to do with Sylv?'

Nobody responds to her. She doesn't seem to notice as she moves around the room, letting her fingers rest on a book, then on the dishevelled duvet, then on the water glass on the bedside table. All at once she stops, looks at the police officers. 'Shit, I guess I shouldn't be touching any-thing, sorry. I'll leave you to it, shall I?'

'If you don't mind,' says Gus. 'Before you go, do you know anything about Sylvia's social media accounts or her email? And her mobile number?'

Mavis pauses by the door. 'Oh, yeah, sure. You'll find all that stuff in a notebook in the desk drawer. Sylv was use-less at remembering passwords. She didn't use her name for Facebook and such. In the cyber-sphere she was Gretel. You know, the little girl who got lost.'

Chapter 35

As they walk, Donna mentions how much Mavis impressed her. 'It's good to see a young woman like her headed into the legal profession.'

'Because she's black, you mean?' asks Theo.

No! Yes? Maybe. She can't gauge whether there's criticism in his tone. *I can't not notice the colour of her skin.* She realises, whatever she might have claimed, she has never been 'colourblind', only now race has become writ large. *It probably always was for Theo,* she contemplates to herself. She says out loud, 'I was actually thinking of myself at that age. Married and settling into domesticity. I don't think I could have been as cogent as she was.'

He nods. 'I certainly hope her talents are being recognised and nurtured, and will be as she goes along.' It sounds as if he thinks his weren't, and aren't, not so much.

Mavis's instructions take them to a house shaped like an armadillo, sitting in the middle of its own plot by the river. With its glass and girders and charred wood cladding, it could be featured on one of those TV design programmes. Perhaps it has been. Despite its modernist pretensions, it still has a path cutting through a lawn (planted with oriental grass) and this arrives at a front door.

It takes a while for Sebastian Hound to answer the bell. He

is wearing a chunky knitted pullover in olive green, an open-neck off-white shirt and jeans bagging at the knees. On his feet are corduroy carpet slippers. Donna notices the thinning hair and the pouches in the face. 'The hound' is beginning to resemble his name. Theo explains who they are and that they have come to speak about Sylvia Franklande. When Sebastian Hound begins to suggest they should make an appointment at another time as he's busy, Theo cuts him off.

'I am afraid not. This is a criminal investigation, and we believe you have some information pertinent to the case.' The other man remains blocking the doorway. Theo then adds that 'sir' wouldn't want to be obstructing police officers in their duty.

Sebastian moves slowly and leads them through a wide hall into a high-ceilinged space. It has large windows at either end. Through one is the Humber, a sward of platinum. The arch of the Humber Bridge (though three miles away) is clearly visible. The weak sun glints off the metal uprights and the long curved suspension rope. The other window gives a view of North Ferriby, its church spire in amongst the huddle of housing, with the rise of the Wolds in the distance. At this end is the seating which Sebastian indicates they should use. It all looks very 1970s to Donna – vibrant orange upholstery and chrome. She's relieved to find style has not trumped comfort. The short walk and air has given her a lift. Still, she fears if she lets herself sink into the cushions she might nod off.

'You said this is about Sylvia,' says Sebastian. 'Is she in some kind of trouble?'

Donna knows her DI will be weighing up possible

approaches. Should they get Sebastian to talk first before revealing what has happened? Even if it doesn't feel entirely fair to hold back, would they learn more?

Theo says, 'When did you last see Sylvia?'

Sebastian takes a moment to ponder this. 'Who has said what to bring you here? Has Sylvia said something? Or is it that Mavis?'

Donna wonders if 'bitch' or 'witch' might have been deleted before Mavis's name was spat out. Neither she nor Theo say anything; they retain their relaxed posture.

After several seconds are ticked off by an analogue clock which might have come from a 1930s train station waiting room, Sebastian crosses his arms and says, 'Monday a week gone. In the evening. She came here about six. And left, I don't know, just after midnight. Now will you tell me what is going on?'

Donna asks, 'Could you tell us what kind of relationship you have with Ms Franklande?'

Again he doesn't respond straight away. 'We're very . . . fond of each other,' he says carefully.

'You're in an intimate relationship?'

'It gets intimate at times. We're not girl- and boyfriend, if that's what you mean, DC . . . ?'

'Morris.'

'DC Morris.' He smiles winningly at her. 'Sounds rather ridiculous at my age, anyway, I'm hardly a boy.'

'Was it monogamous?'

He shrugs. 'Sometimes.'

Can you be monogamous sometimes? 'And you've known each other how long?'

232

He gazes up to the ceiling. 'Three years, maybe? Time unwinds in a different way once you're out of your thirties. Don't you find, DC Morris?' His attention is once more on her.

She responds to his smile, even when she would rather not. She continues, 'Could you tell us what happened that Monday between you and Sylvia?'

'No,' he says, tautness back into his face and voice. 'Not until you tell me what this is about.'

Donna glances at Theo. It's his call what to do next.

After a pause, he does shift slightly forwards. 'I am very sorry to have to inform you, Mr Hound, Sylvia is dead.'

Sebastian doesn't immediately react. He sounds cautious when he says: 'How? An accident? In a car or something?'

'We don't know for sure. We're investigating.'

'You must know if it was an accident—'

Theo cuts into his bluster. 'We are investigating. And you would be helping our investigation if you could tell us about Monday night.'

For a moment, Sebastian stares at Theo. Then he jumps up and talks to the window. 'She came over, we talked, we went to bed, she got up and she left.'

Donna realises he can probably observe her and Theo reflected in the glass. 'What did you talk about, Mr Hound?' she asks.

'Is that relevant?'

'It might be. We won't know until you say.'

Sebastian rubs at his forehead, then his hands settle on his hips. 'Usual stuff. She asked me about my exhibition, the first one for ten years – it's been touring. I asked her about her course. Maybe we talked about some film or other. I really can't remember the detail.'

'It was only a week ago yesterday.'

'Yeah, well, maybe I didn't think I'd ever be questioned about it,' he snaps.

Theo calmly picks up the questioning. 'Ms Lewis suggested Sylvia ended your relationship.'

'Mavis Lewis is jealous. Wants me. Or wants Sylvia. Wants one of us, I don't know which, all to herself. She is always prophesising the demise of our relationship. Sylvia probably said that so she could get out of the house without an argument.' He ambles to his seat. He looks pointedly at the clock.

'Ms Lewis also said you got angry with Sylvia not a fortnight ago and broke some of her ceramics?' continues Theo steadily.

'Did she?' Sebastian throws one leg over the other; his foot jiggles.

'Is that what happened?'

'No, of course not. I'm an artist.' His chest appears to expand as he says this. 'I wouldn't mess with another person's creative work.'

'So why would Ms Lewis say this?'

'I told you, she's jealous,' he growls.

Donna wants to move. She is stiff, the immobility of the morning is getting to her. Plus, she believes, she has been gathering up the energies of those they have been talking to. Mavis's grief. This man's sharpness, barely smoothed down by his charisma. Donna wants to walk outside and (metaphorically) throw the emotions in the river. No, actually, she wouldn't mind giving Sebastian Hound a good dousing while she is at it. Despite this, she asks evenly, 'Did Sylvia speak to you about going to Scarborough?'

'Scarborough?' says Sebastian, as if it were the moon.

Donna can see he is play acting.

'Your exhibition has been in Scarborough,' says Theo flatly.

'You've been reading up on me, Inspector. Or did you go and see it?'

'Had Sylvia?'

Sebastian shakes his head. 'She saw it when it opened in London.'

'Did she talk about going to Scarborough on Sunday the nineteenth of January?'

Donna can hear the edge in her DI's voice.

Perhaps Sebastian perceives it too. He leans his elbows on his knees, his palms open and empty towards them. 'OK, look, when she came over that Monday night, she seemed a bit down. Sylvia has her moments, lord knows. At least I hope he does, because I don't, I don't really understand what goes on with her. Used to do that fucking counting thing. I gather her childhood was something of a 'mare. And I happened to mention, I reckoned I might have met her sister, at the opening of my exhibition in Scarborough. I thought it would cheer Sylvia up. Whenever she does speak about her, which isn't often, she says they were close when they were kids. I get the impression Sarah took care of her.'

'Why now?' asks Theo.

'What?'

'The opening of your exhibition was some weeks ago. Why tell Sylvia now?'

Sebastian shrugs. 'It just came out that way.'

Or you were holding on to that tit-bit for when you needed something to persuade Sylvia to stay, thinks Donna.

'I didn't expect her to go haring off up there. I told her I would find out an email address from the art gallery curator and she could get in touch like that to begin with.' Again, those large, powerful hands spread wide towards them. 'Sarah seemed pretty screwed up, when I met her anyway. I thought it best to approach her cautiously.'

'And did you get the email address and give it to Sylvia?'

Sebastian Hound shakes his head. 'Didn't have time. I haven't seen nor spoken to Sylvia since that Monday.'

Donna comes in with questions about where Sebastian was Sunday evening, then whether he knows Orson Reed or Professor Zavier Cullen. The replies: 'My local.' 'No.' 'No.' He pushes himself to his feet, says he needs his lunch and then to get on with his work. Donna is aware of his bulk towering over her as she remains sitting. She asks whether Sylvia has left any of her belongings in the house and whether they could have a look around.

Again the double negative. Sebastian says with some force: 'I need you to leave. This is a lot for me to get my head round. My work will help me process it all. We can speak more another time.'

Donna and Theo get up. Theo says: 'We are sorry to be the bearers of bad news, Mr Hound. And we will certainly want to speak to you again. Meanwhile, an officer for Humberside will be in touch about taking a DNA swab from you, merely for elimination purposes.'

Sebastian Hound does not return his smile.

Once more on the doorstep, Donna realises Sebastian Hound did not ask again about how Sylvia died. Perhaps he had felt too overwhelmed. Perhaps he did not need to.

Chapter 36

Whether or not Sebastian Hound was really desperate for his lunch, Donna is pleased to be sitting down to hers. They have met up with Gus at a riverside pub. They are seated by some patio doors which have been partly opened. A short stretch of grass ends at the muddy banks of the Humber. It has slunk lower with the tide, exposing thick chocolate-coloured mud and the wooden stumps of boatyards long gone.

Gus explains what they are before admitting to being 'born and bred' in Hull. 'My granddaddy and his brother opened the first ice-cream parlour here, fresh from Naples.' He adds quickly: 'I've been away. I did my probationary in Bristol. I was with the Hampshire force.'

'What brought you back?' Theo asks. They are waiting for their food to be served.

Gus grins. 'The bright lights.'

The waiter arrives bearing plates. Donna has chosen fish-cakes and chips. It smells divine.

After taking a few mouthfuls, Gus says more seriously, 'I had some family stuff to sort out.' He pauses before adding, 'Mum died of cancer and now Dad's been diagnosed with dementia.'

Theo and Donna pause in their munching and say almost in unison, 'I'm sorry.'

He moves his head from side to side, perhaps in resignation. 'Hope to move on soon. I'd prefer a bit more challenge.'

'I guess every place is challenging in its own way,' says Theo.

'The challenge here is not to stand up too tall. Verticals are noticeable.'

Though Gus grins, Donna wonders if there is a warning in the comment. *If you're going to be different, don't be too obvious.* She senses something is being telegraphed between the two young men she is sharing the table with.

Once they have sated their physical appetites, they begin to chew over the morning. Gus has collected various things from Sylvia's room. He has her laptop for analysis and has already requested her phone records from the number supplied by Mavis. He has Sylvia's toothbrush carefully bagged, to confirm the ID with DNA. Plus he has taken notebooks and other paraphernalia connected to her creative vocation. He says he will process all of this over the coming days. They discuss the two versions they've been given of Sylvia's relationship with Sebastian Hound. Donna is inclined towards Mavis's description.

'If we're talking about someone who followed Sylvia up to Scarborough and bashed her over the head with a piece of wood, my money is on Hound,' she says. 'And when it comes to violence against women, lovers have to always be top of the list.'

Theo says: 'We still need to check both their alibis. And talk to Sylvia's other friends.'

Again Gus accepts these as tasks for him.

239

Theo seems pleased with this arrangement.

Means they'll have to be in touch, thinks Donna with secret delight at being there at 'the beginning' of what she now considers a blossoming romance.

Gus continues: 'Could the attack on Sylvia be random? Her phone went?'

'But not her money, nor her jewellery. We are asking about her phone with known fences,' replies Donna.

'It doesn't look like you are finding any new connection with your other case – Orson Reed's death,' says Gus.

'The DCI is still betting on a lovers' tiff there too,' says Theo. 'We need to get Tony Prichard on dry land.' He glances at his watch. 'I guess we should be getting back.'

'What was it?' asks Gus. 'When Mavis said Roland Franklande had been paying his sister's rent?'

He had noticed too, thinks Donna.

Theo has been signalling to the waiter to come over for payment, checking his phone and pulling on his jacket. He stops. He leans forward on his elbows. 'According to Brian's report, Roland hadn't seen Sylvia since she left his flat in Leeds twenty years ago.'

'Maybe Roland lied,' says Donna.

Theo nods.

'Or he hadn't seen her,' says Gus. 'He'd only been paying the rent. In other words he was playing your officer.'

Theo sounds glum. 'And Brian allowed himself to be played.'

240

Chapter 37

Sarah calls mid-morning, she says she won't take up more than an hour of Alice's time. Maybe less. She sounds vulnerable. Alice agrees. She changes her mind as soon as she puts the phone down. However, her call back to Sarah goes to voicemail. She leaves a message saying she would rather not. Ten minutes later, apparently unaware of this, Sarah is at Alice's door, having been let in downstairs by someone exiting. What Alice could say to a digital recording device, she cannot say to Sarah's face. She is whisked away towards the crematorium in Sarah's swish Audi sporty-number. To her own surprise, Alice finds herself relaxing into the leather upholstery (warmed by some interior mechanism), basking (just a little) in Sarah's gratitude.

They park and follow the tarmac path through manicured lawns to the brick building on the brow of the small hill. Rising up behind are more substantial, tree-covered banks. The dark skeletons of beech and birch are in amongst the smoky-blue of the pines. The sky above is the shell of a dunnock egg. Sarah has to pause by the plan at the entrance of the garden of remembrance. She has forgotten the position of the plaque. When they find it, it is low down on the wall, near a moss-dank corner. It says: 'June Franklande 4th June 1951–6th January 1994. Dearly beloved, sadly missed.'

Once again Alice is hit by the coincidence of dates. The twentieth anniversary. Sarah bends down to place the biggest bouquet of flowers Alice has ever seen. It is wrapped in cellophane with a gold-edged black ribbon. As Sarah straightens, Alice reaches for her hand, and they stand together in silence for a moment.

Then Sarah sighs. 'It was Roland who chose the phrasing. He said it was what was expected.'

Alice gets the impression Sarah might have chosen something different.

She continues, as if to herself: 'I didn't come for the funeral. Roland had it all done and dusted before I had time ... I had no money ... Sylvia didn't seem to want me to come.' She takes a moment to slow her breaths. 'I shouldn't have left her alone with him.'

Left Sylvia alone with Roland? Or her father? Alice glances around the courtyard. 'And your Dad?'

'No plaque for him,' Sarah says grimly. 'He's scattered somewhere.'

'Maybe those roses have grown because of him,' Alice says gently, indicating some healthy bushes gracing the edges of the garden.

'Maybe. But he would have wanted a plaque. He didn't like going unnoticed.' She gives a slight snort of laughter. 'Ironic. Mum would have been happier to be compost for roses.'

'And Sylvia?' Alice asks tentatively, holding her breath.

Another slight grunt of derision. 'If we'd done it properly we could have had one of those fancy family tombs with a stone angel on top.' She pauses as if to gather herself. 'There was no body. Both Roland and I were away, not expecting to come back. Her best friend and the school did something, a memorial event, and they planted a tree. Roland and I, we said we'd remember her in our hearts. And I did.' A fierceness comes into her tone. Her free hand goes to her mouth and then covers her face. She sobs. Her shoulders heave.

'Oh, love,' says Alice. She pulls Sarah into her arms. Sarah softens into the embrace.

After that, it is impossible for Alice to leave. She becomes ever more reluctant to do so. First she suggests a coffee, which becomes lunch. Then they agree to a walk along North Bay. Finally Alice accepts the offer of dinner at Sarah's house. A couscous Sarah had learned to cook in the south of France, which she easily adapts to Alice's vegan preferences. The conversation flows equally smoothly, encompassing tales from Alice's growing up and her travels, which intersect with Sarah's experiences. They move onto books, art, films, likes and dislikes. Yes, they tiptoe around Sarah's childhood and her work, but somehow this doesn't prove awkward. They end up seated on the sofa in the front room, a bottle and half of red drunk, the last half to finish.

It is eleven-thirty p.m. when Alice half-stumbles her way up the staircase to her flat. *An extraordinary day,* she says to herself. As she reaches the landing below her floor, a door flies open.

'Where have you been?' Fareeha has on a thick dressing gown over PJs, woollen socks and slippers. She hustles Alice into her apartment. 'I've been trying to get hold of you. I was worried. And now I can see you've just been gallivanting.'

Her face cannot make up its mind whether to be mad or amused. 'Sit down, I'll make you the Fareeha-guaranteed-no-hangover-cure or you'll feel dreadful in the morning.'

Alice plonks herself down prone on the sofa. She checks her phone, which has been on silent, and discovers several messages and texts from Fareeha. 'What did you want?'

'I'll tell you later. First, who is the mysterious woman?'

Alice thinks about prevaricating or even lying, but knows she is in no state to hoodwink Fareeha. 'Sarah Franklande.'

Fareeha hands over a steaming mug of peppermint tea, spiced with ginger and mixed with honey from a local supplier. She shifts Alice's feet a little, as she sits at the other end of the sofa.

'Do I know her?' Then something dawns on her. 'Wait a minute.' She reaches for her phone and scrolls through, before turning it towards Alice. 'This Sarah Franklande?'

Alice takes the mobile and tries to focus on the e-newsletter from enviro-net talking about 21st Century beginning fracking in North Yorkshire. There is a photo and it is of Sarah. Alice continues to search through the text.

Fareeha snaps: 'It is her, isn't it? And you've been making out with her, haven't you? Don't try to deny it.'

Alice finds the quote from Sarah. It brings back what she said to Alice in the bar the week before about the necessity of fracking as a 'bridging' energy. Alice puts the phone face-down on the floor. She fingers her forehead which is beginning to ache. 'I was only getting to know her, for information,' she says weakly.

'Bullshit.'

'Orson had said ScarTek was mixed up in fracking.'

While speaking, she is reminding herself of why she had first sought out Sarah; because, quite frankly, it had all been forgotten in the last twelve hours.

'And now we know,' says Fareeha emphatically. 'I hope there's nothing really going on between you and her.' After a pause, she puts her hand on Alice's foot and gives it a gentle squeeze. 'Oh babe, you're in deep, aren't you?'

'No,' says Alice, pulling herself upright and taking a swig from the mug. 'No, I am not. I was only doing it for the cause.'

'The cause.' Fareeha smiles sadly. 'The cause doesn't require us to sleep with the enemy.'

'I didn't sleep with her.'

'No, I don't suppose much sleeping was done. And just because it's not on a bed, doesn't mean it's not sex. Oh, Alice . . .'

'I'm fine,' she says sharply. Though she is a long way from fine. The warm glow from being with Sarah, utterly doused, the pounding in her head getting worse, the wine sitting sourly in her stomach. 'What did you want, anyway?'

'I'll tell you after you've slept.'

'Tell me now.' She raises her voice more than she intends to.

Fareeha holds up her hands. 'OK, OK.' She takes a deep breath. 'I'm moving out, on Thursday.'

'What? That's the day after tomorrow. You can't. What about the rent?' *What about me?* Alice snaps her knees up so Fareeha can no longer cradle her feet.

'Mum and Dad, well mainly Mum, have convinced me I can pay it and not live here. I won't have to pay any rent at home. They'll help me out financially if necessary. Oh, Alice, please don't look at me like that. I just need to be away from here. I need to go home.'

To calm and compose herself, Alice drains her drink. She hugs the residual warmth of the mug to her chest. She knows Fareeha is right, she needs to go home and be looked after. But still she doesn't want her to go. Even so, she's Fareeha's friend; she should be supportive. Her thoughts circle themselves, made more addled by the wine, by her confusion over Sarah.

Fareeha says with enforced lightness: 'Let's not talk about it now. You should get to bed. Everything will come right in the morning.'

Will it? 'You sound like Little Orphan Annie,' says Alice with disdain, referring to a musical they'd seen on the TV and detested. *Orson had detested.* Alice had cried.

Fareeha shrugs.

Alice senses a chill growing between them. She blurts out: 'And what about you sleeping with the enemy? Orson had his doubts about Ian.'

'What do you mean?' Fareeha asks. Then she shakes her head. 'Let's not get into this now. Neither of us is in a state to think straight.'

'If not now, when? You're fucking off in a day's time.' Alice leans forward, the movement making her feels slightly sick. 'Orson told me not to share stuff with Ian, stuff about ScarTek. Now why would he do that?'

'Because he was paranoid,' says Fareeha testily. 'Come on, Alice, Orson loved all that cloak and dagger stuff. He hungered after the extreme, to be more way out than anyone else. All his life, he was much too far out. Ian had nothing to do with ScarTek.'

'Didn't he? So where is he? Maybe, maybe, he did meet with Orson at the harbour, just to have a chat and something went wrong—'

Fareeha launches herself to her feet. Her tone is clipped. 'Do not, Alice, do not say anything like that about my baby's father. Now I think you'd better go, before we both make accusations we're going to regret later.'

Alice looks at the stony features of her friend and feels her insides crumble. Before she knows it, she is all tears and snot, apologies hiccupping out of her and, thankfully, thankfully, Fareeha's arms are around her.

Chapter 38

The identification of a body by another person is not generally necessary, nor always desirable, as illustrated by the incident with Pat Flither. However, if relatives want to see their deceased loved one, then every effort is made to make it possible. Roger and Ursula Reed have asked to see their son. Donna is given the task to take them. She leads them down into the basement and into a small room. Here Professor Jayasundera is waiting. His greeting is warm, his condolences sincere. He has a kind face. His skin is the colour of aged cherry wood, rather bleached given the lack of sun this winter.

Mr and Mrs Reed have been warned that Orson was badly damaged during his time in the water. Perhaps they are as surprised as Donna when the prof pulls a curtain along one wall which has been screening a window into the pathology lab. Some skilful patching up and subdued lighting and Orson resembles the photos Donna has seen. Almost. Almost appears to be enough for Roger and Ursula. Both say their son's name in unison under their breaths. It feels to Donna like a part of an unspoken prayer. Ursula puts her fingers to the glass. 'He looks so peaceful,' she says.

'Wasn't peaceful, though was it?' says her husband gruffly.

The moment of accord is gone.

Ursula drops her hand to her side, her head drooping forwards. Roger turns to Donna and asks why no one has been arrested for his son's murder. His wife says weakly that it's not been three weeks, give the police time. Donna steadily assures both of them that everything is being done to find and charge Orson's killer. She repeats this twice more, using different phrases, without giving further information.

'There now, darling,' says Ursula to her husband, once more in control of herself. 'We have to leave it to them.' She takes Roger's arm.

'Why haven't you got us on the TV, to do an appeal?' Roger asks Donna. His face goes the shade and texture of stewed rhubarb. It is hanging in pockets around his bloodshot eyes.

Donna agrees this can sometimes help. She doesn't add more often if the victim or relative is particularly pretty or vulnerable, though.

'Let's leave it to them,' says Ursula more firmly. She glances back through the window, then says she would like to go. 'I need some air.'

Before accompanying them to their rented car, Donna quickly asks Professor Jayasundera if she could have a word with him. He agrees readily. He suggests he finishes up down here and meets her in the café by reception.

For 'finish up', Donna thinks, *read put Orson back in his chilled drawer.*

Appropriately, their way out takes them up to ground level. Ursula asks about a possible funeral date. It doesn't sit comfortably with Donna to be vague. She politely turns the conversation to the Reeds' plans for the day. Even as she does so, she is thinking about another chilled drawer containing Sylvia Franklande's body. No one has asked to see her.

Earlier in the day, Donna was reading through the file covering the deaths of Philip and June Franklande. A closed case now sprung open by the killing of their youngest daughter. Donna was surprised at the thinness of the Manila folder and the sparseness of paperwork. Some of the reports were produced on a typewriter; there were even a few handwritten annotations. A couple of the staples holding statements together have created rusty lines on the paper. It was only twenty years ago, but it was like looking into ancient history.

Initially, what Donna found chimed with what she already knew. On 6 January 1994, both elder siblings were absent, Roland in Leeds, Sarah in Spain. Sylvia had been at a sleepover with a friend, returning on the 7th to find her parents' bodies in the kitchen. She had come in through the front door, gone down the hall and, having seen what must have appeared like carnage to her young teenage brain, had high-tailed it the way she had come to raise the alarm with the neighbours. The report from the first officer on the scene had mentioned the possibility of murder, then suicide, citing the position the gun was found in. This conception of what had happened did not appear to have changed much, with the evidence collected being used only to corroborate it. The pathologist was not categorical on the murder-suicide. However, there was no forced entry. The only fingerprints found in the house were from the Franklande family and all the children had alibis. The only fingerprints on the shot-gun were from Philip Franklande. DNA profiling was still relatively new in 1994, but the tests carried out did not contradict the fingerprint evidence.

Furthermore, there was an explanation for the violence in the form of several typed statements and a scribbled note. A friend of June's said she'd been talking about ending her marriage. Then there were some sheets of paper clipped together, an incident which included raised voices and loud banging reported to the police by a neighbour dating eight months previous to the deaths. Sarah's mother had been taken to hospital with a dislocated shoulder, sprained wrist and bruising on her face. The doctor had said the injuries were probably the result of an assault. Sarah's father had been brought in for questioning and said his wife had slipped on the stairs while carrying an overloaded laundry basket. The scribbled note said: 'Domestic violence? Mrs Franklande backs her husband, NFA.' Donna had searched through the file for other similar incidents, recorded but not pursued. She could not find any. Non-computerisation made it harder to cross-reference, of course. But how likely was it that Phillip Franklande had started hitting his wife so many years into their marriage? And how likely was it that in a small town, no one knew enough to take action?

Beyond this, there were several things that Donna noted as needing further exploration. There was the vestigial of a trainer print by the back door which came directly into the kitchen. It was never properly explained. It was eventually attributed to Sylvia, even though she was clear about coming in and running out via the hall. Plus the size of the footprint

251

was larger than Sylvia's. Then there was Roland Franklande's alibi provided by Leonard Arch, with whom he shared an apartment. Not significant at the time, perhaps, it has taken on a new importance in the light of the current cases. A quick google of ScarTek's website identified Roland as the company's accountant. *The two are still at least acquainted then*, Donna logged. *Another thing Brian failed to uncover.* And finally, those photos Sylvia was holding when she died.

Donna watches Orson's parents walk slowly across the car park. Ursula has tethered herself to her husband with her arm looped through his. Their steps match each other's. Donna fervently hopes the togetherness is more than a habit. She finds Professor Jayasundera in the café and gets herself a herbal tea before joining him at the little table.

'Roger Reed,' Professor Jayasundera says, 'is unfortunately heading for a cardiac episode.' Then he smiles gently at Donna. 'And you, DC Morris, need to get your iron levels tested.'

His gaze is an unsettling mix of warmth and incisiveness.

Donna says quickly, 'I'm fine.'

Jayasundera shakes his head. 'Do it for me, DC Morris. Anaemia is no joke.' He takes a bite from the currant bun he has bought to accompany his mug of coffee. 'Now, what can I do for you?'

'Sylvia Franklande.'

'The young woman brought in the day before yesterday? A whack on her head from a piece of wood. I found splinters. Nasty. From the position of it, I would say she was walking away. It's all in my report.'

Donna nods. She explains about the deaths of Philip and June Franklande twenty years ago and about her questions concerning the investigation.

'I wasn't around then. And, of course, nor was Theo. It was his predecessor, DI John Hoyle.' The way he says the name suggests what he thinks of the man. 'I did a few years under him. Not a man known for his perspicacity, nor his diligence. I recall he was disturbingly indifferent to what he used to call "domestics". He felt they were a waste of time pursuing as we'd never get a wife to stand up in court and give evidence against her husband. Though 1994 was earlier in his career, perhaps he was different, maybe he was more engaged. However, we also have to consider that forensics have moved on a lot in the last twenty years – we've got much more sensitive techniques. My advice is to get everything called up from the evidence lockers and re-looked at.' He pops the last piece of bun neatly into his mouth and wipes his hands on a napkin. 'I like a cold case.' He says he must be going and stands. 'Make an appointment with your GP, DC Morris. Please,' he says as he leaves.

Chapter 39

Alice is on the point of refusing. But the restaurant owner (also the chef) pleads and, she argues to herself, the money will go towards her 'moving to the sun' fund. The morning before, she waved off Fareeha after helping her with her final packing and cleaning. Alice spent the rest of the day and most of the night in the studio. All her work developed with deep shadows and gloom. It suited her mood. She returned to her escape plan to give herself something to look forward to.

This morning she is slow at waking and at turning on her phone. When she does she finds four texts from Sarah which she avoids reading. Then the phone call comes in with the request for her to work. It is probably the only thing that would have got her out of bed.

Her boss for the day sends a taxi and it drops her off at the country restaurant on the edge of the moors at eleven-thirty. She likes the owner. He sources his food ethically and locally and always has a good vegan and vegetarian option. She is looking forward to her vegan brownie and raspberry sorbet. There are five serving staff covering twenty tables, plus the maître d', Kalena. She runs a tight ship, and though Alice doesn't know any of the others, they are soon working as a team, sharing brief exchanges of humour or encouragement as the lunchtime crowd moves in.

In the middle of the rush, Kalena points Alice towards table thirteen where service is needed. She looks over. Immediately she recognises Leonard Arch, with his trademark outlandish cravat. He is sitting with a man of about the same age, who is larger and chunkier and has a double chin and thinning mousy hair. Alice hesitates. Kalena asks whether she wants to swap the table. She says no. Would Arch recognise her? Of course not. Nearly three weeks have passed. Plus, to him, she was merely a short piece of skirt and a bosomy low-cut top. Now she is in the more practical dark trousers and shirt with the restaurant's signature waistcoat in a bright primary colour (red for Alice). She goes over. The two men hardly glance at her as they order one of the most expensive wines on the menu. They explain they will hold off ordering food as one of their party is yet to arrive. Alice returns with the bottle and glasses, along with olives and cubes of locally made cheese. Arch makes a big show of tasting and approving the wine. He still doesn't look Alice in the face. When she leaves them, the two men slip into whatever conversation they were already having.

Alice's attention is taken by other tables. Then Kalena tells her table thirteen is ready to order food. Alice turns. Sarah is sitting next to Arch's companion. Immediately the resemblance reveals itself. Sarah and Roland. Sharing a pleasantry. Alice turns to Kalena, tells her she needs a break. Perhaps she betrays something like panic on her features. For, without missing a beat, the maître d' nods. She says one of the others has a no-show and can cover. Alice escapes out through the kitchen, picking up a sandwich and glass of water on the way. Her route to the little garden at the rear of the restaurant takes her through the car park. She notices all the Mercs and Jaguars, the three Audis in amongst them with the personalised number plates: LARCH 1, LARCH 2 and LARCH 3.

With her coat, scarf and hat on, Alice sits at the table/bench in the garden. The sandwich is mushroom and tarragon pâté, tangy with a lemon sauce. She eats hungrily.

'I thought it was you.' Sarah's approach has taken Alice unawares. Presumably Sarah has come into the garden via the exit by the customers' toilets. 'You haven't replied to my texts.' She perches on the opposite bench. She has on a smart fawn-coloured trouser suit, over an ivory-tinted blouse. Its open neck reveals a gold chain against her collarbone.

Alice recalls nuzzling against the surprisingly soft skin in its cleft. She says tartly, 'I've been busy. And so have you.'

Puzzlement seeps into Sarah's set features. 'What do you mean? I've been at home. I haven't even been into work. You'd know if you'd read my texts.'

'You made a statement about 21st Century Energy's plans to frack.'

Sarah sounds weary, and her gaze goes to her hands clasped on the table. 'Oh, that's gone out, has it? I did it a while ago now.'

Alice continues sharply: 'ScarTek is working hand-in-hand with frackers. Orson knew it.'

'Did he?' Sarah appears to stiffen.

'And you lied to me.'

'I did not.' She seems on the point of leaving, then she droops. 'I may have been, um, economical with the truth. I hardly knew you then.'

'And now? You're just going to let it happen?'

'I don't know.'

This is a surprise. Alice expected a long explanation, excuses.

'We . . . ScarTek . . . should, maybe . . . be reviewing its approach.'

'It can't be something I've said.' Alice remains cross.

Sarah reaches out to touch Alice's hand. Alice snatches it away and stands. 'I have to get back to work.'

As she walks away, Sarah says, 'You reminded me, reminded me of a bigger picture, one I used to be more connected to.'

'Before you were seduced by the money,' Alice flings over her shoulder.

At the door to the kitchen she pauses and looks back. Sarah has stayed sitting. She is bent over, as if Alice's words were heaped on her shoulders.

Then Roland appears from the rear of the restaurant. 'Sarah. Where've you been?' He sounds irritated. He comes to stand in front of her, his bulk leaning over her. 'Leonard is waiting to order his dessert.'

'And we can't keep Leonard waiting,' Sarah snaps.

'What's the matter with you?'

'I thought we were meeting today to remember Sylvia, not for a bloody booze-up.' She snatches a glance at him. 'Don't you care, Roland? Sylvia, our sister, is dead.'

'Of course I care.'

'I miss her so much it hurts.' She puts a hand to her chest. 'I let her down, Roland. Where do you think she was all those years?'

Alice wants to go over and give her a hug.

Her brother obviously does not have the same impulse. He crosses his arms. He leans back on his heels, his legs planted wide apart. 'Sylvia made her own choices.'

'Did she, though? Did any of us? Or are we all just part of the inevitable Franklande tragedy?'

'Don't be so melodramatic, Sarah. Is your life a tragedy? Is mine?'

'Without our parents. Without Sylvia.' Sarah sounds on the verge of tears. 'How can you be so unaffected?'

'Don't think you've got the monopoly on grief,' Roland says harshly. He leans forward. For a moment Alice thinks he might be about to strike Sarah. Then his extended arm lands gently on his sister's shoulder. 'But we have to look forward. Look at what we have. I have Joy and the girls. You have your career. Don't throw it all away.'

Sarah looks up, perhaps catching something in his tone. 'What do you mean?'

'Leonard says you've been asking awkward questions about the Cullen Report.'

'Not awkward, just pertinent.'

'It's not your job.'

Sarah rises. Now they are nose to nose, Alice sees they are both as strong as each other.

'Don't tell me what my job is.'

'It's all done and dusted.'

'No, Roland, it is not,' she barks back. She strides past him towards the restaurant.

Then Roland's whole persona appears to metamorphose. His hands clench, his shoulders become blocks, his face turns the colour of chopped liver. 'Don't do anything you may have cause to regret, Sarah,' he shouts with venom.

The words appear to roll off Sarah's back, but Alice feels the full force of them.

Chapter 40

A night without sleep. A throbbing head. It's as if Professor Jayasundera has given her permission to come undone. Rather than go to work, Donna goes to the GP. After an hour she has a slot. She merely meant to ask for the blood test the pathologist had recommended. However, once she starts to talk about 'it', how the changes in her body have stopped her in her tracks. In that small consulting room, the only external window narrow and grey, Donna heating up with every phrase, the words fall over themselves to be heard. Donna begins with the physical – the blood, the lack of temperature regulation, the aches, the tiredness, the memory lapses – moving onto the anxiety about making a fool of herself, of letting the blood leak. The embarrassment. The shoots in confidence in her abilities.

'I feel, I feel wrung out,' she says, tears threatening. 'Like an old dish-rag. I don't know myself any more.' She pauses. The doctor hands over a tissue and Donna wipes her eyes, blows her nose. She says, 'I know it's only a natural stage in a woman's life, but I . . .' *I can't go on,* she wants to say. She doesn't. She doesn't know this GP. Donna worries she has already said too much. She doesn't want health issues to scupper her probationary year.

The doctor waits a moment, perhaps to give Donna the

chance to say more. Donna suspects they have already gone over the regulation seven minutes (or whatever it is) for consultations. However, the GP appears unhurried as she sets out what they are going to do, which includes various tests and a referral to a consultant. The doctor conducts an examination and then takes blood for testing, saying the results should be in by Monday. She tells Donna to go home and rest, today and tomorrow, asking whether she needs a sick note.

Donna shakes her head. She has no intention of taking time off work, until she steps outside and walks to the Esplanade above the restless sea. She sits on a damp bench, looking down through the gardens. The low cloud clogs the stretched branches of the beech, birch and oak. Below the water is obsidian, cracked and fermenting. Waves jostle each other and are then forced together, var-umph into the sea wall, juddering the ground under Donna's feet. *I cannot get up, I will never get up,* she thinks. The desire to spend the coming hours curled up in bed suddenly overwhelms her.

She pulls out her phone. Harrie picks up. The thought of giving any kind of explanation to the younger woman is, all at once, impossible. *I was like you once,* Donna thinks. *Blithely unaware of how treacherous my body could be.* She asks to be put through to Theo. He listens as she explains she is unwell and, following advice from the GP, wants to take sick leave until Monday. Her voice wobbles ridiculously. Her DI gives his agreement quickly and succinctly, adding a request that they talk when she returns. She cuts the connection.

Her stomach contracts. How could she admit any of this to Theo? She leans over, wanting to weep. She might

261

have stayed frozen like that, except a young man in paint-splattered coveralls pauses on his way past and asks, 'Are you all right, love?' This galvanises Donna. She straightens. She says she is fine. She realises she is in no condition to walk home. She allows herself to call a taxi. Once returned to her little house on its little cul-de-sac at the back of the town, she showers and falls thankfully into bed, then mercifully to sleep.

The next day, Friday, slinks by. Donna moves from bed to sofa, bingeing on TV programmes charting people's lives through moves to other countries or from town to rural; through objects needing repairs; and through building projects. The weather is dull, making staying inside all the more tempting. However, mid-afternoon, she feels the need for some company. When she spots Rose in her own back garden, Donna goes out into hers for an over-the-fence chat.

The majority of Rose's garden is a jungle of wildflow-ers, milkweed and lavender. She hands over similar seeds to Donna, explaining the benefits to bees and butterflies. Donna promises to make representation to her landlady. As she did about Rose's idea to build a hedgehog run through all the gardens on the road. Rose has already got agreement from the other residents, and Donna can now add her own. Rose is a 'no time like the present' type of person, which means Donna finds herself helping with cutting through the fence she hoped to be leaning on and chatting over.

As she works, Rose is uncharacteristically loquacious. She asks for news about Donna's investigations into the kill-ings of Orson and of Sylvia, which she has heard reported in local media. Rose recalls the deaths of Philip and June Franklande. She even knows someone who knows somebody who knows someone who knows Miriam Toogood. 'She must be distraught,' Rose finishes.

Donna nods. It was other officers who visited Sylvia's best friend from childhood, and they said as much. Donna explains she cannot reveal any more than has been made public.

'Yes, should have thought of that, sorry. It's only that . . . well.' Rose straightens for a moment. 'It's been playing on my mind.' She shakes her head. 'It's not as if thousands and thousands of people aren't losing their lives all the time. Chemical plant explosions, water being diverted for industrial processing, fires in clothing factories. Oil spills. You'll have heard of the *Deepwater Horizon* disaster?'

Donna says vaguely, 'In the US?'

'Gulf of Mexico. Off Louisiana. April 2010. Mismanagement. Saved money but cost lives. Yes, you'll have heard of that one but what about 1989, Shell, Ogoniland, Nigeria? A series of oil spills and a massive explosion. People died. And people died in the resulting protests. We declared ourselves twins to the Ogoni Nine, protestors condemned to death. Didn't do 'em any good. They died for their beliefs. And, I'm asking myself, is that what happened to Orson?' She stops talking to put her energy into easing out the chunk of wood she has sawed. Once she has completed her task to her satisfaction, she straightens. She says gloomily: 'Orson said we old fogeys were being naive, we had lost our edge. He wanted to completely upend the system to tackle climate change. Problem is working out what to replace it with and where to start. It's all connected. Intensive farming, we lose our birds and our bees, and our capacity to grow nourishing food. We demand more and more and somewhere an elephant's habitat is being destroyed in order to feed the desires we are told we ought to have.' She takes a breath. 'It's the most disadvantaged who always suffer the most. The elephant'll be trampling the crop fields of some village which can least afford it. We could all agree that we have to consume less and have a more sustainable agriculture. But Orson said the way we were going about it was continually restacking deck chairs on the *Titanic*.' She sounds sorrowful.

Partly because she knows this sense of having let someone down, and partly because she is genuinely curious, Donna says: 'I thought the green movement is having some effect? Hasn't the UK got targets now, for carbon emissions?'

'Which merely means we'll export the polluting processes somewhere else – India or Africa where they can't turn down the finance,' says Rose. 'No, I don't often think it, but today I do: we, the human race, are fucked, and maybe it's no bad thing.'

Feeling like she's grasping at straws, Donna says: 'I heard something on the radio – there's new innovations coming through all the time. Isn't it what we're good at as humans?'

'Maybe,' says Rose. Perhaps silenced by her own thought processes, she is reverting to her more usual reticence. In a few words she finds out about Donna's trip to the GP and acknowledges it with a curt, 'Good.' Then she picks up her tools and the chunk of wood she has extracted saying, 'Must get on,' as she turns away.

It isn't the uplift Donna had been hoping for. She has

Christopher and Elizabeth. She is too invested to truly believe the human race is 'fucked'. She returns to the sofa and the TV. This time a police drama, something she would not normally watch, as they are frequently wildly divorced from her daily experiences. What suspect crumbles and confesses like that? Hardly any.

Donna wakes with more energy on Saturday morning. Whatever her state, she would have made the journey to see Elizabeth. However, it is a relief to enjoy the drive and arrive without the usual fatigue. It does flit through her mind that she sees her daughter more regularly than her husband. She had spent eight days with him over Christmas and New Year, only that is three weeks back. *Should I be missing him more?* she thinks. Then she bats back, *He could always come up here.* I'm going to suggest it – though he's shown no interest so far in a visit to Scarborough. *Why am I always running down to him?*

As she goes through the entry procedures, she has a vague sense this might be the day for her revelations. It has become clear to her that Elizabeth will be her first confidant. Despite everything, her daughter remains the best at truly listening to her. But Elizabeth is also accomplished at scuppering her mother's plans and sticking to her own when she needs to. Today she needs to talk about the coming parole board.

Elizabeth pleaded guilty to attacking the grown-up daughter of the man she was milking for drugs money. Elizabeth's lawyer had put forward mitigating circumstances: she was provoked and she was acting in self-defence.

Donna thought her daughter was lucky to have been sentenced to five years, cut to four and five months because of the time she spent on remand. She was moved to the more open HMP North Yorkshire a year ago, after spending fourteen months in a prison closer to her parents' home in Kenilworth. Her parole board has been set for three weeks' time. She deliberates over the various possible outcomes at length. It boils down to: immediate release – impossible; cut in sentence – impossible; day release – the slimmest of possibilities.

Donna can see Elizabeth is pinning more hopes on this than she is letting on. Jim is quick to catalogue their daughter's failings – she lies, she manipulates, she can be violent, she has no direction (oddly, perhaps the worst on her father's inventory). He does not recognise, as Donna does, their daughter's stoicism, her inner strength. She has taken her punishment with a kind of grace. She has got stuck into the hard, physical labour at the prison farm, out in all weathers, without a murmur. She has joined in with the Buddhist, and other, courses she has been offered. She rarely mentions 'getting out'. However, as Elizabeth scours away at the questions – mostly unanswerable – of whether and how she might be offered day release, Donna can see she really wants this. *She wants her freedom.* Donna is surprised she could ever have doubted it. Maybe it is she who doesn't want her daughter out. In prison, Elizabeth is protected, her health has improved no end, her friend, Iris, has a good heart.

Donna admonishes herself. She glances around the institutional functionality of the room they are in with its fetid air. *How could I not want her away from all this? How could I not want her somewhere pretty?* Not that Elizabeth's domiciles immediately before prison have been that. Nor entirely safe.

'You know I'll do whatever I can,' says Donna into a space left by her daughter. 'To assist you.'

Elizabeth nods. 'You moved all this way, didn't you, to be close to me?' She smiles broadly. The hour has zipped by and others are beginning to say their farewells. A guard comes over. Donna expects him to tell them to make tracks. Instead he hands over a paper bag to Elizabeth. She thanks him and he withdraws. 'I've got something for you, Mum. They had to check it for contraband and stuff. This is for you.' She pushes the bag towards her mother.

Donna peeks in. She is holding her breath. Her worry turns to delight when she sees a small earth-filled bowl, and from it several snowdrops lifting their heads, their delicate petals flaring like whirling skirts in the heat.

'I grew them myself, for you.'

'Oh, Elizabeth.' Donna breathes out the words. 'They are beautiful.'

'They are, aren't they? Harbingers of spring. And so resilient: frost, snow, nothing stops them from popping up again. They can be our mascots, Mum. You like them?'

Donna looks up into her daughter's beaming smile. 'Yes, very much.' She realises her vision has smeared and digs in her pockets for tissues to dab at her eyes. 'It reminds me of the Christmas you grew me a hyacinth in your wardrobe.' She watches as her daughter's grin presses together into a line. What has she said wrong now? 'What?'

'Oh, Mum, I nicked it off the kid next door.' Elizabeth

scrapes her chair back and walks away. 'Love you,' she says over her shoulder.

'Love you too,' says Donna, to the snowdrops.

The flowers sit on the passenger seat on the way home. Donna imagines what it would be like to have her daughter there instead. She notices how the anxiety returns. *I can't keep her safe,* she thinks, sadness creeping in. On the moors around her, the bracken has turned to rust, the grass to bog, the few trees huddle in close. Then, as she crests one of the inclines, the ruined Whitby Abbey appears on the horizon. Through its glassless windows is the backdrop of pewter sky, dripping into the flint sea. The abbey's Gothic arches stretch heavenward and, for the briefest of moments, are gilded by a sliding finger of light which then dissipates.

On the radio, someone is quoting Martin Luther King Jr talking about the 'appalling silence of the good people' when it comes to the fight against racism. It brings up the unwanted recollection of her and Theo's recent encounter with the Humberside traffic officers. As far as she knows, he has not made any complaint; certainly she has not been asked to make a statement. Discomfited, she switches the radio over to a music station and hums along to pop tunes from the 1980s. *What can I do, anyway? It's not my place.*

Chapter 41

The way to a creative person's heart is to praise her work. Either Sarah knows this, or she really does appreciate Alice's photographs. Sarah has persuaded Alice to let her come to the studio with the hook of possibly ordering some images for her house. *This is purely business,* Alice tells herself. If it ever was, it doesn't remain so. She is soon deep in conversation with Sarah about chemical reactions. Alice has been experimenting with anthotypes, using ingredients from nature to create photographic images. She has had variable results. Sarah not only takes her ideas seriously, but also has useful suggestions.

It doesn't take much to move from there to having a cup of tea to go with the (vegan) cakes Sarah has brought along. Alice brings mugs of a minty brew to the table where Sarah is again leafing through Alice's portfolio. She stops at a print, leaning in to study it. A light-brown strand of hair slips from its ponytail and lies across Sarah's cheek. The colour of alabaster, it is paler than Alice remembers. The skin under Sarah's blue eyes is puffy and stained a deep mauve. The quirk at the corner of her mouth tugs it flat.

Alice senses the drop in energy. She puts the tray down and peers over. The picture is one she took last spring at Spurn Point on a particularly bright day. A little gull is caught in flight, sun rays picking up the white tips of its wings forming almost a halo. It was one of those fortuitous camera clicks which can never be deliberately calculated. 'Sylvia,' says Alice, not censoring as the name comes to her.

'How did you know I was thinking of her?' Sarah goes on quickly without waiting for an answer. 'Miriam Toogood got in touch. I was so pleased she did. I didn't know her that well when we were young, she was just the kid my sister hung around with. But I realise now she was — her whole family was – really supportive of Sylvia. Especially when I left . . .' Her voice peters out.

Alice waits, sensing there is more.

Sarah hugs herself; her voice is strained: 'Miriam explained there was a kind of code in the . . . the note Sylvia left when she . . . .' She swallows. 'Sylvia put Gilbert Grape under her name because she thought Miriam would understand she was running away and intended on coming back. Only Miriam didn't pick up on it and grieved like the rest of us. When Sylvia contacted her a few years later she explained she had done it to spare Miriam the pain. It hadn't worked. It meant it wasn't always an easy relationship with Sylvia over the years. But Miriam was able to tell me about Sylvia's life. She had a happy one, by all accounts,' she says softly, letting a finger stroke the outline of the gull. 'I am so, so very glad. But then I think, why didn't Sylvia contact me? Why did she choose Miriam over me? And why, why did she come back to Scarborough last Sunday? I keep turning it all over in my head. If she had just told me!' She slaps the heel of her hand into the side of her head. 'I feel so guilty.'

'Why?' Alice wants to hold that slapping hand and kiss the harshness out of it.

Sarah takes a breath. Then she turns and walks to the windows overlooking the garden. 'Oh, you know, I was her older sister. Why didn't she want to talk to me? I should have done more. I should have kept her out of harm's way. Usual stuff.'

There's something in the tinny rushed tone which makes Alice wonder whether this is actually what Sarah had been on the point of sharing with her.

Sarah turns sharply, returns and picks up the mug of tea. 'Grief, they say, takes you in the weirdest ways.' She sits on one of the tall stools by the table. 'What about you, Alice – how are you doing? You are grieving Orson.'

Alice sips from her cup to delay speaking. The mention of Orson brings out the big fat elephant that has been standing restless in the corner all this while. ScarTek. The reason she can't, absolutely can't, won't, let herself fall for Sarah Franklande. 'I miss him, I miss him every day.'

'I miss Sylvia too,' says Sarah. Then adds gloomily: 'But then I think I don't even know who I am missing. I didn't know my own sister. She chose to stay away from me.'

This notion weighs in heavy between them.

'Perhaps,' says Alice tentatively, 'you know, she was always meaning to get in touch, but never quite—'

'Found the time?' The flesh at the top of Sarah's nose pinches.

Pain? Or crossness? It's not clear to Alice.

Sarah appears to shake herself. 'I'm talking too much about myself. I find it easy with you, Alice,' she says with a

271

faint smile. 'Have they, I mean do you know what . . . have the police told you any more about Orson and what happened to him?'

The question clangs into Alice's sternum. *What do you want to know that for?* It rubs out the intimacy which had been developing just minutes before. Yet Sarah is looking expectant. Caution and disenchantment mix in Alice's tone. 'Nothing, they're telling me nothing. It's almost as if they are avoiding me.' Which is true: she has left two messages for DC Donna Morris asking about the missing Ian and has had no calls back.

'But you must have some ideas? Something personal? Or something to do with his work?'

'I don't know who would want to kill my friend, if that's what you mean,' Alice snaps back.

Sarah drops her gaze. After a hesitation, she says more gently: 'I'm sorry, I was being clumsy. It's just, you know, if you want someone to talk all this through with, I'm here.'

'I don't.' *Not with you.*

After a pause, Sarah says, 'Should I go?'

The desolation in her voice nicks at Alice's heart. 'No,' she says quickly, realising the truth of it. She wants to recapture the last few minutes, shake them up so they tumble out in a different way. *Maybe she was trying to be empathic. Grief takes us all in different ways. Straight-forwardness is no bad thing.* When Sarah shyly brings the cake out of her bag, Alice is able to greet the peace offering with an impish smile.

Chapter 42

Monday morning, Donna is much restored. Even Brian coming across the CID room towards her doesn't dent her mood. And he appears to want to appease her. He invites her to come with him into a side room to watch a computer streaming of the interview with Tony Prichard. He came to the station at eight a.m., saying he wanted to make a statement. Harrie and Theo were called in, and the questioning has been going for about thirty minutes. The camera angle shows the backs of Donna's colleagues, both ramrods leaning slightly forward. Tony Prichard is not as stocky as his father, perhaps a smidge taller and he has all his hair. It is brown and sharply cut. As Donna watches, he glances upwards and she sees the family resemblance in the navy of his closed-off eyes. Tony Prichard is the furthest he can get from his side of the table without actually forcing his chair through the wall. His arms are crossed. Every ounce of him is resentment. Yet he presented himself willingly. She voices the contradiction to Brian.

'T'spect both his parents pressured him to come in. And he didn't expect the third degree. Looks like he's admitted to meeting with Orson on the fourth.'

They listen as Harrie continues to interrogate Tony's movements. He and Orson met at around eight p.m. Yes, it was pre-arranged. Just for a friendly chat. In the Bolts.

The Bolts. Donna reminds herself she has not tested out her theory about Doug and his telescope.

Despite Harrie's prodding, Tony is hazy about the conversation he had with Orson. Maybe it was about a second-hand car one of Orson's mates had to sell.

This, thinks Donna, *is the most unlikely untruth Tony could have chosen.*

As if agreeing with her unspoken thought, Brian says, 'Not the sharpest tack in the box.'

'What was your relationship with Mr Reed?' Harrie asks.

'What do you mean relationship?' retorts Tony. 'I knew him, that's all. We'd spoken a half dozen times, around and about. And he had a car he wanted shot of. Didn't sound like what I was after, as it happened. So we parted ways. I didn't have a relationship with Orson.' He hunches over. Donna can no longer see his face. 'What's folks been saying? It's crap, anyhow. Ask the barmaid at the snooker hall. That's where I went after. And I gave her a good time, if you know what I mean, the best time, till I had to leave for my ship. You ask her.'

'We will, Mr Prichard,' says Harrie. Her tone is flat.

Donna feels her disappointment. Tony was otherwise occupied when Orson was murdered; the relationship between the two of them becomes irrelevant. Harrie moves on to asking more generally what the younger Prichard knows about Orson Reed. Nothing much, it seems.

'That's that, then,' says Brian. He turns down the sound. Donna would like to have heard more. But Brian rotates in his seat to face her. He blocks out what is happening on the screen. 'I hear you've been digging around in the files to do with the deaths of Phil and June Franklande.'

'I was asked to, yes.'

'DI John Hoyle was my first boss here. He was a good bloke. I liked him. He closed the case. I don't suppose he would have done if there was anything outstanding.'

There's a severity in his features that compels Donna to placate him by saying she is sure everyone did a good job. Though she does not believe it. 'Professor Jayasundera says there have been developments in forensics which might turn up something new.'

'Like what, specifically?'

She shrugs.

'Come on, Donna, aren't we on the same side?' He taps his knee with a clenched fist.

The room suddenly feels cramped and airless. 'The prof is re-looking at everything from the evidence locker and at the original pathology report. As far as I know he hasn't come to his conclusions yet.'

'Waste of time,' Brian mutters.

'I think it's reasonable to consider whether Sylvia's death is connected to her parents'.' She really wants to get out of here now. Only Brian is between her and the door.

'Do you, indeed? Isn't it more reasonable to look at current circumstances than something which happened twenty years ago?'

'We're looking at everything, aren't we? Theo always likes to cover all angles.'

He gives a rather derisive grunt. He stands.

Because of his abrasiveness, Donna has decided not to ask him, only then she thinks she might not get another chance. 'How did you know about the report on Neal Williams?'

He stumbles slightly backwards and the chair crashes into the desk. 'What?'

'When Terry Prichard said Neal Williams had been beaten up, you immediately knew there had been no police report.'

'No I didn't,' he barks. This time both his fists clench. 'I said I didn't know of any. You're not looking into that as well?'

'Theo asked me to. I did add it to the case log. I have arranged to meet with Mr Williams tomorrow.'

'You can't trust a word he says. Not after all this time. I'm telling you, Donna, if you go on mithering 'bout Neal Williams, it'll be nobbut trouble for yessen.' The vernacular comes out as he becomes more agitated.

'What do you mean?'

'You'll look a fool. Not good for a probationer.' He pivots on his heels. 'Let it drop, Donna, forget about it,' he says forcefully as he slams out the room.

An hour later, Brian has regained equanimity when he, Donna and Harrie cram into their DI's office.

Theo and Harrie look weary after their encounter with Tony Prichard. It has taken one phone call to the barmaid at the snooker club to confirm his story. Orson Reed's death was no lovers' tiff – not with Tony, at least. Whether they were in fact lovers is no longer pertinent.

The initial discussion is about Sylvia. Theo reports her ID has been confirmed with DNA. Plus Gus has followed up on various matters. Mavis was at the film club. Other friends of Sylvia have gone more towards Mavis's narrative about Sylvia and Sebastian's relationship.

'Hound as controlling,' says Harrie.

'He smashed up Sylvia's pots,' says Donna. 'He tried to ration her contact with her friends. It's the classic abusive behaviour.' *A repeat of her father.*

And, as if to repeat what must have been said about June Franklande, Harrie says, 'Don't know why she stayed with him.' She sounds slightly cross, maybe about a youngster getting caught in the same-old snare.

Brian chips in, 'And how is Hound's alibi?' He is studiously not making eye contact with Donna and has ensured Harrie is sitting between them.

'Shaky,' says Theo. 'He was at his local as he said, but not all evening. Witness statements are vague. However, ANPR has him heading north on the A165 at around seven p.m.'

'On his way to Scarborough,' says Brian.

'Possibly. Her phone records show Sylvia did call him on the Sunday morning. DS Spinelli is speaking to Mr Hound today. Perhaps Ms Franklande's death will turn out to be straightforward. Unlike our Mr Reed's. If we tentatively discount a brawl following a chance meeting or a jilted lover we don't know about—'

'Should we be doing that too quickly?' asks Brian.

'You're right,' says Theo. 'Until we know what happened, we won't dismiss those possibilities entirely. But you would have thought after twenty-three days, we'd have had some intel along those lines. What other areas of interest are there?'

'Orson's environmental work'; 'ScarTek', say Harrie and Donna in unison.

'Why ScarTek? asks Brian, for the first time glancing over at Donna, his features tense.

'There's the Cullen Report and Orson's accusations over his tutor's suicide. He targeted Arch at the penthouse party.'

'Does the Cullen Report mention ScarTek? No,' says Brian, his tone forthright. 'Did Orson mention ScarTek to Humberside? No. Could shouting at a well-known local figure who happened to be at a party he gatecrashed be called targeting? No.'

Hearing what she knows interpreted this way under-mines her certainty. Donna closes her mouth. Maybe she has been unduly influenced by her distaste of Leonard Arch and her neighbour's rant.

'We do need something concrete,' says Theo peaceably. 'Donna, can you talk to Mr Reed's friend again, please? What was her name?'

'Alice Millson?' says Donna. 'But . . .'

'Yes?'

'DCI Sewell . . .'

'Don't you worry, I will deal with him. Now anything else?'

Donna brings up her question about the strip of photos found in Sylvia's hand and the date stamped on the back. 'The images certainly look like they could be of Sylvia and her sister when they were younger, yet in the police report Sarah said she was in Spain on the sixth of January 1994. Also the date of the parents' murder.'

Brian jumps in. 'You're saying Sarah was in Scarborough on the day her parents were killed and she lied about it?'

'I'm saying these photographs put a question mark around where she was on that day in January 1994 and she may not be telling the whole truth.' *Why did Sylvia fake her own suicide?* The puzzle keeps re-occurring to her. *What or who was she trying to get away from? Her parents' death? Her brother? Her sister? Or was it something else entirely?*

'A question mark?' Brian sounds exasperated. 'She's got to be the prime suspect now. At least for her parents' and her sister's deaths. Plus if Orson Reed did have dealings with ScarTek, then how much more probable is it that he spoke to the chief scientist on site rather than the owner who is here, there and everywhere? Sarah has no alibi for Saturday the fourth, either.' He sits back, sounding mildly triumphant. 'We've got to bring her in.'

'OK,' says Theo slowly. Then ignoring Brian's objections that he should be interviewing Sarah, Theo says firmly: 'Donna, you and I will talk to Ms Franklande, after you have spoken to Ms Millson. I want to clarify any connections with ScarTek first.'

Chapter 43

Alice isn't capable of dissembling. Not effectively. Donna could see that. But just because Alice believes every word she says, doesn't make it true.

Doug, on the other hand, has proved himself proficient at lying. On her way back from talking to Alice, Donna passes Doug's front door. She pauses, debating her rationale. It occurs to her that this is the first time she has done something on her own initiative, without Theo's express instructions. *Like Brian. And look how that turned out.* This thought stays her hand approaching the bell-push. She's mainly been telling herself that she might as well pop by as she is in the area. Now she admits the real reason for this detour is to postpone the 'little chat' her DI scheduled for when she returns to the station, to discuss her days off sick. Energy is coursing through her veins currently; she can hardly reconcile how she is feeling now with her collapse last week. Yes, she wants to put off talking about it all, even to the sympathetic Theo. She presses the bell. She waits. She is about to move on, when the door opens.

Doug Prichard is dishevelled, as if he's just been woken. He hesitates before letting Donna in, leading her through to the sitting room.

Then Doug leaves her for a while. 'You'll have to excuse

me, DC Morris, I wasn't expecting company. If you want a drink, help yourself – kitchen is through there.'

But Donna is drawn to the window. She focuses the telescope on the Bolts. Despite the drab day, they are relatively well illuminated, especially where the glow from rear entrances into the chippies and hostelries spill out.

When Doug returns, he's wrapped himself in a thick cardigan and his steps are less certain than Donna remembers. 'Chemo does dreadful things to yer digestion,' he mutters as he slumps into a chair.

'I heard you were in hospital,' says Donna. She stays standing by the window. 'I hope you are feeling better?'

Doug shrugs. 'Now, what do you want?' His voice is scratchy, querulous.

'I want you to tell me the truth.'

'I'm not aware I've been telling ye any lies,'

'Let's start at the beginning, shall we?' Donna makes herself comfortable against the windowsill. 'You tell me when I've got it wrong. On the fourth of January, you said you were at home around seven. Your sister-in-law and her daughter were here. Did you get bored and have a look through your telescope, seeing what boats were in, what were out? Then you catch sight of something going on in the Bolts, you focus in, you recognise your son, Tony, and his boyfriend, Orson Reed.'

Doug shifts uneasily in his seat.

'Didn't you like the idea of the two of them being together?'

Doug scowls. 'I told you I'm not feeling me best.'

Donna is less than convinced this is the reason for

281

Doug's discomfort. 'Were they having an argument? Did you hope they were? Maybe it meant they were breaking up? You didn't think any more about it until you realised it was Orson Reed, not Col, in the harbour. If you ever thought it was Col.' Donna waits for a reaction. There is none. 'Maybe you thought if the body was buried as Col Flither, it would make Pat happy and no one need know about your son and Orson.'

'There was nothing to know about Tony and Orson,' Doug growls.

'Still, you worried about the argument and whether it was the reason Orson Reed ended up stabbed in the harbour. Did you tell Tony to leave until things calmed down?'

'He'd already gone, offshore. And one of yorn came round and said the body was Col. It didn't seem significant.' Doug stops for a breath; his hands shake and he grasps one in the other.

He's really not well. Donna eases up. 'You still should have told us. Especially once we knew our deceased was Orson Reed.'

Doug slumps a bit more. 'Aye well, happen I should. My lass told me Tony'd had it with Orson. I don't know what the two of them got up to, I don't want to know, but none of us liked Orson's attitude. Thought he could tell us all about the sea, did he? Had he spent a night out there, in a boat smaller than this room here, the waves coming over the gunnels, wondering if you'd see home? Because that's what it's like for us. No, he hadn't. Orson wasn't one of us.' He pauses. 'Tony spent his last night ashore with that lass he'd known from school.' He licks his lips. He nods when Donna offers to get him some water, and drinks it with relief when it is brought to him. 'I wanted to speak to Tony first, get his side, afore everything got out of hand. I told him to come back, come back and explain 'isself and he did.'

'Eventually.'

'As soon as he was able.'

Donna sighs. It was this part of the story she'd come for. Now she has it. However, maybe there is more. The telescope has a fine view. 'You told us you went to bed at around ten. Is that correct?'

Doug takes a moment to respond. 'I don't sleep well, DC Morris. I'm up and down most nights. I watch for who's in and who's out the harbour.'

Donna waits, her breath held.

His gaze goes past her, through the window. The cloud wouldn't let him see 'fair down to Flamborough', but maybe he can imagine it. 'There was something lively going on at that new penthouse nonsense they've built. They reckon they'll coin it. I don't see it mesel.'

'What did you see, in detail?'

He shrugs. 'There were some fancy motors, that I can tell you. One pulled up, while I was watching, oh I dunno, bouts eleven, mebbe a bit later.'

The time Orson went out of CCTV range.

Donna leans forward. 'Type?'

'Of car? Dunno, lass. Ask me for a type of boat and I'll tell ye, but not car.'

'Number plate?'

'One of those personalised ones.' He blows out a breath. 'It'll come to me.'

But it doesn't, not immediately. They wait together in silence.

Finally, Donna says, 'How about the second of January?'

With a modicum of impatience, Doug says: 'Pass me that notebook from next to ye on the ledge. I keep a note of what I see of the harbour's comings and goings. It'll remind me.' Once in possession of it, he turns some pages. 'It was the night the harbour CCTV was vandalised.'

'Did you see anything?'

Doug slowly shakes his head.

'You'll tell me if anything, anything at all, comes to mind? Here's my card.' She places it next to the telescope.

Doug's head dips forwards. His fingers grip each other tighter.

Donna recognises pain. 'Should I call someone, to come and be with you?'

Doug glances up. His rheumy eyes are now more pale blue than navy, wreathed in wrinkles. He shakes his head. 'Thanks lass. I'll phone my daughter when you're gone.'

It's his signal that she should leave. As she is about to open the front door, Doug's shout reaches her. 'The number plate,' Doug says. 'Some kind of tree. Birch, no beech, no . . . larch.'

Chapter 44

I've got enough to bring you down, you bastard. It's what Orson said, hours before he died. *Was killed.* Alice runs this through her mind. *Isn't this enough proof?* Conjecture was what DC Morris had called it. Despite her external mumsiness, she has the capacity to be severe, Alice discovered when they spoke during a break in Alice's shift at a seafront café.

She is back in her flat. Flopped on her bed. Tired out by seven hours serving tables. And remaining polite when she didn't feel like it. *Moping,* Fareeha would have said. But Fareeha has gone and is too busy to speak properly on the phone. *So yes, maybe I am moping.*

How she would like to discuss her conversation with the police officer with Orson. *Which makes no sense, cos if I could talk to Orson, I wouldn't have been questioned by DC Donna Morris. Questioned? Yes it was more that than a chat.*

She rubs her forehead. Finds it hot and sweaty. Decides on a shower. While the water beats on her shoulders, she turns over what she divulged during the cross-examination. She talked about Orson's suspicions concerning ScarTek. Firstly that it was in cahoots with 21st Century Energy, Leonard Arch using his influence to get the licences in place for fracking to start. Then ScarTek would supply the chemicals. Secondly, Orson was sure Arch had put pressure on

Professor Cullen to change his report. She admitted having a copy of the unaltered version (thank goodness she had had the good sense to give Sarah a copy). She agreed to take it into the police station.

Alice turns off the shower and walks back into her bedroom-cum-everything wrapped in her fluffy towelling robe. DC Morris was not impressed that Alice had not come forward proactively with this information. But then she called it conjecture anyway. Orson could have his suspicions, but where was the proof he had spoken to Leonard Arch before the 4 January or ever contacted ScarTek?

I don't have any. Alice boils the kettle to fix herself some peppermint tea. She wonders if she could text Fareeha again, tell her she really needs to speak to her. She clutches her arms around her chest. The spaces left by her two friends feel raw and aching. *I suppose Fareeha is with her family.* Then this treacherous little notion twists into the wound: *If she has gone to Ian instead . . . if she is covering for him . . .* Alice cannot finish these sentences. DC Morris said there was no news on Ian Renshawe. *But surely the police can find anyone these days?*

Stop! None of this is making her feel any better. Doing something purposeful might. She finishes her drink, gets dressed and goes to her shelves. The Cullen Report is with all the other bits and pieces taken from the CARPE box files, including the mobile phone. She fingers it. Could anything on it negatively implicate her? Or Fareeha? Or Orson? On the other hand, just possibly Orson used it to contact ScarTek. Could there be something on it which proves a link? Could this clunky outmoded bit of kit incriminate Leonard Arch? She picks it up, weighs it in her hand. *Is it worth the risk?*

Chapter 45

Donna realises she has slowed down talking to Doug. *To the pace of the dying.* When she returns to the CID room, it feels as if she is caught up in a maelstrom. How satisfying the German word in the English language. Theo is talking to the IT forensic officer. From what Donna can gather, the young woman has unearthed a Gmail account for Orson containing an exchange with Sarah Franklande. Theo is questioning why it's taken so long to surface. The officer is explaining ways of encrypting and hiding accounts, making them hard to find.

Donna stops listening. She logs onto the DVLA, while checking her phone, which she has had on silent. There is a message from the surgery telling her to call immediately. She does so, as she continues to search for the LARCH personalised number plates. She might be perfecting doing two things at once; however, her brain doesn't keep up. It is only after the GP disconnects that her words crystallise into digestible lumps: 'You have severe anaemia'; 'You must come in and get a prescription for iron tablets'; 'I will put a priority on your appointment with the consultant.' Then the information comes up on her computer screen. Three cars registered with LARCH. LARCH 1 to Leonard Arch. LARCH 2 to Roland Franklande. LARCH 3 to Sarah

Franklande. All on high-end Audis. She thinks back to her and Harrie's interview with Leonard Arch. She cannot recall what he said about how he got to the party. She manages to bring this up on the log, while also phoning Doug. He confirms he can't remember any numerals, at the same time as she confirms Leonard Arch had said the mayor's wife had driven him from the country restaurant to the penthouse. Donna logs onto the ANPR and puts requests on all three LARCH cars, for the fourth and nineteenth of January, just to be sure. *Belt and braces*. It's another English expression she savours.

All of a sudden, Donna feels shattered. Her brain is fizzing, and the heat in her core is beginning to rise.

'Are you OK, Donna?' asks Theo, coming up.

She nods.

'Good, because I want Sarah Franklande brought in straight away. Not only has tech come up with an email exchange with Orson for an appointment on the fourth. But also, a review of Sylvia's emails has found she contacted Sarah at ScarTek, and they had an agreement to meet on the nineteenth. At the South Bay huts. Please ask two uniformed officers to go get our Ms Franklande. Then I want to see you in my office.' He strides off.

She steels herself, tells herself firmly this is not the moment to collapse and picks up the phone to despatch.

The summons to Theo's office turns out to be about what's to come, rather than the promised cosy chat about Donna's time off sick. She is relieved. Nor, when she has shared what she has learned, does she get a reprimand about going to see Doug without prior permission. Though she suspects it won't be forgotten.

Instead, they discuss tactics with Sarah. Which thread to pull at first? Which would loosen and disentangle the quickest? Reception calls up. A Ms Millson has dropped off a package. Once it has been brought up, Donna finds an explanatory note from Alice with a copy of the Cullen Report and a phone. She sends the latter off to tech and flicks through the former to the page Alice has marked. 'Here, here,' she says, excitement sparking. 'ScarTek as one of the possible polluters. I am sure I saw this at Sarah's.'

'This one or the official one?' asks Theo. He starts tapping at his computer.

'Can't be certain.'

He turns his screen towards her. 'This is what the official one looks like, the cover at least.'

'The one Sarah had on her kitchen table had the same outside as the one I'm holding. I'm sure of it.'

'We'll have to ask her about it, then. See what she says. Are we ready?'

'OK,' she says a tad tentatively. She badly needs to freshen up, take time to compose herself and, if she can, get up to the surgery.

'What?' Is there impatience in his tone?

'I need to eat.' Even to her it sounds as if she has just come off starvation rations. She worries whether she has been too vehement.

Theo chuckles and the tension is popped. 'You're right, we'll be working into the evening. Go. We'll reconvene in an hour.'

***

The hour is a lifesaver. Donna manages to use the showers in the basement of the police station, have a falafel wrap and smoothie from one of the local cafés, as well as pick up her prescription and take the first of her iron tablets. As afternoon tips into a dusk which smears the horizon with damson jam, she returns fortified.

Sarah has been brought into one of the interview rooms and is sitting waiting with a PC who has supplied her with coffee. The PC leaves when Donna and Theo enter. They sit across from Sarah at the table with its scarred top. Donna senses the other woman is sizing her up. *And why wouldn't she be? If I was in her situation, it's what I would be doing.*

Theo is explaining who everyone is, setting the tape going and saying Ms Franklande has agreed to come in to help with the investigations into the deaths of Orson Reed and Sylvia Franklande.

There's a slight hitching to the corner of Sarah's lopsided mouth and into her nose at the mention of her sister. Donna finds it difficult to interpret. Hurt, perhaps, or something else.

Theo is establishing that Ms Franklande does not want a solicitor with her.

'Do I need one?' The hitching is repeated. 'I wasn't aware I was under arrest.'

'You are not. Even so, you can have someone with you if you want. This has been explained to you, Ms Franklande?'

'Sarah. And yes, it was explained to me. Though I am not sure who you call in these circumstances.'

A good friend? A lover?

As Theo asks her about her movements on Saturday 4 January, there is a slight loosening of tension around her shoulders. She requests permission to look at her calendar on her phone. She says at the beginning of the afternoon for a few hours she had a meeting at the Art Gallery about the preview. In the morning she probably did some chores and shopped.

'And after the meeting, into the evening?' Theo prompts.

She shrugs. 'I went home. I ate. I read. Listened to some music. That kind of thing.'

'You didn't see anyone? Speak to anyone? Go on social media or your emails?'

She shakes her head. 'I don't like social media. And I always give myself a break from the computer at the weekend.'

'There is no one who can corroborate where you were during the evening and night of the fourth of January?'

'Should there be?' She sounds inquisitive, a bit cross.

'And you didn't drive to the harbour?' asks Donna.

She shakes her head. 'If I was going there, I wouldn't drive, I would walk.'

Theo continues, 'You told DC Morris, you do not know Orson Reed.'

Here is a slight hesitation. 'I think I said I know of him.'

'But you haven't met him or had any communication with him?'

Sarah shakes her head. Her hands grasp each other on the table top, one thumb picks at the skin of the other.

Theo pushes the printed-out copy of a series of emails towards her. 'Is this your email address?'

She looks, nods. At Theo's request, she reads on. Her

eyes widen. 'But I didn't send this nor receive anything from Orson Reed. How did you get these?'

'They were on one of Orson Reed's email accounts.'

She grasps the sheets and leafs through them slowly. 'He's accusing ScarTek of a cover-up over the Cullen Report and of being instrumental in Professor Cullen's death. This is outrageous.' She sounds outraged.

Theo continues evenly: 'Did you agree to meet Orson Reed on the night of the fourth of January, as indicated in those emails? Did you in fact meet with him?'

'No, no, I did not.' She throws the pages of emails at him. 'And I have never seen those before in my life.' She sounds haughty.

'Do you know what this is, Ms Franklande?' Donna pushes forward the copy of the Cullen Report.

Sarah takes a moment to glance over the cover, then says dully, 'I can read.'

'For the tape, would you agree that it is the report written by Professor Zavier Cullen on pollution in the seas around Scarborough?'

'Yes.' She sounds wary.

'And you had a copy of it on your kitchen table when I visited you with DS Harrie Shilling on the twentieth of January?'

'Yes.'

'A copy of this report?' Donna opens it at the requisite place. 'Which says quite clearly here that ScarTek is a possible polluter and recommends they take action or risk prosecution from the Environment Agency?'

Sarah doesn't respond.

'This particular paragraph didn't appear in the final report. Mr Reed suggested it was because of pressure put on Professor Cullen, who subsequently committed suicide.'

Sarah frowns. 'I wasn't in Scarborough working for ScarTek when this report was published.'

'But you were here when Mr Reed started to throw around accusations that your boss and the company you work for had been instrumental in having the report redacted and in Professor Cullen's death. Accusations like that, even if unfounded, can stick. Perhaps you met with Mr Reed to try and persuade him to temper his campaigns against ScarTek?'

'But I didn't get to see this version of the report until after he died.' She spits out the words. She dips her head. Scrapes at her top lip with her teeth.

'When did you first read it?'

'The weekend before you came to see me,' she mutters.

'Where did you get it from?' She's not sure if this is important. *But braces and belts.*

A pause. Then Sarah says quietly: 'Alice, Alice Millson sent it to me. We, we met . . . after Mr Reed sadly died. She told me about the draft report and I asked to see it.' She thrusts her chin in the air; her irises are an icy shade of blue. 'If ScarTek has made mistakes in the past in its environmental policies, I am determined to see we make the necessary corrections.'

'So to be clear, Ms Franklande,' says Theo, 'you were unaware of Mr Reed's campaign against ScarTek and of the unredacted Cullen Report before he died. And you did not arrange to meet him on the fourth of January this year?'

'That is correct, DI Akande,' she replies calmly. 'Now,

are we done? I am sorry Mr Reed was killed.' For a moment she does indeed look saddened. Then she finishes on a deep breath. 'But it has nothing to do with me. Are we finished?'

'If you could stay, Ms Franklande,' says Theo. 'We have some more questions to ask.'

'But I can leave if I want?' Sarah says, readying herself to stand.

'You can. However, I might have to arrest you.'

She slumps in her chair. 'I don't believe you,' she mutters.

'There's the door, Ms Franklande.'

Sarah doesn't move. After a moment, she straightens herself up. 'Can I at least have some water?'

Theo agrees and calls through for three cups to be brought in.

They sit in uneasy silence while this is done. Donna cannot make her mind up about Sarah. She knows she has lied to the police in the past; the photos found with Sylvia prove it. But is Sarah lying now? Donna is as eager as Sarah to drink the water when it arrives. Then she begins with rechecking what was covered when she and Harrie visited Sarah at her home, the evening after Sylvia's body was found. Sarah's responses, given dully and reluctantly, are no different. She has no alibi for Sunday the nineteenth of January. She last saw her sister in September 1993. She did not know Sylvia faked her suicide. 'Miriam Toogood told me she had a good life.' Her voice is soft. 'Sylvia was happy.'

For a moment, Donna is hooked by Sarah's demeanour. *She did love her sister.* Then she gathers herself. 'Until Miriam Toogood spoke to you, you did not know Sylvia was living in North Ferriby?'

Sarah sits back. 'I've said not. Are you saying I am lying?'

'Your brother Roland was paying the rent for Sylvia,' says Donna, keeping her tone unruffled.

This has the effect of a body blow on Sarah. She folds over, whispers no, that can't be.

'Are you saying I'm lying?' says Donna, realising as she does so, she's let Sarah's disdain get to her, when she should not have done.

Sarah smiles ruefully. 'I was hoping you might be. Well, DC Morris, if my brother knew where Sylvia was, he didn't tell me. That's the truth.'

The truth. An elastic concept, Donna muses. She has always thought of herself as a truthful person, knowing she is not. She watches Sarah for a moment as she finishes the water in her cup. Something appears to have occurred to the other woman and as she thinks more about it, the flimsy plastic collapses in her grip. She's paler than Donna remembers, her light brown hair pulled tightly into a messy ponytail. The skin is slack and shadowed under her eyes, and the twist in her mouth droops. 'Ms Franklande, January 1994, the evening your parents died, you told me, and you told officers at the time, you were in Granada, Spain.'

Sarah does not respond. She is staring down at her lap. Her body tenses.

'And yet we found these with Sylvia.' Donna puts the facsimile of the couplet of photos on the table.

Sarah slowly shifts her gaze to them. She reaches out with her fingers to the face of her sister and strokes it.

It's as if her movements are rusted, thinks Donna. *Rusted with pain.* 'Ms Franklande, this is your sister and you? The date on the back says the sixth of January 1994. You were in Scarborough on the sixth of January 1994?'

After a pause, Sarah nods. 'And you've caught me out in a lie, DC Morris. It doesn't mean I've been lying about everything else.'

It doesn't. However, Donna knows only too well how one lie leads to – necessitates, even – another. 'Tell me what happened in January 1994.'

'I, I came because she asked me to,' Sarah starts, and once she does begin, the story flows. Sylvia called her, upset. At first Sarah resisted her sister's requests. Sarah had finally got away from Scarborough, from her family; she wasn't going to be dragged into it all again. But in the end she came, of course she did, Sylvia needed her. Sarah had little money. She hitched a bit in Spain, then got a coach the rest of the way. It took her two days. As she speaks her features become weary, her shoulders stiff. She carries on: she got in at five-thirty in the morning on the sixth of January. She went to a beach hut owned by a neighbour who had shown the Franklande kids where to find the key. She slept for a while until Sylvia arrived. 'We spent the day together, just hanging out, doing daft things.' She indicates the photos.

'Where was the beach hut?' asks Donna.

'What?' Sarah seems caught in the cobweb of memory. 'South side, near the old lido. They're boarded up now.'

Where Sylvia's body was found.

If Sarah knows this clash of past and present, she does not show any evidence of it. Where Sylvia was found has been reported by the local media. Maybe Sarah has not felt able to keep herself informed. *Or has not needed to,* Donna reminds herself.

'Why was Sylvia upset?' asks Theo.

Sarah sighs. 'Afraid was Sylvia's middle name. We talked, it's all she wanted, needed – to talk to her big sister.'

'What about?'

'School, friends, Mum, Dad . . .' She stops. 'It was nothing specific. I imagine by now you've read the reports on file. Ours was not a happy family. But really, truly all Sylvia needed to do was talk.'

'To you,' says Theo.

'Yes, yes, to me. She'd always talked to me about everything.' Her shoulders sag. The edge of her mouth twitches.

Donna recognises the dynamic, the older sister who becomes the parent. *It can get too much sometimes. Had it got too much for Sarah?* 'How long did you stay?'

Sarah explains she took the afternoon coach, around three. 'I didn't even want to come back. I wasn't going to stay longer than I absolutely had to. Anyway, I had an offer of a job, in a bar, I had to get back to it . . . to my life, my own life. Sylvia had to sort her own out. She had to.' Donna asks for more detail about the return journey. Sarah says it was by coach and ferry to Paris and then hitchhiking. 'I was lucky with my lifts, I was in my hostel in Granada early morning of the eighth. Roland called me later in the day, I think. A Scarborough officer the following day.'

'And you didn't think to tell them about your visit?' asks Theo.

She shrugs. 'It didn't seem relevant. I thought it might

waste police time. I knew I hadn't done it and I didn't know anything about what had happened. Anyway, to be honest, I don't remember them being that bothered.' After a pause, she says more forcefully: 'I didn't know it was going to happen. I didn't know they were going to die. Do you think I would have left Sylvia to face it all if I had?' It sounds like a well-worn narrative, one Sarah has given herself to assuage guilt. She crosses her arms. She says more conversationally: 'You know, I came to this station once, in the early nineties. It was all new then, shiny.' She glances around the room. 'I tried to speak to someone about what was going on at home. They didn't even note it down.'

This thumps into Donna's chest. She is pretty sure it has done the same to Theo. It doesn't show on his face.

However, he says: 'I'm sorry, Ms Franklande. It would be different today, under my watch.'

She regards him for a moment. 'Maybe. Maybe if it had been different then, all of this could have been avoided.'

Donna wonders if 'all of this' encompasses Sylvia's, even Orson's, death.

Sarah says: 'Are we done? I am getting tired.'

Theo brings out the printouts from Sylvia's email account. 'You were in touch with your sister in the last few weeks,' he says.

'I was not,' she says. Then she leans forward to peruse what she is being shown. 'No,' she says emphatically. 'No, I did not receive this and I did not reply.'

'And you did not make the arrangement to meet Mr Reed?' says Theo, letting incredulity seep into his voice.

For a moment, Sarah is flustered. She rocks slightly in

her chair. She twists a scrap of hair at her temple, almost to the point of pulling it. She chews her lip. She says slowly, as if to herself, 'Both sets of exchanges were on my work email address.'

'What are you implying?' asks Donna. Intercepted or manufactured communications – it's what she knew as a child. *But here in the UK?*

Sarah looks up. She shrugs. 'I was thinking maybe they went to my spam. But then, who did the replies?' She straightens and says more forcefully: 'Because I certainly did not. I did not arrange to meet Orson Reed. I did not arrange to meet my sister.' Here she takes a breath. 'I did not kill either of them. Now ' – she swallows – 'can I go? Or are you going to arrest me?' There's that downward twitch of her mouth.

Donna glances over at Theo. *Are we?* she broadcasts wordlessly. *We've got the email exchange. We've got possible motive. Though why Sylvia? Unless she and Sarah know more about their parents' deaths than they have let on? But we've got nothing to put Sarah at either scene.*

Possibly a similar thought process is going on for her DI. Eventually he says: 'No we are not going to arrest you at this time. However, we would like to take a DNA swab.'

Sarah considers this request. 'Should I be taking advice before I give an answer?' When she gets nothing from Donna nor from Theo, she says with irritation: 'Whatever. I have nothing to hide.'

As Donna gets her swab kit ready, she thinks how this clangs with improbability. *Doesn't everyone have something to hide?*

Chapter 46

They land in a nondescript housing estate on the edge of Leeds. 'Why would you swap Scarborough for this?' asks Donna, knowing she'd happily been landlocked for all her life up to five months ago. And Scarborough would not have been her first choice. If it wasn't for Elizabeth.

However, PC Trev Trench humphs his agreement.

They had a good drive over. Donna asked Trev's opinion of DI Hoyle. 'He was Marmite,' said Trev. 'And he knew it. And he didn't care.'

'Which were you, Trev? A Marmite hater or lover?'

'I mostly put up with whatever is served on me toast.' He paused. 'I'll tell you something, there was some who were sad to see Hoyle gone and young Brian was one of them. He really believes he'd have had the promotion by now if Hoyle had stayed.'

'Is he right?'

'I doubt it, lass. Not these days. Too many checks and balances. Now, go back to the eighties and nineties, and our Chesters would have had a fair point. There was a lot more of "you scratch my back and I'll scratch yours" then. People – businessmen, crooks, and, yeah, some of our own amongst them – who wielded more influence than was good for them.'

Donna thought about Leonard Arch and DCI Sewell and asked herself how much had changed.

'Brian wasn't reet pleased I am coming with you today,' Trev continued more slowly, as if uncertain whether to reveal this.

'Yes, he told me to lay off Neal Williams.'

'And Roland Franklande. I heard him tell Harrie it should have been him who was going. She said the boss wanted another eye on proceedings.'

Donna could imagine that didn't go down very well. She appreciates the trust being placed in her and Trev. 'I'm glad it's you.'

Neal Williams lives on an upper floor reached by flights of external stairs and a gallery. All the flats appear well kept from the outside. Neal's is smartly appointed inside. He leads them into a living room which has a balcony overlooking a park. As she admires it, Donna admits to herself the view could make up for the lack of sea. Maybe.

Once he has served his guests refreshments, Neal sits on a stool which he has brought in from the kitchen, while Trev occupies the small couch and Donna the armchair. Neal is a slight man with the kind of freckly, pale skin which goes with his auburn colouring. From the bike in the hallway and the chit-chat, Donna has discovered that since moving away from Scarborough, Neal has taken up triathlons. 'I used to be a bit overweight, body conscious, you know?' he says. 'But then my therapist suggested exercise, said it might help with my anxiety. Started in the gym, until I found the running club. And now I love it. It helps. It helps me feel in control. You know?'

'You moved to Leeds last year, Mr Williams?' asks Donna.

He nods.

'Eighteen months after the assault?'

He nods more slowly. He clasps his hands together. 'I wasn't going to see you. But I spoke to Geof – that's my therapist – and we agreed it is time to speak about it. Formally, I mean.'

'Can you tell us what happened, Mr Williams?' Donna says gently. 'In your own time. In your own way.'

'I'll try. Only I don't remember much. Geof thinks maybe I was drugged. Rohypnol? He says the way I have lost whole stretches of time suggests it. Saturday March thirty-first 2012, I went to the Weighed Anchor about eight-thirty p.m. I was expecting to meet someone.' He pauses. 'I hooked up with him on Grindr. I thought that was the way you did it, back then. I was only just growing into my sexuality, you know? Bit of a late developer.' He gives a disparaging snigger.

Don't put yourself down, thinks Donna.

'Colossus, he said his name was.' Neal's mouth twists. 'Daft? Right?'

Donna isn't certain whether he means himself or his Grindr date.

'I was wanting an adventure,' he continues defensively. 'Anyway. Never turned up. And when I looked for his profile again, it had gone dark, offline.' He takes a breath. 'The Weighed Anchor was partying that night. I snuck myself away at a corner table – for one – and drank too much too quickly. I remember going to the loo and coming back and finding a full glass of vodka and orange on my table. I remember really clearly thinking, but didn't I finish my drink before I went to the loo? Then thinking, couldn't have done. No one would buy me a drink. I was feeling sorry for myself, you know? So I gulped it down. And then things got really weird. I mean I had been stowing them away, but I've never felt so dizzy, so disoriented on drink before. I stood up, thought I'd better get some air, and it was like the whole floor began to sway, everything was distorted, I couldn't focus properly. I must have staggered out. I know I knocked into plenty of people, spilled someone's pint. That's what I was told when I went back weeks after with Orson—'

Donna feels jolted: 'Orson? Orson Reed?'

Neal nods. 'I met him through Terry, Terry Prichard. Me and Terry go way back, school mates – at least, he was at school with my brother. Terry and Orson hadn't been there that night. Terry rang me up a few days after the . . . you know . . . attack. It was just a social call. Only when he heard how bad I was, he came round and I told him what had happened. Orson was with him. Terry wanted me to go to the police. Orson said there was no point. He said we should do our own investigation. I didn't want to do any of it. I just wanted to forget, you know? Anyway, there was no way I was officially reporting it. I couldn't remember enough.' He sounds distressed.

'Just tell us what you can remember, Mr Williams,' says Trev soothingly.

'Not much more than I've already said. I was out in the car park. It was dark. Raining, even. I'm stumbling about. Then this arm comes round me and I think it's someone

going to help me. I think I say, "Thanks, mate." Only it isn't.'
He takes a couple of deep breaths and closes his eyes. His
hands clasp at his elbows, locking his arms across his chest.
He says quickly and softly: 'I'm on the ground, face down,
my trousers are down and someone is on my back, banging
into me. You know?'

'Raping you?' asks Donna, her voice also low. Her chest
constricts.

He nods. 'Then I'm on my back and fists are coming into
my face like it's the rain punching me. Then nothing again.
And it must have been quite a bit later. I'm on my side and
there's this awful stink under my nose. I guess I'd thrown
up at some point. I manage to drag myself up. I get home
somehow. Into bed. I don't undress and I must have been
fully clothed again, cos that's how I wake up. I feel like shit.
I mean, I've had hangovers before, but this was something
else. And when I look in the mirror, well.' He stops and
swallows. 'I was a mess. Someone had laid into my face,
black eye, split lip, the lot.'

'Did you seek medical help?'

He shakes his head. 'I've been in the St John's Ambulance
since I was a teen. I patched myself up. Even so, Terry was
shocked when he saw me.'

There's a silence for a moment. Donna needs it to digest
what she has heard. This is not the first time she has taken
a rape testimony. Nor the first time she has listened to
someone talking about being given Rohypnol before being
assaulted. However, she is still appalled by it. She glances
over at Trev. His features are set, his mouth in a glum
line.

Neal opens his eyes and stands quickly. 'More tea?'

Both Donna and Trev decline. Neal says he will get himself some water. When he returns, glass in hand, he remains standing.

Donna bestirs herself. 'And you didn't see your attacker?'

'Attackers,' says Neal. 'I didn't see either of them. But they were different. The one with the fists was taller. I've tried and tried to bring something to mind which could help identify either of them. But I could pass them in the street without knowing. It's what made me leave Scarborough.' A shiver runs through him. 'But I'd . . .'

'Yes? Anything you can tell us, Mr Williams, would help.'

He takes a deep breath. 'The man who beat me up was shouting. "Poofter." "Bastard." Stuff like that. I'd recognise his voice. I think.'

It's not much, but maybe something.

Trev picks up the questioning: 'And did you ask around at the pub?'

He nods. 'With Orson. He said we could sort it without involving the police. Terry said that was stupid. But in the end, there was nothing to be done as no one came up with anything and I, well, I just didn't think I had enough. And who'd have believed it, any road? I mean, men don't get raped.' He gently shifts from foot to foot.

'Yes they do,' says Donna.

'We'd have believed you, son,' says Trev.

A ghost of a smile comes to Neal's lips. Then disappears. Fatigue takes over. 'There's nothing you can do, though, is there? Now, I mean. It's too late.'

'Not necessarily,' says Donna more robustly than she actually feels. 'We have your report and we will investigate.'

'Thank you,' says Neal softly.

'Could you give an estimate of when you think the assaults might have happened?'

Neal shrugs. 'I guess I was drinking for an hour and a half, two hours?' So maybe ten to ten-thirty? I got home before midnight. I remember seeing the clock.'

'I don't suppose you have any of the clothing or footwear you were wearing that night? Or the mobile you contacted Colossus on?'

He shakes his head. 'Threw them out. Orson helped me. Wanted to start again, everything new.' He glances around.

'Nice place,' says Trev.

'I was lucky,' says Neal. 'Mr Arch helped me out.'

'*What?*' Donna tries to control her tone and her expression.

'Yeah. I was really struggling after all this happened. My work was suffering. Mr Arch called me in to talk to me. I thought I was going to get a ticking off. But he was real sympathetic, you know? Asked me what was wrong. I couldn't tell him. Just said I wanted out of Scarborough. And he said he'd give me some severance. He didn't need to. I mean I was leaving the job. But he gave me six months' pay to tide me over.'

'Leonard Arch did? Wouldn't that be something HR would organise?'

Neal considers this. He shrugs. 'I guess because it's his company, you know, maybe he's more involved. Though I hadn't actually met him before – he didn't interview me for the post in the first place or anything.'

'But when he heard you were struggling, he called you in?'

'Yes. Nice man.'

It doesn't fit with Donna's impression of Arch. *But people are many sided,* she reminds herself.

'It was his accountant who sorted it out.' Neal pauses. 'What was his name? Frank . . . Mr Frank-something.'

'Franklande? Roland Franklande.'

'Yes, that's right.'

Arch and Sarah's brother paying Neal Williams off? What is going on here? It's as if sirens are going off in her head. Then she realises Neal has said something about maybe Orson being able to help them with the investigation as he'd done the asking around. And Trev explains gently that Orson Reed is dead. Neal is disbelieving, then upset. He says he didn't know, he'd cut off all ties with Scarborough.

Finally, he sits on the stool and says, sadly: 'Poor Orson. Accident was it?'

'No,' says Trev. 'I'm sorry to say, Mr Reed was murdered.'

'Murdered?' says Neal. 'Can't be. Orson knew how to take care of himself. He knew how to fight. Not like me.'

Chapter 47

They make the trip into the centre of Leeds in silence. Donna supposes Trev is as affected as she is by their meeting with Neal.

Finally he asks, 'Do you really think we can do anything after all this time?'

It feels strange – pleasing – that someone of Trev's experience should be asking her opinion. 'I'll do my damndest,' she says. There's a sharp twinge in her jaw as she releases the tension in it.

He nods. Maybe this is all he needed to hear. He is driving, so she sends a message to Theo explaining why Professor Jayasundera should do a further toxicology investigation on Orson Reed's bloods. This time for Rohypnol.

Roland Franklande's office is in a substantial Victorian building resplendent with carved curlicues, pillars and representations of industry, trade and empire – perhaps built for a wool merchant to boast of his burgeoning wealth. Inside the ceilings are high and windows are large. Franklande Accountancy has the middle floor. Donna and Trev are shown through reception to an open-plan area where mostly young people in suits are working at computers or speaking on phones. There are several glass enclosed offices around the edge. Roland's is down a carpeted corridor, behind solid walls and door. It has retained many of the features from the nineteenth century, including an impressive marble fireplace. Roland Franklande would not look out of place in a top hat, thinks Donna, as he greets them with firm handshakes. He is tall like Sarah, heavily built, with sparse mousy hair. Donna has now seen photos of Phil and June Franklande. The two older siblings take after their father, in appearance, at least. Sylvia was the spit of her mother.

Trev and Donna are offered seats drawn up to the expansive desk. Roland sits the other side. It is a workaday desk, with a double-monitor PC, several folders of paperwork, an A4 diary. Roland uses the intercom to order coffee. While he does so, Donna's gaze roams. She notices a framed photo on the mantelpiece. It is of a woman, perhaps in her thirties, with two pre-teen girls. There is greenery and a lake in the background. Roland's partner and her daughters, Donna assumes. They are all smiling gleefully.

Roland leans back into his leather executive chair. 'What can I do for you, DC Morris, PC Trench?'

Donna brings her focus back to him and summons up her energy. She will be glad of the coffee when it comes. 'Thank you for seeing us, Mr Franklande.'

'Always glad to help the police, but I've already gone through everything with . . . ah . . . your colleague.'

Not quite. 'Unfortunately, our work involves a fair amount of checking and rechecking, as I am sure yours does, Mr Franklande.'

He gives a curt nod. His outward appearance is relaxed. However, there is also an edginess in the air. Donna can sense it invading her guts.

'On the seventh of January 1994, your sister, Sylvia, found the bodies of your parents, Phil and June. They had been shot, most probably at some point during the last twelve hours. That was the pathologist's estimate and also Phil had been seen in the pub the previous evening. Where were you during the evening and night of the sixth of January 1994?'

'Here. In Leeds. At the time I was living in a house off Headingly Road.'

'With Leonard Arch?'

'Yes. I mean the house had been split up into various, what shall we say? Dwellings. It was all very Heath Robinson. And cheap. Leonard and I had a couple of rooms on the ground floor.'

Donna wonders if they could possibly find any other of the erstwhile occupants. And whether any of them could remember back to January 1994. She jots down a note. 'Have you kept in touch with anyone from that address?'

'Apart from Leonard?' He shakes his head. 'We were all students or passing through. It's being gentrified up there now; the house has been turned back into a family home.'

Donna strikes through her reminder. 'And Mr Arch was your only alibi for the night your parents were killed?'

'Do I need another one?'

There's a detachment to the way he is responding to her questions. Perhaps it's because the events are twenty years gone. Or maybe it's his way of coping. Whatever the reason, it continues as Donna questions him about the aftermath. She takes him slowly through every part of the story, and he does not veer from what he has said before. Finally she says, 'So the last time you saw Sylvia was when you put her on the train to Scarborough on the eighteenth of January 1994?'

'Yes.'

'Yet you were paying her rent for her in North Ferriby.'

Roland does not respond immediately. 'We did not meet. It was a purely business arrangement. An exchange of emails when she moved in and then a regular bank transfer.'

'You knew where Sylvia had been for the last four years and you did not see fit to tell us at your last interview?'

'You already knew where Sylvia had been living. Your colleague . . . What was his name?' He rubs his hands against his thighs and then brings them to grip the arms of his chair.

'DC Chesters.'

'Yes. He made it clear this was not at issue.'

Did he? 'When did you discover Sylvia was still alive?'

He glances up to the corner of the room, as if retrieving a memory. 'Four years ago. She came to me when she needed money. She emailed me here at work.'

'And you gave it to her? You weren't angry with her?' *Families can forgive even the most outrageous lies?* Donna wants this confirmed.

'How I felt,' Roland says carefully, 'is hardly relevant. Though, if you must know, it was Joy who persuaded me to do as Sylvia asked.' He glances at the photo on the mantel-piece. It is in the perfect position for it to be in his sightline often.

'So when was the last time you spoke to Sylvia?' Donna asks, putting the emphasis where it is needed to make her point.

'I told you: four years ago. Look, I was grateful Sylvia was alive, of course I was, and pleased she was safe and happy. But she made it clear she didn't want us to be' – he pauses – 'to be in proper contact. And who was I to argue with her?'

Her brother?

At that moment, Roland's secretary bustles in to leave a tray of coffees in china cups. As Donna takes her first satisfying sip, Trev asks, 'You didn't want to have more of a relationship with her? Pick up where you had left off?'

'I can't say we were particularly close as children. She hated living with me in Leeds. Can't blame her really, it was an awful dump when I think back to it. I'm not sure we had much to pick up. Anyway, she didn't want anything more. She was very specific about that. I wasn't even to know her exact address.'

'And did you tell your other sister, Sarah?'

Roland shakes his head, takes a gulp from his cup. 'Sylvia was most emphatic about that.'

'Mr Franklande.' Donna puts her cup and saucer down. 'Where were you on the night of the nineteenth and morning of the twentieth of January this year?'

'When Sylvia was killed?' He looks down and places his cup carefully back into its saucer on the desk. 'I was at home with Joy and the girls.'

'We will have to check.'

He nods and reels off a mobile phone number.

'How about the night of Saturday the fourth of January this year?' asks Trev.

Donna has the sense she and Trev are holding their

breath. The ANPR results have come back. Will they catch Roland Franklande in another lie?

'The same, at home. I don't go out much.' He gives a little supercilious smile.

Yes! Donna holds back her own smile.

Trev says, 'We have evidence of you being on the A64 heading towards Scarborough at eight fifty-seven that evening.'

'Ah?' He closes his eyes, then leans forwards onto the desk as he opens them again. 'Yes, you are correct. I realised I had to get some papers over to Leonard's. I went there, left them, and went home again.'

'You went to his flat in Whitby?'

'That is correct.'

'You did not go to Scarborough?'

His gaze goes to the photo. 'No.'

'Mr Arch wasn't at his flat – he was at a party in Scarborough.'

'I only left some documents for him to sign. I didn't need to speak to him.'

'And you went straight home?'

'Yes.'

The ANPR had not put LARCH 2 in Scarborough that evening. But there were back routes Roland could have taken from Whitby. LARCH 2 had been recorded returning on the A64 at seventeen minutes after midnight. Trev explains this latter point to Roland.

He puts his fingers to the bridge of his nose and says: 'You are right, PC Trench, my mistake. Leonard had left me some things which I read through, to, ah, see if I needed to take them back with me. Perhaps it got as late as that.'

'Spending your Saturday night working?' asks Donna.

'That's what he pays me for,' says Roland. 'And anyway, we're friends. Have been for years. We help each other out.' He stops suddenly, as if regretting this bit of chit-chat. 'DC Morris, PC Trench, I am sorry – I really do have a meeting coming up. Are we finished?'

'Not quite,' says Donna. 'Do you know Orson Reed?'

'I do not believe so.' He pauses, then adds: 'Wasn't he the unfortunate man who ended up drowning in Scarborough Harbour? Leonard did tell me.'

'You have never met him, spoken to him?'

He shakes his head. His hands go back to the arms on his chair. 'Did Mr Arch know him?'

'You should ask him.'

Donna waits.

Finally, Roland says: 'I do not know all his contacts or acquaintances. However, as far as I know, there was not an Orson Reed among them.' He stands up.

Before he can say more, Donna asks, 'How about Neal Williams?'

Roland shakes his head.

'He was an employee at ScarTek. You paid him severance pay on the instructions of Mr Arch, September 2013.'

'Sounds like something Leonard might have asked me to do.'

'Wouldn't it have gone through ScarTek's human resources?'

'We are the accountants for ScarTek. The payment may have seemed to come from us, but it would have been properly handled as a company disbursement.'

'You don't know why the payment was made?'

He shakes his head. 'You could ask to see ScarTek's books.' The look on his face seems to say, *Good luck with that!*

Donna takes a deep breath. She knows what the answer will be as she asks Roland Franklande for a DNA swab.

He strides to the door, pulling it open, as he answers: 'I don't think that would be appropriate at this time, DC Morris. We can, perhaps, discuss this further when I have taken legal advice. Make a further appointment through my secretary.' He turns full square to them. 'Now, I really must insist, you leave. I have things to get on with.' His expression is implacable.

Chapter 48

It's been a long drive. A long day. Donna tells Trev he can get off. She can tell he is eager to; he has his daughter and grandchild coming to stop the night. In the past, especially when she was a PC, she was careful to keep within her shift hours, unless there was a very strong reason not to. Jim and (some of the time) the kids were at home. Now there is no one waiting for her to cook or broker a tenuous peace. Her body is a tad weary; however, she's not in the mood to rest – her mind is too busy.

The CID office is deserted apart from the duty DS in his enclave and DS Gus Spinelli. *Well, well.* Donna smiles warmly. He is perched rather uncomfortably by her desk with a mug of coffee in hand. He motions to three evidence envelopes on her desk, explaining they are items from Sylvia's room he wants a second opinion on. Pleased he wants hers, she signs for them. He then tells her he has re-interviewed Sebastian Hound, who fessed up as soon as he realised he was seriously being considered for Sylvia's murder. He admitted the call from Sylvia had been to break things off and he had sought solace with one of his mistresses. She was a married woman, which was his explanation for keeping quiet about it. This time the hound's story checked out. The final bit of news Gus imparts is about the re-investigation into Professor Cullen's death. The suicide verdict remains intact.

All this could have been achieved via internal despatch and email. They both know it. So Donna asks teasingly, 'You come to inspect our manor?'

'DI Akande invited me.'

'And now he's abandoned you.' Over the years, Donna has realised the British do not always appreciate bluntness. She does not always get it right. She is wondering what this situation calls for.

However, Gus smiles. 'A call from on high. Your DCI on the blower.'

'Delayed gratification, then.' Donna is still feeling for the borderline.

'Ah well, a perennial for a police officer.'

They chuckle together. In her marriage, Donna has greeted being left hanging because of 'work' with greater equanimity than Jim has. This thought leads her to say, 'I suppose it might be easier when it's two police officers in a relationship, knowing the demands of the job.' She sees the startle in Gus's expression and realises she has made a misjudgement.

He says, 'I was meaning in investigations.'

Donna's neck and face grow hot. She begins to apologise.

'No need,' he interrupts. 'It's nice you know. Shows he's not hiding anything. Not that I am. It's only, the worst is . . .'

Donna holds her breath.

'Admitting I'm with a DI from North Yorkshire. The Humberside girls and boys won't like that.'

The release in tension allows them both to laugh more than they might have done. They don't notice Theo coming in until he is standing by them. *How much has he heard?* Donna practically snaps to attention. Gus goes back to his perch on her desk, his half-empty mug pulled to his chest.

Theo's smile is tight. 'Sorry to interrupt the festivities. Donna, would you come with me, please?' He turns to Gus. 'We'll be five minutes. You OK?'

Gus nods. 'No problem,' he says calmly. He takes out his phone. 'Got some emails to catch up on.'

Donna follows Theo to his office. Once they are seated he explains what the phone call from DCI Sewell was about.

Donna is stunned. 'You're kidding.'

Theo relaxes back. His expression is less taut, suggesting his edginess was because of the DCI's news, rather than because of her and Gus's conversation. 'I don't think "kidding" is the DCI's style, do you?'

'Ian Renshawe an undercover officer infiltrating environmental organisations?'

'I don't know what I'm most angry about – not being told he was on my patch or the fact that he went way beyond his brief.'

Donna knows which she is steaming about. 'Fareeha is pregnant. Who is going to tell her?'

'Not you nor I,' says Theo peaceably and yet firmly. 'Is that clear? I understand the DS—'

'Ian Renshawe isn't even his real name,' Donna realises crossly.

'He is being spoken to. There could be disciplinary action.'

After a moment, Donna says: 'Thank you for telling me. I don't suppose the DCI wanted you to.'

'He said it was on a need-to-know basis and left it up to me. I know I can trust you.'

This feels good. She nods. 'Why did he decide to tell you?'

'I can't say for certain,' says Theo, sounding like he's thinking it through as he speaks. 'Partly because I kept asking, partly, perhaps, because he knows I ought to have been told. And . . .' He hesitates, as if weighing up whether to go on.

Donna fills in for him. 'The traffic officers. You told him, and he doesn't want to go any further?'

'He's leaving it to me, but he's set out several reasons why I should hold off.'

'You don't think he'll support you?'

Theo puts his forearms on his desk, his hands caught together in a tight grasp. 'No, Donna, I don't.' He takes a deep breath, then stands. 'Home time for both of us, I believe.'

However, as she waves off her DI and Gus, Donna isn't quite ready to leave the investigations until tomorrow. An hour later she has updated the case logs from today, including opening a new one for Neal Williams. With the hound and Ian Renshawe out the way, the pool of persons of interest for the murders of Orson Reed and Sylvia Franklande is getting smaller. And they all seem to be snapping at each other's tails. Sarah and Roland Franklande. Brother and sister. Plus, somewhere in the murky shallows, Leonard Arch. *Where does he fit in?*

She looks in the evidence bags. Two contain notebooks, one a cassette tape. Gus admitted not tackling the latter. She calls tech forensics to find out if they have a cassette player. The young lad at the other end says he can probably dig one out. He also says he is working on the mobile Alice Millson brought in. It belonged to Neal Williams.

Neal's? It was found with Orson's stuff? Donna tells the lad the bare bones of what she has discovered today. She asks for a verbal report. He promises it by the morning.

Next she asks the duty DS whether there is anyone who can gather and survey some archived CCTV for her from the night of Neal's assault. It seems the 'best woman for the job' has just come on shift. She leaves her to it.

This done, she does think she can allow herself some down time. She is beginning to feel very tired. She returns to her house, has something to eat and goes to bed. She sleeps soundly for a few hours, and then is abruptly wide awake. She peers at the clock. It is four-thirteen in the morning. Even so, she knows she cannot wait. She suddenly feels, with a brightness and energy which are rare for her these days, she's up to clearing the weed from the pool.

The CID office has the atmosphere of the *Mary Celeste*. Abandoned coffee cups, computers gone to standby. Donna reckons she can almost hear the creaking of ghostly rigging. She is glad there's no one to ask her what she is doing there. She can get right down to it.

First, there is an email from Professor Hari Jayasundera asking her to call him 'asap'. She gathers she can do it straight away – he is on an early shift. He sounds wide awake when he picks up the phone and she thanks him for his advice about seeing her GP. 'Good, good,' he says unhurriedly as she tells him about the blood tests, the iron tablets and the referral to the consultant. She is grateful for his easy interest, but also doesn't want to waste his time. 'You've got something for me?'

'I have, DC Morris.'

'Donna.'

'And I'm Hari. Open the images attached to my email.'

Donna does as she is bid. She recognises the chef's knife used against Orson Reed. The others are of a bloodied footprint and of a shotgun. She guesses these latter two are from the evidence locker attached to the killing of Philip and June Franklande.

'You sent over a swab of DNA on Monday,' the professor says.

Sarah Franklande's. It will only have been labelled with a code. 'Did it match with the knife?'

'It did not. Not exactly.'

'It was a familial match?'

'Well done, Donna,' he says appreciatively. 'In all likelihood, a male sibling.'

Roland. Roland held the knife which killed Orson. Did he use it to kill Orson? 'Apart from our deceased's, his was the only DNA on the knife?'

'Yes. But remember the knife had been wiped clean. Others may have handled it. Now then, to my other little discovery.'

'You didn't get DNA off the shotgun?'

He chuckles. 'No. After twenty years it would be a stretch. However, what I did find caught in the breech bolt was a hair. Mousy, probably just above shoulder length.'

Sarah? 'This wasn't in the original forensics report.'

'No. It could have been missed by an examiner who was being rushed by an impatient DI.'

'Don't keep me in suspense, Hari.'

She can hear his smile as he says, 'It is the same familial match to the swab.'

Roland. 'What about the other photo?'

'The unattributed footprint by the back door of the Franklande's house. I only had the photo taken at the crime scene and the information from the report. The blood was apparently from the deceased. I can confirm the footprint is a size nine, possibly ten, or what we would now say is a size forty-two to forty-four.'

Donna tries to visualise Sarah's feet. Wouldn't she have noticed if they were anything above a five or a six? Roland's were indubitably bigger? 'I don't suppose there is anything to link the familial DNA match to Sylvia Franklande's death? Wasn't there something taken from the blanket?'

'You have a good memory, Donna. A fibre, perhaps from the boot of a car. No, unfortunately, I cannot make it a clean sweep. However, the test you asked me to do for Rohypnol in Mr Reed's bloods? Bingo.'

'He was given Rohypnol? How soon before his death?'

'Difficult to tell. It is fast-acting, it takes maybe fifteen minutes to have an effect. It stays around in a person's system for three to five days. Luckily we got to take the samples before they degraded.'

'It would have made him easy to overpower.'

'Indeed.'

The professor has no more to say, so she thanks him profusely and lets him go. She pulls over an A4 pad and begins to write. The act of forming the letters with her hand, rather than typing, brings a greater clarity. She starts with Roland Franklande. His hair in the breech bolt of the gun puts him at the killing of his parents. It doesn't have him pulling the trigger, but it's approaching it. And it catches him in another lie. Along with his purported alibi, Leonard Arch. And Sarah? Can they be certain she returned to Spain as she said she did?

Roland was on the A64 going towards Scarborough on the fourth of January, the night Orson Reed was killed. Plus Roland Franklande handled the knife used to stab their victim. Again, not proof he was the violent offender, but close enough?

Then there are the emails between Orson and Sarah, setting up the meeting. Did she lure him there for her brother to murder him? And, if so, what does this all have to do with ScarTek and fears over what Orson might reveal with the unedited Cullen Report? 'I've got enough to bring you down, you bastard,' were pretty much Orson's last recorded words, directed at Leonard Arch. He is safely ensconced in a party with a DCI as a witness. *Who will rid me of this troublesome priest?' Didn't some British king say this centuries ago? And his will was carried out by his soldiers? Sarah and Roland Franklande acting upon Leonard Arch's orders?*

Then there is the use of Rohypnol with both Neal Williams and Orson Reed. Coincidence? Or a link? She writes it to the right side of her paper. For the moment, she can't see where it connects.

The final piece of intel she has to add is the ANPR report for LARCH 1. It was clocked coming into Scarborough at around eight-thirty p.m. on the nineteenth of January, the night Sylvia Franklande was killed. 'We're friends. Have been for years. We help each other out.' Donna notes down what Roland had said. And yet it had been Sarah who had allegedly agreed to meet with her sister through emails. Was she again the lure?

However, something is niggling. The emails Sarah exchanged with Orson and with Sylvia were on her ScarTek account. And she claims never to have seen them. Is she lying? The WhatsApp messages sent to Fareeha and Alice ostensibly from Orson, though he had already been drowned five days. *Someone was already using IT to confuse,* she thinks. *And appears to know how we work.*

Donna is about to turn to Sylvia's notebooks, when she gets a phone call from Doug Prichard. He sounds remarkably chipper for the early hour; maybe he is used to them. In any case, he doesn't seem fazed to find Donna at work. He has recalled what he saw the night the CCTV camera on the harbour was broken.

'A young lad,' Doug says, sounding slightly breathless. 'Face covered by a hoodie. But I did see his shoes. He was wearing two-tone shoes. Does this help DC Morris?'

In a way, thinks Donna, her shoulders suddenly taking on the weight of an anchor. She manages to keep her tone steady as she wraps up the call. Then she puts her face in her hands. *Maybe it's not what it seems,* she tells herself. She could forgive him mindless vandalism at this point. Or another youngster in Scarborough has two-tone shoes. Then she recalls her own rumination: *Someone appears to know how we work.*

She needs a break. Outside she is glad of her woollen jacket, scarf and hat and of her sturdy boots. The air is frosty rather than damp. Not wanting to lose too much time, she hurries past B&Bs closed for the winter, taking the quickest route to a view over the sea. She reaches the (over-grandly) named Queen's Parade. To her right lumber the ruins of the castle keep wreathed in shadow. To her left is a turreted hotel. Here poet Wilfred Owen spent his last sojourn before being sent back to the front, only to be killed in the dying days of the First World War. He was a resident during January. He had looked over this seascape. There is no moon to light the waves below, rumbling like a battalion of gun carriages. For a moment, Donna imagines an army of the drowned in those midnight waters. If they raised their arms in appeals for assistance, she would not see them. Resolutely she dismisses the notion from her mind and retreats.

On the way back to the police station, Donna manages to find a café just opening up for the workers on early, or late, shifts. It furnishes her with an egg and bacon butty, deliciously salty and ketchupy. She demolishes it quickly. She had not realised she was so hungry. Back at her desk, she finds the CCTV officer with news. She shows her the footage from a street round the corner from the Weighed Anchor at ten forty-three p.m. on the night Neal Williams was assaulted. There's a high-end Audi. The number plate is clearly visible. The face of the person in the passenger seat less so. Donna might not have recognised the features if she hadn't known them. *'He seemed to crash, right after he failed his first sergeant exams and Theo got DI.'* Harrie's words come back to her. Donna adds the name to her notes in capitals with a spurt of anger.

She goes to find the tech forensics officer. He has found Colossus, the Grindr hook-up which had brought Neal to the Weighed Anchor. 'They don't use their own names,' says the lad helpfully.

Donna is on the edge of being sarcastic. She holds back. She needs this young man's skills.

He continues to do whatever he and the software he is using does. 'Interesting,' he says.

'What?' She tries to train her eyes to see what he is seeing in all the text and digits occupying the double screen in front of him.

'Colossus closes off his profile for a while. I can see Mr Williams trying to contact it up until summer 2012. Then he doesn't use Grindr again. In fact, nothing goes on with this phone after fourth of September last year—'

When Neal left Scarborough. 'Threw them out,' he'd said. 'Wanted to start again, everything new.'

'For about six weeks. And on the third of November, Mr Williams contacts Colossus, who has reactivated his account again.'

No, Neal didn't. He didn't have his phone. It takes a moment for Donna to marshal her thoughts. *Had Orson taken it upon himself to find out who Colossus was? And had he succeeded?* If so, his attack on Leonard Arch takes on a different meaning.

326

The officer suggests Donna contact the regional team dealing with sexual assault. Colossus may already be known to them. She nods. But she's already pretty sure she knows who raped Neal Williams and who had beaten him up. And the knowledge runs through her as if it were a blazing sabre.

Back at her desk, she puts a call in to Theo. He does not pick up. She leaves a message. She looks down at Leonard Arch's name speculatively added to the left of the page on her pad. Up until now, encouraged by Sewell, they've been thinking of Arch as more of a witness than a suspect. She realises they haven't done something basic – checked him on police databases. It brings up two things. He has a shotgun licence, which he first obtained in 1993. Plus, a report from Spanish police. Arch had been in Ibiza in 2001, and was one of a group of men questioned over the rape and sexual assault of a young woman. No charges were brought. However, the victim had been given Rohypnol. Donna circles the section she has right aligned in her notes and connects it to Arch's name with a large arrow. Plus she annotates with: 'access to shotgun in January 1994?'

Both her body and mind are fizzing. She still has to go through the notebooks and cassette (now she has a player from tech forensics.) The tape first. There are two voices, a young female and a male. The lass helpfully identifies them at the beginning: 'My name is Sylvia Franklande. I am going to interview my brother Roland, but he doesn't know it. I'm going to hide the microphone.' Her tone is fluty, slightly breathless. *Excited? Or afraid?* The quality of the recording deteriorates markedly, it becomes muffled and crackly. Donna can make out Roland's entrance into the room and him possibly slumping onto a chair. There are some exchanges about their days. Sylvia asks why her brother is so late coming in. He sounds pretty drunk and disinterested in his responses. The TV goes on in the background, making it even harder to hear. The tape has almost got to the end of its thirty minutes, when Sylvia says, 'Don't you ever think about them?' She sounds desperate. Maybe she realises time is running out.

'Who?' replies Roland

'Our parents, of course.'

Her brother either doesn't respond or perhaps makes a gesture. Donna can imagine a shrug of his large shoulders.

'Roland, I know what you did.' Sylvia's voice is tight.

'What are you talking about?'

'Mum and Dad. You did it, you shot them—'

'Don't be ridiculous.' His tone is suddenly louder.

'Your jacket was there when I . . . found . . . found them,' she finishes quickly. 'It was spattered with blood.'

Slight pause, then: 'So what? I left my jacket the last time I visited.'

'No, no you didn't, you didn't even take it off. I remember.'

'Well, I remember leaving it. And who is everyone going to believe?' Another pause, then: 'Aren't we better off without them? Eh, Sylv? You, me and Sarah, we're going to be all right.' His voice has softened, it's almost beseeching. It's also clearer on the tape. Perhaps he has turned towards her.

'You killed them!' Sylvia's shout is strangled in her throat.

'Oh, fuck off, will you? Leave me alone. Haven't you got any fucking homework to do?'

'But Roland—'

'I said fuck off out of here.' Roland's roar almost knocks Donna back. She can imagine the terrifying effect it has on the traumatised Sylvia. There're noises, maybe of the young woman running out of the room, then the TV sound goes up and, seconds later, the tape clicks off.

Donna takes a moment to absorb this exchange. *It's not enough. Is it? Does Sylvia have more?*

She turns to the notebooks. One pad is full of sketches. Although she can appreciate the young woman's talent for capturing an emotion or a gesture with quick, free-flowing strokes, she can't extract anything useful to their investigation.

The other pad is full of words. Donna can identify the formation of ideas for ceramics, alongside quotations from artists and notes on technique. There are dislocated sentences which don't appear to mean much – except, she supposes, to the author. Then from the centre of the note-book, Donna finds herself caught up by a story. She realises it is a retelling of Hansel and Gretel. Only Gretel is happily living in the woods with the witch – a too-good witch, her husband and daughter. However, Hansel arrives and forces Gretel to come home with him where he has not only baked their mother in the oven, but has also carved up their father. It is quite graphic and Donna feels slightly sick, thinking about how Sylvia had seen too much too young. Donna finds another version of the ending where Gretel's guardian angel is with Hansel, her wings dipped in blood. Finally, a few pages on, a continuation: Gretel runs away, having tricked Hansel into thinking he has killed her. The handwriting is stronger here, more purposeful. It describes Gretel arriving at an everlasting orchard and being welcomed by friendly sprites. Sylvia writing her own happy ending.

Donna sits back. *And she found it for herself. Until she got back in touch with Hansel and – what? – blackmailed him for her rent? Or was it her email to her guardian angel which put her in real danger?*

A phone call from Theo breaks into her thoughts. She tells him about who she saw on CCTV sitting in Leonard Arch's car. There's a long silence. Then Theo says: 'I'm coming in. Call Harrie.'

Chapter 49

'I can't believe it.' Harrie sounds waspish. Maybe it is the early hour. Perhaps it is the brief headline Donna had hurriedly delivered over the phone. 'Are you sure it was him, Donna?'

The force of Harrie's desire that she be wrong gives Donna a shudder of doubt. Should she have rechecked before bringing them all in? 'Yes,' she says with some uncertainty.

'He wouldn't go that far. He's been angry, yes, but jeopardise the investigation? Jeopardise' – she pauses to swallow – 'us? There must be some other explanation.'

'There may be any number of explanations.' Theo emphasises the last word. 'Let's stick with what we know.' They are gathered in his office, the four of them, including Gus. Everyone is studiously avoiding commenting on him being there. Theo is standing apart from him, his arms crossed. 'Go on, Donna.'

She can hear the simmering anger in her DI's voice. She knows it isn't directed at her; however, she still has to take a moment to settle herself. *Don't shoot the messenger,* she silently transmits as she begins: 'March thirty-first 2012, ten-o-nine p.m., DC Brian Chesters approaches the Weighed Anchor, apparently very drunk. Ten forty-three p.m. he leaves the area in Leonard Arch's car. In between these two times Neal

Williams is raped and beaten up by two different men after probably ingesting Rohypnol from a spiked drink. Leonard Arch was investigated by the Spanish police for a rape involving Rohypnol in Ibiza in 2001. Doug Prichard identified DC Chesters as the person who vandalised the CCTV camera on the harbour a week before Orson Reed was killed. Mr Reed was given Rohypnol the night he died. Unless, Sarah has another male close relative, we have Roland Franklande's probable DNA on the knife, which also has Orson's blood on it. Also probably Roland's hair caught on the shotgun that killed his parents. Leonard Arch had a shotgun licence at the time. There's the tape which suggests Sylvia suspected her brother of their parents' murder. And Arch is in Scarborough the night Sylvia is murdered.' She doesn't mention Sylvia's story. It doesn't seem to conform with Theo's injunction to concentrate on what they know. It would hardly stand up in court. Would any of it? She finds she has run out of oxygen. She takes in and lets out a long breath.

'And where is Sarah Franklande in all this?' snaps Harrie.

'We can't be certain she was in Spain when her parents died. Plus there're still the emails from her to both Orson and Sylvia.'

'She's the bait?'

'Possibly.' After all, she outlines what she has read in Sylvia's notebooks.

'A fairy tale?' says Harrie, clearly not impressed.

'If Sarah is the guardian angel, then her wings are bloody too.'

'That's a pretty big if. And it could mean anything. As a child, Sylvia saw a lot of violence.'

'Roland Franklande. Sarah Franklande. Leonard Arch. And . . .' Theo's features appear to harden. He spits out through gritted teeth: 'DC Brian Chesters. All four of them are in the frame. We'll need to talk to all of them. However, with the DNA evidence from the professor, we've got enough to actually arrest Mr Franklande. We can then search his house, car and get a look at his digital trail, which should be interesting. I'll talk to our colleagues in Leeds about detaining him. And speak to the DCI about a warrant to access ScarTek's server. We need to know where those emails purportedly to Sarah came from. Donna, get onto the sexual offences team about Colossus. Harrie . . .' The doling out of tasks had lightened his tone, but now the grimness returns. 'Get Brian in here.' He looks around. 'Anything else?'

'Alice Millson.' The name lurched into Donna's mind as they were discussing whether Sarah was in on the murders or not.

'What about her?'

'She gave Sarah the unedited Cullen Report. She was a confidant for Orson.'

'You think she might be in danger? Check on her.'

They all begin to move and disperse. 'I'll get the coffees in then, shall I?' says Gus, with good humour.

Alice is slightly earlier than expected. She woke abruptly, pulled out of an erotic dream in which she and Sarah were together in a universe where their differences did not exist and the days were literally sun drenched. In the real world, dawn is raising its indolent head and there are clouds overhead. Those on the horizon are stacked nimbus, thick as bracket mushrooms. Sarah is standing outside her house. Her stance is rigid. She is talking into her phone: 'OK, Roland, I will catch you later.' Then she sees Alice and snaps shut her mobile. She hardly bothers with a greeting as she hustles them both into the car.

'Your brother?' asks Alice as Sarah negotiates the traffic within the environs of the town, before picking up speed on the road south.

Sarah shrugs. 'He wants to meet up today. I told him I was busy. He thinks the world revolves around him.' She sounds irritated.

Nevertheless, Alice has several more goes at establishing a conversation which result in her merely asking questions to which Sarah gives short answers. After a while, Alice gives up. She stares out of the car window at the wind turbines stranded in the saturated fields and glumly wonders why she has come. She thought she and Sarah had made a connection on Saturday. Even so, it took some persuasion by email and text on Sarah's part to get her to agree to this trip to Spurn Point. A day out for the both of them. Sarah said she wanted to go, to remember Sylvia in a place she loved. Sarah also said she wanted specifically to go with Alice. And Alice could take some photos. Alice found it impossible to rebuff such urging. *Too late now to change your mind,* she tells herself, settling herself into the comfort of the warmed leather seat. Her phone pings. It's a voice message. She listens to it. It is DC Morris, asking her to call.

'Who's that?' asks Sarah, her tone and posture taut.

What's wrong with her? 'It's nothing important.'

There's quiet between them again. Then Sarah suggests

Alice finds some music, and, after much fiddling, she chooses some Capercaillie.

'Nice,' says Sarah. After a pause, she says, 'I'm sorry.'

'For what?'

'For being, mmm . . . what did Sylvia used to say? For getting my knickers in a right twist.' She flattens the vowel in 'right' and Alice can hear her as a teenaged Scarborian. Alice smiles to herself. Sarah continues: 'It's just that I'm worried about the tides. I looked it up: after the storms at the end of last year, Spurn gets cut off with a high winter tide.'

'We'll do something else,' says Alice easily. 'Would that be so terrible? We can still enjoy ourselves.'

Sarah takes a moment to consider this. Then she says quietly, 'Yes, you're right, we can make it up as we go along.' She says it as if it is a novel notion. Then she laughs. 'Why not? I think Sylvia would approve.'

They are once again driving south through the flatlands – monochrome except where a strand of light filters through and glitters on the puddles or bounces off the scything blades of the wind turbines. Theo is driving with Harrie up front, Donna and Gus share the back seat. Brian cannot be found. Roland's partner told the Leeds officers that Roland is on his way to North Ferriby, to 'sort things out' with Mavis Lewis. The choice of words do not inspire trust. The possible risk to another vulnerable young woman and with an arrest warrant in hand, Theo decided he wants Roland Franklande detained as soon as possible. With DCI Sewell's blessing, they are on their way into Humberside jurisdiction.

Donna sits back and watches the countryside roll by. She takes a sip of water. What they are driving towards remains uncertain. She eases the slight jitter in her stomach with the thought that she can rely on Theo, Harrie and Gus. *And they can rely on me,* she thinks. *Today.* It's this team aspect of police work which drew her into the profession and has helped her to stay.

Nobody is saying much as the tarmac unloops beneath them mile after mile. The louring sky gobs several times on the windscreen. Gus's phone chirrups. He has intel from his colleagues and an ANPR check. Roland has bypassed North Ferriby. He's on his way to Spurn Point.

Donna asks what everyone must be thinking. 'What's taking him there?'

'Just a minor bit of precipitation,' says Sarah as she pulls into the car park at the visitor centre. 'As my aunty used to say.' She peers through the windscreen with its wipers going at double speed. 'Shall we get some refreshments first?'

Alice chuckles as she agrees. Sarah is wearing jeans and a tangerine-coloured pullover today. Even so, she hardly looks kitted out for the weather. 'There's no bad weather,' she says, as they scurry along the path. 'Just the wrong clothing.'

'I think my aunty said that too,' says Sarah. 'I've got boots and waterproofs in the car. Don't you worry. I've tackled the High Sierras, I'll have you know.'

The atmosphere between the two of them has eased. Sarah treats them to teacakes and coffee and they spend some time exploring the exhibits, both as keen as each other to absorb the facts about the area and the wildlife. Finally, they agree they want to take a look at it for real and head on outside. Sarah does have all the gear, though it's not as grubby nor as battered as Alice's. *Meaning*, thinks Alice, *she can't have used it much or is better than me at caring for her clothes.*

As they walk past the barrier towards Spurn Head, they hear a vehicle draw up into the car park. They don't look back. They follow the roadway between tall dunes. They are a shield against the elements. Leaving them, the full force of the wind suddenly hits Alice, along with the bellow of the sea. She halts. Before her is the slender strip of beach left by last December's storms. It is all that attaches the rest of the peninsula to the mainland. Gritty mini-typhoons spin across the flattened marram grass. A black-headed gull is suspended in mid-air as if on a wire. It is screeching. For a few seconds, Alice doubts the wisdom of going on. Yet when Sarah asks whether she wants to turn around, Alice shakes her head. They link arms and forge onwards. Their gasps become shouts, as if their lungs and vocal chords are released to finally express themselves within the natural cacophony around them. It feels so good, and they are both laughing boisterously as they reach the other side.

Here, once again, dunes give them some protection. Sarah saunters along the track, while Alice pauses to snap close-ups of a twisted and rusted remnant of what could have been a boat trailer. Then she becomes fascinated by the patterns whipped into the sand. She hunkers down in the dunes to get the best shots, noticing the light meter calling for a higher and higher aperture. She is vaguely aware of a large motor vehicle passing behind her. When she straightens and regains the tarmac, however, there is no one around. There is just the keening of the wind, the darkening sky and the taste of the salt. *Where's Sarah?* In a fraction of a minute she is both scared for herself – has she been abandoned? – and for Sarah. Has she come unstuck somewhere? She calls out Sarah's name. There is no response beyond the wind and a gull's cry.

She walks on, nervousness and her pace shortening her breath and quickening the beat of her heart. Around a corner and before her is an impossibility: standing in front of the dark bulk of a parked Land Rover are Sarah and Roland. *Have I been set up?* Alice remembers the phone call earlier – *'Catch you later.'* She feels trapped, as if in a spider's web. She doesn't know whether to go forwards or scarper. She stays put. The wind carries the shouted exchange between the siblings.

'What do you mean you were in Scarborough?' Roland is saying.

'Sylv begged me to come. She was afraid. Afraid of you. What you might do.' Sarah matches her brother in height. She tilts in. 'What *did* you do, Roland?' There's something of the taunting teenager in her tone.

'What did you? Apart from lie to the police?'

'You're the liar, paying Sylvia's rent all these years. Why didn't you tell me?'

'She didn't want me to. She didn't want to hear from you.'

This seems to knock Sarah. She takes a pace back. 'You turned her against me. What did you tell her? That I didn't want to see her?' She re-gathers herself. 'Every day, every day, I look in the mirror.' What she is saying rises and falls with the bluster. 'I see him. I wonder if I have inherited more than his height. His colouring. Do you, Roland? He was a brute. Maybe he deserved to die. But why Mum?'

'You always stood up for her; she never did for us. Pathetic.' Roland grabs Sarah's arm. Pulls her roughly. They are almost nose to nose.

'She was fucking petrified all the time,' Sarah screams. Then it is something about a gun, where did he get the gun? 'From Leonard's swanky gun club? The police didn't even check, they didn't care. And Sylvia, what did you do to Sylvia, Roland? She came to Scarborough the other day looking for me, didn't she? Why couldn't you let her talk to me? Did she always know, or suspect, what you'd done? Rent money was silence money?'

Roland throws his fist which catches Sarah on the side of her face. She would have fallen if her brother hadn't been holding her.

Already rising, panic sets in. Alice turns, pulls her phone out of her pocket, punches 'return call'. Then her mobile is pulled from her fingers. She shrieks. The phone is dashed to the ground and smashed under the heel of one finely crafted two-tone brogue.

When they enter the car park, they clock the cars of both Sarah and Roland Franklande. In the visitor centre, the staff tell them Sarah has been in with a young woman who sounds awfully like Alice Millson. They are described as a couple enjoying themselves. They were last seen exiting the centre saying they were going to walk towards Spurn Head.

The four police officers, the only occupants of the café, discuss the situation. Donna is asked whether she knew about a relationship between Sarah and Alice. She shakes her head. It throws up so many possibilities, her mind is spinning. She tries to articulate some of them. Sarah and Alice together involved in Orson's murder? Alice somehow and for some reason throwing suspicion on Sarah? Sarah a danger to Alice? Or the other way round? Could their presence here be a coincidence? And what of Roland Franklande's car?

As this is being mulled over, a wiry man in his mid-forties comes in with his dog. He accepts a large mug of coffee from the woman behind the counter who obviously knows him well. He then grumbles to her about the folly of someone driving onto Spurn in the weather they are having. This attracts Theo's attention. Introductions are made. The dog is Bristle. The man is Eric Stable, a centre volunteer as well as a police community support officer. He says: 'It was one of yours, as it happens. A police Land Rover from North Yorks. Driving like the clappers.'

Brian? No one says it, but Donna reckons the others are thinking it too.

Theo tells Gus to sort some backup. He then talks to Eric about getting onto Spurn. Eric says it would be foolish: the tide is coming in and it's high. They would only get stuck.

Donna's phone sounds. She answers it. There's what sounds like moaning, followed by the throat wrenching scream of the terrified – a gap filled with static – followed by an impact, before the connection goes dead. She looks at her screen. It shows Alice's number.

Now there is little further discussion. Eric brings round

340

the centre's vehicle, the sort of four-wheel-drive off-roader with large tyres and an exhaust pipe winding up to the roof. It lurches and wallows across the uneven ground. Donna holds tight to the strap by her side. They pass across what Eric terms the 'wash-over', the narrow neck left by the December storm. A wave slaps hard against the vehicle window. It's as if they are unmoored.

The man has more strength than Alice anticipates. He is able to twist her arm behind her back and half-drag, half-carry her to the other two. Roland is standing with hands on hips, his portly abdomen heaving for breath. Sarah is leaning over, recovering from being struck. She sees Alice and whispers her name, along with 'sorry'.

'Who's this?' says the man holding Alice. 'Alice? Not Alice Millson? Fuck!'

How does he know my name? she thinks crossly, even as her collar bone and elbow joint are beginning to burn.

The man continues: 'This is crazy, man. This wasn't the deal. Getting rid of two of them, it's just not viable.'

Rid of?

'No, no, no, you're on your own.'

Roland turns, his skin the colour of boiled lobster. 'Don't you think of backing out – you're in too deep. I go down, you go down. Understand?'

'You don't know the DI, he won't let it go till he gets it figured. Fuck.' The man is practically moaning. 'This is too much. You don't know him, man.'

'Then we'd better make it look fucking good, hadn't we?' Roland's voice is controlled now, down an octave. His gaze is on the man holding Alice. Too late, he realises his sister has regained some of her own puff. As he turns to take hold of her once again, she straightens and flies at Alice's jailer. He almost topples. His grip loosens. Alice runs.

With the rapidly diminishing causeway behind them, Eric pulls over. He and Theo deliberate. Without more details on who is where doing what, staying in the vehicle is safer for the officers but could be more dangerous for those they are searching for. The backup is on its way. But they can't wait for it. And it may not be able to pass through the breached causeway.

There is a debate about whether their quarry is armed. As Harrie points out, it's possible Roland Franklande has used a shotgun and a knife. On the other hand, there could be one, perhaps two, people in danger of their lives. They can't just sit there. They all have their stab-proof vests hastily snatched from the cars and put on under their waterproofs.

'We go cautiously,' says Theo finally. 'We follow Eric and do everything he says; he knows the ground the best. And no heroics.'

Eric parks the jeep across the roadway, in case any of their quarry tries to get away, though, by now, they'd be stopped by the tide submerging the neck of the land. He leads them carefully down the tarmac. He is keeping his attention forwards. Donna and Gus are to focus to the left, the other two keep a watch on the right. The sand mounds slither and drift, as if they are alive. In a dip, Donna sees the white ridges on the charcoal waves, foothills to the cloud mountains at the rim. Pulses of rain are pitched from the sullen clouds and are scooped up into curtains of lead rods.

Under the corset of her jacket, her core is primed, tight as a fuse twisted onto a firework. Trepidation mixes with excitement. She watches for anything out of place, any incongruous movement, certain that each of her colleagues has got the others' backs.

Grit and gravel scatter as Alice runs. She hits sand. It gives way at every step. She has the impression she is going nowhere. Despite this, she keeps moving her legs, one foot pushed in front of the other, then another step, and another. Her pulmonary pumping thumps against her ribcage. Air comes in as ragged breaths. Icy droplets scrape against her cheeks. *Are they coming?* She dares not stop to listen or glance back. Sweat trickles from around her breasts down her sides. Clammy. Cold. Why did she wear her yellow mac? Even in the fast fading light, she must stand out like a flare. *Are they coming for me?*

The land around her has widened and flattened. Off to her left is the striped cone of a lighthouse. To her right is the shelving beach being gobbled by the swell. She turns more inland, following a path between sea buckthorn. The berries are orange against the slender olive leaves. The bushes form a corridor. Her run becomes more of a trot. She was an adequate sprinter at school. But it's been years since she has had to put on any turn of speed. Then she sees it, the half-collapsed bunker under what would once have been a gun emplacement built during the Second World War. Pushing through the undergrowth, she is able to stumble into a semi-buried area. It smells of damp and sheep shit. She sits on the hard ground. She drags in air. She can't hear anything above her own body's circulatory systems and the heaving of the wind. She knows she isn't safe, yet hasn't the energy to move. She rests her head against the concrete. She wraps her arms around her body. She jams her teeth shut so tight they begin to ache. She mustn't make a sound. She mustn't give herself away. *I've got to think straight. I've got to find a way out of here.* She has also realised she has been going in the wrong direction. Away from the visitor centre. Away from other people.

She wonders whether she should have stayed to help Sarah. It all happened in an instant. She was so terrified. She has never been as frightened before in her life. *I am not brave,* she berates herself. And now, what has happened to Sarah? Alice could not forgive herself if it was something awful. Sarah dead? She shakes the idea from her head. It brings up a silent sob. Yet, she also cannot stop herself from wondering whether this has all been arranged? Whether in some bizarre way Sarah was working with her brother and two-tone shoes to get rid of her? She pulls her knees up to her chest as she shivers. She is growing numb. She rests her forehead on her crossed arms.

Her breathing quietens sufficiently for her to make out noises beyond herself. Slowly sounds begin to emerge. There's a rustling. Gusts of rain-laden air pelt the stone structure above her. But. She holds her breath. There. There. And there again. No doubt, feet have sent pebbles a-tumbling; they skitter into her own boots. She can't make out what it is. It's darkness against darkness. The form is keeping low against the bushes. It lifts something curved and sharp. Alice bends forward, arms over her head, bracing herself. Warm breath condenses against her neck. Her clenched hand hits out hard, meets wool-covered bone and the sheep retreats, bleating, scattering more stones in its wake.

'Fuck, fuck,' Alice repeats softly to herself. If there is anyone out there, she's just given herself away.

They reach the North Yorks. Police Land Rover parked askew at the edge of the roadway. Still all they've seen has been birds and a few of the squat, brown, horned Hebridean flock who naturally maintain the flower meadows with their teeth, hooves and manure. Finally, as Donna and her colleagues creep to a corner created by a dune and a mass of bushes, Eric waves for everyone to stop. There are two figures by the lighthouse. Plus there is a light which looks like it might be from a torch further on. It is time to split up. Eric has binoculars with a night-vision function. Theo uses them to assess what is happening at the lighthouse. He cannot be certain, but it looks like Sarah Franklande is curled on the ground and her brother is laboriously trying to improvise a noose from one of the metal brackets on the wall. Gus and Harrie are despatched in that direction. Eric, Bristle, Theo and Donna follow the individual with the torch who Theo thinks is Brian.

Being now clear where their targets are, the three of them move more swiftly, their gaze intently following the path of the light. It is fluctuating through the grey squalls. Donna thinks maybe they are mistaken. It is from a boat

345

in the estuary. Or even a decoy of some sort. However, she does not slacken her pace. She concentrates on keeping her breathing long and even. Bristle, who up until now has remained tight in to his master's shin, is allowed to go a little way ahead. He stops at a tunnel of bushes, pointing with this nose. Eric indicates he will go further on and come at the pathway from the other end. Donna follows Theo as he moves up the track, slowly, sometimes pausing to listen.

Then comes the scream. The same as the one that had torn across the airwaves from Alice's phone to Donna's. She and Theo begin to sprint. They reach the concrete construction. A form is dragging at another dressed in buttercup yellow. Theo launches himself forward. There's a tussle. Arms. Torsos. Legs. All in a muddle. Until Donna can make out Alice scrambling to her feet and flinging herself out of range. Donna practically catches her in her arms. 'It's OK, it's OK, I've got you,' she says softly. Out of the corner of her eye, she sees Theo catch an elbow on the bridge of his nose and stagger backwards. Brian turns to flee. Within moments he is brought down by Bristle. The dog grabs Brian's ankle in his jaw, and then, once Brian is prone, sits triumphantly on his back. Bristle barks delightedly.

Chapter 50

The tension in the room is as thick as the filling for a Yorkshire curd tart. It's six a.m., and there's a hint of luminosity in the grey through the oblong window high up in the wall of the cramped interview room. Donna and Theo have both had a few hours' sleep. It doesn't look as if Brian has had much during his night in the cells. Next to him sits Reggie Harvey, more spruce than any of them in his tweed suit and trademark bow tie (today striped yellow and red). Donna has already met him several times across this very table. The solicitor who relishes a lost cause, and frequently salvages them. For his acuity and tenacity, like her fellow officers, Donna respects Harvey, grudgingly at times.

Her DI is making no attempt to keep his irritation out of his voice. 'What you're telling me, Brian, is you were there to protect Sarah Franklande and Alice Millson?' His fingers go to the bruised bridge of his nose.

DC Chesters resolutely keeps his gaze away from Theo's face. Harvey has undoubtedly told him to do a 'no comment' interview and Donna supposes this is becoming a more appealing option. Even so, it seems, he is willing to make one more attempt. 'I'd have been mad to take the police vehicle if not.'

Mad. Yes. Was he cocky or panicking?

'Which you did without authority,' says Theo.

'So discipline me,' snipes Chesters, much of the assurance he had at the start of the interview gone.

'That will be the least of your problems,' mutters Theo. Then he straightens himself up. 'Let me get this straight. You misused police data – namely ANPR – then misappropriated police property – namely a Land Rover – and took it upon yourself to follow two suspects in a murder inquiry. You arrive into the middle of an altercation between brother and sister. You assault Ms Millson.'

'I did not—'

'Remember we have her witness testimony,' says Donna.

Brian lifts his head, his eyes narrowed.

She pictures the cogs of his mind whirring.

'I had no idea what her role was, what she was doing there.'

'She said you were talking about "getting rid of" her and Sarah Franklande. What did you mean by that?'

'I had to play along a bit, work out the lie of the land.' He sits back and crosses his arm. 'I let her go—'

'She got away,' says Donna firmly. 'And then you left Sarah to her brother and went after Alice.'

'To make sure she was OK.' Desperation is seeping into his tone. 'I had no backup—'

'Because you didn't call any.'

'And when it arrived,' interjects Theo, 'you shoved an elbow in my face.' Even as her DI keeps his tone severe, Donna sees there is ghost of a smile, perhaps of disbelief, on his face.

Brian does not notice. He looks wildly around the room.

'It was dark, I didn't know who you were.'

'There are a lot of black men wandering around Spurn Point, are there? I said your name, Brian.'

'I didn't hear you.'

'You are lying.'

Brian flinches, is about to retort when Reggie Harvey lifts his hand as if halting traffic.

'DC Chesters has told you what happened from his perspective,' Reggie says. 'Have you any more questions for him?' He puts the emphasis on the word 'questions'.

'Yes,' says Donna. 'How did Roland Franklande get from the Spurn Point visitor's centre to where you say you encountered him?'

Brian shrugs.

'For the tape,' Donna raps out.

'I don't know.'

'Are you sure? Because Ethan Buckle has got his people crawling all over that Land Rover. Are you sure he won't find evidence that Mr Franklande sat in it?'

'He may have done, after I went off,' Brian says quickly. There's a slight curve to his lips.

Sarah Franklande may or may not be able to help with this little detail. However, for now, she is still recovering in hospital. The tension deflates a little.

After a pause, Theo asks, 'Where were you on the second of January?'

Brian shrugs, then straightens and says clearly: 'I don't know. I would have to check my calendar.'

'You were seen,' says Theo, 'vandalising the CCTV camera on the harbour.'

This could be a surprise. Brian's knuckles crack. 'Who?'

Neither Theo nor Donna responds. They both know Doug's sighting wouldn't be good enough for the CPS. Reggie Harvey senses the game and lifts his hand again, only he's too late to stop his client.

He shrugs slightly less nonchalantly. 'Charge me then, with criminal damage.'

'Why did you do it, Brian?' asks Theo, sounding genuinely empathic, though Donna is aware the gentleness is hiding the ire.

'Because I fucking felt like it. I was fed up, OK? I'm a good copper.'

'Was,' says Donna.

'Am,' Brian shouts. Then slumps in his chair. 'It was my promotion, if Hoyle hadn't gone, if they didn't want to show how fucking right-on diverse they all are.' He falls silent, chin on his chest.

Theo sounds saddened when he says, 'You're not doing yourself any favours, son.'

'I'm not your son.' Brian glares at his DI. 'OK? I don't owe you nothing.'

'No,' says Theo softly. He appears to check through his notes. Donna suspects he's giving himself time to collect himself. 'We have arrested Roland Franklande for the murders of Philip and June Franklande, and the murder of Orson Reed, plus the attempted murder of his sister Sarah and conspiracy to murder Sylvia Franklande with Leonard Arch. We are preparing to interview him. We have executed a warrant for the IT server at ScarTek. We are carrying out a forensic re-examination of the blanket found wrapped

350

around Sylvia Franklande. A fibre has been matched to carpets used in high-end Audis. We have requested the DNA sample Spanish police hold for Leonard Arch. We will be bringing him in for questioning.'

In other words, the net is tightening.

Brian doesn't look up. 'You haven't got him yet though, have you?'

Leonard Arch has indeed done a vanishing act. At least for now. Possibly left the country. Theo looks over at Donna.

Donna takes a plastic sleeve from under her notebook. It contains printouts of bank statements, which she shows to Brian. 'These are for your account. Where did these payments come from? Two thousand pounds. Five K. Here and here.' She prods at the paper.

'I won on the horses,' Brian says without moving. 'I gamble online. I'm good at it.'

Theo shakes his head. 'Remember what we used to say about people making things up as they go along? How we would laugh at the mistakes they made. Remember, Brian?'

He makes no response.

Taking her cue from Theo, Donna continues: 'We are already examining Roland Franklande's various accounts, DC Chesters. I imagine we will find the answer there.' She is rewarded by seeing him tensing. 'However, it wasn't money that first reeled you in was it?' She takes out the photo. 'Do you know who this is?'

Despite himself he does lift his gaze. He shakes his head. He hugs his arms tight around his chest.

'For the tape, Brian Chesters says he does not recognise

Neal Williams. Where were you, Brian, on March thirty-first 2012?'

'My father's funeral,' he growls.

She keeps the shock from her face and recalls their conversation the day they interviewed Terry Prichard. Brian failed his sergeant exams and his father died. *Not an excuse, a reason.* 'And in the evening?'

'I got blathered.'

'You did indeed. We have CCTV of you approaching the Weighed Anchor on March thirty-first 2012 at ten-o-nine p.m. and you are obviously drunk.'

'It's not a crime to be drunk.'

It's like he can't turn off the goad button. Donna keeps her tone steady. 'It is a crime not to report a crime. In fact, as a serving officer, you had a duty to step in when you found Neal Williams being raped.'

'I didn't see nothing.' His voice is less certain.

Donna lets the silence stretch. Then she says, 'Instead you beat him up.'

'You can't prove nothing.' It's as if he is muttering to himself. Reassuring himself.

'Try me.' Donna knows at least 50 per cent of interrogation is gaining psychological advantage. She leaves a pause. 'Mr Williams says he'll recognise the voice of the man who assaulted him. We have you being driven away from the scene by Leonard Arch. It's only a matter of time before we link Arch to Colossus. Do you think he'd rather be done for raping someone or assaulting someone? He'll hang you out to dry.'

Brian twists uneasily in his seat. 'No comment.'

Reggie Harvey appears on the point of applauding – his client is at last following his advice. He says conversationally, 'I think we could all do with a break and I would like to consult with my client.'

Theo nods.

Chesters pulls himself up to standing. 'You'll have a hard job pinning anything on Leonard Arch. He owns this town. He's got councillors in his pockets, the DCI is his mate.' This reinjects a bit of swagger as he heads out the door, followed by his solicitor.

He leaves behind him the burden of his betrayal. Donna can feel its wrecking ball thumping into her abdomen. Theo sits poker-backed, his face showing the strain. Neither finds the words to express the sadness, the anger, the wretchedness. Brian was someone they counted on. He was one of their own. Instead, they both somehow pack it away internally. Carefully. As if it has sharp edges.

Theo is the first to speak: 'Their alibis are like one of those towers made of playing cards. Once one gets pulled, the whole lot will go. But which one of them is going to be the first to give a tug?' He stands. 'Or knock it accidentally? Let's go and find out how Harrie is getting on with Roland Franklande.'

Chapter 51

Theo and Donna watch the video link to the interview of Roland Franklande by Harrie. Beside her sits another DC. Neither Theo nor Donna mention the painful irony: they have just despatched to the cells the DC who would normally have been with her. Brian's absence takes up more space than his presence would ever have done.

Gradually and painstakingly, Roland is taken through the events of January 1994, of the fourth of January this year, of the weeks leading up to Sylvia's murder and finally onto what happened at Spurn Point. He has obviously decided to follow his smartly suited solicitor's guidance, as he answers 'no comment' to everything put to him.

Harrie suggests he was in the room when his parents died. How can he explain his hair in the breech lock of the shotgun?

'No comment.'

'Where did you get the gun?'

'No comment.'

'Did your friend Leonard Arch give it to you?'

'No comment.'

And so on, until Harrie turns to the night Orson died: 'Were you in fact in Scarborough, not at Leonard Arch's flat as you have claimed?'

'No comment.'

'How do you explain your DNA on the murder weapon?'

'No comment.' His clothes are more dishevelled than they were when Donna last saw him. However, his demeanour and responses remain stony.

His tone doesn't change as Harrie asks him about the conversations with Arch the police have found on his phone in the week before Sylvia died and on the night she was killed. Harrie tells him about the fibre and (stretching it a little) the possible DNA match for Arch on the blanket.

'No comment.'

And on to the encounter with Sarah on Spurn Point. His violence. Harrie suggests he deliberately went there to 'get rid of' Sarah, who he feared knew too much. Having knocked her out, he was going to make it look like she had hanged herself through guilt over the murder of Orson which she had not committed.

'No comment.' 'No comment.' 'No comment.'

It's like he has detached himself from the reality, Donna thinks. Her phone buzzes, she checks it, sees it is Elizabeth and goes out into the corridor. 'They're going to postpone my parole board,' her daughter roars at her. *Oh Lizzie, I haven't got time for this.* Donna realises how fatigued she is. She puts fingers to her forehead, which is beginning to ache. Gently she teases out what has happened. One of the other women called Iris a black bitch and Elizabeth floored her. 'They said I should have reported her. But they never do anything about the racist abuse around here. She won't be doing it again, that's for sure.' Elizabeth is still shouting. Donna wishes she wouldn't. She asks quietly what she can do. Elizabeth continues in a raised voice: 'Can't you pull some strings? Please, Mum. Please.'

'I don't know, love—'

'I knew it. I knew you didn't really care. It's all show with you, isn't it, Mum? But when the chips are down, when I really need you, where are you? Nowhere.' It's desperation talking. Even so, it cuts straight through Donna's heart.

'I'll try, I'll ring the governor, OK—'

'Just don't bother, don't fucking bother.'

'Lizzie . . .' But she's talking to the dialling tone. She holds down a scream. She has the impression she's a dung beetle. No – that bloke who got to push a stone up the hill only to have it roll down again. OK, an amalgamation of them both. Either way, she gets covered in shit.

Slowly, she returns to the CID office, wishing she could go home. Harrie and Theo are there. Roland Franklande is in discussion with his solicitor.

Theo tells Harrie to check whether there are any updates on forensics or Arch's whereabouts. Then he asks Donna to come to his office. He's decided they have time for their little chat. Reluctantly, she follows him. She had hoped he had forgotten. He has not. Her two days off sick. He is not deflected by her assertions that she is fine – partly true, the iron tablets have, at least, given her some energy, only they are now troubling her guts. And no blood for days.

Theo sits back in his chair and pins her with his gaze. She squirms, looks to the window, the rooftops shiny with the drizzle.

Theo continues: 'I grew up in a household of women who

did not hold back on what they were experiencing. And I am glad. My mother and sister are nurses . . .'

Don't liken me to your mother. I am not old enough to be your mother!

'My mother . . .'

Here we go.

'. . . had an easy time of the menopause. But she tells me it is not always so: some women really suffer. If any of my staff are suffering, for whatever reason, I want to know about it. Donna, do you understand?'

She turns back to him. His features are set in an encouraging mode.

'There is nothing to be ashamed of,' he says.

I am ashamed!

'We are all human with our frailties. We need each other.'

This brings her up short. She wonders if there is something else in this statement. Is he asking her for something? Maybe because of her recent conversation with Elizabeth, the traffic cops come to mind. Has she done enough about what happened with them? In truth, she's done nothing. Despite the result, she admits to herself a grudging pride in her daughter's action and sense of justice.

Theo continues: 'Plus, we can take practical steps. I want you to have an appointment with occupational health and, together with them, see if we need to put anything in place.' He cuts off her denials with a curt, 'That's an order, DC Morris.'

It's meant in a teasing way. However, Donna feels the weight of the command. 'Can I go now?' she says, a tad crossly.

Theo's forehead scrunches. Perhaps he is considering

whether he has said the right thing or whether he needs to say more. Whatever, he carries on more gently. 'You went to see Doug Prichard without my permission, Donna. Please do not do this type of thing again.' He breathes heavily. 'I've had enough of my officers going rogue.'

'I didn't mean . . .' says Donna quickly, not wanting to be linked with what Brian did.

'I know you meant no harm and it was, in the end, helpful. But I need to know what is going on, at all times. It's too easy for things to unravel.'

There's wretchedness in his tone. She apologises for her actions. He nods. She waits for him to dismiss her. He appears to be brooding. She hopes not on her and her future career prospects. She decides it would not be a good time to bring up Elizabeth. Luckily, they are both saved from saying anything more by Harrie coming. Roland Franklande is ready to make a statement.

Once again Harrie goes into the interview room and Theo watches the video link with Donna. It is the solicitor who reads out Roland's words. It makes everything feel staged. Everyone knows it is.

Roland admits to arriving at his parents' house to find Philip Franklande had shot his wife. Father and son tussled for the gun. It went off. In a panic, Roland ran. He did not think Philip had been hit, the gun was at the wrong angle. However, he was afraid for his own life. All he had known from his father was violence. In his naivety, he accepted the police's findings, 'which they seemed eager to promote', and his best friend's offer of an alibi.

This locked him into a lifelong sense of debt to Leonard Arch, as well as fear of what Arch might reveal. Roland had agreed when Leonard had asked him to meet with Orson Reed to discuss with him the complaints he had about ScarTek's relationships with an energy company.

At midnight on a Saturday night? Would anyone believe that?

Arch had given Roland the knife, merely as an 'assurance policy'. Orson was behaving in a very strange way; he didn't seem to be able to control himself.

The Rohypnol Roland himself must have given him.

He became abusive. In self-defence, Roland struck out at him with the knife. Orson staggered, slipped and fell into the sea. Thinking he could do nothing, Roland once again fled. He believes Leonard Arch had tried to protect his friend by fabricating false emails between Orson and Sarah, assuming Sarah would have an alibi which would put her in the clear.

Roland Franklande agrees he did speak to Leonard Arch in the weeks leading up to 19 January 2014. Most of the conversations were business related. However, on one occasion, Arch told him that Sylvia was attempting to reach her sister via Sarah's work email.

Did Arch monitor all his employees' emails, or just Sarah's? Was that how he found out the man he raped was a member of his staff?

Sylvia was aware that her brother had been present at their parents' house when their parents died. She had even once accused her brother of being more involved than he was. Neither Roland nor Leonard wanted 'such tittle-tattle being raked over and communicated to Sarah'. Arch suggested he meet with Sylvia, as he was less emotionally invested, to check out her intentions. The plan hatched by the two men was that Arch would simply speak to Sylvia, using his famously adroit negotiating skills. Roland had been horrified to find out it had all gone horribly wrong – a terrible misunderstanding between Sylvia and Arch resulting in a terrible accident.

Could hitting someone over the head be an accident? Donna thinks about her own daughter. *The intention not. The result maybe.*

Roland's statement continues. He deeply regrets the death of his sister Sylvia. He had arranged to meet his sister, Sarah, at Spurn Point—

Arranged? If so, Alice hadn't mentioned it.

A place much loved by Sylvia. Unfortunately, Sarah was emotionally overwrought and they both hit out, verbally and physically. It was most unfortunate. When the police officers arrived, Roland had been making his sister comfortable, while he worked out how to signal for help, since the tide had come in and he had no phone signal. He had thought to use the brackets on the lighthouse to improvise a flag.

Donna almost laughs. *No?*

The solicitor continues in his ponderous tone, with a completely straight face. 'I, Roland Franklande, deeply regret the hurt that has been caused. My condolences go out to the family and friends of Orson Reed, as well as the friends of my sister Sylvia. I too sincerely feel her loss. My hope is that over time I can rebuild my relationship with my sister Sarah. I have nothing more to say. I will respond "no comment" to all further questions.' The solicitor closes his folder and for a moment there is a – possibly slightly stunned – silence in the interview room.

'Poor man,' Donna says. 'Seems like he never meant to kill anyone, but somehow all these people ended up dead.' The heavy sarcasm suits her mood.

Theo flicks his finger against his thumb. 'But has he said enough to set the stack of cards tumbling?'

It is mid-afternoon before Donna returns home. Despite her fatigue, she forces herself to her laptop and phone. She won't use her fists like her daughter, but she has decided to do something. At last. After finding the information she needs on the internet, she sends off the email she has been planning in her head since the morning. Then she steels herself to ring the governor of HMP North Yorkshire. She will inveigle and flatter like a police officer. Or beg like a mum. Whichever works best.

Chapter 52

Two funerals in a week – it is too much for anyone. Alice pulls on her purple Docs as if she is going into battle. She dismisses immediately the notion that she could duck out of this one. She's going to a funeral for someone she has never met because, despite everything, she is in love. She pauses. The foundations are shaky. There's many a flimsy floorboard. Not least when Sarah finds a smidge of under- standing for her brother: 'He was terrified of losing his little family.' *Yeah right.* But then, it must be tough to know your family is either bad or dead. And Alice instantly forgives her again. And again. *Is it enough? For the future?* The morning of a funeral, she decides is not a good time for making long- term decisions.

Fareeha tried to push her on it, at Orson's funeral. It was so good to see Fareeha. And little Malala. How glad Alice is that Fareeha has a daughter. Less of her father in her? Though Alice knows this is ridiculous, she feels it. The adorable baby is named for Malala Yousafzai. However, the meaning of the name carries within it the grieving, the loss in the making of the sweet soul. Still nothing from Ian Renshawe. *And the DC – what's her name? Donna . . . Donna . . . not-summer.* She had assiduously avoided Alice and Fareeha, rushing away quickly after the committal.

But Fareeha's presence rescued the day for Alice. In the planning of it, she had practically come to blows with Ursula and her 'oughts' and 'shoulds'. She had wanted to invite family members whom Orson abhorred because of their political views. Luckily, he had left some instructions, which they found once they got access to his caravan. A green burial. Even a guest list. The guys at the Curry Shack – Orson's favourite and where he ate his last meal – did the refreshments for the wake, held in one of the barns at Viv's. Ursula reluctantly agreed – she had wanted a swanky hotel. It had all been an awful strain and not how Alice wanted her friend's send-off to be. She still worries she didn't do enough. The one moment that felt right was when the string quartet (led by a cousin of Orson's), playing a haunting lament under an awning in the middle of the muddy field, became briefly mingled with hail brought in on a north-easterly squall.

Today's cremation is a very different affair, organised by Sarah with a lot of input from Mavis and Sylvia's other friends. No one is in black for a start. There is upbeat music, a slide show of Sylvia's artwork, moving tributes. Having only thought of her as dead, Alice is suddenly presented by a vibrant young woman with a life to live. Tears stream down her face, like they never did at Orson's ceremony. They are for both Orson and Sylvia. *And for me.* Alice feels her fingers and then her hand being grasped by Sarah. The two women bend into each other's embrace.

Much, much later, they return to Sarah's house. Sarah is exhausted; her paleness allows the bruising remaining on her face to show through. She walks gingerly, continuing to compensate for her healing cracked ribs and sprained ankle.

She turns to Alice. 'Don't look like that. You were right to run. You couldn't have done more.' She gently puts her hands around Alice's cheeks and kisses her robustly on the mouth. 'No guilt. Remember what we promised?'

Easier promised than done. In the front room, Alice notices the print of the little gull with its radiant corona is hanging over the mantelpiece.

'I put it up last night,' says Sarah. 'I couldn't sleep.'

'And you've sorted the books.' They are properly organised on the shelves Alice helped Sarah buy.

'Do you want tea?'

Alice shakes her head. Two funerals in a week; she is drowning in it.

'G and T then?'

'Yes, but I'll get it. I can't manage your measures just now.'

Sarah sinks heavily and thankfully into the sofa.

In the kitchen, having done the mixing to her taste, Alice opens the cupboard under the sink to throw the tonic bottle into the recycling. In the crate she sees the headline on the local paper.

She stomps back to the sitting room. 'Why didn't you tell me about Arch?' She hands over a glass to Sarah.

Sarah takes a sip. 'I didn't think it appropriate to mention at my sister's funeral the man charged with her murder.'

Although she now knows it's covering nerves, Sarah's primness irritates Alice. She plonks herself down in an armchair. 'What's going to happen to your job? To ScarTek?'

'As a matter of fact, I had a brief conversation with Mavis today. I am so, so glad she was in Sylvia's life. When

I . . . I . . . wasn't.' This time Sarah takes a swig. She goes on: 'Anyway, this morning I asked her to advise us on an employee buyout. Think of it, Alice: we could turn the company to genuine environmental aims.'

'Your idea about using bacteria to digest plastic?'

'It would only be the start.'

A minuscule and tardy start. Alice grits her teeth on the remark. No arguments about ScarTek. Not today.

After a pause, Sarah pulls an object out of her pocket and holds it out towards Alice.

She hesitates.

'The key,' says Sarah. 'To this house. It could be our house, Alice.'

After a moment, Alice takes it. It feels warm as she closes her fingers around it.

Chapter 53

'Mum you are a miracle worker.' Elizabeth joins Donna at the table beneath the window in the visiting room. 'How did you manage it?'

Threaten an equality and diversity audit by the Howard League? She is not sure which of her threats or entreaties made the difference. She is only relieved one of them did. Elizabeth's parole board postponed, but only by three weeks.

Elizabeth is grinning. She says: 'I am sorry, I shouldn't have shouted at you. Especially when you were at work.' Not exactly the first-ever apology, but rare enough to be welcome. 'And you smashed it, Mum, didn't you?'

Donna does not quite know what to say. Having Arch on remand isn't the end of the story, not by a long chalk. Especially as he and Roland are now trading accusations about who was threatening whom and who was responsible for what. Plus Brian hasn't said anything further. However, she is struggling to find any words at all for another reason. She has determined, this is the day. She has deliberately manoeuvred herself into a cul-de-sac, by pre-warning her daughter.

Elizabeth helps her out, demanding: 'You said you had something to tell me? What is your news? You are leaving Dad?'

Donna shakes her head. Elizabeth looks less disappointed than expected. There's an alertness, a buoyancy which is new. No, not new. Donna hasn't seen it for a while. For years.

'Come on, Mum, don't keep me in suspense.'

Donna breathes in the warm, curdled air formed by too many bodies and too little space for the emotions they are exuding. She wishes she could be out tramping the moors with Elizabeth, their words half torn away by the wind. *Oh, why am I making a meal of this?*

'Mum? It's not cancer, is it?' Elizabeth's voice is suddenly taut. She leans forward, a pinching in her forehead.

'No, darling,' Donna rushes to reassure. 'Nothing like that.' She realises she has to start. She is frightening her daughter. She tries something simple. 'You know last April we celebrated my fifty-second birthday?'

'Yes.' Elizabeth's frown deepens.

'Well, it wasn't, it was my fifty-first. I was born in April 1962.'

'You've been lying about your age?'

'Yes.'

'And this is what you had to tell me?' Elizabeth's tone sounds as taut, but no longer from concern: irritation is seeping in.

'Yes. No. It's why . . .' She stumbles to a halt.

'Mum, just bloody well tell me will you? Christ.' Elizabeth leans back in her chair and slaps at the table between them.

Donna forces the words out and they flow forth higgledy-piggledy, detritus ejected from a storm drain. 'I also said I was – only I wasn't – born in West Berlin. It was in Germany, you see, but the GDR. Then, in 1980, I ran. I ran away from our home in East Berlin and I lied, I lied about my age and my name. Erika Neuhausen. I said it was Donna Newhouse. It got written into my passport and that was it. I said my parents were dead, only they weren't – not then, anyway – maybe they are now.' That splinter of sadness in her chest gets tweaked again. She goes on: 'I don't know, I don't think I cared then, not really, about what happened to them. I just wanted out. So I went.' She drops her gaze to the table. The untruths she has told come to a halt on its cold surface, ready to be turned over and sifted through.

Elizabeth takes a moment. She leans in again. She whistles low. 'Wow, Mum, you are kidding me, right?' She pauses and then says, more seriously: 'You're not, huh? Wow. Wasn't there like a wall? Did you go over the wall? Or under it?'

'Through it,' Donna says quietly. 'Hidden under the back seat of a car.'

'Wow.'

Neither speaks. Elizabeth searches in her pockets and takes out a plastic packet of tissues. She holds it up so the officers can see it and come over if they wish. One of them nods at her and she slides it to Donna. She extracts a tissue and dabs at the tear dribbling down her cheek. She wants to curl up, be hugged and be told it's all right. *Mum and Dad, they used to do that.* She reminds herself she is over fifty and she is visiting her daughter in prison. This is no time to crumble. She blows her nose and looks up.

'What do you think?' she asks, as if soliciting an opinion on a new dress.

The slight frown has returned to Elizabeth's face. 'To be honest, I don't know. It's a lot to take in all at once. You're a year younger. You escaped from communist East Berlin. You're really called Erika Neuhausen. And I might have grandparents I never knew about. Yeah, like a lot to compute, Ma.'

'I know. I am sorry, darling.' More apologies. Donna has spent her life apologising to her daughter, mainly not completely genuinely. In the past it seemed easier and a way of bringing Elizabeth down from whatever drug-induced rage she had got herself into. This time, however, Donna does feel regretful. She wonders whether by not being entirely herself, she had somehow been instrumental in Elizabeth's troubles. She has always felt implicated on this front – what mother avoids guilt? Now there is perhaps more reason to.

'Why now? Why tell me now?'

'The case I had last year. It brought it all back to me. I had buried it, somehow.'

'Buried your real identity? Buried your parents? What – forgotten them?'

'It was like they all belonged to someone else, not me.'

Elizabeth nods slowly. 'I guess I can understand that. I look back at some of the things I did and think, was that really me? Bashing that ... that ...' She pauses. 'That woman over the head with a chopping board, for one.' Her voice has gone low. They are both studying their own hands, clasped a metre away from each other. 'Marion,' Elizabeth continues even more softly. 'She's called Marion.'

Yes Marion, the daughter of the elderly man Elizabeth was conning to feed her habit. Donna can't think of another

369

time when she has heard Elizabeth use the name rather than some invective. *I shot someone.* This is the bit she's not saying. *Shot at someone*, she corrects herself. *I didn't kill him. Or at least*, her mind adds the reminder, *no proof either way.*

Elizabeth is regarding her mother.

Donna wonders if she can see into her head. Has her expression betrayed her?

'All those secrets,' Elizabeth says. 'How did you hold onto them all those years?'

A good question. Donna makes an effort to breathe.

'Denial is a wonderful thing.' After a pause Elizabeth continues more slowly: 'I guess that was why you were always more understanding of me than Dad. You knew, you knew, I can't quite work it out, but you knew—'

'I knew, I know, about desperation.'

'Yes.' Elizabeth grins. 'Yes that's it, isn't it, Mum? And you knew doing bad things doesn't a bad person make.' She glances away at the window. Gradually its turning into a Kazimir Malevich painting – a black oblong. 'I wish you'd told me earlier. It might have made a difference.'

Her daughter prods expertly at her mother's culpability wound. Consciously? Possibly. Donna understands the need to divest responsibility. It was the regime. It was because her parents stopped listening. It was her age. It was Ed. It's hard to stand up and hold herself accountable for all her decisions. She does not always manage it. She can forgive Elizabeth for wanting to say, *Here, have some of it*. But then, forgiving Elizabeth is habitual. Even so, she halts the apology slipping down her tongue.

Elizabeth turns back. 'Well,' she says peaceably, 'it is

what it is, as they say, we are where we are. You should write it down, Mum. It would make a great story.'

Donna shakes her head. 'I'm not a writer. You do it, Elizabeth, you've always had a way with words.'

'Yeah, I can spin a yarn, can't I, Mum? Done that enough times. Maybe I will.' Her tone becomes harsher as she finishes. 'Got lots of time on my hands here.' Perhaps at the thought of the time she still has to spend in prison, or of the time she lost with maternal grandparents, her expression turns gloomy.

The visiting hour seeps away into a dull silence between them. Normally Donna would try to lift things with comments and questions about books, about memories of happier times. Today, she does not have the energy.

Finally Elizabeth says crossly: 'I don't know, Mum, you're not who I thought you were. I've got grandparents I never knew, for God's sake. Maybe other family. Have I, Mum?'

What's wrong with the one you've already got?

'I'm still the same person,' says Donna, feeling defensive. 'I still love you, Lizzie, you know that.'

'Yeah, whatever.' They have minutes before the buzzer sounds to end their time together. Elizabeth stands abruptly. 'See you next time,' she says over her shoulder as she leaves.

Yes, I'll be here next time, thinks Donna, deflated in her seat. *I'll always be here next time. It's my job.* She realises she is clutching at the edge of the table. She imagines it heaped with all those bits of life – hers and her daughter's – which neither wants to grasp for fear of being irreparably scorched.

Chapter 54

Despite the awakening in the earth – marked by the green spears of daffodils lancing through and a few miniature yolk trumpets – it is turning into a season for interring.

Three funerals in a fortnight. Donna appreciated how the last two had reflected something of the youngsters being eulogised. She was glad to see Fareeha Gopal with her newborn held snugly to the front of her body in a papoose. She looked healthier than Donna remembered, her skin smoothly bronzed, her dark hair shining. She was wearing a white salwar kameez, with a gold-edged dupatta. Had she heard from Ian Renshawe? The thought of questions about him from either Fareeha or Alice meant Donna's attendance at both Orson's and Sylvia's funerals was brief. She was not going to be tempted into defying Theo, though she truly wished she could.

Now she joins Trevor and Theo for Doug Prichard's send-off. This time it wasn't necessary. Trevor was going anyway, his family being originally 'bottom-enders', and Theo decided he wanted to be there (as well as be seen to be there). It is Donna's day off. However, she has realised she had, somehow, developed an affinity for the old man which she wants to honour. Plus, she can't deny her curiosity: how will a stalwart of the fishing community be venerated?

It is a solidly traditional ceremony. The horse-drawn hearse has passed through streets lined with people, their heads bowed in quiet contemplation, to St Mary's on the hill by the castle. The coffin is borne into the church by men from the community, including Doug's son, Tony. The prayers, address and hymns are determinedly old-school, including a surging rendition of 'For Those in Peril on the Sea'.

Afterwards, Donna finds Pat on one of the benches along Paradise, the street skirting the churchyard. Rather than be buried at the out-of-town cemetery, the only one where space is still available, Doug's body has been taken to be quickly cremated. Later it will be scattered at sea. Pat says of the service, 'Happen, Doug would have been proud of that.' In defiance of the spring sun, she is bundled up in a dark, heavy coat. She goes on, perhaps to Donna, perhaps to the distant watery horizon: 'The sea took my boy from me. I've no bones to anchor him here with me.'

It is as if Donna looks into the void at the centre of the woman sitting beside her and feels the vertigo. She pulls herself back. She has her daughter, her son, her husband. 'I am sorry,' she says, knowing it is inadequate.

'Aye lass,' says Pat. 'So am I.'

Trev says he will join the wake at the Leeds Arms. Theo offers to buy Donna a coffee from the café on the harbour. She often walks around the area anonymously. It is not possible with Theo. There are those who do a double take, which they then attempt to hide, and those who openly stare. There are those who know who he is. From them there is a friendly greeting. The youngster behind the counter is one of these. 'There you go, honey,' she (or he) says, handing over the drinks in china mugs.

They take them up onto the harbour wall to lean against a balustrade. The sea is a rippling silk parachute dyed a dark indigo. And through the gin-sparkling air they really can see 'fair down to Flamborough', its cliffs a shadowy Roman nose against a sky the colour of a turquoise. Standing here in the open, the sun isn't warm enough, but on this corner of the North Yorkshire coast, you learn never to miss the chance to stand in its glow. Even so, both Donna and Theo put on their woollen hats and are glad of the heat from the mugs held in their gloved hands.

'I've heard from DCI Sewell,' says Theo. 'He's willing to advocate for my complaint against the Humberside traffic officer.'

'That's great.'

'I think he needs me on side now.'

'Being at a party with a suspected murderer not good for the image?'

Theo nods. After a pause he says: 'I also understand there's been an intervention. From someone working for the IOPC.' He breaks off. Perhaps waiting for Donna to comment.

She does not. She was surprised the woman from the Independent Office for Police Conduct remembered her. They had met several years prior, the woman had been the trainer on a course Donna had attended. They had gravitated together, being the only women over forty-five and the only people worried about getting home in time to cook an evening meal.

Theo continues: 'There have been other complaints about this officer. From colleagues, harder to define, harder to prove. Mine will push things along.'

'Good.' She drains her cup.

After a moment, Theo says: 'I don't know what you did, Donna. But thanks.'

It was easy for me, Donna reminds herself. *It'll be Theo putting his head above the ramparts.* However, she feels pleased.

Theo leaves her shortly afterwards to go back to the police station. Donna lingers. She hears the bray of a donkey from the beach. She saw them earlier, fluffy with their winter coats. Another harbinger of spring in her adopted town. She begins to walk out along the harbour arm. Yesterday, on a stroll by the beach huts the other side of the bay, she thought about Sylvia. Today, when she reaches the spot where she consulted Ethan Buckle, or an approximation of it, Donna pauses for a moment to remember the young man who was so brutally despatched – like 'a clarty long tail'. She recalls the words of Terry Prichard. No, Orson didn't deserve that. No one does. But then no child should have to see their father beating their mother to pulp, either. She moves on.

She should be getting home, to her little house. She has cleaning and cooking to do. Jim is arriving later. He has finally agreed to visit her in Scarborough. Only overnight. She has engineered it because she thinks in her own place, on her own turf, so to speak, she will be able to tell him about her past. At least some of it. Maybe. The dry run with Elizabeth has not filled her with confidence that things will turn out well. And then she will have to speak to Theo about how to approach HR and the inaccuracies in her police paperwork.

Her eyes catch a movement out in the bay. She switches her focus. Yes, there it is again. And again. A fin scything through the water. The surfacing and diving back of a porpoise. Trev said they could be seen at this time of year. And here they are. And here she is. The sole witness. She feels the privilege of it.

Acknowledgements

Thank you to Krystyna Green, Hannah Wann, Amanda Keats and all the crew at Constable/Little, Brown for making this happen. It is quite literally a life-long dream.

Thanks go to my husband, Mark, my sister, Ros, and all my lovely friends – readers and writers alike – who supported me with my writing. It's been a long road travelled, but generally a good one. The title of this novel is a riff off the fabulous poem 'Not Waving But Drowning' by Stevie Smith. I am grateful for her words and her inspiration.

Author's note

This is a work of fiction. All remaining mistakes are mine. The publication of Reni Eddo-Lodge's excellent blog post has been moved forward a month to help with the timeline. Scarborough, North Yorkshire, exists and the vast majority of settings I have used are real. On the other hand, HMP North Yorkshire is not a genuine institution. There is no prison slap bang in the middle of the Yorkshire Moors, though it sometimes feels as if there might be.